What Happened in Vienna, Jack?

What Happened in Vienna, Jack?

Lies and Consequences Book 1

Daniel Kemp

Published 2017 by Creativia
ISBN: 978-1979217996
Cover art by Inkubus Design

Other Work By This Author

The Desolate Garden
Percy Crow
Once I Was A Soldier
A Shudder From Heaven
Why?
Reasons

Three Children's Stories In The Teddy And Tilly's Travel Series:
  The Man Who Makes The Clouds
  The Mermaid Who Makes The Seas
  The Mother And Son Who Make The Fun

Prologue

My father was a field-promoted captain in the Royal Artillery Regiment during the Second World War, but after the surrender of Italy he was attached to Military Intelligence interrogating captured Axis troops, remaining stationed in that country until 1945. Back home he served a further seven years in 'The Colours' before applying to join the London police. He was turned down because he had one false tooth! The Metropolitan Police had the choice from so many returning British Forces personnel that such a small inadequacy of a missing tooth was deemed to be undesirable in a perfect police force; however, that presumed perfection was not evident in later years. I was born four years after my father returned home.

I cannot speak of the integrity of the police in London before I joined in 1971, but through the late '60s and early '70s reports of the alleged corruption in the Met were regularly carried in the national newspapers and openly spoken of. It ranged from the ordinary constables, in a patrol car, stopping a drunk driver and accepting the equivalent of a week's wage to drive that drunk and his or her car home, to high-ranking criminal investigation detectives taking bribes from violent robbers to turn a blind eye, or, in some notorious cases; covertly assist! No station or department was immune to this endemic practice.

I was at Oxford when the offer to join the 'Job' was first put to me. I declined that offer, favouring to stay and follow my chosen path of studying analytical chemistry and my secondary recreational pastime; the science of psychology. Three weeks into my final year at university, my father died of a sudden heart attack. He was forty-nine and employed at the War Department. My mother died two months later from a broken heart.

The security of a degree became less important to me on accepting another approach from a senior Metropolitan police officer named Barrington Trenchard. He spoke passionately about his desire to root out this criminality that was being linked to Members of Parliament. He wanted me and knew my weakness.

My self-importance had led to some written articles of mine being published on the utopian dream of right and wrong. The complexity of realism that he threw at my argument destroyed the idealistic world I lived in. Both the ordinary men and the extraordinary, who wished to serve the cause of justice were being challenged by the ensnarement of those who wished its desecration.

Sometime after Trenchard's presentation, I became a fully signed-up and committed custodian of justice. As I was coming straight from university I was to be fast-tracked, becoming an inspector within five years, but no one mentioned Jack to me, nor the tracks he travelled to impose his kind of virtue.

I was about to find out that justice could be found in more places than a court of law, and bribes come in more ways than mere money.

Friday In London

Chapter One

Models

The doorway was set back in an alcove between a world-renowned French restaurant and a newly opened Chinese one that had crispy roasted ducks hanging from a rail in a steamed-up window. There was only one bell push that did not have the word 'Model' added above it with their country of origin; just the name of Jack Price. I pushed it. Moments later a buzzer sounded and I was climbing the bare wooden staircase to the third floor. The corridor leading to his black-painted apartment door was narrow, lined by peeling garishly wallpapered walls and crumbling ceiling plaster, the same state of disrepair I'd seen on the staircase. The place reeked of damp, garlic and cooking oil.

I was twenty-three and attached to the criminal intelligence section of Scotland Yard, or C11 as it was known when I first came to meet Jack. He was thirty years my senior. He had been in the wrong place at a time when my department was executing an operation against an organised gang of robbers under the command of a known Irish Republican Army member on a cash-carrying security van in Charing Cross Road one day previous to this meeting. I had shot dead the Irish brigade commander, and another armed robber was wounded as Jack looked on from across the street. The year was 1972. However, seldom are things quite as they appear in life and this was true in this case.

Although I had followed the standing orders of the day I was naive and to some extent gullible. If those are faults, then I plead guilty!

"Are you sure that warrant card is not a forgery, young man, as you don't look old enough to be out of short trousers let alone a gun-carrying, hot-shot police officer," he said on answering my knock after unfastening three locks, then as I entered he added, "But there you go, all you lot look young to me nowadays. A sure sign of getting old, or so they say."

The apartment was spartanly furnished. No television but a radio instead with a copy of the *Radio Times* lying open on the occasional table it occupied beside an odd looking hard-backed triangular, wedged shaped chair, newly upholstered in a yellow leather lookalike material. There was a single, soft, red velvet armchair almost on top of a five bar electric fire. On the wall opposite the double bay windows stood a cheap imitation light oak sideboard, on which were three mixed size glasses and an open bottle of what appeared to be whisky.

"I would offer you one but I don't want to encourage the young to drink. From experience I know that's a bad habit to get into at an early age," on catching my gaze he declared.

The red, well-trodden, patterned carpet clashed with the heavy dark blue curtains which were closed, even though it was only the afternoon on a moderately hot July day with no sun shining on the windows behind. A yellow shaded chrome standard light and two similarly shaded table ones enhanced the natural light in the room. On the mantelpiece over that electric fire was a grey chiming slate clock, beside which were two wooden framed photographs. The one on the left, in black and white, a young woman arm in arm with, I presumed, a young Jack and the other, in colour, of two children; a boy and girl.

"Your family, Mr Price?" I asked.

He picked up the first of the photographs, held it in his left hand and stared at it.

"That was my wife, Mary. She died six years ago from the loneliness I caused, I think. I was never around much in those days." He kept it close for a second then carefully replaced it in its exact spot as he turned from the fire, walking the few paces towards the sideboard.

"The other one is of my children; George and Mildred, both living in Canada. They upped and left soon after Mary had gone. No love lost between us there. Do you want a drink while you tell me why you're here, Detective Constable West?"

He had an impassive, well-worn, chiselled face, not hard and cold, but one where no emotion or feeling for the past lived. More pragmatic than sentimental. He was just under six foot tall, weighed slightly less than his height suggested and although his complexion was more waxen than florid there were no signs of health issues that I could see.

"I will, Jack, thank you," I replied, about to sit in that hard chair thinking that the soft one was his to relax in. I was wrong!

"No, wrong chair, my friend. That one is mine. Have the one I keep for visitors. Hardly used nowadays, far more comfortable than that old thing," he said.

"You never lived here when married then, Jack?"

"Pretty obvious, that, I would have thought, unless Mary had little taste for the finer things in life like me, which she didn't. Could never quite work out why she married me, as I've always been a bit of a slob around the place. Never one for an Ideal Home Exhibition show house. Now I live as the mood takes me, with no one around to moan. Live on your own, Patrick, or is there a Missus West? Take water, or as it comes?"

I didn't bother to answer the first question.

"Have you any ice?" I asked.

"No, neither does the water come all the way from a pure Scottish glen. Good old murky Thames tap stuff. Take it as it comes, will you?" he asked, somewhat impatiently.

"You've sold it to me, Jack, pour away."

Although I considered myself well-crafted in the insight of a person's personality by the fundamental material things in life that they owned or spoke of, nothing held my attention more than that odd shaped chair. I could not avert my gaze away from it.

"I wouldn't think that you're here to discuss my choice of interior colour nor to taste my whisky, so why are you, Patrick? I have made my statement. By the way, hope you don't mind the familiarity of me using your first name, young man?"

"Not at all! Patrick is on the warrant card, after all. It was my governor's decision, not mine. He wants me to go through that statement of yours and see if my description can be; I'll use his words, 'erased,' Jack. As though I wasn't there, you understand."

"You have nothing to be ashamed of. The man had a gun, and, in my opinion, looked capable and dangerously close to using it. I did say that in my statement. I can't see how you had a choice."

"That's not the problem! The 'Job' has had its own internal enquiry and there's no question over the need or legality of my actions, it's just your wording that we would prefer to alter slightly if that's possible."

"We? I thought you said it was your governor's wish?"

"Always that pedantic, Jack? Had a need to be precise in a previous life, have you?"

He stood, tasting his drink before he spoke again.

"Precision can and often does save lives, but it can also cost lives when it confuses the enigmatic and ambivalent of this life leaving them lost to understand the rationality of thought. Your governor a rational thinker, is he? What's his rank?"

"I've always found rationality to be a subjective thing, Jack, best left to the believer, so I can't answer that. My direct governor is DI Fisher, that's Detective Inspector Fisher, but we all answer to the high Commander of 'C' department; Commander Trenchard. He's got something that you have, a precious thing at that."

"What has Mr Trenchard got that I have, Patrick?" straight-faced he asked.

"You both have the George Medal. He got his one a lot later than you got yours, though. I believe you were one of the first recipients of that honour, Jack. 1942 you got it, was it not?"

"It was, yes! Research that on your own initiative, did you, or your revered 'C' gently nudge you into doing the shovel work?"

I was sure I saw the glint of a smile in those hard, hazel-coloured eyes below his high forehead and receding hairline as he placed my glass in my hand and his on top of the *Radio Times*, moving the full glass ashtray aside to make room. His dilapidated surroundings were not improved by his clothes; striped pyjamas under a dark blue stained dressing gown and neither socks nor shoes. He had not shaved for days. From Trenchard's description I had expected a man of means, well-appointed and well positioned in life, but on the surface, he was none of that, lonely, down on his luck and living a shabby life in one of the most squalid areas of London. A place frequented by transient visitors seeking temporary pleasures; Soho.

"If you don't mind me saying, Jack, this is not the sort of place I thought someone of your past would be living out his final days." I tasted the Scotch, finding it raw and stinging on the throat. "That's a bit fierce," I added.

"Tesco's own brand. I think they have a still in the back of the shop," he laughed and I almost believed him. "Are you a connoisseur of Scotch whisky as well as being very self-opinionated and presumptuous? Disturbing for someone your age. For all you know I might have a place in the South of France and a yacht on the Med, this being my London pied-à-terre when I have the misfortune to visit London town. As for living out my final days, have you inside information on that too?"

"Not of that rank yet, Jack. Maybe someday, though! It would be nice to think along the lines of a place in France, feet up, sipping the local wine, watching the French girls go by, but this is all you've got. You're right, though, it is none of my business how you live on the government pension you receive on the twenty-third of each month. I found it to be a tidy sum for a retired minor home office official."

I was not sure if I'd rattled him as I hoped, but there was a change in tone to his next question.

"You will eventually come to the point of this visit, won't you, officer?"

"Ah, touched a delicate spot, have I? Sorry if I have. It was not meant to offend. The enthusiasm of youth added to a poor background in diplomacy, I guess. I think it comes from those hard-nut instructors of mine. One knocked me out for being indelicate in the way I put my supposition as to his birth, but he never went on to teach me how to call a superior officer a bastard without causing offence."

"You should always add the word 'sir' after the insult, Patrick. I always found that helped."

"That would explain a lot, especially if you forgot to take your own advice. A short period of service in the secret mob but no explanation as to why they dumped you that I could find, and I had clearance from way up high, Jack."

"The obdurate Mr Trenchard, I presume."

"Got it in one. You two go back a long way, I understand. I had the impression that he doesn't much care for you. Said he saw your name on the witness statement then recognised that distinctive signature of yours with the capital P and R of Price. Added rather brusquely that he hadn't seen it for many years, and that observation was not followed up with any words of admiration or effervescent compliments. He was very silent after that, not usually so monosyllabic, my commander, but I gathered that you must have worked together at some point."

"Are you always so insightful, Patrick? I do hope that you are. Wise head on young shoulders comes to mind. How is old Barrington nowadays?" he asked as he rose to refill our glasses.

I didn't answer his question, instead I asked one of my own. "Care to enlighten me as to why the extra capital letter in that surname of yours, Jack?"

"Stands for Police Reject, Patrick. Thought of applying once before a better offer fell into my lap. I realise that it was only conjecture on my part about being rejected, but it seemed to fit at the time, so I kept using it."

Chapter Two

Three Months Earlier

There had been four gunmen and two drivers, both of whom had stayed inside the cars at their respective steering wheels of a red S-Type Jaguar and blue 3.5 Rover, one in front of the security van and one behind as it started to pull away from the last bank on its route. Two of the robbers had pickaxes with their guns and the other two just firearms; sawn-off shotguns. The pickaxes went through the wind-screen before Henry Acre fired both barrels of his gun at the roof just above the uniformed driver and his mate. He reloaded and was holding his weapon pointed at the passenger's face as I shot him dead. The second sawn-off holder turned in my direction, levelled his gun and was then wounded by an armed colleague from the Flying Squad. Acre immediately died at the scene. Greenlee, the one wounded, was taken to University College Hospital where he was still receiving treatment. None of the other four in the gang had a chance to use any weapons. All were arrested and taken into custody before I removed my heavy disguise. It was then that Jack Price had noted my description, the one he gave in his written statement taken at Tottenham Court Road nick a few hours later. I knew of Acre's intentions to shoot the driver as it was I who had infiltrated the Kilburn Six, as they were known, some months prior to the robbery. That's why Trenchard insisted that I was included at the scene, at least that's what I was told.

My father was a born and bred Londoner but my mother was Irish through and through, hence the name of Patrick, my red hair and my natural Irish accent which, after a few months of ironing away any flawed nuances, was perfect enough to get an invitation to Edward (Teddy) Greenlee's table in the Nag's Head pub, Cricklewood Lane one Thursday night, three months, more or less, to the day of my calling on Jack.

Bill Hewitt, an Irish-Canadian, had unknowingly invited an undercover policeman into the heart of a conspiracy. The other three at the table that night: William O'Brien, Roy Murry (known as the Beret, which he wore come rain or come shine) and Ward Morrill, were all Irish by birth. Murry and Morrill were the two drivers. I had the innate endearing Irish ability of friendly conversation, aligned with good humour along with a deep pocket that my cover legend provided. My peripheral acceptance within the group was guaranteed as I worked at a second-hand quality car showroom where I could get legitimate cars without the need to 'ring' them. Henry Acre, whom I met later, was notably different from the others. Whereas they all were vicious he had a criminal record more akin to a savage animal than any human, and that's what worried Bill.

"He's going to shoot one of the guards regardless of the outcome, Pat. I can sense it. It's a statement he wants to make, not just pull off a robbery. Some time ago he told me of his Republican friends trying to drag me into the Provos, but I'm not a bomber. I'm a tea-leaf and a good one at that. I'll take my share then leg it back to Toronto away from politics, cos that's what turns him on in all of this. The money is less important to him than the statement. You mark my words!"

On the strength of the assessment made by Hewitt, coupled with Acre's previous two convictions of grievous bodily harm, one using a firearm, we were instructed to shoot if the situation looked life-threatening. As I was the only one with a clear shot I followed the orders given by Detective Superintendent Ball, the head of C1, the flying squad.

"Have you shot someone before, young Patrick? I only ask as you seem so unaffected by it all. As though it's quite a common occurrence in your everyday life as a police officer." We were well into our second glass of throat-blistering liquid as Jack asked his question.

"Mind if I smoke, Jack?"

"Not at all! I'll give the ashtray an empty just for you." On his return with a now sparkling clean one, I offered him a Dunhill cigarette which he accepted before I answered.

"First time, Jack! And yes, it never touched me. My hands were as cold as ice as I squeezed that trigger, not one shake anywhere. How about you when you faced down that neo-Nazi in his black-shirted uniform on the steps of the public toilets in Whitechapel? Did you shake? Were you scared stiff?"

"Different days then, Patrick, maybe we had different reactions too. Long forgotten times and best that way."

"You were the same age as me, were you not?"

"I was twenty-three, I believe, at the time. So, if you're twenty-three, then, yes, I was."

"Signed on in any particular branch of the services, or waiting to join up with the Americans and win the war, Jack?"

Now he did laugh, a high-pitched loud one at that. It suddenly struck me that I could not hear the sound of sex coming from below his flat but could hear the traffic on Shaftesbury Avenue, some fifty yards away.

"If Barrington Trenchard has sent you on this mission of yours then I'm sure he must have filled in some details, Patrick. Are you fishing for bigger game in order to persuade me to visit Tottenham Court Road nick again, because there's really no need?"

Another bottle of golden colour liquor appeared without a label attached, as our two glasses were refilled.

"I was trying to get more background on you as you'll have my life in your hands. Not only would I like you to change your statement slightly, I need an introduction to someone you both know. Only Trenchard is on the same side of the fence with no camouflage to work behind nowadays."

"Who might that be then?" he asked as my packet of cigarettes was further used.

"A Charlie Miller! I was told he is a top rank Met Police officer. My Mr Trenchard believes he knows the porn magazine trade in London inside out. Apparently every shop we raid is suddenly emptied of pornographic material before we arrive and it's Miller's department who organise the raids. Whoever he's in with is always one step ahead of us and we would like to stop that with your help. That was to be my next mission, hence the reason for the disguise. Not that it worked that well did it? We just need you to take out all reference to what I look like."

"A bit odd that your lot would expose you in such a high profile way just before another operation, don't you think?"

"That's why I joined the police, Jack. To uphold the law. Mine's not to reason why."

"And why did Barrington Trenchard send you looking for me, do you think?"

"The only reason I can think of is that he suspects you might know Miller and know his tricks."

"Hmm," was the only reply as he sipped his drink before adding, "anything in it for me, this help you ask for?"

"About the same reward you got from MI5 when they dispensed with your services, Jack. Nothing but our thanks."

"I did get the pension that you remarked on, Pat, plus I got the chair I'm sitting in."

"Strange gift, the chair I mean. Far from normal government furniture, I would have thought."

"And you wouldn't be wrong in that. It was presented to me when I came home from abroad and they billeted me at an outstation of Five in Pinner, Middlesex. It was part of my job to grade the pupils at the nearby Harrow School as to their prospects towards a career in the intelligence gathering industry."

"Funny shape for a chair," I said, to which he made no comment.

"Give me half an hour to dress, shave and what have you, then you can buy me dinner. I hope, but doubt, you've got a huge expense account as I'm as hungry as an old war horse, and the club I and Miller use doesn't open until nine o'clock. We'll have hours to fill with food and drink before you'll have a chance to meet one another. Go find Fifi on the floor below, tell her I send my avuncular love. Her real name is Gloria, comes every day from Bethnal Green. The door painted pink is hers. Likes a quick turnaround of clients, does my French neighbour, so she won't keep you long." Again he laughed, but even more so when I declined that invitation.

"Scared I might hear of your sexual prowess, or lack of it, are you!" he said as he left the room.

"While you're away I'll try to think of reasons why you only empty ashtrays when you have a visitor. Not many call on you, I'm guessing," I countered.

Chapter Three

Curzon Street

My newly acquired unkempt friend had metamorphosed into a Savile Row-tailored dressed man about town in a purple chalk-striped linen suit with a red silk handkerchief in his jacket pocket when he next appeared.

"Will this shatter the image you've formed about me, Patrick? I do hope so, otherwise I'll have nothing to smile about when I think of Barrington in his stiff collars and club ties. I too can put on a charade when required. Still wear that university club tie, does he? Not entitled to, you know. He never played rackets at Cambridge and as far as I know he never did play the game at all. It was his great-great-great-grandfather who played it whilst in the old Fleet Prison in 1832. He was put away for being unable to pay the debts of the company business, but Trenchard likes to gloss over that."

"I don't know much about the man, Jack."

"That I can believe, Patrick. Now's the time to fill that missing space in your education then. Come on, let's go taste some fine wine and talk about bent coppers."

"Do you know who Miller gets his money from?" I asked, genuinely surprised.

"There are many more than just Miller on the take and I know most of them, maybe not all though. How much time have you done on the streets young man?"

"None, Jack! I went straight into the 'Job' from university. I finished my full tutorial, got the 'A's' I wanted then joined the police on a whim. Thought it would be much more exciting than delving into furtive minds or sitting in a sterile laboratory. I was told that I could return to Oxford for a Master's if things don't work out, but I want to right the wrongs of this world, Jack, before I settle into a sedentary career. The 'Job' shoved me into a section of the criminal records department at Scotland Yard from a shortened initiation course to profile criminals. It was a start. I did only a five-week stint at reading The Instruction Book. That was too easy to learn verbatim for me. The Kilburn job was my first. Did the firearms course at Gravesend, apt name when you think of it, before they let me loose. All of that's part of the reason for the C11 attachment. Trenchard wanted me on that security van heist, as he knew I could identify Acre and not just from photographs."

"You're very young to have been trained on firearms, Patrick."

"I didn't know guns had a discrimination policy against age."

"As far as I knew the Met did. Two years before you can play with them," he replied, then went down a different track. "You said Fisher was your DI, did you not? Only we might run into some others from the Yard tonight. Thought about that at all, have you?"

"I've never actually met Fisher, Jack. Only heard him on the phone and read his written orders. Been exclusively tied to Trenchard's desk since day one. He is the only serving officer that I've met at the Yard. I've been kept out of sight since joining. Never actually worn the uniform! This opportunity of going solo was put to me just after the interview board. I grabbed it with both hands. They assigned two physical training instructors from Hendon to meet with me twice weekly in an old railway shed outside King's Cross, but apart from the time I spent with them, I studied all I was given in a flat not far from here in Covent Garden. The car front where I now work is part of C11. Buried deep beyond anyone's knowledge, as far as I was told."

"Where's that apartment of yours?" he asked, rather quickly I thought.

"Number six, Rose Street, Jack. Did you want an invitation?"

"Did you rent it directly, or was it provided by someone?"

"Came with the job. Trenchard sent me to a letting agency and then I rented it in my name."

"Who was on that board when you joined?"

"Trenchard was one, but the other two I didn't know. Looked like civilian brass to me. I never had a formal introduction."

"Old Barrington certainly threw you in at the deep end, didn't he. It's not in my hands that your life lies, Patrick, it's in the hands of the intelligence set-up that you're wrapped up in. Personally, I wouldn't trust it, but I no longer play that game. As far as anyone is concerned I'm out socialising with the man who possibly saved my own life three days ago but I won't introduce you as that. I'd only say that you're a friend and leave it there. But if pressed, I wouldn't be wrong in saying that the man you shot could have shot me and others. The robbery has been spoken about in these parts. There's a very close knit society amongst the prostitutes and us layabouts. I have a reason to be out with you if I need one!

You've got to understand something before we go on. What I know about people has come after donkey's years of listening to what I'm told. To them that tell the story, I'm just an old sop who likes a drink or two, easy on the eye and of no consequence. You're a stranger in a world where the only knowledge you have of it, has come from what you've read, fantasied about or been told. Soho is not just on the surface, Patrick, it goes a lot deeper than that. Now you've come to dig a hole into the soul of the sex trade. If you're successful you're likely to put a lot of people out of work. Afterwards, if you ever want to hide away where no one looks further than their own nose, then don't look for a farmhouse set in acres of open ground, hide in a city with plenty of noise, that's where you'll find the real silence."

It was he who fell silent as we left his apartment on the top floor of number twenty-six Romilly Street and walked north along Dean Street towards Soho Square. Then as we turned into a side street he spoke again.

"I'm guessing here, Patrick, but did Trenchard recruit you at university with a whiter than white campaign speech? —Let's clean up the streets of London together, making it safe for the working man, my young intellectual friend. Paint the town white with an Irishman as the artist."

"Not quite as pretentious as that, Jack, but that was his stated purpose without the Irish bit. Frankly that's what enticed me to sign up. I hate dishonesty in any form. If I can help him achieve that aim, then why not try?" He didn't answer my question.

"That club I mentioned earlier, as being used by Miller and others of his fraternity, is owned by a one-time friend of Trenchard's and a distant acquaintance of mine. A man known as Alhambra. That's not his real name, of course. Barrington knows it as do I, along with the majority of what used to be the intelligence community. Mind you, if the rumours are true, he's moved on and upwards to other things nowadays. Some in these parts say that it's him that runs the porn trade. That could be why his club is so popular, but I have no first-hand knowledge of that. Trenchard could well be intrigued by me telling you that name, or, he might just want to hide it away and ignore it. Be careful how you play it, Patrick. As I remember Trenchard has allies in very high places."

* * *

"You off to the Ritz for the night, Jack, or on the pull?" asked a very beautiful woman, whom Jack introduced as Amelia, as we entered a wine bar in Wardour Street.

"If you are out looking for company then I'll take your arm. Oops, sorry, I didn't see your friend? He looks tasty!" she said before adding, "I'll take him off you when you've had your fill."

"My new lover, Amy! Keep your hands to yourself."

"Yeah, if either of you were that way inclined then I'm an elephant flying on a cloud." Her long blonde hair trailing down her slender back was the last I saw of Amy, leaving me to admire her wiggle and shapely legs as she departed.

"You two know each other well then, Jack?" I asked, rather unnecessarily.

"Somewhat, yes! She owns this place along with half of Soho. Don't let that sensuous, female body fool you. She is a he, Pat! Goes by the name of Jimmy when the moon's asleep. Never go on first impressions alone, they can be painfully misleading."

I looked around but I could see no men in the bar; only women. Or were they women? Certainly the cleavage of the girl that brought our drinks over to the candlelit table Jack had selected in the corner facing the doorway had me fooled if she was not. I never asked, but the uncertainty didn't impinge on my imagination.

"Have you a fetish for full ashtrays, Jack?" I asked, noticing the overflowing one on our table, at which he laughed before he explained.

"My wife hated me smoking, even tried to force me to quit. I told her I would cut down, but never quite managed to. Whenever we were out, and I had to wait for her, I would sit at a table where there was a full ashtray so she wouldn't be able to count how many fags I'd smoked by the time she had finished her shopping. It's a habit I haven't been able to shake off. You used the word camouflage a little while ago, so call it that if you like." He continued to laugh until the business of the evening was once more addressed.

"What did Trenchard tell you about me, Pat?"

"Nothing really from Trenchard. Just what I've told you: said he'd seen your name on the list of witnesses, recognised that distinctive signature of yours and knew you from the old days. That was it. I thought you may have been in the police until I followed his orders of visiting a building in Curzon Street, in Mayfair, where everyone I came across told me that was about to be closed down. I showed some guy in a uniform a letter from Trenchard and was allowed to view a file on you. It didn't tell me much either, other than you worked in the secret intelligence service during the war and for a bit after. It ran out of paper in 1948."

"I didn't work in the SIS, Pat, I worked for the likes of Barrington who worked in it. There is a difference. I never went to the right schools, you see, nor lived in Guildford to become staff. I did the mundane that they were too busy talking about."

"Want to tell me how you started, Jack, because there's nothing in your file. A list was all I found. Date and place of birth, parents' names and your retirement date; June the first 1948," he laughed.

"Is that what it said? Even that's a lie! I did another five years after that. Not all that time for Five. I was pushed upstairs somewhere along the line, up a number to Six and sent abroad to Austria. It was when I came home from Vienna that they put me out to grass. I was married then, but the time abroad cost me my wife and the time back here cost me my children. Mary and I married in the autumn of 1944. I was twenty-five, with her being three years younger. George was born the year after and Mildred the following one. That was the year they started to send me away from London more and more. If they hadn't, then who knows how many kids I would have fathered that would have grown up to hate me."

There was no change registered on his face that I noticed nor any alteration in his voice that I detected. The sadness, if there was any, was swept away long ago.

"Mary and I never got back together when I returned. I moved out and let life go on for them. In 1966, when she passed from this world, both my son and daughter emigrated without a word to me. We've never spoken to this day."

I was looking hard for some recognition of regret, some trace of human emotion that my psychological training could pick on and develop, but there simply was none. He had detached himself from the world that he had once lived in, in a way I had never thought possible.

Work had been his love, coming first before any pangs of conscience about a destroyed passion of a once solid and tangible relationship. The unattainable and the touchable both ruined, but only one clung onto. It wasn't indifference, otherwise, he would never have broached the topic, nor apparent apathy, just self-control being demonstrated naturally and not for effect. What an asset for someone in the espionage game, I thought, and could not hide my juvenile admiration.

"What a spy you must have been, Jack." He smiled at that, but kept whatever reaction he had to himself.

Chapter Four

Leonard Miller

We left the wine bar with its dark mysteries undisturbed after finishing a rather good bottle of Beaujolais, then doubled back on ourselves towards Old Compton Street.

"Let's eat, Pat! By the time we finish a good slap-up meal, Alhambra's club will have opened and you can start on that journey of yours." Without another a word we suddenly turned abruptly left into a dead-end alleyway, and stopped.

"You thinking that we're being followed, Jack?" I asked, "I haven't noticed anyone."

"You wouldn't if they were good, Pat. And if they were super good they'd know that this place leads nowhere, so they wouldn't turn in here. But I don't warrant the super good anymore."

The regret in that admission was covered by a contrived smile that now lined his forehead and creased his mouth. Almost a minute passed before he spoke again.

"Simple precautions can save lives, young Patrick. Your man will be at our next port of call. We need to be cautious. If it's true that Alhambra does indeed run the porn industry then Miller has his hands deep inside his pockets. He sits alone every night at the same table just inside the doorway of the restaurant we're going to use. I use the place regularly. Sometimes he will just nod his head at me, but occasionally he will speak. Tonight, if he does, you will say nothing nor look at him. Just stand silently on my left side looking straight in front. I will say that you're a person I met a few days ago and leave it at that. If he invites us to sit, which I very much doubt, you will excuse yourself, saying you need the Gents as you have an upset stomach. Stay in there for at least ten minutes. He's normally gone by a quarter to nine on the dot for his journey home to his wife and three children in Blackheath. He has a very grand looking place there. He's a fool, Pat, but not a stark raving idiot. He'll smell you out as plod if you get too close. His name is Leonard Miller; Detective Chief Superintendent at West End Central nick. High cheese as you said and a tough target to hit, but if you are as passionate about all this as I believe you are, then you will find a way. Ready?" he asked as we departed from our lonely alleyway.

"No one following us then, Jack?" I asked.

"Seems not, Pat," phlegmatically he replied.

* * *

He was a big man, but it was not until he left that I saw his overall build. The first, and the only thing I saw, as I stood where Jack had told me, were his feet. They were enormous!

"You're looking very smart tonight, Jack. Out on the town, are we?" asked a gruff, guttural, cockney voice as we entered.

"Something like that, Leonard. We will be at the Guitar later. Will you be in there tonight?"

"Nah! I'll be home with the trouble and strife soon. She misses me rotten if I'm away for too long. Have a nice evening with your friend, and say hello to the maestro for me if you get a chance, Jack." He was too busy with his meal to glance at me.

We sat a table at the far end of the half empty restaurant with my back turned to where the detective chief superintendent was seated. I caught sight of him as a reflection in the emblazoned Restaurant 'Da Fiono' windows. Wide shouldered, much taller than average with a head of hair that betrayed his age. From his rank, I had deduced that he must have passed fifty, but the thickness of his grey hair, swept back behind his ears, was that of a much younger man. He stood as an athlete would, straight with no slouch of any kind and looked light on his feet. He was dressed immaculately, but seemingly with no pockets of his own unless he had paid before our arrival, as he offered no money to the waiter who obsequiously brushed the front of his suit jacket. He made no sign to us as he left, right on the time that Jack said he would.

"You are a very observant man and one for precise details, Jack. Did that come from over here or the time you spent abroad on HM business?"

"Never gave that much thought. Both would be right in their own way," he replied as a waiter hovered to take our order. I took a menu but had not finished with Jack at that point.

"What would you like to do first, Jack? Tell me how you started that work you did over on foreign soil, or about Alhambra and that man who's just left?"

"As I told you, the man who just left is a fool, but he'll take some catching. I'll give you his full address in Blackheath Park later. He has the first floor as his family home, but look at the deeds lodged with Land Registry. The Millers own the whole building and the one at the back of the plot that's being built. The construction company is not in his name but it's his all the same. Take a drive out there one day if the urge grabs you, and see if you could buy that place and maintain his lifestyle on the salary he draws. He would probably say that his wife is on the game as his way of explaining it. He's not your worry, though. Alhambra is another kettle of fish all told.

He fought on the Nazi side in Spain during the Civil War, taking that name from the palace in Grenada. He was born to English parents in India. Very good breeding with better-placed connections than most. He was one of the first Nazi sympathisers I came across when I started work for those inside the SIS whilst still at school. Again, you must control that enthusiasm of yours. Order some grub first. We might have a long night in front of us. We'll talk as we eat, but first some more vino to smooth my throat. *Un chianti per favore, Alfonso. Il tuo migliore, come il mio amico sta pagando.*"

"Learn Italian in Italy, Jack?" naively I asked.

"Somewhere colder than that, Pat! Learned it when I was in Austria. I had a teacher who had a huge wood-burning stove going all day and every day. Sometimes I sat on it until my arse was cooked. Outside it was cold enough to freeze the balls off brass monkeys. I even heard them fall sometimes!" I was getting used to his humour and that smile of his.

The bottle was served, uncorked, sniffed and tasted, then when approved poured into the appropriate glasses. He excused himself from the table to wash his hands, leaving me alone with my thoughts. His return coincided with the arrival of the first offerings of food.

"Was it simply my persuasive powers that led you to agree to helping so much, Jack, or something more than that? After all, I only asked you to change a few written words. We didn't have to do all this tonight."

"Why not tonight? I was hungry anyway and you're paying, I've already told the waiter that." It was my turn to laugh which I did gladly.

"I think I can see a bit of me in you, Patrick. I was eager to help my country at your age, do the best I could in flying the flag. Patriotism, idealisms of freedom from oppression and all that shit drove me on. For me, at that time, the establishment stood in the way and shut me out. Ever seen and read the inscription on Edith Cavell's statue opposite the Portrait Gallery? She was a spy, you know. Ran a small but significant group from a Belgium hospital in the First World War where she worked. We made a great propaganda thing out of the firing squad death. Used photographs of her on recruiting posters. That is something we're good at; turning the truth our way at pressing times. Barrington's name is enough of an incentive to wind me up and start the motor running again. Enjoy the ride while you can, but learn where the brake pedal is, and check that it works every so often, Pat."

Not having heard him elaborate on any statement so much as that before, I wondered why now there was a necessity.

Chapter Five

The Savoy

"I was a page at the Savoy Hotel when I was fifteen, Patrick. My dad had died the year before and although I was in a grammar school with ambitions of perhaps making it into a university, Mum needed the extra money that I could provide with that job. I was a bit ruthless in those days; it was the tips I was really after. Saw the advert at the bottom of a newspaper I was delivering on my paper round one morning and applied straight away. I had to bunk off school to get there. The only qualifications it said that were needed was you had to be clean and not too tall. I passed on both those counts. I think the man who was in charge was called Snow, but it could have been Scott. Nearly forty years have flown past since I was given that first pair of white gloves. They gave you three pairs a day you know, so none got dirty or grubby. Good little earner, that job! Bit wearing on the old feet, though. Must have walked miles each day through the corridors and reception halls. There were eight of us, I think, delivering messages or going out for cigarettes or flowers for the guests. Gave you a cloak to wear if you had to go outside through the main doors. Great fun I tell you, especially if it was an American guest you were going out for.

They tipped well, but no one tipped like a US celebrity. Had a few in my day. Don't ask me for their names as most of them I'd never heard of, but Mr Snow, or whatever his name was, said they were really important and to look after them. Added a big wink when he said that. That was enough for me. I do remember one celeb, a young girl, a year or so younger than me who was over here to sing on the stage at the Adelphi. She was with her parents and every morning I was instructed to take breakfast to her room. I was the only one allowed to do that. Her mother gave me two tickets to the show, and, don't faint, a five-pound note! More than a year's wage. I went with my mum, who was so proud of me knowing this American girl that she told all our street that she was off to the theatre to see Judy Garland. She bought a hat for the occasion from that fiver. My mum would fill a hot bath tub every night for me after that for my sore feet. She and I feasted well on the strength of my tips and the stories I told about who I'd met at Savoy."

"Was it at the Savoy that you were first approached to work for the secret mob, Jack?"

"Observe and listen, they were the first orders I received, Pat. *That's all we want you to do.* So said Mr Stewart Campbell, my first handler in early 1933. He wanted me to pin my ears back for mentions about Germany and the name of Hitler in particular. Then they wanted more. They always did! I was promoted in-house a year later to the reception desk and that's where Alhambra comes into the equation, although, he wasn't called that then, of course. Trenchard came a few weeks later. 'The Strummer' was Alhambra's code name between Campbell, Trenchard and me, and I was to handle him carefully, they told me. Taking note of callers, telephone numbers if I could, along with which guests he mostly spoke to or mingled with. Trenchard was a junior at Five then. I called him a runner as he was always in a hurry to get somewhere else. He passed on instructions from Campbell and sometime later one of them ordered me to enlist in the Blackshirts of Sir Oswald Mosley. I was on my way to one of the rallies held in the East-End, calling for him to be released from internment, when I came across that man at Whitechapel with the gun. I knocked him out, but my cover was blown in Mosely's New Party so they assigned me elsewhere. I was sent to a Royal Naval yard to work in order to unearth a Communist spy, but I can't tell you of that. Mind you, by that time I had every name signed up to Mosley's way of thinking, some would blow your mind wide open, Pat. What I will say is that I told Campbell about John Cairncross way before his name cropped up with Burgess and the other lot from Cambridge. Dropped Victor Rothschild's name on his lap as well, but what I said was ignored because, as I said before, I never lived in Guildford and only went to a common old grammar school. I was not one of the chaps. Wrong side of the country for inclusion into their club."

"Why would they wipe your file clean from 1948 if you didn't finish with them until '53? That doesn't make sense unless you did some really important covert stuff for them and they wanted to hide you."

There was a wide smile from Jack as he finished picking at his food, neatly placing his knife and fork beside each other and laying them diagonally across his half eaten meal. At first, I thought the smile was because the pasta he'd had and the wine he'd drunk both met with his approval, but there was another reason.

"Do you remember me saying that the chair you paid so much attention to was given to me when I retired from the service, Pat?" I nodded in agreement. "Well, that wasn't entirely true. I took it as my going away present! Walked out the office, past a startled janitor and boarded a bus carrying it. A right two and eight of a mess I made of it on that bus, I can tell you. The conductor said it was too big, but it wasn't at an angle. I only travelled as far as the train station and he let me ride on the platform with it. Caught the train into Marylebone then had to walk all the way home to Baker Street with it across my back. It has been everywhere with me since then. Had it re-covered more times than I can recall. Did you wonder why it has three sides?" he asked. To which I replied that I had.

"Barrington brought it in with him one day. Wanted to make some derogatory gesture in front of all the others, put me in my place kind of thing. Said that one side was us, the Brits, one the Americans and the other represented the Russians. But although I asked him what he meant by that, he wouldn't say. Trenchard was by then in Special

Branch, heading up 'A' department; internal affairs. Sort of rubber-heel mob, creeping around with their noses up each other's arse. They were amateurs, Patrick. Made loads of noise and unnecessary commotion. I was under surveillance by them. When I complained, I was informed that I was suspected of having been turned in Vienna, where I had diligently served my country. They had no evidence of that, because it had never happened, but I was told it was—standard practices, old chap. *We use the same procedure on everyone who has returned from foreign lands. We suspect first and regret the inconvenience later; if we must!* and *don't take it personally.* But I did, in a big way! Can you see the irony in all of this?"

I answered that I couldn't and he'd left me behind somewhere. As two glasses of Marsala were delivered to our table that I had not seen Jack order, he explained how he had come to that conclusion.

"There you are, a university graduate helping another graduate to bring down another who has enjoyed privilege, but having to engage me, an old washed-up spy from the wrong side of the bed. One whose affiliations were once questioned but never answered." He tasted his wine as I tasted mine before continuing.

"Trenchard needs not only you but me too, Patrick. On your own, I doubt the two of you would have got close. Even if I'm wrong you most certainly would not have any inside knowledge of Miller so soon. From him there must be a direct money trail to Alhambra. The trouble for Barrington is yet to be revealed, but it will be, believe me. I will introduce you to the ultimate prey right after we drink up and leave. That's where things will start to get hairy. A simple point I would like to raise before we set about our quest. How do you suppose a known fascist who still advocates his hatred of Jews and all blacks, yellows and browns can get a licence to run a club in London? Let's forget about his trade in pornographic books and concentrate on why he's not locked up for his political statements. Whose pockets do you think he's lining?"

"Could be freedom of speech, Jack? Something along those lines, perhaps?"

"If only! Soho might be a closed shop to outsiders, but it's nothing compared to Freemasons, Westminster and the law, Pat. You're on a loser, my son. You're the tethered lamb to bring out the snakes while the lions gorge on the buffalo around the next bend. If you want my advice, which you haven't asked for but nevertheless will get, then call it in now. There's a phone box we pass before we get to his club. It's never been raided, not even Barrington would dare to do that."

"Why, Jack? That would seem the obvious place to start." Another smile preceded his reply.

"You are an ant in this world, Patrick. You are expected to show the corruption in the police that every Tom, Dick and Harry walking the streets of London know about. Appease the public mind. You are not expected to find politicians having it off in the back rooms of a Nazi's club in the Capital on a Friday night whilst claiming allowances for legitimate entertainment. Follow Miller's money lodged in his local bank under his sister's name of Carolyn McKay; her husband, incidentally, is the MP for Darlington. Call in the Sweeney, Pat. Tell them you believe there's an IRA gunman in the Guitar. Use whatever your Kilburn cover name was and they'll come running. Then comes the hard bit. You'll have to get away. Out of the Job and far gone. You look perplexed at that, why? You don't believe me?"

"Can't see that I'd be a pariah by outing the corrupted, Jack. Just can't see that at all!"

"No, you're not as cynical as me. Do you know who's the Member of Parliament for Herne Bay, Pat? But don't worry, they won't arrest him. The Prime Minister has a green pass on sex. You might be made Commissioner overnight, or you might not. Depends on how much they value your silence. Don't just settle for a chair, Patrick, idiotic ideals are worth more than that. Go somewhere abroad. America would be my choice. More liberal minded over there. Write a book about it all and get it accepted into Hatchards. They have Royal patronage, with three Royal warrants displayed announcing their self-importance. But if they try to slam a D notice on it here in England you'll have no worries as you will have readers crawling all over you in the States. I never had the bottle, nor the intelligence to do that and it's too late now."

"What happened in Vienna, Jack? Were you turned?"

Saturday In London

Chapter Six

A New Life

Unlike other branches of the criminal investigative departments within the Metropolitan police, C11 did not have a central office at Scotland Yard. There were many scattered around London and beyond its perimeters, all trying to keep their anonymity. Trenchard had an office to himself just off the Haymarket in Suffolk Street in an otherwise unused four-storeyed terrace house. My orders were to write a report on what happened with Jack and leave it on his desk first thing Saturday morning on my way to Kilburn and my car salesman role. To have left that position so soon after the bungled security van robbery would have raised suspicions, thereby endangering future operations for me, and the front.

I wrote my report in long-hand, paying heed to Jack's warning of careful appraisal of the information he had disclosed, before leaving my flat at around eight that morning. My omission of the Prime Minister's name was not done through any sense of loyalty to him or his position, more in a way as self-protection. If Jack had been wrong then I would have looked a complete fool in reporting a rumour and if he'd been right, then I figured that my life would have been over in one way or another. There were a couple of things I had to do before I got to Suffolk Street, but as I was in no hurry I played Jack's game of shaking off any would-be followers by occasionally doubling back on myself before retracing my route. As I crested the Duke of York's steps, turning to see if anyone else was climbing them and then stopping to light a cigarette when there were none, a young scrawny boy no older than fourteen thrust a sealed envelope at me, saying, "This is for you."

At that he ran off in the direction of Carlton Gardens, leaving me speechless. For some inexplicable reason I never opened it; I waited until I was inside Trenchard's building.

If you're after sun, sea and sex then do nothing about this note, but as I know you're after much more than that be at No 74 The Albany, Piccadilly by nine. Amy sends his regards!

It would be easy to say that I abandoned the significance I previously placed on morality by an iniquitous value I suddenly placed on prestige, but that was not strictly true. I never believed that virtue would give me power in the first place and it was the lure of power that had me in its grasp. Not for one second did I question the authenticity of this note coming from anyone other than Jack. Ethics are fine in idealism, but dishonesty and pragmatism are the only tools that will sustain power once it's been achieved. Every sinew in my body ached for the excitement that could be supplied by Jack Price. He held the power that I craved and I wanted to snatch it from his clenched fist. It had taken me about a minute to decide what to do with the information that Jack had given me about the Garage club and Miller's conspiracy; it took less time to decide about this invitation. Had I taken more time to make a considered choice then maybe my future might have been different, that's if I ever had a say over my future at all.

In order to start a new life the old one has not only to die but be buried safely away from view and interference. That may appear to be an obvious statement; however, never having had the need to change, it was not one I considered. As far as I was concerned the suitcase I carried was light on relevant history books or files of past achievements, and what there were could easily be hidden on the bottom layer, but there were others who carried not only a key to that case, but the pen that was writing my life story day by very day.

In less than five minutes after opening that note I was knocking on the designated door in the private, exclusive courtyard of The Albany. It was promptly opened by a colossus of a man with deeply scarred tissue on the left side of his face with the blackest of deep-set eyes I'd ever seen. I don't know why, but I thought the scarring had been caused by an explosion of some sort.

"Put those clothes over there on and be quick about it, young sir. There's a cab to catch and a new life to begin." He pointed at a brown long-haired wig, a pair of false spectacles, a blue jacket and black shoes with built-up heels that made me look two inches taller. Without a single question or utterance I obeyed. The only sound in that room was the scraping noise of one set of clothes being shoved into a plastic carrier bag whilst another set was put on.

* * *

"Did you have someone at the rear entrance of The Albany?"

"We did, sir! We had two men trailing West this morning and as soon as he entered the courtyard one of them was around the back to that innocuous-looking rear exit. We've used that building ourselves once or twice. Great short cut if you know it's there. They jumped into a cab, but the cab they used is not registered at the Public Carriage Office nor is the number plate assigned to any vehicle according at the Ministry of Transport. We've lost him!"

"What about Price? Is he still at that place of his in Soho?"

"Left DC West in Soho Square a little after ten o'clock last night, returning straight home. We tried his door this morning at eleven, but after getting no reply we forced it to gain entry. There was a step-ladder in the rear bedroom leading to a trapdoor into the loft. From there he had access to the roof area. He could have gone anywhere from up there, sir! The man who met West this morning was easy to recognise. The head porter knew he wasn't a resident. Said he'd come to deliver a package to Sir Horace Butler. He insisted on taking it himself. Flashed a wallet at him with what the porter said was a police warrant card. Added he had the key and was expected to enter if Butler wasn't there. Our man at the back in Burlington Gardens copped him straight off. West was disguised, but it was him all right. The man with him was Job, sir. No mistake with that one. Pointing his camera at everything, he was. Probably got our chap in one photo at least."

"What has this Sir Horace Butler to do with any of it?"

"I doubt he has anything, as we can't trace anyone of that name."

"Blank wall then?"

"Seems that way, sir, yes!"

"I wonder where West will surface and for what purpose?"

"*Tantum tempus narrabo*, sir."

"Indeed it will!"

* * *

Once I was dressed, the man who had met me ushered me along a curved covered veranda to a doorway opening onto Burlington Gardens then, after producing a heavy camera from the holdall he carried, started to snap away at everything at ground and rooftop level. A black London cab drew alongside us almost immediately and we were in, turning left at Regent Street towards Oxford Circus. We turned left again, and as we reached the Bentley car showroom at Berkeley Square my fellow passenger alighted, and stood on the corner photographing every vehicle with occupants that had followed us along Bruton Street. No one at this stage had spoken a word to me since leaving The Albany. That did not change until Scarface was back in the cab again.

"It's clear behind. Waterloo next stop! There was one I recognised who made us as we came out the back, but that was to be expected," he said directly to me.

He had a quiet, deliberate voice which coupled to his size was reassuring in a manner that I had not anticipated. There was the trace of an accent to his speech that I could not put my finger on, but if I had to take a guess then Afrikaans would have been my choice. I was shaking, but not uncomfortably through fear. It was the adrenaline of excitement pumping through my veins. I sat patiently waiting for an explanation which never adequately came.

"In the inside pocket of that jacket you're wearing is a rail ticket and twenty-two pounds in assorted coins and notes. I want you to check it now and then sign this receipt."

"Where am I going?" I asked.

"Tells you on the ticket. I'm not your nursemaid. You are expected to do something yourself." With neither a soft voice nor a bad-tempered one he told me, he just said it. I followed his instructions and whilst I was counting the money he passed me a slim wallet with an opened envelope.

"There's a driving licence in here under the name of Phillip Marks. The envelope is addressed to you under that name with a letter from your fictional boss inside. You won't end up with the name of Marks, nor that address, but it will do if you fall over, injuring yourself and need police or ambulance assistance until all of this is sorted out. It's best that neither of us know much about each other. Jack wanted me to pass on a message, said you'd understand that it came from him and no one else. Said Twickenham was in the right direction for Guildford."

The imagination I'd locked away inside now had its chance to be explored, but if it was an illustrious fanfare I had expected to be playing on my acceptance within Jack's nefarious world then I was disappointed. However, that focused regret over a prosaic welcome was misguided. I should have shown more recognition to the abandonment of my innocence than the unquestioned approval I tacitly gave him.

"Will Jack be meeting me at Twickenham station?"

"Can't say for sure but I doubt it. Mr Price doesn't care too fondly for the daylight hours."

I looked directly into those shadowy eyes, finding nothing remotely excitable in them, just a professional doing a job of work. He was roughly forty years of age, smartly dressed with hands and feet that matched his enormity. For some reason I found it odd that he was clean-shaven, as a beard would have covered those hideous scars of his. Fingernails that were immaculately manicured, but the skin on the back and palms of his hands was coarse and gnarled as though well used to manual tasks. The holdall at his feet looked of military issue which fitted how I saw him. I could not make out the driver's face as his interior mirror was tilted upwards towards the roof of the cab, but from the little I could see of his silhouette there was nothing distinguishing about him. Younger than my companion by a few years with the same colour hair; black. A hooked nose but apart from that, nothing. My agitation had captured Scarface's attention.

"The first time into action is always the hardest. The realisation that the unknown waits around the corner is the making or the breaking of a man's spirit. You either bottle it or make it into something. You've been selected for something big, young man, be happy that it's you Jack wants."

"I wasn't aware that I was being recruited and I'm certain that I don't know why some ex-undercover spy would want me. You, yes, but me! What do I have that's in demand?"

"Perhaps it's your innocence. We all had that once."

"Where did yours get left behind?" I asked with rising confidence.

"Vietnam, when I got out!"

"I didn't know we had a military presence in that war."

"We didn't, but some over here had an interest in what was happening over there, so they sent me along with some others. We all came home, Phillip. Don't you worry about a thing. Jack is a very precise and careful man."

"Am I to become anonymous like the department that you work for?"

"No, Phillip! Anonymity means that there's no name. You will be given a name to suit the circumstances you're needed for. People like me have no need of a name."

"Was Jack in charge of your venture into Vietnam then?" I asked, but he gave no answer, just stared straight ahead.

* * *

"Why is Job his name? Do you think it was mixed up with a job sometime in the past and his name was just wrongly interpreted?"

"Would that be important if it had?"

"I guess not, but it could be!"

Chapter Seven

No One Is More Important Than Each

The house was a small, red-bricked terraced affair with a well-cared-for short, front garden in a dead end, tree-lined street no more than five minutes ride from the station. The twenty-minute train journey had passed uneventfully with only a few passengers travelling southwards at that time of morning and even fewer alighting at Twickenham. I was met by a medium-built man, dressed head to foot in black leathers on a motorcycle who, apart from asking my name, spoke not another single word as he passed me a blue helmet then took it from me when we arrived outside number 14 Merton Road. It had been raining hard on the journey from London and the trees were still shedding water in the wind. Jack Price stood sheltering in the open doorway!

"Why am I here, Jack?" I asked as he stretched out a welcoming hand.

"Because you wanted to come, Patrick, it's your dream job," he added as I accepted his greeting.

"Did I make that choice when I was asleep and before you changed my name?" I asked as he smiled in that condescending fashion I was beginning to know.

"Your name is to be Shaun Redden but we'll come to that in time, and yes, you made a choice the minute you met me. I note that you decided not to mention Edward Heath being in Alhambra's club when you reported to Suffolk Street. It was a lie of course, but you never knew that. You did the right thing without thinking too deeply. Firstly we survive and secondly we think of ourselves. Do you follow that?"

"Not at all! One follows the other. One cannot survive without thinking of oneself first. How did you know that I never mentioned Heath in the report I handed in this morning?"

"I had it read, of course. You don't think I'd let something like that go forward without my approval, did you? By the way did you spot those two men following you, or, were just allowing them to believe you hadn't?"

"Truth is, Jack, I never saw a soul."

"Hmm, although I always appreciate the truth I was hoping that you had spotted them. You don't have to beat yourself up too much, though; they were good. Quite professional."

"I didn't warrant the very good then?" He chose not to answer that question.

"No one is more important than each, Shaun. You will learn that. That's what we do! We look after those who need looking after that nobody else wants to touch," he declared, making no further comment on my report.

"You never answered my question about being turned back in Vienna. Shall we start there, Jack?" He closed the door behind me without answering that question either. Although I was irritated by his reluctance to respond to my queries, it wasn't simple petulance. It was because I imagined there still to be a choice available to join him or not, but if there had been a choice, I was never strong enough to exercise it.

"Leave the paperwork you were given on the stand in the hallway, Shaun. It's time for a new beginning. Come through."

I slavishly followed him along a lighted narrow corridor lined with torpid, hanging boating prints on sleepy, white painted walls into a double lounge with a casement window to the front and two other such, but smaller, windows to the rear overlooking a grassed garden with a high wooden fence. All three windows had curtains that were drawn back. In the centre of a speckled linoleum-covered floor was a square dining table surrounded by four, red padded upright chairs. There was one other piece of furniture in this part of the room; a side-board, on which were two packets of unopened cigarettes and a half full metal ashtray. A yellow settee, with two matching yellow arm-chairs, an oblong occasional table and a television set were in the other half of the lounge.

"Tea or coffee, Shaun?"

"You mean to say that there's a kitchen to add to the opulence of this house, Jack? Are there many more rooms full of surprises?"

"It's not much is it, but it does for what's required. There's a kitchen along with three functional bedrooms and a bathroom upstairs with all the necessary facilities. Enough practicality for the short time you'll be here. We prefer to move around quite frequently."

"By 'we' you mean there's more than just you and the three I've met so far then?"

"More than you'd imagine, but not too many to clog the system."

"Does Trenchard know that I'm here?"

"Nobody knows exactly where you are other than me, Shaun. But that's not the question you should be asking."

"What is then?"

"Why did Trenchard select you in the first place?"

"You invited me here, Jack."

"True, but it was he who dropped you in my lap. I can't imagine him having the brains or balls to do that alone. I had a tip-off to be in Charing Cross Road from an entirely different source unconnected to you or him and what's more, I never made a statement to any copper. You didn't think of checking that, did you?"

I was struck dumb, having believed everything Trenchard had told me, even the signature.

"I've told you how I knew about the timing of the robbery. How about C11? How did Trenchard know?" he asked.

"That's easy! I told him, Jack. The car front where I work took the cars in as part exchange on the Wednesday and as always they were parked in the company's lock-up yard half a mile away from the showrooms in Iverson Road. The keys were left behind the sun visors with the yard locked. That night I gave Murry a copy of the gate keys I'd already made. The yard was not going to be used that Thursday as both mechanics, who were brothers, were going to their mum's funeral. Neither car was missed until Friday morning, by which time they had been impounded. The local uniform made enquiries on Friday but it was written up as incompetence by someone from the garage or the showroom. I was never questioned about it."

"Well, you're here now, Shaun, so let's leave the full reasons for why till another time. Is it the tea or the coffee you want?"

As I answered 'tea' I heard a water tap begin to run and then, seconds after, a kettle start to boil. Next came a woman's voice with a heavy Irish inflection asking, "Will you be taking sugar in that tea, Shaun?"

Taking the chair at the end of the table that looked directly at the closed kitchen door, I answered, "No, thank you, but if there's any whisky a drop would not come amiss," then turning my attention back towards Jack I continued, "perhaps, the whisky might help me make sense of all this."

"I think it might take more than one measure in your tea, Shaun. Think on this whilst you're waiting; why did Trenchard want you and me in the same place, do you think? He's obviously getting instructions from outside offices and I reckon they have been running you since your days at Oxford, but every cloud has a pewter lining as they say. At least you're at the same place both they and you want."

"Speaking of places, was that place of yours in Soho, Jack, just a façade with the family snaps laid on to fool me?"

"It was a place I use occasionally if the purpose suits me, but the photographs were not meant to confuse or coerce you in any sense. I don't believe Barrington was relying on any sympathy you may have had for my marital status swinging your vote in my direction."

"He knew of it though, the flat and your family, Jack?"

"I have used it before and my family issues are not a secret, Shaun," he answered.

"I'm becoming a mite peeved by this Shaun business. Can we make a start on clearing that up?"

"I will get to it, but for now I'm sizing you up. Are you here for the excitement I can undoubtedly provide, or are you a mole sent to infiltrate my organisation for the benefit of Barrington Trenchard and his friends? I watched you before the event in Charing Cross Road, during it and then, more importantly, after it. Not once did you hesitate or show any remorse for killing that man, Shaun. Does Trenchard want to give you a role where you're the sheriff, judge and hangman all rolled into one?"

"How did you know of me before I shot that man, Jack?"

He had my fascination and attention and he knew it as he took his place at the opposite end of the table, studying me carefully.

"Have you ever noticed how a poor child will scream his head off if deprived of a toy, but the child from a wealthy house will merely complain slightly, knowing that he will easily find one of many thing to play with? You're not screaming a single decibel, Shaun, in fact, you're wallowing in all of this mystery having found yourself in the biggest stack of toys imaginable. I did think you might do more than just ask where you were being taken this morning. But no! Not even a whimper of protest. Not wishing to repeat myself, but not a single tear shed for the Irishman you shot dead? And don't tell me it was in the line of duty. I've seen men take lives, Shaun. I know a cold-blooded killer when I see one. Now is the time to see if you have a calm head in times of crisis, or merely the fool impressed by gun-firing adventures." He was smiling confidently as he spoke.

If he had worn last night's clothes as a uniform to impress, then today held no reason for the making of impressions. He was in casual clothes, albeit bespoke rather than bought off-the-peg. It was the truth he spoke about me trying to fight against the temptation he offered, but it was a losing battle and one I had no heart for. Reaching for the ashtray, he placed it on the table and offered me a cigarette. I tried to hide that previously mentioned obedient compliance of mine as I took it, placing my own brand in front of myself with my one prized possession, a Dunhill lighter, on top. It was a defiant statement; denying I had been bought for the price of a single smoke.

"Did you really believe that I would swallow the Edward Heath story, Jack? Because if you did then you're the fool here, not me. Why are you avoiding that question of mine about Vienna? I'd like to know if you were turned and if so, whose side I'm being recruited to work for."

"I'll have to work harder on telling lies, Shaun. I must be slipping in my dotage!" laughingly he replied.

Again my question about alliances was avoided as the mysterious kitchen voice entered carrying a tray laden with a teapot, mugs and milk in the bottle. The door crashed shut behind her, making her entrance even more theatrical.

"By turned, are you suggesting that a true Englishman such as Mr Price might have had his fidelity diverted from the imperial path of colonialism towards what could it be now; the hammer and sickle of Communism, or perhaps you're implying a sparkling star and striped future of abundance and gratitude? If so, then I'll answer for the man who sits before us accused of treachery. No, is the answer. Here's your tea, Shaun! I'll be fetching your bottle of Ireland's finest whiskey sometime later tonight after I've formally been introduced to my younger brother. I'm Fianna Redden, by the way."

My head was swimming with the colourful imagery and the lyrical prose delivered from a derisive face that stared unerringly at me without blinking her cold fixed eyes. As the tray was placed on the table, she continued without an intake of breath.

"Born in 1947, before you'll be asking me age. Originally from Carrick-On-Shannon, Co. Leitrim, but coming here by way of varied paths that started at an orphanage in Athlone. Before today you were only Irish through your mother, Shaun, but today's your lucky day. Now you're the Irish brother of an Athenian goddess." At last she looked away, standing to her full height and bracing her back defiantly as she admired the reflection she made in the window.

"Perhaps it could be said that I'm not blessed with that goddess's wisdom, but certainly her beauty, if beautiful indeed she was! Stand and kiss your sister at once, or I'll be pouring the tea all over yer." she finished.

Her heart-shaped face, with its small, dimpled pointed chin, shone in the watery sunlight. Her predatory amber, wide-spaced eyes were transparent pools of gold that adorned her freckled fair skin, lined with laughter lines which etched the story of a full life. Seemingly someone who gave away smiles like they were wishes. Yet there was a subtlety to that amber gaze trying to conceal the most sorrowful face I had ever seen. Here was a woman who had lost what she knew she could not afford to lose, and the knowing did not soften the desolation.

"Did she have a temper, this goddess from Athlone?" I asked as I stood and faced her.

"Now there's a silly question for a handsome man to ask a woman and no mistake. Did you see Maureen O'Hara in *The Quiet Man*, Shaun? I'm her reincarnated. Of course I do, and a wicked one at that. There will be no sense in the finding out."

I had seen a poster of that film and as she stood a pictured formed in my mind's eye of her being carried in John Wayne's arms with her flowing, long wavy red hair swaying on the way to the altar. I gently kissed those pale lips, trying to taste the sweetness of a life that had drained away somewhere far from this dead room. I found none, nor could I find simplicity in those eyes.

"Was your scepticism born in that orphanage, Fianna, or did you find mistrust and suspicion somewhere else on your journey?" I asked, holding her small waist as lightly as I could.

"There we have it, Shaun! Your brain and my beauty! Our parents must have been something to see." She pulled away from my light grasp and I watched as she took her seat between Jack and me, neither of our eyes diverting from her. It was then that I noticed the small, yellow-metalled jade ring she wore on the first finger of her left hand. My thoughts were ended abruptly by Jack.

"You will have time after I'm gone to assimilate and memorise what Fianna will tell you about your shared background. Learn it well. Unfortunately I must be somewhere else by one o'clock this afternoon so cannot join in the pleasure. There are documents and details in the room above where you'll sleep tonight, Shaun. Fianna can teach you all of that. I'll be here in the morning, bright and eager to start again. For now I'll paint the broad outline of what you'll be doing for me and what I represent. He took a long draw on one of my cigarettes before continuing.

"All I told you of myself last night was the truth, but only part. I never left the intelligence services. I just moved along corridors and changed offices. Where I am now I don't have a fixed abode with telephones and chairs as do the institutions that you know, we move as the circumstances dictate. As I said, we dirty our hands in places they've never heard of at dinner parties in Guildford; however, often we enjoy more wholesome meals than them. We have no official title only the letters that spell our name; No One Is More Important Than Each: NOIMITE. Without the whole we are nothing. There are only two permanent staff. The man who you met at The Albany, Job, is one, I am the other. Everyone else is transient. No one is told more than what is immediately in front of them to do and I expect complete adherence to those instructions. We do not use the serving military, nor present operatives attached to any government intelligence services. Private security, retired army and local resources are our main supply of manpower. Excuses there to Fianna! I'm not forgetting you, but there aren't many women available to us."

Her curves, tall figure and angelic face left my circuitous mind wondering what was meant by 'available' as the returning rain danced in the grass beyond the windows, bending them down then up under the weight of its fall. They had no choice but to bend, I wondered if it was the same for Fianna.

"Are the two of us just temporary accomplices in the plan you have then, Jack? To be dispensed with when it's all over, or are we to be permanently counted amongst your number?" I caught sight of Fianna's turning head in his direction as I asked.

"You do not disappoint me in your directness, Shaun. Uncertainty is always better to be dealt with at the table than to be cited after the negotiations. But I cannot be unambiguous in this. Time is an entity that none of us have control over. Neither of you are transitory in what lies directly ahead, the absolute opposite is true, but this story has been playing without an end for longer than both your ages, thirty-five years to be precise. It's impossible for me to guarantee the unknown."

"Is it performance related, Jack?" I asked, to which he simply smiled.

Chapter Eight

The Chancellery In Vienna

"In late November 1937, whilst the war in Spain raged on with ever increasing casualties and the emergence of a wide-reaching war in Europe was a foregone conclusion, a meeting took place in an office within the Chancellery of Austria, in Vienna. It had three high profile attendees with all the fuss and palaver that comes with such people and their travelling entourage. They were served their refreshments, requirements and everything else they asked for by a Jewish man, who for the sake of this story I'll call Mr X. The guests I'll call A and B and their host will be C. You may be able to work out who they were a bit later, that's not so important as secrecy. I can't imagine Trenchard not insisting on you becoming a signatory of the Official Secrets Act. I trust you are aware of the consequences of failing to comply with that Act of Parliament. Fianna has worked alongside us for a little while, so is aware of our rules. Any breech of that Act, or our rules, will be severely punished, Shaun." He stared at both of us before continuing without waiting for a response.

"As the meeting drew to a close four females were introduced to the gathering on the insistence of guest A. Guest B made no complaint. After both guests had their fill of sexual pleasures guest A suggested younger participants to indulge themselves with, to which, to his only credit, guest B first declined. Guest A wanted young fair-skinned girls with blonde hair. It was the host who suggested the victims; one of whom was well known to Mr X. Despite strong but whispered protests from Mr X, Mr C would not change his views. C held his exalted position because of family connections and was seeking further patronage from A, willing to pander to any request. What then transpired between those girls and guest A, was condoned by both the host and guest B, who although as I said was initially reluctant, eventually gave in to temptation. I think your minds can fathom out what happened without me going on any further and spelling out the sordid details.

The girl that X knew, with her entire family, was hastily sent to America that night to join similar refugees from Austria who had emigrated long before this day. Unfortunately, that girl was pregnant. She gave birth to a healthy female child in August 1938. The child was kept. Unwisely, in my opinion!" The telephone we had passed in the passageway began to ring. He stopped speaking and checked his watch.

"Would you be a dear and get that, Fianna. I'm expecting Job to call with an all-clear."

"Will do, boss," she replied and left the room with a serious expression on her face.

"Just like you said, it was Job and everything is tickety-boo, boss."

He picked up where he had left off.

"Mr X survived the war, being one of the very few lucky ones who had held a pre-invasion government position, to be completely unscathed or touched by Nazi hands. He came from a moderately wealthy family and was a forward-thinking man, having made friends with a Catholic priest when he heard of the execution of a very close friend; the father of the girl he knew. X was subsequently hidden by that priest when Austria acquiesced to German demands." He paused, his previously unremitting poker face becoming etched with regret and sorrow.

"All four women along with the two other young girls who had been part of the obscenity of that day, were shot on the host's instructions, with both guests looking on. All were Jewish! Mr X's position within the Chancellery had given him a chance to save the pregnant girl and his skill at forgery saved her life. He changed the family's name and their stated religion to Catholic, thereby extraditing their flight to freedom without any undue hassle." Another pause.

"The father, X's close friend who was murdered, of the two children of this family had died some several months before all this happened and the mother died a few years after arriving in America, but her son and daughter, plus the granddaughter, are all alive. The son has gone on to own and control a pharmaceutical company who are in talks to merge with a similar West German chemical giant as we speak. Those discussions have been going on for months and are drawing to a close. The host of that 1937 meeting also survived the war, being released from the concentration camp in which he was confined relatively free from suffering in 1945. He emigrated to America a year later and is the only living person outside of the family other than me to know the name of who raped that thirteen-year-old along with the identity of the other guests. Both the German intelligence services and those of America are now closely delving into the family history. They only want suitable bed partners trading together, not ones with the history as told to me by Mr X in the Cafe Landtmann when I met him there in 1945. I had been sent to Vienna to bolster our newly appointed legation sorting through the various applications to travel to the UK. Three days after our meeting Mr X was hit by a car whilst crossing the road to Aspern airport on his way to start a new life. He never recovered consciousness from that assassination"

"Who killed him, Jack?" I asked.

His chair made a rubbing noise as he pushed it backwards and rose from the table.

"I have no idea, Shaun, but for our purposes we have put together a realistic story that fits. Now I must go, leaving the upstairs paperwork to fill in what I've omitted to answer of your questions. By this time tomorrow you will either be leaving England for America or walking away from my offer entirely. The choice lies with you and in what you will read. If you stay there is an element of danger with nobody beside you to make the instant decisions you will have to. Spontaneity and your ability to adapt will be your only weapons. If you leave then the question of what to do with you will arise. I'm hoping that no answer to that problematic situation will be needed."

He opened a drawer of the sideboard and withdrew a buff-coloured file sealed by a blue ribbon, placing it on the table in front of me.

"Read what's in here, Shaun." He took his jacket which was hanging behind his chair and made to leave, before adding, "There are some 'take-away' restaurant cards by the phone along with some money for incidentals in the other drawer here. Use what is necessary, but please, ask for receipts. There is a bottle of Jameson Irish whiskey in the kitchen. Try to leave some for when I return, I might need it."

At that he left, walking in the now drizzling rain to a blue Vauxhall car parked about twenty yards away. He was alone when he drove off. Fianna and I were still seated at the table. I offered her a cigarette and took one myself.

"So, you know the details, Fianna and decided to stay. No implied threats required in your case. Is Fianna your real name, by the way?"

"That's a yes to all of it, Shaun, and before you ask, the name Redden is real as well. The thing is, I changed back to my proper name from another that's not important now. I'm in for the whole craic of the trip."

"How do you know, Jack, Fianna?"

"I don't really. Met him a few months ago when he approached me with his story."

"And where were you when he made that approach?"

"I was being detained at Her Majesty's pleasure."

"Under an assumed name, I take it?"

"Ah, you are a wise one, Shaun. There you have me!"

"Which prison were you in?"

"No, I wasn't in prison as such, Shaun, at least not when your man Mr Price found me. I was in one before I was released to a big fellow with scars on his face and a mean temper of a man. Now that came as a surprise, the release I mean, just settling in to the new prison, I was. He took me to a different kind of internment, without the bars and locks. I was told by Scarface that I'd be needed to do a job of work and he didn't elaborate on what would happen if I didn't. Had no need, if you're following me."

"Would that job be anything to do with a security van?"

"There we are again, you with your brains and all that. We've turn the square into a circle and danced in its centre, Shaun, me boy. An Irishman with the English name of Henry Acre was the chief Apache. I take it that's the Irishman you shot dead. I met him the once and spun him the story I was told to tell. They were very thorough, Mr Price and Mr Scarface. *Not too much detail, just enough to be convincing*, they said. I was to be an Irish patriot with a love of the money and the drink. The background they gave me all stacked up to Acre's satisfaction," she winked.

"I haven't far to look for the source of Jack's tip-off to be in Charing Cross Road then!"

"No, about two foot away."

"Was it Jack that planted you inside that team?"

"A girl gets a living wherever and from whomever a girl can, Shaun. You're not going to give me some holier-than-thou speech, now are you? Cos if you are, I'm walking out."

"No, I'm not, but where's the incentive for you to do that kind of work?"

"I was inside for life, Shaun. Banged up in 1968 with no remittance for good behaviour. Smashing my head against the walls I was. I killed the man who killed my brother, but don't you go worrying any, Shaun, as it was a Bridget Slattery who did the murder and the real reason was never divulged. The real Shaun went missing when he was eight. No dead body was found, but I knew what had happened. I waited nine years to find the priest who'd done it, but I never let on why it was I killed him. Wanted no sympathy from any bloody English court."

"There are consequences to everything, especially if they're violent. More men could have lost their lives because the robbery went ahead. The one that you and Jack set up."

"Am I to feel sorry for that? As sorry as you are for shooting dear Henry dead, Shaun? If it's floods of tears you be wanting then you'd be waiting for a long time as there will be none from me. I'm all dried up in that department. I don't do crying anymore for anyone. Run for home and share your sorrow with the Met Police boyos if that be your wish."

We continued our sparring in the kitchen which was as frugal as the rest of the downstairs part of the house. I could smell milk and cornflakes on her breath as I obeyed her orders, and she dried the cups that I had washed-up.

"Arrived earlier than me and shared breakfast with Jack, did you?" I asked somewhat annoyed and hungry.

"No, I was brought here last night. Getting first sight of what Mr Price referred to as functioning bedrooms; folding camp beds and an overhead light. There are blankets though. No frills up there, Shaun."

"Start on the Scotch, did you, or can I have the honour of deflowering that?"

"Don't let me stop you, but it's not Scotch, it's Irish. And also while you're about it put away your testosterone for the ladies who might fall for your innuendos. I wasn't made to propagate life. I prefer the company of females to that of the male gender. Be careful to put the seat down in the loo as well, that's after you've made sure to lift it up when you wee. Very particular I am about such things."

"A brother and sister relationship without incest, well, I'm glad we've cleared that up. Save on the bruises from a camp bed. Was yours and Henry's relationship so squeaky clean?"

"I can play roles when asked. Never said that I'd never been with a man, now did I? When I was growing up I had a fancy of being a film star. I had a flair for the acting, so I did. Perhaps, if things had been different, I might have got there, but at least I know where your affections lie. You like the pretty girls and the shooting of Irish terrorists with a boss named Trenchard squeezing your trigger finger. Is that the full pack of cards from me long lost brother so dear to me heart? Would you be on your way to prison if you hadn't answered Jack's call?"

"Might be better than a bullet in the head if I don't fall in line with his suggestions that I've yet to read. Do you believe all that bullshit he just told us?"

I didn't refer to the previous night nor how I'd come to know of Jack. It wasn't suspicion that held back my full confession nor was it the fast approaching sense of doubting my newly acquired antecedents. It was, I think, a fear of two things: her displeasure of me and my acceptance of this new challenge too readily.

"From the little I know of Mr Price the one thing I'm sure he's not is a bull-shitter, Shaun. You, on the other, I'm none too sure of."

"Thank you!"

"You're most welcome."

"Why are you in for the ride, Fianna?"

"Oh, there's many a reason for that, but perhaps if that daughter of Mr whatever letter he was is a lesbian, then I might just have a bit of fun to look forward to. Jack might want me to look after her in her time of trouble. I'm good at cuddles if it's the right one I'm cuddling. But if you're going with the expectation of killing someone, let's hope it's more than the lower half of your anatomy that's loaded and it's a gun you'll be carrying; as Mae West would say."

"I don't think that was quite what she said, sister dear."

"Be away with yer. I knew that, you dumbhead." The smile that filled her face was so bright that a book could have been read in the darkest of rooms from its light. I stood in its reflection and marvelled at her personality.

"Will it be the whiskey you'll be wanting, or, shall I go to the shops and buy some food for me brother's tea? I passed a grocery shop, not a distance away from that car you were so interested in when the motorbike brought you here. Don't look so quizzical, Shaun. I was born nosy. It's got me into trouble more than the once. Named O'Callahan's, it was. The shop that is. Could be the real thing or the headquarters of the local Republican Army. Want me to see while you're having that read? Ask about any Henry Acres being shot while I'm about it and who shot him, shall I?"

"Ha, bloody ha!" I replied, adding, "I'll phone the local nick and ask about Bridget Slattery while you're shopping me."

"Shall we be leaving the past to the historians then, Shaun? Would that be your wish?" I nodded to that suggestion hoping it could be so.

"In the document you've read are there any names to the letters Jack quoted before he left, Fianna?"

"Only the one! The host of the gathering, Mr C, was a Kurt Schuschnigg. Mouthful there and no mistake."

Sunday

Chapter Nine

Mr X

The outside early Sunday morning silence would have disturbed the quietest of libraries with its concealed secrecy until, that is, I heard the footsteps. Next came the squeak from the gate as it opened then closed on the noisy catch, followed by heavier footfalls along the paved garden path. I never heard a car. The closing of the front door reverberated through the house on his entrance.

"Are we awake?" he called out, to which Fianna replied, "I am, but can't say about the boy."

The smell of frying bacon had wafted into the bedroom where I lay rekindling fond memories of home, but I had not slept with many warm homely thoughts beside me that night. Certain conclusions that I'd drawn from both listening to Fianna's tale, and reading Jack's, had caused me to worry about the task that lay awaiting me; but I had no doubt that it was something I wanted to do. A wiser man may have come to a different answer, mine was, "Yes I'm awake, Jack, and can't wait to get started." Inwardly I wondered if I had been drugged whilst being persuaded from being a person who wanted to uphold the law to someone who was to become at best a withholder of the truth, but by the time it took to go down the stairs to Fianna's breakfast those thoughts had disappeared.

"Morning, Jack! How do you want me to kill Mr Kurt?"

"Bejesus, my lot of papers must have had a page or two missing and no mistake, but I'm glad I wasn't wrong about you, Shaun," Fianna stated as plates of sizzling bacon with thick buttered slices of bread were placed on the table where Jack had already taken residence.

"Are you not eating, Fianna?" Jack asked without glancing in my direction.

"Mine's coming," she said. "In time for the fireworks, I'm hoping."

"I think I've worked out who was Mr A. B is a bit of a puzzle." Not waiting for Fianna's return I began. "I guess you'll be telling us about any trips you may have taken to the Bahamas, Jack? That's if you have a mind to, of course. Or was it in Paris that you two had a heart to heart? I wonder where his wife was when he was playing games in Vienna? Oh, and if I'm right, didn't he die back in May this year? Are we to hear of the escaped family today and what it is exactly you want us to do with them?" I changed track when she came back into the room.

"Did you buy any mustard last night, Fianna, or must I go without?"

"I did not, brother, as I had no inkling of your liking for the stuff."

Phlegmatically ignoring my question, Jack replied, "You two seem to be getting along fine." He had that wide grin cemented to his face, the one I was to remember for years to come.

"Is it to the Bahamas that we'd be going after this trip to America then, Mr Price? I quite fancy a trip there. Mind you, Paris would be nice as well. I've heard it's good at this time of year. It would do at a pinch," Fianna, standing with both arms folded across her chest reminding me of a school mistress, both asked and announced.

"While we're at it, could I also get the history on the green jade ring you're wearing?" I responded.

"You gave it to me the week before you disappeared. That's what started my fears. The priest said you'd run away and 'twas better you'd gone as you were a troublemaker. No one cared enough to see through his lies, 'cept me! It was I who cradled you in me arms when you cried every night till he called for you that last time. I gave myself a birthday present when I turned twenty-one. A nice long, sharp carving knife which I held in my lap after slitting his throat with it. Sat there in his room at St. Mary's Church, Liverpool awash with his blood for hours waiting for the police to come. He had skipped away from Ireland when I was alone in that home so I had to bide my time, but I got him in the end. Are you sure it's to be you doing the killing, Shaun, and not me?"

"I won't be asking for any tomato sauce now then." I remarked flippantly.

"I'm surprised you never asked Fianna that question about the ring last night, Shaun," Jack replied.

"I had too many other things on my mind. Like why now, for one?"

"Now is the right time, as I told you," he answered.

"You mean he might meet the same end as his ex-aide; hit by an errant driver if he doesn't agree to your demands?"

Fianna was enjoying her breakfast as much as we were, showing less interest in what was being discussed than in the cup of tea that was beside where she ate. Death, by whatever means, held no diverting fascination for her, it seemed. How different from last night?

I heard her singing a sad story of love from the bathroom whilst I was studying Jack's paperwork. I'd taken little notice of the words as it was her divine refreshing tone and the softness of her voice that made me think of standing in a meadow of long grass with a gentle summer breeze fluttering everything around. Until sadly, my dream burst as if it was a bubble from her bath.

"Did Jack tell you, Shaun, that I'd killed a priest?"

* * *

"Before you two came into our sights we had no one who could effectively do what's required," Jack was quickly into his stride expounding on the task ahead. "The priest that Bridget Slattery murdered was the same one who gave my man, Mr X, sanctuary in Austria during the war years. He went to Ireland, and more specifically St. Patrick's orphanage in Athlone, straight after it ended in '45. The legend we've put together for you, Shaun, involves that priest and the originally named Sternberg family, known now as the Stockfords and more particularly the man I met, Mr X; Alain Aberman. Kurt Schuschnigg might die sooner than his allotted time, but not at my bequest, nor that of anyone I'm directly associated with. I also doubt it will come about at the request of either Richard Stockford or his sister, Leeba; the girl who bore the child conceived in Schuschnigg's stately rooms, but you're going to say Schuschnigg orchestrated Aberman's murder because Father Finnegan told you so as way of a threat against both your lives." He finished speaking, walking over to his jacket which was lying on the settee.

"Here's some more reading for you to do. Not as much this time, just an outline of what the priest told you and how it was said. The why you've come to them now is self-explanatory. Shaun ran away in fear when Finnegan threatened you and it's only now that you've met up again courtesy of two strokes of luck. One: you, Shaun, read of Kurt Schuschnigg in *The Evening News* of last Friday being presented with an award for literature, his published biography, on his seventy-second birthday, one week's time from now. And two: three weeks ago you, Fianna, were told by the family reconciliation services in Manchester of your brother's new address. Happy families all round. We're not as dumb as you may have thought, Shaun. We may even be smarter than you, my boy. The pseudonym of Bridget Slattery was immediately undone by those higher powers I've previously referred to, leaving us waiting for a suitable brother to appear since Fianna went into prison. You not only solve our frustration but open untold doors for yourself on completion of this matter. As to what's in it for Fianna, that depends on many unquantifiable things at this moment, but there is a place in my department for the both of you." He sat, and Fianna and I stared at one another in bewilderment.

"How could two children remember a name such as Schuschnigg, Jack? I wouldn't know how to pronounce it now, let alone when I was a toddler." I stated.

Once again he avoided answering a direct question, leaving me both confused and astounded.

"Your flight leaves Heathrow at five-thirty tonight, I will not be at the airport to wave you off. I've somewhere I must be now, but I shall be back before you depart. There's a cab booked for four p.m. By the way, as far as we know none of the surviving family know who the father of Leeba's daughter was. She, as all the others, wore a blindfold throughout the ordeal. Incidentally, and a point to remember please, Penina, Leeba's daughter, does not know that Leeba is her real mother. Both Leeba and Richard have told Penina that she is their younger sister born to their mother, Mayanna Stockford, after their arrival in America. That's the status quo and it must remain the case; understood?"

It was Fianna who responded first. "Oh, I understand, Mr Price. Too right I do! In order to stop the Yanks and some Red bastards finding out that this Leeba was raped at a party thirty-five years ago, a seventy-two-year-old man has to be murdered. That seems a good enough reason to you, and Shaun here don't seem too bothered by it all as well. I'm thinking to myself that there could just be another reason that you're not letting on about. But I'm a simple Irish girl with no mind to the politics of men, so I'll be keeping me mouth closed and doing me duty in the kitchen as you two discuss the murdering and the like."

"There I was a moment ago thinking you had no morals or misgivings over the death of people, Fianna. Was I wrong?" I asked her.

"Only God is justified in taking a life, Shaun, and sometimes even He can get that wrong. Men, and sometimes women, interpret His wishes purely to fulfil their own ends. The church is more full of corruption than piety." She lit a cigarette before she spoke again.

"What I did was worse than what you did. Maybe it was right for you to kill that Henry Acre with him being a terrorist and all that, but it was not right what I done. It's true that filthy-minded priests that abuse kids are beyond God's forgiveness, but they are not there for the likes of me to deliver vengeance upon them. I'm a heathen that's going to hell anyway, what's another body on my conscience? This man's already knocking on the gates of Hades, so I'll hold his hand as he passes through if that's what you need, Mr Price."

The harsh reality of acceptance was reflected in her sad eyes and expressed in her short speech, leaving Jack outwardly unmoved, but not me. I was still imprisoned by conscience, but as yet in no need of the word penitence.

"Fianna has eloquence on her side, Jack. Care to enlighten us with the real reason behind this masquerade?"

He didn't! We were left to examine the passports, travel documents and other things that he left, with his noisy footsteps echoing along the path on his way out, as our own squeaky gate to hell closed shut on another unanswered question.

Sunday Night / Monday Morning In America

Chapter Ten

Celluloid Characters

I made my first contact with the Stockford Pharmaceutical Company just after ten-thirty on Monday morning, New York time.

"Good morning! You have reached the office of Mr Richard Stockford's private secretary. My name is Sandra. How can I assist you today?"

"Good morning, Sandra, I'm Shaun Redden. I have a message for Mr Stockford from a mutual friend of ours, Sir Horace Butler. If he is available could you put me through, please?"

"I'm afraid Mr Stockford is engaged with other members of the board, but I can pass on a message if you'd like me to?"

"That would be fine, thank you. Tell him that the identity of the person involved in the accident with a Mr Aberman has been discovered and Sir Horace is eager for the two of us to meet. I'm staying at the Metropolitan Hotel, on Fulton Street, in Brooklyn, but I don't know the phone number here. I'm over from the UK with my sister Fianna for a few days. Room number 306. It is quite important that he gets the message, Sandra."

"I'll certainly see that Mr Stockford receives it, sir. Your name was Mr Redden, I believe?"

"Yes, it is, Sandra."

* * *

In 1936 the two brothers of Gregor Sternberg rolled up their film production and distribution company in Vienna, relocating in the fast expanding Hollywood area of California where they began all over again. It was not only the love of celluloid that took them, but also the rapidly growing anti-Semitism in Europe.

Alain Aberman, although Jewish by birth, believed that his position as first secretary to the Chancellor of Austria would safeguard him through what he described as a passing phase in history. That was the belief he held and the one he told his good friend Gregor until, that is, Gregor was arrested for assisting not only his brother and their families to escape from Austria, but also fellow wealthy Jews. All allegedly for money! Gregor was never dishonest. Such an act of opportunism would have been abhorrent to the Austrian-born captain in the Fifth Rifle Brigade as much as it was to Alain. When Gregor Sternberg was shot for that alleged crime Aberman hastily altered his religious convictions and all the records of him being of the Jewish faith.

During the hours of the debauchery that Gregor's daughter and the other women and girls suffered, Alain forged Schuschnigg's signature on the documentation Mayanna and her two children would need for their diplomatic covered escape from Vienna aboard a flight to the East Coast of America in the name of Stockford. He then contacted Father Finnegan, asking for help. He never told Finnegan any of what he told Jack. That had come straight from the horse's mouth one Wednesday afternoon at the end of the war over coffee in the Cafe Landtmann. Nowhere in Jack's report did it say that Schuschnigg had killed Aberman. What it did say, however, added up to a plausible reason.

On release from his last concentration camp, Schuschnigg was repatriated to Austria and invited by the Americans to join the then fledgling Austrian government. He was, according to Jack's story, waiting in the American Embassy in Vienna when Alain Aberman made his own personal travel application. He could not check the documents that Alain had submitted, but he could have him followed when he left. It was the following day that Aberman was killed. Kurt Schuschnigg refused the invitation offered him to serve in government, preferring to emigrate to America and start a new life. According to Jack's report that's what he did. The fear of his betrayal of innocence and the wish to survive a revengeful witness can be written convincingly into any good conspiracy and that was what Jack was relying on.

* * *

The phone rang in my hotel room twenty minutes later. It was Richard Stockford.

* * *

Whether or not it was the truth that Fianna told me on our flight to New York I had no way of knowing, but that wasn't of primary importance, the fact that she was convincing was. She and the younger Shaun had been taken into the orphanage when their parents had perished in a fire that destroyed their home above the bakery in which they worked in the small town of Carrick-On-Shannon, when Shaun was seven years old and Fianna two years his elder. Their mother, Rebecca, had been overcome by the smoke fumes and their father, Michael, had died from the burns he suffered when rescuing his two children. Fianna had a burn on her upper arm as a remaining legacy of that fateful night, but Shaun was spared any injury. He was to face agony later.

Father Finnegan had already established his place at Athlone by the time the two children arrived, but his penchant for naked boys dancing before him was unknown by anyone else connected to the home. At each of his weekly dancing sessions the male selections were made to recite the initials of Schuschnigg in a song he composed:

I know a devil called S c h u s c h n i g g, who once killed a man that he could clearly see.
He ran him down in a big fat car, so the story he could have told would never go far.
If you close your eyes then maybe you will see, that the murdering devil of S c h u s c h n i g g still lives in me!
Shaun told Fianna of the song, and she too had nightmares.

Jack's version of the story now deviated from the truth. Whereas the real Shaun was murdered by Finnegan, I, as Fianna's brother, simply ran away in fear. The name and the song stayed branded onto my subconscious as though put there by a scalding iron, only to come alive again when reading that name in the London evening newspaper. Fianna stayed at the orphanage for a few more months after my disappearance then she was placed in a normal home owned by a family called Gleeson who lived in Dublin. She had a list, compiled by Jack, of positions she took as employment which she assured me she had memorised.

The murder of Father Finnegan was carried by many publications with speculation being kept to the minimum that his murderer, Bridget Slattery, never added to. Fianna, under that assumed name, was deemed to be psychotic and committed to a variety of mental institutions before playing a leading role in Henry Acre's death. Why Finnegan had only murdered Shaun from all the others was not known nor commented on. Like Fianna, I had a separate letter from Jack that was for only my eyes. I believed every word.

He confirmed my suspicions over the father of Leeba's child, along with my supposition that the once King, Edward VIII, of the British Empire, was guest B at the Chancellery. The reason for that meeting was to discuss the new order of things when, as all three men expected, Britain was overrun by the Nazis. Hitler had a daughter and the world knew nothing of it. Jack implied that would change if Schuschnigg ever opened his mouth. As I read on I understood why he had not, but also why now he might.

The atrocities that the Nazis inflicted upon the Jews is a well-documented subject, often in graphic detail, but one programme that I had never seen mentioned was the propagation of Jewish children by at least one Jewish parent. The Nazis were nothing if not pragmatic. They knew the extermination of the Jewish race, although taking time, would inevitably lead to its extinction. The babies born in the concentration camps were to be the future; human beings bred solely for medical experimentation. Ideally they wanted pure Jewish bred children from fine ancestral stock!

One of those used in this programme was Kurt Schuschnigg. He descended from a very distinguished Austrian family, having traceable roots back many centuries, including attachment to the Habsburg monarchy. No precise records of births were kept by the Nazis, therefore no exact number of children fathered by Schuschnigg could ever be known, nor their names and sex. Perhaps, Jack suggested, the Gross-Rosen concentration sub camp complex-born thirty-two-year-old chief executive of the German chemical company in talks with Richard Stockford was not one of them, but he wanted no chance to be taken over Schuschnigg involvement. Loose ends, as he called them; ones that need to be tied together, he added. I wondered why it was necessary for Fianna to help in connecting those loose ends.

By now you're entitled to accuse me of being stupidly naive and I will plead guilty to that offence. I cannot even offer youth and inquisitiveness as a just defence, as having studied psychology I should have been asking more questions than I had. On self-examination I could say that Jack had replaced the father I had known so little of, and it was in his reports I'd found the purpose I was searching for. But I very much doubt anyone would fall for that one. Jack was like a smooth pebble in my mouth, helping me to keep my aspirations moist whilst travelling through the dry desert of life.

* * *

Fianna was starting to conduct her own examination of motives on boarding the plane.

"Is it not bothering you, Shaun, that you're here at all?" she asked, to which I answered, "Should it?"

"If I was you then, yes, I would," she replied before continuing, "and a bit quicker than yourself. Before you say a thing that you might be ashamed of, let me put a few pointers your way. You're a policeman who just happened to shoot dead an Irish army brigade commander and then fell into the path of the mysterious Jack Price. How convenient was that for the both of you, huh? I've had me ups and downs with the police in my time but I'm more used to the ones like the Scarface I met and told you of than handsome burly ones like yourself. I reckon your man Jack turned your head, with you falling in love with the adventure stories he told of a hero rescuing some dumb maiden in need of a good seeing to. I hope I'm none too vulgar for you, Shaun, but it's the way of the world nowadays. I have a couple of questions you might like to chew on as we take to the air," she said, her eyebrows raised in a questioning fashion.

"Why pick you to shoot a Republican Army man? You're young and a bit too inexperienced for my thinking. I would have thought there must be loads of coppers better qualified and already tested in killing. While I'm on the subject of shooting people dead, you seem mighty cold about it all. It's as though you do it every day of your life. Like making a cup of tea first thing in the morning, or tying your shoelaces. It's not natural, Shaun. Did you not feel anything when you shot him dead?"

"Not a thing! I knew he wouldn't hesitate firing his own gun and killing that guard. He had a history of violence that stretched back many years, plus someone in the gang had told me that he intended this hold-up to be more of a political statement than just a robbery. I had my orders and followed them. That's what people like me do, Fianna. We uphold the law."

She looked away and laughed, more mocking me with derision then scornfully, then she asked, "So, doing away with this old man Schuschnigg is lawful, is it, Shaun? Is that what you're telling me?" She never waited for any reply.

"Scarface is the killer type, he could easily do Schuschnigg anytime, come to that so could Jack. Why use us to load the bullets? Another question for you while I have your attention."

If the truth were known, neither of us were paying full attention to what was being said. We had been airborne for a few minutes and for at least one of those minutes staring at the 'Do not Smoke' light. As soon as it was switched off we both reached for our cigarette packets. It was Fianna who exhaled first.

"Why this story of us being brother and sister and Finnegan being the piggy in the middle who connects us? It seems too complicated and unnecessary just to bump someone off. Where's the need to tell the Stockfords anything? There's been an undisturbed secret for thirty-five years. With the proper names being changed it's nigh on impossible to link any Sternberg to a Stockford. Why rock the boat now, Shaun?" I had no answer to her puzzlement and in actual fact her worries were my own.

"I've got a question for you, Fianna. Who turned you into a lesbian?"

"Get away with you, Shaun me boy. Save the masculine flirting for the girls that care. Tell them of your talents and I'll say no word of your windy habits in that camp bed of yours last night. Sounded like you had a machine-gun up your back-side. I blamed myself, by the way. Should have made allowances for a soft, half-baked Irishman from London town and not Londonderry! I would have done better ordering a mild Chinese curry and not a hot Indian one as I did for me brother's tea. Are you next going to tell me what I'm missing out on, Shaun, because believe me; I'm not missing a thing!"

"There either speaks the voice who experienced disappointment, or…" I was not allowed to finish.

"Or the experience of male incompetency that you could more than adequately replace, Shaun? Was that roughly what you were about to say?"

"Actually no! I was going to be somewhat derogatory and ask if they really were men you'd been with. But your assumption about my long term motives were correct though."

"So you fancy me then, Shaun, do yer? Is it the challenge of the spiritual conversion that I represent or just the physical pleasure that you'd be after?"

"Would it be immodest to say the only conversion that would follow the sex would be a conversion to the enjoyment of that sex? But that's something we'll never know, will we?"

"You'll never know, but I do, and no mistake. I was almost raped when I was fourteen by three boys, but then fully raped days after." Her sarcasm had turned to anger. "Don't bother to tell me you were about to offer the mystical awakening of love for a man instead. That really is bullshit! All men are animals." Abruptly her brief denunciation stopped, but I wouldn't leave it alone.

"What made you fall in love with an animal, Fianna?"

"There was nothing that made me, Shaun. It's just there was no one to stop me."

Chapter Eleven

A White Picket Fence

"I didn't go to a family called Gleeson when I left that orphanage. That was Jack's deception. I was fostered out to a home about ten miles away from it, where I had to attend a day school, one change of bus away from the pretty white picket-fenced house of Imelda Duggen and her husband Keith. It was in the early days of spring, when I was on my way to catch my first bus home from school that the attempted rape happened. The bus only ran every half an hour and I missed it by seconds, seeing it drive off as I rounded the corner leading to the stop. I had stayed late for an art class. I wanted to be a painter at that age. It was so mild that the jacket I had worn in the morning, when the dew hung on until the warming sun melted it away, was no longer needed. It rested under my arm that carried my school bag. There were three boys about my age coming towards me. All of them were in high spirits, joking and giggling amongst themselves. Their faces got more threatening as they neared me.

"Are they real those tits of yours, or just apples stuffed down your blouse?" the middle one asked. Seconds passed before I could answer. "Go away," I said, but by now they were beside me and no one else was about.

"I bet they're only pimples and it's all padding to make them look that big," the shortest one baited, and stupidly I reacted to his derision.

"No, they are not," I replied without fear of what was to come.

The tallest of the three boys said, "We don't believe you. Show us then." There's no point in asking me why, but I cupped my breasts in my hands and shook them. "You'll just have to dream about them then, won't you." I had been around boys all my life, never frightened by them but shortly I was to find out that these three were different.

"No, we won't, Rory, will we? We're going have a look now." Rory was the tall one. Foolishly I thought I could outrun them across the field to my right and for a while I did, but then I tripped on some roots I hadn't seen, falling face down on the grass. We were behind a big, spreading bush under a tree. One of them fell on my back and pinned my arms to the ground.

"I'll have her after you," he said, spreading his weight over me, forcing the air from my lungs. I knew exactly what was about to happen, but I tried desperately to appeal to a better nature that just wasn't present.

"Leave me alone," I pleaded. I felt more hands pull my briefs clean off, ripping them as he did so. The one on my back was now sitting on my shoulders. It was then that I felt naked flesh pushed against my legs. Then I felt cold hands on my hips as the boy between my legs attempted to lift my bum up. From somewhere I found the strength to lever the one off my back, sending him flying to one side. Then I twisted and kicked the boy, Rory, who was trying to penetrate me in the face, leaving him sprawled out with his trousers and pants trapped around his ankles. His nose was bleeding. As I got to my feet I swung my bag at the third one, who too had his pants around his ankles. This one fell awkwardly, screaming in pain holding two fingers of his left hand. I prayed to God for a knife that day, Shaun, and had he granted that prayer it wouldn't have been fingers I would have cut off! I picked up my coat and bag, and made off across that field.

"I'll kill you, you bastards! You wait and see," I cried through my tears in their direction, hoping it could be so.

When I arrived home it was Keith who called the police after Imelda had told him almost all of what I had told to her. I was pretty in those days of 1961, Shaun, and yes I followed the fashion of the day imitating what I saw on the TV. Keith disapproved and had remarked in the past about my choice of clothing along with what he called my general behaviour. Imelda thought it best not to start him off again.

"*Her clothes are too tight and too short. She acts and dresses like a tart. She'll get into trouble that one; you mark my words, you'll see*," he had said more times than she liked to remember.

It was she who poured me a bath, taking my grass-stained skirt, blouse and cardigan from me as she did so. Then she asked, "Was it so warm this morning that you had no need for tights or panties, Fianna, my dear?" She was now thinking that maybe all along her husband had been right.

"I left them there in that field. They were ripped off. There're no good now are they?" I replied maybe a bit too harshly, but I was unaware of the thoughts mulling through her mind.

The absence of that particular clothing was the same issue that the policewoman put to me.

"They say you were not wearing any underwear, Fianna. What's more they contend that you lifted your skirt, exposing yourself to them, when you were walking towards to the bus stop together. This, they say, led them to believe that you would be a willing participant in what they had already proposed. They add that you had plenty of time to catch that bus at six forty-three had you not previously invited them to join you in the girls' toilets at the school where you performed an act of masturbation in front of them. They also allege that later in the park, where you had agreed to have sex, you changed your mind and they stopped; never pressing you on that promise." The policewoman waited for my reply; I had none other than a complete denial, but that did not stop the accusations.

"They deny attempting to rape you. One of the boys' fathers is saying that you are malicious in making this complaint, attempting to cover up your own guilt in misleading his son and the other boys. In essence he's saying that you are trying to protect your own reputation by slurring their names. You had second thoughts, in other words."

She leant forward across the dividing coffee table and looked me directly in the eyes.

"What they are saying, love, is that you started it all by provoking them, leading them on to believe that you wanted sex. You never screamed nor fought back, any bruising that you may have was caused accidentally when you invited one of them, (*she checked her note book*), James Craig to sit on you just before you had a change of mind. He claims that you broke his fingers when you snatched your bag from him when he was about to place it under your head. He alleges that it was your suggestion by the way. I have to tell you that unless an independent witness comes forward it is your word against theirs, and there are three of them, remember. Attempted rape is a serious crime. One that we investigate thoroughly, including all allegations of it. Unless you can prove that the boy, Rory Mulligan, ripped off those missing briefs of yours then I'm afraid my advice must be to forget it. If you go to court, no jury will believe you. They're going to be more inclined to believe three stories rather than one, especially if it's unsubstantiated by evidence, Fianna."

"They are either very good liars, Mrs Duggen, or it's true that Fianna led them on," the welfare minded policewoman quietly told Imelda as she left, with opportunistic Keith overhearing every word."

* * *

Sitting back heavily into her chair, she recalled what I can only describe as a story from hell. As much as I tried to listen without showing emotion I couldn't. I reached for her hand and she took it.

She told how life became unbearable after that, both away from home and in it. No longer could she attend school without feeling shame. Not simply for what had happened, but for what she saw as her stupidity. *If only I had stopped and had thought of those torn briefs, then things would have been different*, she had told herself, quick to level the unjust blame where others too directed theirs. She was called 'that whore' by the judgmental neighbours and girls living nearby, or 'easy' to the lustful onlooking boys that were only aware of a side of the story as told by Rory, James and Michael.

"It will be best to go back, Fianna, you can't mope around here all day," Imelda advised her after two days of self-examination which she had spent on her own, venturing only as far as the corner shop where she encountered some of the sanctimonious who lived close with their smug vilification and censure. Reluctantly, accepting Imelda's advice, she found the courage to return to her studies, hoping that things were not so bad at the school. But hope didn't last long. The bus rides were the first obstacles to face. That was where the first opinionated groups were gathered and they were short on mercy that first day.

"Can't keep her legs closed, can't keep her mouth shut. You're nothing but a little tart," bravely called out an anonymous voice shifting behind acquiescent friends when Fianna had turned around to confront him. Abject loneliness was how she felt, without anyone standing beside her shouting the innocence of credibility. Then pride left her. She felt let down by everyone, including most importantly herself. She would not stay, nor travel on to find more abuse and denunciation. To the pretty picket-fenced home she returned. The only place of comfort left to her. Or so she thought.

Something more sinister than the loss of self-belief and confidence entered her life shortly after her decision to confine her studies to that foster home that she called home. Keith Duggen started to hang around more often than he used to do, and Imelda began to question why. He had less puritanical intentions than his outbursts would have his wife believe.

Why do you think I'm at home, woman, it's dead at work. There's nothing coming in. Do you think I want to stay around here all day with that girl, listening to her music playing? I asked her yesterday to turn it down, I couldn't hear all the news about the rail strike that is crippling the country.

He offered a different excuse one Monday morning for not going to the warehouse where he worked. This time a sore back was the reason for absence. *Done too much in the garden over the weekend, I think*, he said, as he waved goodbye to his wife on her 7am departure to the bank where she was employed as assistant manager. He made toast and a pot of tea, found a tray and carried his bribe to Fianna's room. She was asleep. Gently he laid the tray on her bedside table, carefully avoiding her now redundant pink alarm clock that stood alone. She was dreaming of young devils as an older one stood gazing at her, imagining her naked body and what he would do with it as he silently slipped from his nightclothes and pulled back the single white sheet that covered her. Fianna awoke as his tobacco-smelling hand clasped her mouth and his flabby body descended alongside her stricken figure.

"He lifted my nightdress and with his other hand pushed his prick inside of me, tearing me apart!"

"Be a good girl and I'll be good to you. Be a bad one and I'll rip your head off then burn your body before anyone notices that you're gone!"

He was a lot stronger than a boy and more determined than they had been. There was nowhere to hide for her and no early escape from what occurred nor, as she was vehemently told, *future beatings and punishment if Imelda ever found out.*

"It will be our little secret, or I will tell Imelda that you forced yourself on me. No one's going to believe you; you have bad history, girl. Be sweet to me and I will be sweet to you."

Twice more he visited her bedroom that day, and several more times during the next two he took off from work with that sore back. Fianna was condemned to her fate until late on Wednesday night when she was awakened by a silent Imelda with a soft finger, instead of Keith's stinking hand across her lips.

"I haven't got loads of money, my child, but what I can spare I'm going to give to you. I think I know what's happening here with you and him and it's not right. I'm not strong enough to stop him and neither are you, my child. I can't let it all come out. I'm too old to start all over again on my own. I'm a coward at heart, you see, and couldn't stand the scandal. I'm sorry, but you will have to leave, and I have no idea where you can go."

* * *

"That's when I found my animal, Shaun, and I took centre stage in his jungle. I travelled to Newry, to a sect I'd heard off on the fringes of the city. It took days to get there, but the hope of finding some peace drove me on and kept me going. They were not a religious group as such, more a free thinking lot where the church played no part. They believed, so they said, in looking after each other in the cruel world of commerce and world politics. Their motto was; from each according to his ability, to each according to his needs. I didn't know it was a Communist slogan and if I had known it would have made no difference, as those words appealed to me as if they had been written with me in mind. Jack was not there but possibly he got that silly phrase of his; no one is more important than each, from them, or the Russian in Vienna. Only I hope his words are more sincere than theirs.

At first I was welcomed with open arms, they genuinely seemed to want me, but it wasn't so much me as my money they wanted. Imelda had given me about thirty quid, which was a fair bit of money in those days, especially for a fourteen-year-old to be carrying. Their philosophy of one for all and all for one stretched into everything they did, including the share of work and wealth. Me, the silly fool that I was, believed in every word they said. I gave them what I had left, leaving myself no option but to rely on their generosity and skill in providing. I was a long way off of being wise in those days, Shaun. We all lived on a farm owned by the leader of the group, a man named Donegal Fitzpatrick. He seemed a lovely man at first. The tall, dark, handsome type you read of in magazines and see at the picture houses. A Clark Gable kind of figure! Yes, no need to look so quizzical, I hadn't been put off men at that time in my life and you can draw whatever conclusions you like from that.

The spring and early summer were okay, with the dozen of us who were there finding plenty to do around the farm, but come late July all that changed, and not for the better. There were eight men, aged between twenty and forty, not counting Donegal, and four of us women. I was the youngest, with the other three in their late twenties and early thirties. Two were sisters apparently, but none told me their surname. I was told to call them Kelly, Ruth and Philippa. They did all the cooking and most of the trips into Newry, driven there by Donegal in his car.

I thought that although we were almost self-sufficient those journeys were to buy the stuff we couldn't grow on the farm like tea and coffee, but that wasn't all they went for. Fitzpatrick was no glamorous film star, he was a sordid pimp, Shaun. And the men; they were his enforcers, if he had the need of them. This I found out in the third week of that nonstop rain-sodden July when I'd just passed my fifteenth birthday. Donegal took me along with the other three women one Friday night to begin my career as a prostitute. I took to it like a duck to water at first, but then I guess I was lucky in the punters he found for me. It was not only in Vienna that the men favoured the young!

Ruth was not so lucky one night. The man she was with took back his money and slashed her across the face with a switchblade knife. Donegal and his men found that man later. They left him with both knees broken after beating him with pickaxe handles. So, Shaun, I've had plenty of men, knowing how to pleasure them whilst giving them the impression that I was enjoying it, but I was not. As I told you; I'm good at playing roles. A born actress. How good are you?"

"Were you playing at love when you fell for that Donegal, Fianna?"

"I didn't have to play at it, Shaun. He made me feel safe and wanted. That must be strange for someone like you to understand. I doubt you've ever been confused by life and certainly not used as I was. There you have me; a murdering whore full of evil and lacking affection for men as well as having no common sense."

"So, apart from murdering a priest what else have you been up to in the remaining unaccounted-for ten years, Fianna?" I asked.

"You wouldn't want to know, Shaun, believe me on that one."

Chapter Twelve

Pavelić

We met Richard for lunch at the Manhattan offices of his pharmaceutical company. When we left not only was I unsure about Jack's true reasons in sending us to America but also Stockford's involvement in the plan.

His offices had displayed the usual luxurious grandeur of success, with award-winning plaques hanging on walls alongside certificates of excellence and floor-to-ceiling glass looking out on the skyline of Manhattan, but we were entertained in a smaller, windowless place beyond that spacious plushness. A singularly private room lined throughout by bare polished dark wood, bereft of family photographs and paraphernalia. Here was the solidity of a single mind. A place of quiet refuge to escape and rest. Apart from the table around which we were to sit, there was only one other piece of furniture, a reclining red leather chair, beside which was a rolled-up heavy woollen blanket. I was trying to imagine the kind of life that requires a minimalistic sanctuary to find sleep when I began reciting Jack's tale of Aberman's death to his hard, impassive face which never altered even as I finished.

"You'll excuse me, Mr Stockford, but you seem little concerned about Schuschnigg killing the man who was instrumental in your escape from eventual death in a gas chamber. It's as though it never happened," I declared, bemused by his non-interest. "I thought you might want him dead, and that was one of the reasons I was sent." Fianna glanced angrily at me on my mention of death.

Sandra, the woman I'd spoken to earlier, was pouring wine. He dismissed her then, removing his heavy-rimmed spectacles, and wiping his eyes, he laughed derisively.

"I am a peaceful man, but if I were not it would serve little purpose wanting Schuschnigg murdered, Mr Redden, as he is already in his grave!"

"But I read an article of him being presented with an award for literature on his seventy-second birthday in the *London Evening News* over a week ago, Mr Stockford. Either you're mistaken or the paper has got it wrong," I said, utterly surprised by his reply.

"No, there are other possibilities, Mr Redden. One being that you were told of this presentation in order to prove yourself to me. My only wish would be that you could pronounce his name correctly, but as it was an Englishman who first told you of him I'll make allowances."

Again I looked into Fianna's eyes, and this time all I saw was a look of intense sorrow.

"What's another possibility, Mr Stockford?" I asked, to which Fianna supplied an answer.

"Jack as we all know him, or Sir Horace Butler as he's using for this exercise, is a storyteller, Shaun. It's how and why he lives the life he does. He weaves truth with lies making up a believable story, but the selling of interesting novels is not his goal. He sells new lives to those who he believes need them. There was never an entry in that London newspaper about Schuschnigg. He wanted us both in America for completely different reasons than the one he told you, and Richard is our way in. I really am the Bridget Slattery who murdered Finnegan and I would never have got a passport in that name without Jack. He has a special mission for me. I am in no position to refuse."

"What about the stories of your life in that orphanage and then when you left? Were they lies too, Fianna?"

"I can do without the family reminiscences." Stockford took command of the situation, as I continued staring at Fianna.

"You two can patch up your relationship another time. The story you were told about a meeting in Vienna in 1937 is true, as is its outcome; the birth of my niece Penina. On release from his German wartime prison camp Schuschnigg returned to Vienna where he started to make enquiries about Alain Aberman. We can only assume that he wanted to make good the friendship he hoped had survived the war. Alain got to hear of it. Aberman thought that Schuschnigg had died in the war and he believed he'd pushed all thoughts of him from his mind, but that wasn't the case. Memories that he had tried to suppress came flooding back, leading to his seeking out a foreign intelligence agent to tell his story to. He wanted Schuschnigg arrested, along with any of the ensemble who had accompanied the main players to the Chancery eight years previously. By fortune or ill luck it was Jack Price with whom he met. I have absolutely no idea who raped my sister, nor who was at that party. I've asked Jack but he's never told me. That's his hold over us.

Schuschnigg was shot dead in the street by a member of the Ante Pavelić's Ustaše as he walked from the American Embassy the very day he arrived in Vienna from Germany. You look quizzical, Mr Redden. Perhaps you're wondering how I know?" I was, but I was also wondering about the truth of Aberman's death. I must have sounded dumb to him as in a feeble voice I answered, "Yes, I am."

"On the night I and my family departed from Vienna, Aberman met my mother, Mayanna, and told her of his plan to avoid capture. I saw them together, Mr Redden, and I knew the moment I saw them that they were having an affair. It was in their eyes and in the way they held each other. It was not just good friendship that united them that night. In my opinion they were lovers. My mother cried when they parted and cried again on the flight. When we landed in New York, we moved into the same house as I live in now. When the pregnancy of my sister became more obvious, she was kept at home and the two of us were sworn to secrecy. When Penina was born everyone we knew accepted her as Mayanna's child without questioning that. I was told some of the story as I held my mother's hand before she passed away. Leeba moved out after Mayanna died and Penina a little while later.

A man my mother always referred to as an uncle would visit every month during those early years bringing food, books and sometimes I saw him pass Mother money. I never saw anything that resembled a letter pass between them until, I think it was October 1945. We went out for dinner that night, Mr Redden, a thing we had never done. I asked her why that was—'what are we celebrating, Mum?' and she told me why.

At first she asked me if I remembered Schuschnigg. How can anyone forget that fat pig, I answered. I remember him coming after our father was shot, full of sorrow that was feigned and false. Then, when he left I saw him stuffing his pockets with bread that our Mother had just taken from the oven. She said that he had been shot dead three days after the war officially ended on the fifth of September. That's how I know Schuschnigg is dead and Jack is filling your head with stories. I have no common ground with fascist values, but if I ever met that man who shot him I'd shake his hand in gratitude as much later she explained exactly who he was. She spoke too of a priest who was not choosy nor discreet in whom he told of his wartime rescuing of Jews. He spoke to the Allies who were trying to reconstruct the government of Austria, and he spoke to senior members of his faith. One of those was the Archbishop of Vienna, a close confident of a certain Karl Weilham.

The communications that Jack and I have with each other are one-way. I wait for his letters with postmarks from all over the world. I have no idea how to contact him directly. I also trust him in the retention of secrets, but I don't fully trust him in his motives. He hadn't contacted me for years until about a month ago, when he phoned and said he would be sending someone who would know the story of the Sternberg family and how Alain Aberman met his death. That was his code and your story was the other half of it. The use of the telephone was not only unprecedented, but deeply disturbing! He too knew the name of Weilham.

Somehow or other Jack knew of my interest in our family's ancestral history. He instructed me to pick that study up again, this time concentrating on the name of Schuschnigg. I discovered that he has a living step-brother. Born in Vienna in March 1918. Unlike Schuschnigg, the step-brother, Karl Weilham, joined the Nazi Party three weeks after their annexation of Austria in the Second World War. He served in the Wehrmacht on the Eastern Front, then after being wounded, was attached to German Army Group E, serving in Italy and the Balkans.

It was there he met and collaborated with Josip Tito, leader of the anti-German forces in Yugoslavia, a communist and Ante Pavelić, leader of the Croatian pro-German forces. Although Tito and Pavelić were on opposite sides during the Second World War they were on the same side during the First World War fighting the White Russians. Tito went into the Red Army after the October Revolution in 1917 returning to the newly formed Kingdom of Yugoslavia and joining the Communist Party. Pavelić, on the other hand, returned to Croatia to form the Ustaše movement in allegiance with the Fascists of Italy and then the German Nazis.

From an early age Weilham learned how to play both sides in a conflict. He now has an undisclosed financial interest in KGA, the company we are in talks with. I know this as a fact and have the necessary written confirmation. He did not disclose any of this information when he was appointed senior assistant secretary to the Secretary General of the United Nations last year! Tito, now President and Marshal of Yugoslavia, was one of his sponsors having first met our Karl in Vienna as early as 1934.

Tito's wartime partisans helped many Jews escape from persecution, whereas Pavelić, and his Ustaše movement, murdered tens of thousands of my religion. Weilham was in the middle, appeasing both sides through a Catholic association he had developed with Croatia's archbishop, who at best turned a blind eye to the genocide and at worse favoured Pavelić. As soon as the war in Europe ended Tito expressed his repugnance for what he saw as direct Vatican intervention, but absolved Weilham from blame. One year on saw the head of Croatia's Catholic church arrested by the Yugoslavian army and sentenced to sixteen year's imprisonment for assisting the Ustaše. This, and his censorship of Rome, led the Pope to excommunicate Tito and his government. Pavelić, however, was assisted by some of the authorities within the Catholic church in his escape from arrest in Vienna, and his flight to South America. Weilham, the newly installed UN assistant secretary, met with Ante Pavelić in Argentina many times and it was he who was instrumental in securing his return to Europe in 1959 after an assassination attempt on his life.

I've heard stories of some of those who escaped from Austria to Croatia only to be shot by Weilham's friend Pavelić. He, Weilham that is, conveniently denies any knowledge of genocide. The world is corrupt, Mr Redden, and there's little I can do about it other than tell Jack and hope he can. Whatever you do, don't damn Jack's story as a mere fairy tale. He needed you to believe it in order to persuade you to come. Only Jack knows why that is." From the breast pocket of his jacket he removed an envelope.

"All of what I've just told you is written in this letter. Jack ordered me to give it to whoever he sent. I do not understand what this has to do with my family. I can only pray it has nothing."

Not only was Richard's world widening, so too was my own, but not apparently Fianna's whose expression had not changed. It seemed her world had collapsed further than it had when on the plane.

* * *

"I've told you of me, Shaun, now how about you? Let's do a spoof of Eamonn Andrews introducing 'This Is Your Life' without the television cameras. Start with where were you born in real life."

We were about two hours into our flight and I could see no reason to refuse. She had been open in her disclosure, so I followed suit with a description of my early life in Camberwell, London, then on to Oxford and my meeting with Trenchard. I concluded the brief biography with the night in Soho, but omitted any details of what Jack had told me. It was not enough for my fictional sister.

"There's nothing about you in all that lot, just a matter of facts with no feelings, Shaun. Tell me of the girls you've loved and those that got away as well. Have there been many that ran out on you, or was it you who upped and ran leaving them begging for more, brother of mine?"

"Can't remember any girls running away, Fianna. I'm much too debonair for runaway girls. No offence meant there, by the way."

"None taken, brother, but I'll screw up those cigarettes of yours and flush them down the toilet if you don't give me more info."

"I knew some girls at university, but not for any great length of time, I'd be too embarrassed to give details. Besides, I was too busy being a good student to chase after girls. I still want a Master's before settling down."

"Oh, I have a queer as a brother after all, do I?"

"Master's degree, you idiot! It's an educational qualification."

"Ah! There was me thinking you too good looking to resist the cailíns in the world of study. No one catch your eye permanently up there in Oxford, Shaun? No legs pumping hard at the cycle pedals chasing after you, nor bosoms heaving as you disappeared over the horizon?"

I loved the somewhat risqué picture she painted of female students on their bicycles charging towards me. I wished that Fianna had been one of those leading the assault on my virtue, but sadly it was far from the truth. It was me doing all the chasing and more often than not getting exhausted without reward.

"I really did fancy one though. A very beautiful American girl name of Patricia. Patricia Ann Hickling. Came from rich parents, I believe. Far above my level in life."

"You never struck me as one of the oppressed proletariat. Unpolished and a bit awkward yes, but handsome enough to overcome those childish ineptitudes. Were you never educated to rise above your position and send the towers of oppression collapsing to ground?"

"That's a lot of big words for an Irish country girl. Most of them easily forgotten. Am I handsome enough for you to forget your sexual preferences and initiate me into the mile-high club? If so, I'm ready to take instructions, ma'am."

"There'll be no instructions from me, Shaun. Rough and parochial you are, me boy. Is that how your Patty girl saw you?"

"She was never my girl, although I did have ambitions in that direction."

"You never even spoke to her, did you?"

"I spoke, but she never noticed me. Too busy with others, I suspect," I replied regretfully.

"Did you share your lessons with her?"

"They were called lectures, not lessons. She was studying psychics and occasionally our studies overlapped in some small parts."

"You missed out on carrying her satchel then. What a wonderful pair you would have made. Leaving out the sordid details, tell me what you would do if you had a second chance with Patty Ann, Shaun?"

"I've never spent much time pondering the unlikely and I'm not about to change that. You're a dreamer, my girl. A very pretty one, but nonetheless a head in the clouds type. I haven't said it before I know, but you have a wonderful name."

"I told you I'm a goddess, Shaun. Goddesses have no need to dream on beds of clouds. They live on one. You should go and find one of your own one day." She was smiling and so were those eyes of hers.

"Go on, tell me of your first real love?" I wanted those smiling eyes to remain.

Elsewhere there was concern showing on faces rather than smiles.

Early Monday In London

"Earlier today I asked archives to fetch me all we had on Sir Horace Butler and do you know how much information we have recorded under his name, Perkins?

"No, sir! I first came across that name when West disappeared from the Albany on Saturday. Never heard of him before that."

"Not likely you'll hear much of him in the near future either. There was nothing recorded on the card index. It had been completely sanitised. All information had been redacted other than one inscription; file closed by Royal decree."

"What do you make of that, Perkins?"

"We're not meant to know, sir."

"Precisely! And what shall we do about that?"

"Get everyone we have on it straight away?"

"No, that won't work. First we need a key. Get me an appointment at St James's Palace within the hour, if not sooner."

Monday In New York

Chapter Thirteen

The First Touch of Honesty

"Not all of what I told you about the orphanage was true, Shaun. Finnegan didn't like boys dancing naked for him, he liked the girls and in particular me. That degenerate bastard took away my self-respect along with my virginity and that's why Imelda Duggen never found any bloodied sheets in the washing. It was that what egged her husband on, he thought I was what he imagined me to be. He believed what he had said of me being a slut was true all along."

We were in the lift on our way out of the Stockford company building sometime around two o'clock that Monday afternoon.

"Apart from me being your sister, everything else I told you about me was true."

"What happens now?" I asked, only having to wait until the lift stopped at the floor below Richard's to find out. As the doors opened it was I who was asked a question.

"Mr Redden?" He was a short man in his late twenties with a crop of shoulder-length brown hair.

He limped as he entered the lift, but those characteristics were not what I first noticed. The left side of his face was deeply scarred and burnt with raised angry mauve lines from his forehead to below his shirt collar. Parts of his neck and jaw were covered by pale pink skin grafts. I could not take my eyes from his hideous injury as I nodded and helplessly replied, "yes, that's me."

"I didn't think there'd be too many people with red hair travelling from the fifteenth floor. The guy who gave me this envelope was spot-on in his timing." He thrust the small white envelope towards me.

"Do I owe you anything?" I asked, shocked by his condition.

"No, bro, I've been paid! But if you want to donate then I won't stop you. My military service pension don't go far, if you get my drift." I did as I dug into my pockets and found a five dollar bill.

"I'm sorry, I've not got a lot."

"Don't sweat it. Every little helps, I'm not here to mug you." I spent the remaining seconds of our downward journey in abject embarrassment for not having any other money to give him and failing to find any words to account for my meanness. As the lift stopped at the street level I hurried from the building. It was then that I opened the letter.

"It's from Jack. He wants me to meet him," I announced lamely to a following Fianna.

"Somehow I never thought it was from Father Christmas, Shaun. I'll be away to the hotel to await my brother's return," she added playfully.

Jack Price was seated at one of the only two window tables inside the brightly blue painted Salvatore's Restaurant and Coffee Bar, opposite the New York library. On the pavement, either side of the front door, sat eight burly men around three wooden tables. By the boisterous conversation and their mannerisms, it was plain that they knew each other. One I thought I'd seen before; at the airport when we'd arrived, but I couldn't be one hundred percent sure. He was a small, rotund man, no more than five feet tall, dressed in blue shorts with knee-length matching socks. Not someone you would readily forget. They looked accustomed to being there, as I only saw two with coffee and one with food. There was a well-built man in his middle fifties standing in the doorway, glancing from one table to another and occasionally adding a remark to the friendly exchange. He struck an imposing figure, with a full head of hair as black as coal which glistened in the sunlight, making it difficult to focus on his face.

Jack was smartly dressed in a light grey suit, white shirt and yellow tie with a black fedora hat on the table before him. To all intents and purposes he hadn't a care in the world, unlike myself. My list of regrets at accepting his invitation was quickly growing. I could now add shame, as I hadn't the stomach to shake the hand of the departing disfigured war veteran whom I had just left. For a brief second I considered not following his written instructions to meet, turning around to chase after Fianna, but my curiosity had completely taken over, leaving no other option open.

"You're a long way from Soho, Jack? According to Job you preferred darkened alleyways in which to hide rather than out in the open casting your spell over events." I was annoyed but tried not show it.

"Ah, Shaun, and it's good to see you too. I guess you're a trifle confused by what's just occurred," he said on standing to greet me.

"Only a bit, Jack, but as someone just said to me; don't sweat it. I'm in the process of learning more and more about you as each moment goes by. Will I live long enough to know all what you're about?" I passed him Stockford's letter, giving him a chance to clear away Schuschnigg's body and resurrect Aberman in one omnipotent stroke.

"I certainly hope so, but it's mainly boring stuff really. Most of the time I spend reading a newspaper with my feet up. Only once in a while does something as important as this come along and then, well, we will soon find out."

"I'm guessing that you already know all there is to know about this Karl Weilham character and at the moment I can't see the necessity in flying me all the way here just to fill in any of the missing details. As for what's her name being here, again I'm at a loss. Care to enlighten me?"

"Fianna Redden is the name you're looking for. We keep to the script Shaun, all of the time. Are you okay? As you sound a little miffed today."

"I'm sorry, Jack. That was churlish of me. I apologise. I think it was the note that upset my equilibrium a bit. I wasn't expecting to hear from you or see you in New York. I thought Fianna and I were on our own."

"Oh no, that would never do. There's too much invested in this for me to take a back seat. Shall we sit? Would you like coffee? It's rather good in here actually."

Psychology is not an exact science, but to me it can be summed up in one sentence: if you can't change the problem, change the way you are thinking about it. A practising psychologist will never give a defining answer. If the question posed by a patient is: how can I deal with this feeling? The specialist will answer: how would you like to deal with it? I was beginning to believe that Jack had that Master's degree I was after in psychology. He was good! I merely sat and ordered coffee.

"They even empty the ashtrays in here, I see. You're sounding more and more as though you're a resident of Guildford, Jack. Have you got the DSM and Bar in a medal case on display in a cabinet at home? Moved into a plush detached mansion recently and barbecuing the local riffraff for brunch on Sundays, are we?"

There was that smile of his again, not haughty nor arrogant, just one of supreme confidence. This man was used to being alone and relying only on himself. I knew I was being used but didn't want it to stop.

"What's mine and Fianna's role exactly? I guess I'll be needing another name now this one is blown."

"Far from it, Shaun! Yours is buried so deep it's impossible to dig up. We have been extremely diligent in that respect. I told you that we've waited a long time for you and we're not about to lose you now. The likelihood of your arrival in this country with a fictitious sister being unearthed by any American security agency is so small as to be discounted at our end. However, if asked the whereabouts of Fianna Redden in the future by any of them, you will truthfully say that you have no idea where she went." Went! That word hit me hard.

"Nobody knows you're here and there's no reason for that to change." He felt my surprise. "Yes! It is not planned that you'll see Fianna again. I hope you said your farewells."

If ever there was a moment in my life when I felt like screaming it was now. She had left me with no word of her impending departure but must have known all along. Without waiting for any reply from me, he continued with his dialogue.

"She's here for a purpose unconnected to your own. But back to you, dear boy. Let's try to put your mind firmly to rest. Shaun Redden was a real person. Born in Belfast in the same month and year as your true self." He stopped speaking as a man wearing the white apron of a waiter approached with the coffees.

"This is Salvatore, Shaun, the owner of this establishment. Say hello!"

He was the same man I had seen leaning against a door pillar talking to those men outside. Now I could make out his strong jawline, deep set black eyes and the fixed determined look on his face. I obeyed Jack's instructions and I nodded in acquiescence.

"Salvatore was a colonel in Mussolini's army. Amongst many Germans that he served with was Karl Weilham, who you've just heard of, and Generaloberst Alexander Löhr, who you will hear more of. Salvatore has first-hand knowledge of atrocities carried out by Weilham. He was a witness to some of them. He will be your contact here in New York. If you have messages for me then leave them with Salvatore. He has a network of people he can call on if the need arises."

"Did you two meet in the same cafe you met Alain, Jack? Or was it in the place you once referred to as warmer than Vienna?" I asked, recovering my composure.

I'm sure I saw him wink at me as he sipped his coffee. When Salvatore left our table, he continued to beguile me.

"Salvatore and I have shared a few beers in our time in various places but let me get back to your history lesson, saving my recount of playful escapades for another day. Shaun Redden's parents both died in 1965 and there are few people that we discovered who can remember the young Shaun. Those that we did find can be discounted; too old for incriminating memories. He was a loner, was our Shaun. Apparently making no friends we're aware of. One month on from his parents' deaths in a tragic road accident, Shaun signed on as a galley hand on board a freighter ferrying coal from Swansea to Belfast, then iron ore from Belfast to Liverpool and finally plastics from Liverpool to Swansea. On registration he claimed to be one year older than he was, and using his father's name as a reference, nepotism won the day. Clive Redden, Shaun's father, was a seaman employed, when alive, by the Neiptiun Line, owners of the Aura. He was not a baker as Bridget was instructed to tell you." He lit a cigarette and stared at me.

"It was on that last leg of that seagoing triangle that MS Aura sank. There was a terrifying, vicious storm in the Irish Sea that sent the Aura to David Jones's locker along with the six crew members. There are no records of a Shaun Redden, no antecedents to hide, no fingerprints and no legend other than the sixteen-year-old who lived with his parents Mary and Clive. That brief history is in the letter I'll give you when we part. Read it, Shaun, then you'll know as much about him as anyone else does and will ever do."

"What is it you want Shaun Redden to do for you in New York?"

"I guess you mean apart from enjoying your coffee and sightseeing?" His gaze moved from me to the outside as he took a few seconds to answer.

"There are few steadfast rules of the game, Shaun. Most you'll pick up as we go along. All are simple, but equally all are important. One to ponder on as we sit enjoying each other's company. If you believe you're being followed then you must change some relevant detail about yourself." I never allowed him to finish.

"You don't advise jumping into a dead-end alley then, Jack?" He made no reply as he picked up from where he had left off.

"Be it a coat you're wearing, or a bag you're carrying. Dump it. That will confuse whoever's on your tail."

"Am I being followed?" I asked.

"No, you're not as far as I'm aware, but your hair colouring defines you. It has to go, Shaun. Salvatore's youngest daughter is a hairdresser. I've made arrangements for her to dye it and show you how to keep the new colour."

"I could get Fianna to do it if you have a forwarding address, Jack." His benign business-like expression changed into a devilish smile.

"It's a big city, Shaun, with plenty of distractions to take your mind off Fianna. I would start at the Tat & Tail club. Their card is in the envelope with a name you could meet."

"Another contact of yours?"

"No! Simply a friendly girl you might want to get to know. Just thinking of your welfare and how you can amuse yourself."

"How long will I have to find amusement, Jack? How long do you propose I stay in New York?"

"Can't answer that one precisely. Events are moving quickly in the current affair. After this finishes then there are other considerations that require our attention, but for the moment all's in hand with regard to your comforts. At my instigation Richard Stockford has opened a bank account for you, along with finding you an apartment. Don't go getting too excited though. I don't suppose it's a penthouse suite, but it will adequately serve your purpose whilst you're here. We certainly can't afford hotel bills on a nightly basis. I don't suppose there's much in the bank. Enough to tide you over for essentials, I should think. No point raising suspicions by turning you into some sort of playboy," he grinned widely.

"Leeba Stockford will be adding to it on a regular basis for as long as you work for her." The grin turned into a smile.

"She's the founding partner at Stockford & Crawford. They are what's called a boutique law firm, operating exclusively here in New York and specialising in corporate affairs such as the merger that's underway with her big brother's pharmaceutical company and the German KGA company. You're to be their research analyst, Shaun. After your spell in the criminal records office back at dear old Scotland Yard, it should be right up your street and it provides you with great cover. Fancy something stronger than coffee to drink?" Not waiting for my answer, he summoned Salvatore again.

"Whatever happened to only having my wits and intuition to rely on, Jack? It seems as though I now have a branch of the mafia and riches to call on."

"You have exciting times ahead, Shaun. As good a reason for a piss-up as I've ever heard."

Chapter Fourteen

Green Or Yellow?

There was a letter pushed under the door of my in room at the hotel. It contained much, but explained little.

Dear Shaun, I'm sorry it ended this way. That was not my decision. However, I couldn't be doing this face to face, it would upset me too much. I've told you many lies, but that was not my idea either. Now is the time to clear up some of them, if you allow me and if I can.

When I first met you I thought you were up your own backside in a big way. I slowly changed my mind about that. I realise we've only known each other for less than three days but I can say without question you are the nicest man I've ever come across. I truly wish that if I had a brother and that brother was you then, perhaps, things may have worked out differently for me. I reckon you could have kept me safe, but I'm too far into this mess to ever be that and now I have no way out that I can see.

I was recruited into British intelligence when I was a prostitute in Newry, but I told you the truth about not meeting Jack Price until recently. One night my favours were paid for by a rugged looking middle-aged Irishman who spoke with such eloquence that I could almost forget he was a trick. It was not only the sex he was after though. He told me that Donegal Fitzpatrick was in trouble with the local Garda for supplying guns to a group of Irish dissidents, as he called them, in Sligo. I could help him he said, by finding out some information on that group for him to pass on to the police without Donegal having the need to know. It would get him off the hook, he said. Perhaps I believed him the more because he was old enough to be the father I'd never had.

Donegal was screwing me so it wasn't hard to go with him on his deliveries and meet who he met. I got the names of most in that group and in time, some more. In no more than six months the Brits were screwing me in my mind. I was owned by them and had no other place to go. But that wasn't the whole of the story. I never found that out until very recently. The man who slashed my friend's face, and was then beaten up, was heavily connected within the Republican Army. As Donegal expanded his prostitution ring so he met people with differing political agendas. Many were from the Ulster Volunteers. The IRA pulled his strings and when they pulled hard enough he supplied them those Ulstermen's names! But the IRA's alliance with Donegal didn't last long.

They shot him as a traitor when the young Irishman I met that night in Newry fingered him. He ran me for a while until Scarface turned up one day when I was working in a bar in Belfast. It was he who told me where Finnegan was and it was he who taped the knife under a pew in St Mary's that I used to kill him. Said, and I believed him, it was the British government's way of saying thank you for the work I'd done against the Republicans.

I'm not looking for your sympathy, nor for the understanding of me. All I'm trying to do is warn you against accepting Jack Price for what he appears to be on the surface. There's so much hidden out of sight that I fear for you. You are too honest for your own good and you're too ready to be taken in by anyone who shows an interest in you. In that respect we are equals. My case is beyond salvation. I've sinned too many times, but you are just starting out with time on your side to turn around and go home. I know you won't take my advice. I know I would not if our roles were reversed.

To most people that I've met, killing becomes easier the more you do it. With you I'm not so sure that's the case. The lack of emotion that you had after shooting that man Acre was not natural, Shaun. You may think that to be a strength of yours, it's not. Jack Price sees that as your major weakness. I'm in America as your older sister Fianna and although there won't be anyone looking for you to back up my story, please remember the tale about Athlone. Lies get you into trouble if you forget the reasons why you're telling them. If you forget Athlone you'll put my life in danger and then I can't protect you. There aren't many friends in the business you've chosen, don't lose the only one you might have.

You'll probably think that I'm a sentimental fool in asking this of you, but it will mean a lot to me if you kept this ring of mine. I have no family nor likely to have any. Stay safe and distance yourself from Jack Price as much as you're able. He plays dangerous games with other people's lives.

Before you came along I could put up with being me, knowing where my life had to go, but now I'm having regrets and as you once told me, there's no point in wishing for something you can't have. Remember me well as I will fondly remember you. I believe in God. I must, as this life is a living hell.

Bridget x x

PS. If I wasn't queer I could well fancy you myself. Go find your Patty Ann and tell her to treat you well, or she'll have a fiery Irish colleen to look out for.

Her key was at the reception desk and her room had been completely emptied of her belongings. Every tangible trace of her had disappeared apart from that jade ring and her letter.

* * *

We were on the plane when the subject of regrets weighed heavy on Fianna's mind. "This ring never came from the priest, Shaun. I won it in a game of cards. I'd come to the game with the five hundred quid needed to sit at the table and was up that night about a grand. It doesn't matter where that money came from. I'll let you imagine what I had to do to get it, but it wasn't all hardship. I'd met a few women by then who wanted me and were willing to pay for what I could provide. Anyway, I held a pair of aces and the last man still punching held a pair of kings. He'd laid down the best part of fifteen hundred pounds, only having the ring left to see my hand. The pot on the table was worth a fortune, more money than I'd ever seen. The man in charge of the game said I should accept it as the same worth as my wager and I wasn't about to argue with half the IRA Army Council who were sitting around that table, so I did.

I should have known that jade being lucky was a lie as it wasn't for that Englishman that night. I thought it would change with the change of ownership and in some respects that's been the truth. I've known luck, but it doesn't last forever. The wheel spins around and around. Sometimes you're on the top and other times you're at the bottom. The secret is in knowing when to jump off, no matter how high you are."

"That sounds so full of remorse, Fianna. Why?" I asked, trying to entice more from her.

"I once read a series of magazine articles, written by a women riddled with cancer who wanted to tell the world of her chemotherapy treatment. It contained detailed memories of her life that she regretted and would change if she was given a second chance. It was sad and beyond sad. There's no salvation to be found in regrets, Shaun, now is there!"

"I don't know. A trouble shared and all that. It might help if you were able to talk about it."

"Yeah, I can imagine. A friend in need is a pain in the arse and I was never a pain to a friend unless I needed to be."

At the time that negative statement sounded threatening, but having read her letter that threat disappeared.

I folded her letter and placed it in my pocket. As far as I was concerned I was living an exciting life with nobody to answer to. However, parts of that letter challenged that assumption. Should I ignore the tenderness and sincerity she expressed in it simply to follow my self-absorbed interest in the intrigue that was offered by Jack? Should I consciously pay no regard to advice given by someone who put my needs before their own? I had lived alone for some time now, but even when my parents were alive I gave scant regard to their requirements or wants from life. I thought only of me. I was a loner who held no perception of the idea that a stranger could give her heart so readily, so quickly without expecting something in return. Her letter had shaken the foundations of my life.

The two conditions of being alone and experiencing loneliness are completely separate. You can be lonely in the middle of a crowd of people that not only do you know, but normally interact with easily. That can be as a result of a simple or complicated unconnected event, or, a mood swing. Stark, miserable loneliness, where there are no friends or relatives that you can speak to or socialise with, can be agonisingly painful, where all self-esteem vanishes to be replaced by depression and anxiety. Being alone and not only expecting that, but also welcoming the condition as your destiny, requires a special disposition where an amount of selfishness, in not wanting to share your life, plays a significant part. Few possess this ability and even fewer welcome it. Up until this point in my life I had been one of those few.

Fianna, as I preferred to remember her, had been no more than a companion on my journey through the labyrinth of Jack's mind, yet she had touched something in me that I'd never experienced. As I stood with the memories of her swirling through my head I felt both the state of being physically alone and the misery of loneliness at the same time. Memories of people, with recollection of events, fade or change as time moves on. They become misty and indistinct. I decided that by keeping her ring I would be able to keep her presence clearer, but I had not counted on sharing in her personal regrets. Mine was the regret of not knowing her better and the belief that I never would. I checked out of the hotel and trusted in my widening circle of acquaintances for the next steps on my journey, but to use an Americanism; I almost never made first base!

At The Cut Shop

"A Salvatore Guigamo has sent me. You should be expecting me. He told me to ask for his daughter but never told me her name. I'm here to have my hair colouring changed to black," I announced on my arrival.

The receptionist never had a chance to reply. The girl standing behind her responded quicker. "It's not my lucky day, is it!"

Salvatore's youngest daughter was my junior by some years, but the fact that we were both breathing was about the only thing we had in common. She was obese, and bad-mannered. Her size could easily have been ignored as she had the most angelic face imaginable; small and pert with large, sharp, sea-blue eyes, a tiny upturned nose and hair the colour of the deepest, blackest night one could ever have imagined. It was her temper, rudeness and attitude that set her apart from any description of beauty. Those characteristics would have precluded all but the most insane from approaching her for anything other than a haircut. And then it took only the bravest of the brave!

Back in England I was used to the name of unisex to describe hairdressers where both men and women went for a trim or perm. Her salon was called The Hedonistic Cut Shop; perhaps that should have given a clue into what I was in for.

"Were you born stupid or did you achieve that status on the boat that brought you to New York, Irish? You have the very worst skin colouring for black hair and I will just not do it!" was how she answered my request, walking determinedly around the reception desk towards me.

"Go cover it in river mud and let it set," was what she added, stopping two paces in front of me.

Thinking I'd made a mistake in the timing of the visit and not wishing to antagonise her, or her father, I thought it best to make an appointment for a later date. But it wasn't my lucky day either.

"Where the freaking hell are you going, you son of a bitch?" she shouted at my turned back.

"Go plant your ass in my chair." She pointed to the empty one in a line of twelve.

"I can do you a sick green or a yellow submarine colour. Whichever one you choose you'll still look a freak. Your one consolation is you're not infested by freckles like some of you red-haired weirdos. You choose, but you ain't leaving here black." She turned her attention towards the other stylists, who had stopped working to watch the spectacle of her berating of me.

"What are you lot looking at?" It was their turn for a lashing of abuse. "Get back to work or you're sacked!"

I plucked up enough courage to speak.

"Are you always this respectful to your customers, or am I special to you in some way that I've not yet noticed?"

"I'm doing you a favour and being nice. You should see me when I'm a bad-mouthed cow," she added without a glimmer of a smile.

"Green or yellow? What's it to be?"

I sat in silent discomfort for some considerable time with my neck being heaved from side to side as she painted clumps of my hair then wrapped them in foil whilst mumbling under her breath as she did so. As she finished that process I tried to gain favour by paying her a compliment. It was useless.

"Your hair is very nice. I never got your name, by the way."

"Nice! My hair's not nice, that's a stupid thing to say. It's either stylish or not. Everything about me oozes style, can't you see that?"

"Well, it's very stylish then. As, of course, are you," I lied, as the chair was turned and my head was forced under a tap. I wasn't ready for the outcome when I emerged as a dripping wet blond. As I was spun back and faced the mirror again, nameless had wrenched off her hair.

"It's a frigging wig, you Irish Mick! Do you really think anyone who works as hard as I do to please my father would have such perfect natural hair, cos if you do then you're worse than stupid. There's never enough time to do it and then supervise this lot."

Underneath her long, tumbling black wig was a head of short, chocolate-coloured cropped hair. So short any serviceman would have been thankful for surviving the barber's razor. My compliment had only managed to provoke her into more insults.

"My dad doesn't normally make friends with screwballs. Why the exception with you? You sure you ain't his bastard son and he has to be kind? Oh no, I know what you are. You're a leprechaun who arrived with his restaurant's salad delivery this morning? Whatever way you got here, Irish, you're still a fool."

The prolonged noise from the hairdryer luckily drowned out any more conversation until, seemingly finished with both the hair colouring and her assessment of me, she removed my gown before delivering her final blast.

"I've heard a lot said about thick Micks from the Emerald Isle of Ireland and now having met one who must have spent all his youth standing in the rain, all I can say is that I never want to go there or meet any more. It's a pleasure to say goodbye, Mick."

I stood, towering over her by several inches, then picked her up by her braced elbows and dumped her in the chair that I had just risen from. She wriggled fiercely, trying to break free from my grip. I wouldn't let her, as I pinned her bare shoulders back roughly against the plastic of the chair. I had her attention and that of everyone else in the shop.

"In time my hair will grow, but I'll be able to keep the colour by simply colouring it again. A simple practice that even an Irishman can do. You, on the other hand, are just a sour-mouthed bitch who will never change no matter how many different wigs you wear. You're in desperate need of much more than a wig to hide what you are. Your father seemed a reasonable man, you have a long way to go to be like him. I can only hope that one day he'll get over the disappointment and shame he must have for fathering you. By the way, I'd change the name on the outside window if I were you to Chucklehead. It would suit an idiot like you far better."

At that I left the salon, glancing at what I imagined as smiles of approval in the wall-mounted mirrors on my way out, but there was no smile or sarcastic grin from Nameless. I guessed she wouldn't have known the meaning of the word chucklehead and I wasn't about to stay and explain.

Chapter Fifteen

Banks and Boutiques

Having already experienced so many surprises, I chose the bank that Richard had selected for my newly acquired wealth as my next port of call, hoping for the best. Back home I was never used to having more than a couple of hundred pound or so in the bank at any one time. My expectations never exceeded the equivalent. My luck was in! His generosity exceeded my wildest dreams. Whilst I was there I rented a safe deposit box, placing all the written instructions I had from Jack, along with my passport and the jade ring of Fianna's hoping that the luck she had experienced would spill over onto me.

As I left, following the map that Salvatore had drawn on a restaurant order slip depicting my new apartment in relation to both the bank and Leeba Stockford's boutique law firm, I mused over how to spend Stockford's largesse. Would it be on a car? I had never learned to drive in England and driving on the wrong side of the road here in America did not seem appealing enough to squander money on learning that craft. A bed might be needed, but perhaps new clothes? Now that was something worth considering as I had very few with me. All the eagerness of an extravagant lifestyle disappeared as I turned the corner into Baxter Street where an ugly, tall block of greying concrete apartments was staring straight at me as if in reprimand to my desires of pleasure. Eighteen storeys of grime with a minimum of windows and only a tiny number of apartments having a balcony. It was in this building that my life in New York was to be lived. My solitary remaining hope was that it overlooked the park in front of the block, and not the endless buildings behind.

Jack had said that it was furnished, but his idea of furnishing was a long way from mine. I decided not to make my day any worse by looking inside and finding out. Saving any more disappointments for later, I made my way towards Leeba, silently praying that visit would go sufficiently well to lift my now downhearted mood.

Her offices were opposite the US Centre of Citizenship and Immigration in a small intimate building resembling more of an English one than anything I'd seen since arriving in New York. It was brick-built with sash windows and what's more, consisted of a mere two floors with a basement area, all of which were part of the Stockford & Crawford, Attorneys at Law. Inside the ground floor glass door I was immediately greeted by two smiling, well-dressed women seated behind a rich, curving wheat coloured marble desk, bedecked with a battery of telephones and two bulky computer screens that almost filled the whole of the contemporary, stylish reception area.

"Good afternoon, Mr Redden! We were told to expect you sometime today. Welcome on board the S & C. I'm Christa. Jennifer has the honour of accompanying you to Miss Leeba's office. It's very good to see you," she added on answering a ringing telephone.

"How did you know my name?" completely surprised, I asked of the standing attractive Jennifer who, although holding my fascination could not wholly divert it from the title of *Miss* attributed to Leeba.

"By the description we were given, Mr Redden. Height, weight, looks and hair colouring. Plus there's nobody else expected today, sir. Monday is set aside for in-house case appraisals and reconciliation," she explained.

I was beginning to think that being blond along with everything else in my life was predetermined by Jack. For the first time since my remonstration at the hairdressers I wondered what Fianna would think of my new persona.

The previous animosity I'd experience was replaced by Leeba's sincerity and consideration, balanced by a degree of understandable suspicion. After she greeted me with a warm and friendly handshake, I took my place in the chair in front of her desk, trying hard not to stare at the well-stocked drinks cabinet standing beside one of the four windows that looked out onto the street, but my diffidence brought no reward. My thirsty anticipation of alcohol went unanswered; instead I soberly drank the coffee I was offered.

"Let's dispense with the formalities first. Richard has informed me that you are aware of our full family's history. My brother trusts the man who told you our story so it follows that I must trust you, Shaun. I find it odd that a complete stranger knows more about us than we know and even more strange that my brother accepts that situation. However, all that's out of my control. I'm left with nothing but to comply with the arrangements." She glared at me, trying to search inside my soul for hidden secrets, but her glare was tinged with compassion not anger. The title of *Miss* was confirmed by the lack of a wedding ring on her finger, neither did she wear any other jewellery.

"Richard has explained part of why you're here. He left most of that explanation shrouded in mystery. I assume your work will be more investigatory than simple everyday research. As I understand things your main interest, for the time being at least, will be the pending merger of my brother's company with KGA where Karl Weilham is an undisclosed, but legitimate stock holder. I'm guessing that your expertise will not necessarily be aimed at the legitimate side of business." There was a hint of depravity in her voice and mirrored on her face.

"I hope I haven't given you the impression that you're not wanted here, or unappreciated. That is not the case at all. And to show how much we welcome you I've had the office next to this one prepared for your sole use. There's an interconnecting door which will make things more convenient, as I assume that you and I will be meeting many times before you've finished whatever it is Richard wants from you. I've had a list prepared of the company's employees. There are not many, but too many to confine to one's memory in a short time. You may find it useful while you settle in. Is there anything my firm can do for you now to help smooth your way into the life here in New York City?"

She was of medium height with a trim, well-proportioned figure. Shapely legs and a small behind. The conventional lemon yellow business suit of a lightweight material and low cut cream blouse hung snugly to her body, holding my gaze the longer I looked. A sharp featured rounded face with a sloping nose, bronzed complexion with deep, narrowly set brown eyes. She wore little makeup, just eye shadow and mascara; both of which were brown. Her long raven black hair swayed as she moved around the room and the scent of a crisp, sharp, exotic perfume served as the finishing touch to her appeal. She may have been at forty-eight more than twice my age, but time could not dull how seductive she was. By her confident bearing and perfunctory welcome speech I had no doubt that if this woman wanted privacy then the transgressor would be dismissed in a flash. Pushing those corporeal instincts I had just experienced to the back of my mind for another day, I tackled the austere possibility of living a restrained life in a bleak home.

"There is one thing that's occurred me, Leeba. Your brother has rented an apartment for me, a few blocks away on Baxter Street. I haven't looked inside yet, but I doubt if there's much in the way of furniture. Could you point me in the right direction to buy some cheap stuff, such as a bed and a couple of chairs etc."

"There's no need for that, Shaun. That property is one of several that my sister Penina, owns. I know it looks a little rundown from the outside, but I can assure you that it would have been furnished to a very high specification. That whole area is on the up with a facial refurbishment due on the building in the not so far off future. We're Jewish, remember, Shaun. With that comes a reputation of wise and shrewd investments." A heavenly smile accompanied that comment, which only served to arouse my interest to new heights.

"I'm not sure what reputation the Irish have brought upon themselves in this city, but I'm becoming aware that it's not a good one judging by the hairdressers I've just come from. Are they all so obnoxious in this part of town?"

"You must have picked the wrong one, but the change of hair colouring added to the mystique that surrounded you. Richard said that you would be having your red hair dyed blond. He didn't say why that was, but I presumed it was done with anonymity in mind." I was right about Jack then.

"Yes, it was suggested that it might be more prudent. Red does tend to stick out a bit," I answered politely.

"Also indicative of a temper, so I'm told." I never answered that implied question and instead I asked my own.

"I take it your *sister* Penina is a rich woman in her own right then?" I figured that although she was aware of my knowledge, discretion was more favourable than stark disclosure. That was not my only reason. I hoped that a principled approach would add to the mystique she attributed to me.

With her cheeks puffed out in pride and pleasure she smilingly answered.

"Very much so! She's a classical musician by training, on both the violin and the cello. Unfortunately she seldom plays nowadays, preferring to concentrate on musical scores for the movie business. Penina is extremely successful in that regard. She's written for many of the top grossing modern-day movies that have originated in Hollywood. She does stage productions, as well as owning her own recording studio in Beverly Hills. I have a collection of some of the highest profile modern singing artists who have recorded there. It's a prized possession of mine. I'll show it to you one day. When your clandestine work for Richard allows for it."

"That would be extremely nice of you, Leeba. I'll look forward to the day, but my work is not that secretive. I think sensitive would be a more correct definition."

"Is there a difference?" she asked with that smiling laugh again lighting up her face. This time I too laughed, bowing my head towards her in recognition of her humour and her understated awareness of my role.

"You take your time in moving into the office, Shaun. Everything Richard and I thought you might need is in there. I understand that you don't drive. Is that right?" she asked, to which I replied that I didn't.

"In that case you will need our driver with one of the company's cars. Might I suggest that tomorrow you take a drive out to Hartford, Connecticut. It's a couple of hours through pleasant countryside. You'll enjoy the scenery!"

Was that last remark made because she had noticed just how much I was enjoying it already? Was I being presumptuous to assume that she may have noticed, or cared? Her tone of voice had not changed nor had her expression. A misinterpretation perhaps? If it was, then I had relished the thought. She was still speaking.

"Backing on to a golf club, just outside the town, you'll find a very grand house belonging to a man named Haynes Baxter-Clifford. The driver knows where it is. Haynes is a powerful man and one to watch out for. Now would be an opportune time to know who your enemies may be." All remains of that smile had disappeared from her face, replaced by a solemn frown in my direction.

"That sounds very intriguing and also a touch disconcerting. Has that name any relevance to the street where my apartment is, Leeba?"

"Oh yes, a great deal of relevance. He owns the freehold of that whole street and almost all of the freeholds in half a mile radius of it, including this building. With that comes the franchise on construction work in this whole area. It's a very lucrative business, building in New York. He inherited his father's property portfolio when his older brother died in a car accident sixteen months ago. There was a degree of speculation at the time as to what could have caused that accident on a clear road that he knew so well. The FBI conducted the investigation as he was running for the Democratic nomination for congress. Stood a good chance of winning. Haynes knows Karl Weilham extremely well and through him a Marty Killick, the leader of the Nazi party here in America. You looked shocked, Mr Redden. We don't have the monopoly of fringe lunatics in this country, but we do have enough of them in New York. They met three months before Earl Baxter-Clifford died. But that's not the only thing that connects him to our family, Shaun. Haynes and Penina are friends in an intimate sense."

She stood to refill our coffee cups just I nearly ruined everything.

"I thought Penina was a—" I caught myself just in time before repeating what Fianna had implied her sexuality to be.

"A what, Shaun?" Leeba asked.

"Oh, I'm sorry. I thought she was married."

"I don't know where you got that from, but would it matter? What monastery have you been hiding in?" The smile that replaced the frown now widened considerably. "I thought three Hail Marys was the going rate for infidelity in Catholic Ireland as it is over here. If she was married, which neither she nor I am, would it make her unredeemable if she had committed adulatory?" laughingly she asked, adding. "My brother Richard has been divorced twice for having affairs with married women. I believe he's involved with another now. Shall we construct some gallows for him?" Her eyes narrowed into an inquisitive stare, and her grin bordered on the promiscuous.

"I noticed that you're not wearing a ring, Leeba. Are you divorced as well?"

"That's beyond your remit, Shaun. Some things are best not looked at too closely. You're not wearing a ring either, does that mean you're gay?" That question caught me off guard and I had no way in which to adequately answer it. She eased my frustration by supplying an answer herself.

"Don't worry, I'm only joking with you. I have no doubts on that issue."

Was my preoccupation with her getting the better of me or was the seductiveness in her voice and on her face sincere? I decided to bide my time before testing that sincerity just about the same time as she changed direction.

"Haynes is twenty-three years older than Penina, but the reality of the situation has been clouded by what she calls love. He is an evil man who never would have come to prominence without his brother's death. Penina has a fixation that I've never seen in her before. I have substantive suspicions that link him to some of the radical far right parties that cloak themselves in respectability by making financial donations to the down trodden and under-privileged. Penina won't take my suspicions seriously. In fact, she won't listen to anything said about Baxter-Clifford that's not complimentary. She can be very stubborn in certain matters. Personally I suspect him to have been involved in his brother's death, but that's for another day. I have tried to protect her over the years, but now I'm worried. She has no first-hand knowledge of what the Nazis did to the Jews in the war."

For thirty-five years her true Jewish heritage had been denied from her. I wondered why the resurrected memories of such atrocities would be needed now.

"I'm not at all qualified in these matters, Leeba, Surely you need a mediator of some description. Perhaps a therapist, or a historian if the Holocaust needs to be explained?"

I had no idea how to respond and was wondering why I was being told of her *sister's* crush on an older man. Was agism her reason for scolding me before I developed a similar crush on her? A discrimination carved on Leeba's heart?

There was an obvious connection in what she disclosed to Jack's main target Karl Weilham, but all the rest was superfluous and mere supposition, as had been Fianna's when she labelled Penina a lesbian. I thought that could have been because Fianna was aware of the unmarried status, perhaps due to being sexually unattractive to men, but I was soon to change that opinion.

"This is my sister." Leeba turned one of the three wooden-framed photographs that were placed on her desk around to face me. She was everyman's fantasy! I was stunned into almost complete silence. One word was sufficient to disclose my interest. "Wow," I exclaimed.

"Is that a 'wow' in recognition of Penina's beauty, Shaun, or in admiration of the plane she's standing next to? One of her many achievements is to hold a pilot's licence for both a fixed winged aeroplane and a helicopter. That photo was taken at Bradley airport, on one of her visits to Baxter-Clifford. It was her birthday and the plane a gift from Haynes. I think it was two years ago, but let me check that as it could have been three." She reversed the photograph then spoke again.

"Yes, I was right; two years ago. I want you to work for me as well as my brother but without Richard's direct involvement and knowledge. If he knew he would object. I want you to expand my knowledge on Haynes Baxter-Clifford and I want you to meet with Penina in order to do that. Then I want you to ease her away from that man."

"Wow again, Leeba! Ease her away. I'm no Casanova. That's some ask! Look at me, I'm not exactly dressed to meet a rich beautiful woman who's used to the better things in life like aeroplanes, now am I? And while we're at it, how do you suggest I get an invitation?"

"All that's in hand, Shaun. You have the looks and ways of a man who could do the job. Just turn up at his home around lunchtime tomorrow suitably dressed in the very best attire this can buy you. Do you play golf, by the way?" she said, as she gave me an opened envelope stuff full of dollar bills.

"I don't," I answered, staring wildly at the contents whilst my head was somersaulting down a runway.

"That's okay as Haynes does and will be playing when you arrive. You'll have Penina all to yourself for hours. It's the seventies, Shaun.

Women no longer have to wait to be included in men's fantasies. They are free to play out their own when and how they wish."

"Do you include yourself in that freedom for fantasies, Leeba?"

"Yes, Shaun! Very much I do. What's the point of being an advocate for sexual liberation if one can't enjoy all the freedom that's available?" She smiled lasciviously, and I wasn't imagining it.

"There's a performance of Puccini's *La Bohème* at the Met next week. I have a box there. Get yourself a white tuxedo and who knows, I might just let you take me. Oh, and on the way out ask at the reception desk for the key to this building and the one to your office. They have them ready for you."

"I have no idea how long I'll be in this country, Leeba. I could be gone before that opera."

"No matter. It's only money, Shaun, it's not life or death."

I had found money, culture and a seductive woman. What more could America offer me? As far as I was concerned now was not the time to ask about 1937. Now was the time to have fun.

Tuesday In New York

Chapter Sixteen

A Rainbow

I would never have considered myself as scruffy, but on the other hand, neither would I have considered myself to have been well-dressed. I was simply dressed in a manner appropriate to my situation in life. I was, however, a *tailor's dummy,* being able to wear anything and look good in it, but that wasn't something that was high on my list of waiting achievements—until this moment, that is.

My height, a couple of inches over six foot, and my weight of between thirteen stone twelve, and fourteen stone two ounces never changed. I was heavily built in a muscular way. Whilst in London I kept fit by regularly visiting a gym and eating sensibly. The training I undertook was in strength rather than stamina, using progressively heavier weights for my profile, with only squats and the odd cycling machine for cardiac exercise.

With Leeba's money I purchased not only off-the-peg suits, but jackets, trousers, shirts, ties and shoes in various colours. As I walked, glancing at my well-presented reflection in car windows or shops that I passed, I felt good, so much so that I had no hesitation in planning a visit to the Tat & Tail after I made my way to apartment number 430, The Holstein Building, Baxter Street; my home, depositing the new look for me inside. Jack was both right and wrong. He was wrong about the apartment not being on the top floor; it was, and some apartment it was too. Split level with an open-plan kitchen, three bedrooms, two bathrooms, furnished with little regard to expense and overlooking the park below. There was even a table with chairs on the balcony. He was right though about the girl he knew at the club. She was entertaining in all manner of ways, lacking nothing when it came to vigour and staying power.

I had no need to choose which bedroom at number 430 in which to sleep that night, nor did I indulge in any of its luscious furnishings until the morning on my return from the club, where I had fully immersed myself in amusement and vowed to carry on. With the blond hair and new wardrobe had come a newly awakened me who wasn't about to stand waiting at bus stops for the next ride to come along.

* * *

My driver's name was Barkley. Whether that was his first or last name was never made clear throughout our journey to the suburbs of Hartford that Tuesday lunchtime. He spoke very little and whenever he did he referred to me as *sir*. My attempts to dissuade him in this were futile, so I stopped and sat back to enjoy the view. The journey passed quickly and smoothly until we pulled up outside a set of high security gates with an entry phone protecting what could only be described as a palatial mansion of some substance. Barkley made the introductions.

"I have a Mr Shaun Redden to see Miss Penina. He is expected."

I was escorted through the white marble-floored entrance hall to the rear of the house by a frail, balding man in his late sixties with a curving scar on his forehead. He was dressed all in black, which did not reflect the abundance of splendour that surrounded my walk. Penina was lying beside the pool, stretched out on a sun lounger in partial shade. She wore a flimsy orange-coloured shawl over a gold bikini that disguised none of her sexuality. There was a table beside her with a telephone, bottles of sun cream, and a jug of lemonade. Through sunglasses she addressed me.

"My sister tells me that you are my newly appointed personal advisor, Mr Redden. In which areas of my life do you think I need advice?"

"Maybe in the quantity of your fluid intake, but certainly not in your dress sense or style." I stepped forward and poured some of the iced cloudy liquid into the empty glass she held. "May I call you Penina or would you prefer Miss Stockford, Miss Stockford?"

"Those who I like call me Penni, Shaun. What I'm seeing of you at the moment I'm liking, so Penni will do nicely." She removed her glasses and examined me from toe to the tip of my head without moving. My eyes were wandering over her.

"Are you Catholic Irish in religious doctrine alone, or in your taste for life, Shaun? Or are they the same thing to you?" she asked.

"That's a tough one to answer, first up, but I'll have a stab at it. Without knowing the righteous things of life one would not be able to enjoy the sinful ones with the same amount of pleasure. I'm going to hazard a guess and say you know them both, but prefer the wicked to the pure. If that's the case, then I'm of the same persuasion, but far be it from me to show you an insight into the sin-laden world. It is too corrupt for someone as beautiful as yourself."

"Perceptive Catholicism! How rare and refreshing. But you are too young to know of promiscuity. If your perception holds no reprimand for apparently enjoying the sins that you and I do, then I shall listen to your advice, but I'm a totally wicked girl who prefers to direct matters rather than seek guidance from others." From where she lay she passed me that glass. "Drink some, I've had enough."

She was tall, with the most exquisite tan imaginable, blonde-haired, with long slim legs beneath heavenly thighs. A small pinched waist leading up to champagne breasts and a coquettish smile that matched Brigitte Bardot's. A beautiful oval face with a small pointed chin beneath wide, thick lips that screamed, 'kiss me.' But it was her eyes that transfixed my stare the most. The tantalising blue of a spring sky and as wonderfully hypnotic.

"There is something on which you may be able to advise me, Shaun. I cannot see colours in thoughts. I see every shade imaginable when composing music or playing it, but when it comes to the minds of other people, it's only black and white that I see. What advice would you give me to clear that vision?"

"If by that you mean that you can see the good in others that some belittle or malign, then I have no desire to advise you otherwise, but if you saying that there are shades of wrong that you are willing to accept, then that's an illusion that does need rectifying."

"Pontifical Catholicism as well. You are one full of surprises. Have you an answer to the wrongs of this life to go with your cynicism?"

"I could suggest a swim, Penni, alongside some deep contemplation of that question."

"Not dissimilar from the church then with your indecision! Could advise or would advise? Have you brought swimming trunks in that attaché case along with the business papers? Only I don't think it's big enough." She bit her bottom lip then sighed and stood, discarding the shawl.

"Are we alone?" I asked.

"Would it matter if we were not?" she replied, unhooking the top of her bikini and allowing it to fall to ground.

"I haven't got any trunks."

"I hoped you hadn't."

"Are you always this direct?" I asked awkwardly.

"Do you want me, Shaun, or just talk to me?" I needed no second invitation.

The memory of using Leeba's money in such a self-absorbed fashion the previous night haunted me, as the day brought the gift of extravagance in extremes of satisfaction. I felt both humiliation and fulfilment with her sensuality in equal measures. Fortunately my inexperience was not the defect I feared it may have been, but her supremacy surpassed my most frenzied thoughts of how sex would be. We showered then dried each other then showered again, until finally I mentioned the reasons that had brought me to her home. All the documents I carried were business related and quickly dealt with. When I finished reading them to her I added, "If you have no objections I'll be handling you in the future, Penni."

"Hmm," she replied, "I quite like that idea, but I'm picky with performances. I save the most pleasurable for the most elitist people I mix with. I hope you experienced that virtuoso rendering I just gave in colour, Shaun. If not then perhaps another rendition is called for?"

"Some of the colours were a little indistinct, Penni, but those that I saw clearly were of delightful shades."

"Then let us go see if we can discover the full spectrum of colour that exists only in a bedroom, and then you can advise me further on the business matters that so occupy that overworked mind of yours. But don't go jumping too far in front of yourself, Shaun. I know why Leeba sent you. Let's see how good you are at persuasion, shall we?"

Barkley was smoking a cigarette beside the car when I eventually returned some hours later.

"Did all go to your satisfaction, sir?" he asked obsequiously.

"Perfectly, Barkley! Better than I could have imagined. But now I feel the urge to find a square with a nightingale in full song."

"I'm sorry, sir, but I don't know of any of those," he replied.

"That's a pity, Barkley. I felt sure you'd know of one." I laughed loudly at my attempted joke, to which he added a confused smile.

Chapter Seventeen

Sally's

There was a letter pushed under the door at number 430 when I got back from Penina, and a message on the apartment's telephone. The call was from Richard Stockford. Karl Weilham was scheduled to chair a private meeting at the UN this coming Saturday, and Richard was attending. The question of a monopoly on the manufacture of an anti-typhoid drug was to be discussed in view of the forthcoming merger. His company and the West German one were the only two in the world to have developed and distributed Ampicillin, a recent replacement for Chloramphenicol when resistance to that drug had become widespread. He suggested I accompany him. The letter was from Jack. A curt, unceremonious one, not an invitation to a far off meeting. One that demanded immediate attendance.

Meet Horace for afternoon tea. Post Haste!

He was out of sight this time. Hidden in a high-backed alcove at the very end of Salvatore's where the shadows were at their darkest, but even those dark shadows could hide the flush in his cheeks.

"What are you doing, Shaun? Are you an idiot or something worse? You've been out to meet Penina without my authority. It just won't do! Not at all!" The ashtray in front of him was overflowing with used butts of cigarettes as he lit another, not offering me one.

"Leeba asked me to go, Jack, and I couldn't find a reason to say no. I thought you wanted me to know the family."

"Not shag them, Shaun! That's getting too close. Next you'll be falling in love and wanting a green card to stay and settle here raising kids on a ranch in Texas. Is it the cows or the stirrups and six-guns you're attracted to? If you're to stay in this job then you cannot get close to our '*cestui que trust*'." He beckoned a waiter who appeared carrying a bottle of Bells whisky. He already had a glass.

"What does that mean, Jack? Not good at French!" We were interrupted by the waiter.

"*Volete un altro bicchiere, signore*?"

Jack nodded his approval to the suggestion, waiting for the second glass before pouring from the bottle and then addressing me.

"It means beneficiary. Leeba has an altogether different agenda than we have. She's worried about her daughter's entanglement with members of a very nasty far-right organisation here in New York. We, on the hand, take a wider view. We aren't interested in the slightest with Leeba's concerns, Shaun. Please try to remember that no one is more important than each, and not put your," he paused and drew on his cigarette, "manliness in front of the mission again. At least not with her! Keep it in your trousers other than at the Tat & Tail. Do you understand me?"

"She's very attractive, and I didn't have to force myself upon her, you know. As I see it, knowing her and gaining her trust would be an ideal way to get inside Weilham's pocket as you so aptly suggested."

"Would it indeed! We have enough on Karl Weilham to strip him bare already. As for Penina, how would you feel if you had to put a gun to her pretty head? Would regrets force you to fatally hesitate from pulling that trigger? Some unfulfilled passion holding you back and wanting to turn the gun on yourself perhaps?"

"Why do you want her dead?" I asked on standing up, towering over him. "There must be a better solution than that, Jack!"

"Is there, Shaun? You know the full picture do you? Fancy a Nazi leader of the free world, or just fancy screwing the next one, eh? Sit down, drink your whisky and shut the hell up."

"How on earth is Penina to become President of America, Jack, that's just too far-fetched for even one of your stories." I remained standing in defiance.

"You have a lot to learn about life, Shaun. The first being to do what you're told to do!" he was dribbling through anger. I sat. "I just wish that on occasions you didn't show your ignorance quite so readily." Another cigarette and an offer for me to join him. "Weilham more or less runs the United Nations. He has that label of senior assistant but he's more than that. He does the day-to-day important stuff. His bosom pals: Haynes Baxter-Clifford and Marty Killick head up the Nazi party here in America. Both, incidentally, are fabulously rich. Then, lo and behold, abracadabra a magician waves his magic wand and along comes Hitler's beautiful daughter into the political mix. Can you count the dollars going into her presidential coffers? There would be every right-wing zealot and halfwit the world over contributing to her conquering accession."

"You're mad if you believe that's possible! Do those three know about her birth?"

"Am I mad? Did you not notice her eyes and colouring? She's his female offspring, Shaun, and has exactly the same magnetic appeal. And no to your second question; not yet." He held out his hands in a simulated prayer at the end of his declamation.

"But how can her heritage be discovered? Without that she's just another rich girl with an older infatuated man on her arm. Surely any Jewish tag attached to her would scare them away? As far as I know they're all catholic any way. They have been well hidden, I have to say, Jack. Congratulations on that one. Perhaps this Haynes is not looking beyond her sexual attraction and why would he. I certainly wouldn't."

"No, you haven't, Shaun, have you? None of this is secure in the sense that it needs to be. If Leeba is putting her hand into the waters and making the tiniest of ripples, then we must be careful. Very careful! Personally I'm amazed at just how well their secret has stood up. And there are others back home more amazed than me." He poured two large glasses from the bottle that stood between us.

"By others do you mean, Trenchard, Jack?"

"No, I do not mean Trenchard, Shaun. Get him completely out of your mind. Barrington Trenchard is a dinosaur of a policeman and no more than that. He was an operative of little or no importance. I mean," again a pause, this time to compose himself before saying something that he might regret, "It doesn't matter who I mean. Just be careful and keep looking over your shoulder. That flat of yours, did you tell Penina that you're living in one of her apartments?"

"As a matter of fact I didn't, Jack. Why, important not to, was it?"

"Yes, I think it was. How about her brother Richard, mention him, did you?"

"I did not, Jack. As far as Penina is concerned I work for her sister as a research analyst doubling up as a special advisor on business matters that involve her, nothing more."

"She did not offer anything about Weilham, Baxter-Clifford or Killick?"

"Not a word about any of them, but I was keeping her mind focused on something else for most of the time."

He sat back with yet another cigarette clenched between the fingers of his left hand looking into the smoke that circled the ceiling, but it wasn't my acerbic remark causing the distraction. The lines around his eyes and mouth looked deeper than I'd noticed before, as though they had appeared overnight without warning. *Perhaps I was wrong*, I thought, but then I noticed his hand shake as he flicked the ash into the fresh ashtray that the waiter brought over along with two coffees that I hadn't seen ordered. Little things become more noticeable as one gets used to mannerisms. The collar of his white shirt was smudged, as were his cuffs rolled back to his elbows. The skin on his forearms was wrinkled and scale-like in places with the back of his right hand having mauve patches running across it.

"Are you alright, Jack?" I asked, concerned.

"What? Yes, I'm fine, Shaun. I have to go and use the phone across the road. I'll be five minutes. Concentrate all you have on Karl Weilham whilst I'm gone. It's him we have to turn." As he rose from his seat he asked, "They were used notes that Leeba gave you, I take it?"

"Yes, they were. Nothing over a ten dollar bill."

"Oh, and by the way, what's the colour of the front door at that apartment where you live?" It was as though he didn't want to leave without making sure he'd covered everything. Very unlike his normal systematic self.

"It wasn't you who posted the note under it then?"

"No! One of Salvatore's lot."

"It's a dark brown colour, Jack. Why?"

"Get some matches and shoe polish then colour the matches the same shade as your door, or as near to it as you can get. Each time you leave the apartment wedge a coloured match or two into the doorjamb. Up high on the opposite side to the lock is best. No one thinks to look there. That way if they're moved when get home you'll know that you've had a visitor."

"You think there's a possibility of that happening?"

"I don't know, but it's all too close for comfort for me." Was he panicking, I wondered?

"You didn't know that the apartment Richard gave me was Penina's, Jack, did you?"

"I didn't know that the entire building was owned by Baxter-Clifford either, Shaun. Now that does rake at my skin a bit."

"Perhaps it's not only Leeba with their own agenda."

"Perhaps not! I'll go and make that phone call now. Be right back."

There was a slight stumble as he left the booth. If it wasn't from experience I might have thought he was drunk. I followed for a while then stood at the bar, after he had hurried out through the restaurant and then across the road. It was not like him to hurry. Salvatore was behind the bar watching too.

"Have you noticed a change in Jack recently?" I asked the restaurant owner.

"*Mi scusi. Non capisco*," he replied.

Yeah, I bet you don't understand, I silently thought.

Monday Morning In London

Chapter Eighteen

Group

"Fiona, get me the director at the *doughnut* on a red line then fetch a fresh brew and Giles Phillips from Archives, please. Tell Perkins to come as well with that young assistant of his. Clear my appointments for this afternoon. I'll be busy."

Geoffrey Perkins, a man in his early fifties and a reincarnated life-long *oil-burner* was the first to arrive, by which time Sir Archibald Thomas Finn was on the phone to his counterpart at the government's listening post, GCHQ.

"Yes, Joseph! Absolutely everything you can find in the last fifty years, or more if that's necessary. Use a microscope with the finest of lenses possible. We need this information urgently."

"How far did you get at the Palace, sir?" Perkins asked as Sir Archibald replaced the telephone receiver.

"Nowhere. They clammed up tighter than a lion's jaw around its prey, Geoffrey, but they know something about Sir Horace Butler, of that I'm sure. We will have to find it all ourselves, I'm afraid. How far has the training of that assistant of yours got to? Can he be assigned to a desk yet?"

Perkins had no time to volunteer his judgement on that matter as Giles Phillips was next through the door. Giles had been a private man for the twenty-two years since his early divorce from Ann, his wife of five months. He adored the sterility of old documents. He found pleasure in tracing long forgotten codes and names hidden in the barren isolation of his underground retreat without the thought of the revenging daggers that haunted Geoffrey's protégé.

Daniel Cardiff was the last to enter. The IRA were occupying most of Geoffrey's devotional *oil-burners* hence Daniel had been fast-tracked in the two months since signing on straight from Cambridge. He had very little training in covert operations, but oodles of enthusiasm to learn, a dangerous combination that could lead to one of two things: soaring success or agonising failure. There was no middle ground on which to find cover.

"Gentlemen, we must find everything connected to a ghost, Sir Horace Butler is a mystery that demands our meticulous attention." Sir Archibald declared.

* * *

At the end of Craig Court, a cul-de-sac leading off Whitehall at its Trafalgar Square end, was where the offices of the National Strategic Liaison Group could be found, but not by any accidental tourist, that is. It was inside the inner concrete and lead-lined shell of a shabby red-brick building that at the beginning of the First World War years the oil lamps were burned late into the night and early morning analysing threats to the British Empire from its enemies. Other than the identity of those enemies little had changed in the fifty-eight years that had passed since then. Those that plunged their hands into hazy secrets had kept their oil burning until this day. The reasons for keeping secrets seldom change, it's the custodians that do.

There was no sign affixed anywhere on this nondescript edifice to proclaim its importance, nor was there an actual front door, as entry was strictly controlled via the maze of tunnels that connected the building to its more illustrious neighbours nearby: The Admiralty, The

Foreign and Commonwealth Office and Number 10, to name a few. Those who worked here provided the knowledge that ultimately found its way to the desk of Sir Archibald T. Finn before he informed the Joint Intelligence Committee of the Secret Intelligence Service and then the department heads of MI5 and MI6. The NSLG, or just plain *Group* as it was known throughout those who knew of its existence, had no classification within the intelligence community. It was answerable only to the Minister of Defence, or so it was thought.

Daniel Cardiff's first assimilation into the actual covert workings of the NSLG was undertaken by Geoffrey Perkins early that morning in his office on the top floor; it didn't stay in that room for long.

"My late uncle had a butler named Horace, sir. Not sure if he's still alive though. The butler that is, not my uncle." Daniel announced, slightly embarrassed. "Uncle Maurice died earlier this year. I think it was in March."

"Really, and who exactly was your Uncle Maurice when alive, Cardiff?" Geoffrey asked.

"Admiral Sir Maurice Curtis, sir, one of my mother's many brothers. He was the personal private secretary to His Royal Highness Prince Philip until he died. Not Prince Philip, but my uncle! Huge funeral. Most of the Royal Household came, sir. I remember his butler, Horace, but only vaguely, sir."

One hour later Sir Archibald took a government car from the front door of the Ministry of Fisheries and Agriculture to the tall building on the other side of Westminster Bridge. The one that every Tom, Dick and Harry in London knew as the headquarters of MI6. He took the express lift to the top floor, then swallowed hard.

"We think Price was in Vienna twice in his service career. The first time was in '45, then again when he was sent *overseas* in 1948, but the file was closed and sealed with no mention of where he went or to whom he reported. We are now assuming he went back there. To all intents and purposes that's when he died on us. What we are now trying to find out is how he and young Craig's uncle became acquainted. I've managed to find that Sir Maurice Curtis and the Duke of Edinburgh had met at the Royal Naval College, Dartmouth as far back as 1939, but how on earth our Jack Price got invited into that circle, I've no idea."

"He was briefly one of ours, this Jack Price, Archie, after being a resident spotter at 5 for many years. All I can find out so far is that we dispensed with his services in the late forties sending him back to 5. I've checked their assembly roll. No one there is holding his hand. Who did you speak to at the Palace?"

"The present private personal secretary to Prince Philip."

"Did you mention Price to them?"

"I did, yes. They denied knowledge of him quicker than St Peter denied Christ, and they were almost as convincing."

"He's *on the firm*, that's what he is. He's one of theirs, Archie. Were any of Philip's Nazi-leaning sisters or brothers-in-laws in Austria around about that time?"

"I wouldn't think it was impossible. The Mountbattens have Royal connections everywhere, don't they."

"Got any idea where Price is now?"

"Not the foggiest, but we're looking, Dicky. Believe me we'll find him," Sir Archibald announced confidently.

"I expect you're choked to the full on Irish matters, Archie. General Ford's 1st Para not withstanding! You must be running out of room for other enquiries. This all sounds a bit inessential to the points at issue for the time being. I'll have words with the Home Office and have your enquiries shifted from the Ministry Of Defence onto my desk. We can't have Royalty rumoured to be mixed up in anything untoward at present. Very bad timing all round for that to happen. Got any idea as to who fired first over in Derry that the press are get their knickers in a twist over?"

"We're backing the official line, Dicky. Our boys simply returned fire."

Dicky Blythe-Smith gazed down across the rooftops towards the spires of Westminster and wondered how much truth was in that statement.

"Tell me more of this Jack Price, Archie. Rum old bird as I seem to recollect. Saw his file once, but can't recall precisely why that should have been."

Dicky held back the truth when saying that. There was no reason that he could see to be more open at this stage either here with his old friend, or, when eventually he had to present his department's case for handling this 'inessential' matter and not where it should have been handled; the internal service back across the river.

"I met him a couple of times when I was in Ireland," Sir Archibald was speaking. "But then he turned into a bit of a maverick. Runs operations using unregistered personnel, ex-military and the like. That's part of the reason that we became involved at *Group*. His name first popped up on our screens four years ago in of all places South Vietnam. We never wiped it off.

The Tet offensive was underway with the Americans starting to lose troops, hardware and positions left right and centre. I was summoned to a meeting at St James's Palace. Prince Philip's then PPS presided with me and the Foreign Minister in attendance. I was told that GB had two very important observers in Vietnam that needed urgent extraction, but no accountable units from this country could be used. A private agency was to be employed in the task. One endorsed by Prince Philip. We, at *Group*, and General John at *5*, who were to supply the necessary equipment, but were to stay away and make absolutely no mention of it in any Cabinet or Privy Council meeting if we were so summoned. I'm sorry to say that my curiosity got the better of me, Dicky, as I'm sure yours would have. I followed the contraband and requisition forms, turning up Price and a retired Marine known only as Job. In time there were five who flew out from here, touching down at a US airbase outside of Saigon. Price stayed put on station, but Job and his team ventured north and successfully brought the two VIPs out."

"I take it that it was the present PPS and not the one that your young recruit mentioned, Archie?"

"It was, yes."

"And the VIPs? Names of note, old bean?"

"Not ones we had flagged at that time, Dicky, no. One was a rear Admiral who worked for an armaments manufacturer, the other was the owner of Courcy's Intelligence Service; a Kenneth de Courcy. Set up, so the prospectus said, to provide early warning intelligence to businesses and governments."

"Interesting stuff, Archie. Know much about what happened to those two once back here on terra firma?"

"I do. The rear admiral left the company he represented and is now skipper of the Royal Yacht Britannia, but the other, Kenneth de Courcy, is still on all joint security screens. He was listed because of his comments to overthrow Wilson and his socialist government a few years ago. He hasn't stopped in that resolve apparently, just has it on hold whilst Wilson's out of office leading the opposition."

"What brought Jack Price's name to reappear on your screens recently, Archie. What's he been up to that's disturbed your sleep?"

Some people are incapable of listening to what they're told. Others only hear the parts they want to, preferring snippets to the whole, in order to grasp hold of single words or phrase helping to build their own complementary tales, or ones of a contrary nature, around them. Dicky did not fit into either type. He was one of the unusual breed who not only listened intently with the sole purpose of absorbing the orator's entire words but to hear what was not said, either through ignorance or with intent to deceive. He had an astute and quick mind, careful in assessment and razor-sharp in analysis. He would not have been *C* at the international branch of the Military Intelligence Services if he was not so equipped.

As well as a brute of a man in build, he was the same in temper. Throughout their military careers he had outranked his contemporary at the internal security branch, General John Mark Hampton, but since the more colourful arm of the intelligence services had made demands of his talents he had deemed himself as secondary in the hierarchy to his rival's offices. If he had a weakness that's where it lay; a resentment of General John, as his counterpart of *C* at *5*. Caused by a nagging wife who wanted him to have closer ties at home, particularly with the Home Office for the parties they threw and honours they bestowed.

As Sir Archibald's car drove away from the underground carpark, Dicky first phoned the unit head of his own section four.

"I want all you can get on a young Cambridge graduate name of Daniel Cardiff. He's presently working undercover for *Group* as a Grade Two at the Ministry of Agriculture and Fisheries. I want his full family history with emphasis on an Admiral Sir Maurice Curtis, late of the St James's Palace *on the firm* variety. I also want the name of his recruiting agent and any back mention to departments within the Joint Intelligence Committee. I need you to run a trace on someone for me. I'll send you the details in code by in-house messaging. Be a love and mark it urgent and deal with it yourself, Catherine, there's a dear. Oh, and by the way, no phone calls to Curzon Street on this one. No point in disturbing them whilst they are settling into their new abode."

He then poured a large brandy and made dinner reservations for eight o'clock that night. "Yes, for two,' he told the maître d' at Claridge's Hotel. "It's our wedding anniversary, but I don't want any fuss, you understand, just a quiet, peaceful meal, Marco."

Next he buzzed his section head at Pipeline and Acquisitions, Fraser Ughert, five floors below, only two above the ground floor.

"I need a spare native from the Fatherland, who's treading our green and pleasant pastures as we speak, Fraser. Young, responsive, good-looking and not averse to military uniforms and horse whips if the need arises. The more German she is the better. Need to make a present of her to a rather well placed individual who will not be easy prey.

Make it a priority, old chap, and just between the two of us. How's the wife by the way?" He heard Fraser's reply but didn't dwell on it. There were others to call before he could indulge in banal responses.

I ran into you once, Jack Price, a long, long time ago and from what I saw on that day and heard later you're a shifty bloody pain in the arse carrying a bag full of envy on your back. Still there is it, Jack? he silently asked as he finished his phone calls and the last sip of his second swirling brandy.

"Have my car readied, Louise. I'm off to my club for the rest of the day. Would you be so kind as to call Barrington Trenchard. You'll have to call Scotland Yard for his telephone number. Have him meet me there for a late lunch, please. Tell him to bring his memory and any notebook he has on Harrow School with him. Oh, and if he declines the offer, tell him it's an order, please."

* * *

Dicky had been seated in the royal blue, ornately decorated and plush members' dining room at the Travellers Club for no more than ten minutes when Trenchard arrived. During which time he had brooded over the previous evening's conversation he'd had with Sheila his wife. She was trolling on about her favourite subject; Dicky's reluctance to move sideways.

Marjorie and John are off to their retreat in Cornwall again this coming week. According to her he has so much spare time nowadays that he's joined the local chrysanthemum society down there. He's able to delegate most of his work. She said they're considering buying another house in Buckinghamshire as John is spending more time away from his London office than ever. It's all well and good being knighted, Richard, but it's a peerage you need and you'll only get that if you're nearer home, constantly in people's minds. I'm damned if I know any retired Chief of MI6 in the House of Lords. Normally they are put out to pasture and kept quiet forever and a day. Can't you request a transfer across to the side of the river that counts, Richard?

He had reluctantly applied once before, but the parcel containing the keys to the department one numeral below his own had been on the person's lap before his when the music stopped playing. *C* of '6' or *Chief*, or, if one wanted to be pedantic about it; *Captain*, as the first head of the then combined departments was a naval captain, held more celebrity status than General John's office dealing with home affairs, but that held no sway with Sheila. What was brewing in the Irish suburbs of Liverpool or Manchester might not compare with Paris or, even Port-au-Prince at a push, but according to Sheila he needed less excitement and she needed more of the prestige that could be measured by the company one kept. He was in no mood for unnecessary prolonged exchanges.

"Know much about an aircraft crash in 1942 carrying the Duke of Kent, Barrington old chap?" Picking up on where Sir Archibald had left off, but avoiding the real point of his invitation, he opened the game.

"I know more than what's in the file, Dicky, if that's what you mean. And there was I thinking you wanted a chat for old times' sake," he replied.

"Oh, I do, old man, I do. That's precisely what I want to chat about. Thought here would be the ideal place. They serve a really stupendous apple crumble on Mondays. It's one of the reasons I renew my annual membership. If the pastry chef ever moves then I swear I will too!"

Midday Tuesday In New York

Chapter Nineteen

Adam Berman

There was a lot of what Jack had told me that just didn't fit. Why, for example, was there the need for the Sir Horace Butler façade, plus where was the incentive for Richard Stockford's compliance and continued association with Price? If Jack was hiding the fact that Hitler was Penina's father from the family, why would Richard be helping Jack with information on Weilham at the same time as Leeba was pointing me along a different path overhanging with Nazi sympathisers? If Richard and Leeba didn't know the secret behind Penina's birth then why were they helping to keep it? Where was the benefit in blackmailing the Stockfords? I wanted to access a computer away from Leeba's offices, so I used the rear entrance of the Immigration Centre opposite to avoid being seen.

There were several entries under the name of Sternberg as it was not an uncommon surname, but I checked by year and country of origin, soon finding one in 1936 detailing seven immigrants of that name listing film production as their occupation. I looked at 1937, but found no more. However, a Mayanna Stockford with two children, Richard and Leeba arrived on the twenty-sixth of November 1937 from Vienna, Austria. Everything was too easy and convenient for my liking. On a whim I next looked up the name of Aberman.

It was a large, old, Hewlett Packard cumbersome computer, slow with a keyboard widely spaced, worn and sticky from overuse. As I typed the 'A' it separated from the next letter and threw up—A. Berman, I clicked on the name and explored further. Adam Berman came to America via Belgrade eleven years later than Richard and Leeba, but in the same year that Jack Price was last registered as an MI6 operative; 1948. There was another oddity that I hadn't seen on any other page I'd come across before, a cross reference to something called the Central Agency for Jewish Emigration and a redirection to The Government Accountability Office. I made notes and returned to my office across the road. As it was lunchtime I believed the office to be empty, so I used the more modern machine that was installed in my office to probe into those two departments.

On the emigration site I found a description for Mr A. Berman, but no photograph as was the case with other entries on that and subsequent pages. Just height, weight, build and a far from detailed account of his facial features. There was a date of birth; 14 April 1893, but it had not been authenticated. On the Government Accountability page there was less information. Date of entry; 29 March 1948 and then, in the end margin; US citizenship granted 3 April 1948, repatriated to The State of Israel 14 May 1948. Underneath that entry it was heavily encrypted with the seal of the FBI and the words: Further Access Denied!

"Did you find my sister to be pleasant company, Shaun?" Leeba was standing behind me looking over my shoulder and I hadn't heard her come in. "Was she alone?" she added.

"Apart from a creepy old man dressed all in black who showed me through to where she was then yes, Leeba." I closed the opened computer page before she had a chance to see exactly what I was researching.

"He was old Baxter-Clifford's man. I was never able to discover much about him. Penni told me his name was Dieter Chase but I never looked at that site you're on. Maybe you'll have better luck. Who is it you're looking for?"

"One of Weilham's staff, but I'm getting nowhere. Richard has a meeting at an outside office of the UN on Saturday and I wanted a bit of background on who Karl predominately works with." I lied at first but then told the truth.

"I'm pleased we've all now shortened Penina's name to Penni. Although not as beautiful, it's certainly easier on the tongue to pronounce." Leeba was sitting on the edge of my desk. Her thighs had my full attention.

"Penina was our mother's middle name. Penni told me that she had allowed you to use the abbreviated version. Personally I prefer her given name, but it's her choice of course. Talking of adopted names, try Dieter Chase in your search," she suggested.

When she left, I did that and found an entry dated October 1945 of his admittance into America from, of all places, Vienna. I was beginning to wonder if all of this country was inhabited by Austrians. His age then was given as thirty-one and religion Catholic. The description fitted him exactly: black hair, black eyes, five foot nine inches tall, slight build with a curved scar on his forehead. I entered Leeba's office and told her of my discovery.

"Earlier I found a Jewish emigration site registered in Vienna, but originating from Tel Aviv. It listed all those who fled Austria at the end of the war. If you had a photo of Dieter, I could fax it to them and we could check if it is his real name or not, Leeba."

"I'm sure Penni said she had one, with both Haynes and Earl together when they were all much younger. Why don't you ask her yourself? Penni seldom does what I ask her to do, but from you it might be different."

"By that I take it that you think I'll be seeing her again."

"I would think so, Shaun. She was very, how can I say, pleased to have made your acquaintance. I wasn't indelicate, asking for the details of why that might have been, but I'm allowed to guess." She smiled, but I'm not sure if it was a sincere smile or one meant to castigate me slightly.

Midday Monday In London

The Travellers Club on London's Waterloo Place was always busy on Monday's. A favourite haunt of those who sought adventure or a comfortable seat to watch others exchange warm greetings and honest recounts of past achievements. Dicky Blythe-Smith listened patiently to Barrington Trenchard in anticipation of his main meal.

"The official line was that Prince George, Duke of Kent, with fourteen of his staff members, had left from the Mountbatten's estate at Mullaghmore in Ireland en route to Sweden with suitcases stuffed full of one hundred Krona notes to bolster Swedish resolve to stay neutral in the war against the Nazis who were occupying their neighbours of Norway and Denmark. During the flight over the Highlands of Scotland the pilot lost his way due to bad weather and crashed into a mountain. No one survived that crash. The crash site was sealed off as soon as was humanly possible with members of what then was called the Internal Security Department taking over the scene. Apart from the initial headlines in the press nothing was allowed to be further printed. The full notes of the inquiry are not scheduled to be released into the public domain until 2038 and I doubt the whole truth will ever see the light of day."

"But you know the real reason for that flight, Barrington, because at the time you were sitting at a desk of a Privy Counsellor acting as his secretary, were you not?"

"I was, yes, and you know his name, no doubt?"

"I do! Shall we address the reason now?"

"But I never found out from him."

"Immaterial at this stage, old chap. Can you address the subject, please?"

"The real reason for the flight was to secure a base for the Duke of Windsor, the abdicated King Edward VIII, to use under the auspices of King Gustav V of Sweden. It was the intentions of the Windsors to wait for Hitler's victory in Europe then to return to this country, setting up court here with Oswald Mosley as the prime minister and followers of the Mountbatten clan forming the government alongside our German conquerors. As Sweden was populated by more German sympathisers than Allied ones the plan had some merit, attracting financial support from Hitler himself.

The wartime coalition government heard about it in a very strange but fortuitous way. Most of Mountbatten's money was inherited from his wife's grandfather, Sir Ernest Joseph Cassel, a friend and private financier to the previous king, George V. Cassel was one of the richest, most powerful men in Europe. He had converted from Judaism to Catholicism in order to marry, but lost his wife early into that marriage. Later he lost his only child. His entire wealth was left to his granddaughter, Edwina who, by the time she married Louis Mountbatten was a millionaire in her own right, owning large estates in England and Ireland. The marriage ceremony in 1922 attracted all our own royalty and many from Europe. Edwina's father, William Ashley, 1st Baron Mount Temple, was a German appeaser, admiring Hitler for his anti-communism. He was the founding member of the Anglo-German Fellowship, visiting Hitler several times; however, he baulked at the anti-Semitism and broke off ties to that ideological side of fanaticism. After his first wife died he remarried and had a son. I went to the same school as that son, Dicky. It was he who told me of the plot. I immediately, of course, reported it." Trenchard sat back in his chair awaiting Dicky's applause, but none came his way.

"Go on," Dicky ordered.

"I reported the matter to Meredith Paine, then head of your section at Military Intelligence, who along with the Secretary for War, Oliver Stanley, and Churchill agreed that the plane had to be shot down. Now I don't know that as a cast iron fact, of course, as someone as lowly as I was never in the loop, but two and two was four when I learned arithmetic and I doubt that's changed."

"So, in essence you have nothing but a conspiracy theory, albeit one that sounds intriguing, Barrington. Nothing substantial with written evidence and all the interested parties privy to your friend's allegations being now buried in the ground. I very much doubt the old telephone service between here and Helsinki could have been sufficiently adequate to arrange such a convoluted plan as this. Do you think that perhaps Hitler used a direct private telephone line to organise it all?" Dicky asked sarcastically.

"I was told that most had been planned at meetings between the Duke of Windsor and Hitler in Vienna shortly before the outbreak of war. The Duke of Kent was known to have visited Stockholm around the same time as Hitler walked into Austria, with cohorts of both the royals travelling widely throughout Europe and America before and during the war years. But there was something else that my ex-school chum told me. Your written evidence was on the plane. A sealed letter of the agreed proposals was carried by Prince George. It was signed by his brother and countersigned by Adolf Hitler. Not a letter that anyone would want printed in any newspaper, Dicky. Not that suitable, one would have thought?"

"Would such a lowly office-wallah as yourself have been included in the circle of knowledge as to the whereabouts of this piece of evidence after the event?"

"Surprisingly enough, no, Dicky. Never filtered down the lavatory as far as me."

"I've noticed over the years that all manner of things get stuck in the U-bend and in my experience all best left unspoken of. The reason that most people never bother to delve too closely into our sewers is that we give them other things to care about, Barrington. Like the cost of these new-fangled washing-machines, their new car and who's posing half naked on page three of The Sun newspaper. Only wish I was involved in their selection policy on that one." There was the faintest of grins across Dicky's face before he continued.

"We trade on the tacit understanding that love of one's country without the knowledge of what the figureheads of this country get up to in their spare time is the fundamental nature of what we refer to as democracy. That's what guided the populace to war on behalf of our erstwhile leaders. Shit floats if it's stirred around too often. A lesson seldom taught at the refined schools of this sceptred isle, but learned quickly by those of Jack's ilk who were confined inside the less perfumed." Dicky leaned forward across the table, speaking in a quieter tone.

"Correct me if I'm wrong, Barrington, but you only have a year before you reach retirement age, is that right?" Trenchard nodded his acceptance at that estimation.

"Then I expect you're looking forward to the full ministry pension. I'm told that a dependable, index-linked income makes such a difference in the latter stages of life. Somewhere in my memory I believe that you and Jack Price had a falling out that almost cost old Jack his pension. I think, and do correct me if I'm wrong, it was sometime in the 1940s at an outstation of *5's* at Harrow. Are you ready to order the crumble and have a nibble on Jack Price, Commander Trenchard?"

Late Tuesday Afternoon in New York

Chapter Twenty

Parked Cars

I had not thought of Fianna since first meeting Leeba and then, perhaps more significantly, her daughter Penni. I think the girl at the Tat & Tail had acted like the buffers at a train station, stopping my thoughts of her as I had walked along the platform in a trance. The easy availability of Jack's *friend* had concentrated my mind on only the one thing, whereas Leeba had opened it far wider with her sexually attractive maturity and then Penina with her pure exciting intellect coupled with a kind of liberal sensuality I had never thought existed outside of dreams. It was Penni who now stood framed in my office doorway.

Some men that I'd met found most of their gratification in the female form when only naked. I had seen Penni that way and could perfectly understand that view, but for me the woman who is immaculately dressed, whether provocatively in the accepted sense, or in a style that accentuates her femininity, holds an equal appeal, and if coupled with intellect then more so. My philosophy relied on there being as much delight in the chase as in the capture, but overall it was how one acted with the prize that mattered. As I sat and looked at her I honestly considered her to be a prize well worth the chase. However, had I known the full complexity surrounding the Stockford family I would have caught the next plane to central Africa and hidden in a cave.

"You look divine, Penni," was my dumbstruck opening line.

"I'm in a blue and orange cloud, Shaun, hence the colours of this outfit. I need music and a recording contract. I want to go through the EMI one with you. I think it will need a deliciously thorough seeing to!" I was trembling in anticipation, but held myself in check.

"And I need a photograph, if you would be so kind as to provide one."

"Of me?" she asked.

"I have your elegance embedded permanently into my mind. I have no need of a photo to remind me of your beauty but I'll keep one close to my heart if you have one. No, it's that man at your house who introduced me to you. Leeba said that you might have one of him? I have a friend back in Ireland who had a German grandfather he lost touch with in the war years. The way he described him to me matched your man to a tee."

"Not my man nor my home, Shaun. Both belong to Haynes, as I'm sure either my sister or my brother would have mentioned. I believe the man you refer to was born in Serbia. You're wrong on two counts! It's not me that has that photo but Leeba. If she's lost it then why don't you just ask him for one yourself?" I wondered why Leeba would make that up.

"Maybe he'll think I have a fetish for older men like you do, Penni," I replied, trying to defuse the situation.

"I don't think he'd be confused, but I am. I reckon it's older women that you fancy, Shaun," she replied, tantalisingly biting that lower lip of hers, before adding, "and not just me. I have a new apartment overlooking the Hudson River that I haven't seen yet. My car's parked outside. Want a ride and see the reflected colours from my new bedroom whilst we investigate EMI?"

"Have you parked Haynes up somewhere as well? On hold, is he, whilst I'm around?"

"I have no problem sharing you with my sister, if that's what you want, so why be judgemental of me. I'm too creative to be fenced in by any one man. I'm surprised that you would expect that when you clearly would not practise it yourself. You need to exercise that lust of yours for my sister, Shaun, and then decide if only one of us would satisfy you sufficiently. You cannot ban the liberty you wish for yourself from others who wish the same."

"I wasn't suggesting that you stop seeing Haynes, Penni. I was just wondering where I stood," I replied.

"The world is built on self-doubt, Shaun, it's how we are controlled by the state. Imagine the independence one could enjoy without fear of the uncertainty. Take it one step further in your imagination and visualise your own future built with no regard to the consequence to others. Wouldn't that be something?"

"Hasn't that already been dreamt of by the Stalin's and Hitler's of this world , and look what became of them!"

"Neither of them were women, Shaun."

"Do you want to rule the world, Penni?"

"I want the power to rule my world, yes. After I've achieved that, then who knows where I'll end up."

"Haynes is a powerful man, I'm given to understand. Do you think he will provide you with that power?"

"He is, and those who advised you of that are not incorrect. But we all have an inner power. I won't be waiting for him to decree any of his power in my direction. Mine comes from the belief in superiority. I like to think of this world being akin to a colony of ants with rulers and workers. The queen is the dominant creature. It's she who makes the rules. She is serviced by the males, fed by the unproductive females and controls the whole of the kingdom. I would make a few changes to that system. Obviously I won't be giving birth as many times as she does, nor would only infertile females do the work, that would the prime role of those men not privileged by me. I have some work to do on that, but it's coming along. Your present power and influence comes from your previous ability to satisfy me; sexually. Was that to be a one-only-night performance, or are there to be many encores in answer to my cries of bravo? The invitation is still unopened lying on the car seat, Shaun," she stated as she stood.

"I can only hope that the repeats are as good as the original," I replied hopelessly, joining her and taking a ride.

Late Monday Afternoon in London

"Before we begin with Jack, Barrington, fill me in on what seems to be a temporary loss of memory on my part." Dicky began the dissection of the crumble of his apple dessert with the embodiment of any myth surrounding Jack Price.

"Why were our abdicating king and the Führer so close on ideas around that time in history? Where was their common ground precisely?"

Barrington, on the other hand, although also staring on his dessert, had Price on his mind and was finding both hard to swallow.

"Difficult if not impossible to be specific in that matter, Dicky, as most of where they overlapped were simply ideals and philosophy. There was a lot of empathy over here for how Germany had been treated at the end of World War One, stripped naked and hung out to dry, as it were. Then up springs this corporal full of rhetoric about restoring pride to a nation once so close to us and doing away with the Bolsheviks. Our royalty were of German descent, remember. King George V was of the Saxe-Coburg and Gotha house and related to the Schleswig-Holstein dynasty. The whole of European Royalty were inter-married at some point. The revolution in Russia, culminating as it did in the murder of the Russian Czar and his family, sent our lot into convulsions. The ease and the severity of his punishment had fatally disturbed their ambivalence towards the working man. Hitler truly believed that we were not his enemy, having no appetite for a war so soon after the first one that destroyed most of Europe's young men. His foes lay to his east and north with the Communists. The seeds from the Russian 1917 Revolution were still falling on fallow ground, if you can recall. Apart from a few radicals and trade unionists, practically the whole of this country agreed with Hitler's anti-Communist stance and wanted peace on any terms.

We, remember, were financially devastated after that first war both in armed service personnel and money. There was recognition of a Jewish problem with us attempting to set up the Protectorate in Palestine for a future home for the Jews, but his anti-Semitism hadn't fully evolved into what it later became. Quite frankly the liberal intelligentsia wanted to turn a blind eye in that direction and to the possibility of another bloody war. There was another voice in the ring at the time, faint, but nevertheless significant. That of Philip Mountbatten, Duke of Edinburgh and future husband to Queen Elizabeth. Philip's family are more royal than the Windsors, Dicky. Our Queen Mother, bless her heart, although an aristocrat is not of Royal lineage. It was Edward VIII, as David, the Duke of Windsor, now he'd abdicated, who finally persuade Neville Chamberlain to visit Hitler at his Bavarian home and smoke a peace pipe. Dear old Neville came back singing Hitler's praises all the way from Heston airport to the rafters in the House of Commons, telling stories of Adolf's wall painting depicting English private Tommy Taddey's heroics in saving German lives at the Mennin Crossroads in 1918!

Where would I be now if the English Tommy had shot me instead of saving my life? Hitler asked our Prime Minister.

He wants no war with us. Chamberlain went on. *He only wants the Rhineland and Czechoslovakia and to stay friends!*

"Where indeed would we all be?" Dicky interjected. "Did he get shoved up against a wall and shot for negligence, this Private Taddey fellow, Barrington?"

"Hardly. He was the most decorated First World War soldier we had. VC, MC, DSO and more, so I heard."

"Interesting, but I wager it wasn't true. Just another rumour that got enlarged upon as it travelled down the line. Incidentally, was it down to those spurious rumours linking you and Stewart Campbell, that led to Meredith Paine letting go of your hand and shunting you off to Special Branch, or was it your choice to move on? Only, it was thought you could have made my chair one day. It was at the Savoy, wasn't it, that you and he were said to be found in a compromising situation. Allegedly of course. Personally speaking I'd heard them before I ran into Sir Archibald Finn from *Group* earlier today. It was he who reminded me of Jack Price, old sport. Hence the invitation! But back to business, just because two fellows are naked in a hotel room doesn't mean they were at it, in my book. Strange country ours, don't you think? Always ready to believe the worse without question. One man's life is ruined by supposition and another's honoured with medals for saving the enemy. How's that crumble of yours? Mine seems a mite short of apple so far. Is there a shortage in the market that you're aware of?"

Trenchard's nerves were at breaking point. His sanity was hanging by the same single hair that held Dionysius's fate. Dicky's puerile remarks and his earlier implied threat were beginning to rattle and madden him.

"Perhaps Price has bought them all and is at this moment handing them out around to the poor in South London. He's probably holding a banner proclaiming that's it's due to your charitableness, Dicky! What is it that you want from me exactly, as I was busy before you summoned?" His question was ignored.

"By the by, didn't you spend some time in Ireland in the sixties, having dealings with Sir Archibald over there? You were heading up a special police unit as I understand whilst he was running the intelligence show. Had contact with any natives, did you? But no, I haven't really any time for that line to progress further at the moment. Save it for another meal. What I want now is to know whose idea it was to shoot an Irish terrorist and then kidnap the young detective who shot him. Because even someone as dumb as you would not have done that without his arm being twisted. Has someone got him locked up in some Scottish Castle and demanding a ransom, Barrington? Because if so I want him back!"

"How did you come to hear of West, Dicky?" Trenchard asked incredulously, almost having a heart attack.

"We have a seat at the Irish table. There's nothing happening over there that doesn't pass across my desk at some time. The boys with letters after their names have a phrase for it: *Swings and Slides*, or SAS as they prefer. It means that none of us are on the same apparatus in the playground at the same time. Ireland being the playground. A bit confusing actually. Whenever I see it I think it's our Special Air Service they're referring to."

If Commander Trenchard, one time warrior of Her Majesty's secret intelligence service and now the head of police undercover counter-intelligence had a retreat strategy it was left shattered by an innocent conversation between two former associates that he wished he'd never known.

In New York

I learned little regarding Haynes Baxter-Clifford whilst lying with Penni and neither did I see many boats on the Hudson River whilst on her virginal bed, but there were lots of other things I learned that aroused my interest. One of them being that Leeba had dated Haynes before he and Penni had met. But the most thought-provoking came about during a conversation in the most innocent of ways.

We were discussing her recording studio, with Penni in full flow describing the nuances between different sounds, echoes, tones and pitches that can be achieved by expert use of subtle variations and mix. It was variations that were on her mind.

"Do you think that my brother and sister are different to me, Shaun? By that I mean facially and with their colouring." That was a bombshell I hadn't expected.

"I haven't given it much thought to be honest, Penni. Do you think you're different to them?"

"Actually I do. I have done throughout my conscious life. Both Richard and Leeba have brown eyes, whereas mine are blue. They have similar coloured brown hair but mine is blonde and I'm taller than either of them. I reckon our mother had an affair and I'm the product of it."

"If that's the case then I have nothing but admiration for your mother's choice of lover. He must have been an even better looking man than your sister's father." I laughingly replied, feeling relieved.

On leaving her apartment I took a cab and returned to my office intent on finding more on Haynes than the little she had provided. If it was possible to discover closer dealings of any nature between him and Weilham then Saturday might prove more beneficial for Jack and ultimately me. Any deficiency I was suffering from in my sexual education prior to arriving in America was fast becoming the basis of an interesting study, but although it was intensely pleasurable it was not helping in the primary reason for me being here. I did want to follow Jack's instructions, but there were complications that he had either failed to see or disregarded. I wasn't completely sure as to which at this stage.

Leeba had left the office fifteen minutes or so before Penni had arrived, and as the outside door was locked and the reception area empty I assumed that the whole building was the same, but I was wrong. I set about searching through the files of local records on building contracts along with the recorded charities that the Baxter-Clifford company donated money to when Leeba entered the room from the interconnecting door with two empty glasses, along with an ice bucket and an unopened bottle of whisky. Her hair was tied back tightly to her head and the top three buttons of her blouse were undone.

"Do you want the Scotch with or without ice, Shaun, and how would you like me?"

"I'll take ice with the Scotch, but you as straight or whichever way you want. I think ice would be too cold for what you have in mind," I replied as I rose from my chair and locked the outside office door.

"There's no need for that, everyone's gone home. We have the place to ourselves. You've been indulging yourself with my sister for too long, now it's my turn."

She was an intense, passionate lover, quieter and more serene than Penni, but not at first. That had been a noisy explosion of excited ecstasy on the small two-seater sofa where she had pounded at me until breaking open a tiny crack and allowing, in her words, a *dam to burst.* Having experienced that sensation she then took her time. What she may have lacked in finesse compared to Penni she more than made up for in energy.

"I want to wake up beside you in your bed, Shaun. This can't end here like some tawdry one-nighter that Penni would indulge herself in. I want more than that. Much more!"

After my earlier exertions with her daughter, and now her, I was tiring and eagerly accepted her suggestion about the bed, hoping the walk to Baxter Street might exhaust some of her vigour. It didn't.

As I opened my apartment door I checked that the coloured matchstick was still in the doorjamb where I'd left it, but I had no need to fear an intruder, it was my invited guest that I should have been afraid of.

The Travellers Club London

Chapter Twenty-One

Times

Sir Richard Blythe-Smith had one eye on the club's dining room clock and the other one fixed firmly on his quarry; Barrington Trenchard. He deduced that neither were making his life any the easier.

"I would have thought that a security van raid in the West End was low grade material for you to spend much time on, Dicky. How did you hear of that?" Barrington asked, noticing Dicky's glance at the clock and hoping that his tormentor would soon run out of time and give up the chase.

"I got the details from Archie. We did not meet to discuss old acquaintances and rumours of a homosexual liaison you may or may not have played a role in. The man your DC West shot was on General John's books. He told Archie who in turn got fairly perturbed by it all, even more so when he smelled Jack in the mix. Seems that Henry Acre was providing worthy intelligence on some American sympathisers who are funding various activities of the Republican army, including an arm shipment from Libya that was recently seized. General John's department were running him. They knew of the security van heist and approved it. Drew the line short of any killing, but violence was permitted. That way it supplied additional weight to Acre's curriculum vitae. John's plan was to slam Acre into Parkhurst prison on the Isle of Wight alongside the other Irish terrorists banged up in there, sit back and reap the benefits. But then fate played a hand, up steps your boy and blasts him to kingdom come. General John was none too pleased, old chap. Started to call Archie unjust names and you some you deserved, hence the mud-slinging about the Savoy. That's my toe-in into this story, what's yours?"

"If you and Archie are thinking that Jack Price was behind it all then both of you are idiots, or perhaps I should use your word, Dicky; dumb! Do you have to sign for this meal at the table or can you do it on the way out, as I have work to do and people to see."

"As do I, old bean. As do I. But first tell me exactly how your department got entangled in this web? Cross the T's and dot the I's if you'd be so kind. We wouldn't want to be having to do this again in some less comfortable place, now would we? The direction signs carrying the word *Blame* are pointing your way, old bean. Everything is on your plate with the meat smelling slightly rank downwind. If I were you I'd come clean about it all."

Barrington poured the last of the coffee from the pot into his own cup and lit his first cigarette of the week.

"Never realised you smoked, Barrington. New thing, is it?" Dicky asked.

"To be honest, Dicky, I rarely do, but I think the occasion warrants it somehow. I'm beginning to feel a bit caged in."

"I take it Jack never approached you directly then, sort of came by the back door, did he?"

"Nothing suspicious in the information that came to me. I heard of his connection in a phone call last Friday morning from the Home Office. Said I was to dispatch West to Price's address in Soho and harry him a bit." Trenchard was lying, but having committed that sin he had no alternative but to see it through.

"A strange instruction didn't you think?"

"I just follow orders, Dicky. Try not to think too much about them."

"Did you get a name from the Home Office, Barrington?"

"No, quoted current standing orders and left it there."

"How about the following morning? What were you told of that?"

"Nothing specific, only that West was to be reassigned and his name to be erased from our records."

"Was this unusual, no written order to that effect, just verbally over a phone line?"

"Not exceptional, it happens sometimes and it was on the internal secure system."

"Did you surmise anything? Any clue in the voice? Was it something of an occasion to celebrate, do you think, or one where a rap over the knuckles was on offer?"

"Certainly not an admonishment, as West had been exceptional throughout his time with us. He'd come with the highest recommendation from Oxford. I had interviewed him myself. Marked as special by none other than the Commissioner. Full red carpet treatment with kid gloves. At the time I did think it was strange that someone so high could know of an undergraduate, but I never considered an old hand like Jack Price to be interfering."

"This would be our present Commissioner of police would it?"

"Yes! Not sure of the timescale now but he rang me personally and told me to recruit West."

"Give you any reason for that?"

"None at all, Dicky!"

"You never thought to ask." Dicky shook his head with his eyes wide open in astonishment, sitting solidly back in his chair.

"I've never questioned my superiors. I'm just an ordinary soldier, not a leader of men like yourself."

Leaning forward Dicky said, "Archie tells me that this West chappie put his mark on some senior Met officers who are on the take. Could one of them have been close to Price? Know something that we're missing, do you think?"

"I wouldn't have thought. Their files are with internal investigations who are pursuing the matter. If there is anything to find then I'm sure they will."

"You had better get those files back pretty smartly. Go through them yourself, mark them up as possible matching where appropriate and send them over to section four at my place. You can't be the only policeman in London who's worked with our Mr Price over the years. When you get back, write me up a detailed report starting when your Commissioner tossed you Patrick West's name. I want the names of everyone on his initiation board. Who signed his papers and the names of the others in your records office who may have had dealings with him. Also I want a more detailed account than you've given me on why a Commissioner sends you a university student's name? I want that on the desk of section four tonight, Barrington. This takes priority, Trenchard. I'm not saying that your life depends on it, but it damn well nearly does!"

"What am I being accused of, Dicky?"

"I thought I would start at treason and then work my way down."

"Treason! You're being ridiculous. I have done no wrong, let alone am I a traitor."

"The actual indictment is waiting to be decided upon; treason, incompetence or just sheer bad luck. Until we know what Jack's up to and what's the colour of West's underpants everything's up in the air so to speak. At the moment yours is the only throat I can grab hold of. In time, I expect others to come along, but until then I'm going to throttle you so get used to it, old chap. It's entirely up to you as to how painful that could be."

At that Dicky left, making an impromptu call on the head of the Civil Service in Whitehall on his circuitous way to number one Curzon Street; the new home of General John. It was four-forty on Monday afternoon when he eventually arrived at his own department. He was running late.

New York

I too was running out of time. Leeba had finally fallen asleep just before midnight, having exhausted her appetite for the two things that she had denied herself, the first being sex and the second being whisky. She was no regular drinker, but the abstention from sex made her hunger for its experience the more pleasurable. However, it was impossible to say which previously forbidden fruit had loosened her tongue the most. Her dynamic revelations captured my spiritual attention as much as her capacity for fornication had held my physical awareness. Not only did I need the wisdom of Solomon to make sense of what she told me, I needed to understand why she had as well.

As she copiously emptied the bottle her craving for corporeal fulfilment slowly decreased, to be overtaken by a compelling necessity to share more of her knowledge. My body was pleased about the first, but confused thoroughly by the second. There were no recollections of Vienna in anything she told. It was as though she had never been to Austria.

"Haynes and Earl's father, Herbert Baxter, inherited the family logging business when he was twenty-four years of age on the death of his own father in 1914. For the next two years he and his mother ran the company together, setting in motion the process that has turned it from a middle of the road family concern into the highly profitable property development company it has become today. His interest in timber also expanded to such an extent that by the time of his mother's death in 1916 he owned two saw mills in his own state of Connecticut and three in Canada. It was the trade in timber that led to him meeting, and then marrying, Mary Clifford, the only daughter of Michael Clifford, an Irishman who hates all things English. The Clifford's owned real estate stretching across America from California to New Jersey but until Mary and Herbert married, none in Manhattan. Michael Clifford is still alive and meddling in anti-British affairs, but Mary died of cancer a year after giving birth to Haynes.

Herbert Baxter, now with the hyphen of Clifford added to his name, was devastated when that happened, turning more and more towards Mary's father Michael for solace in his grief. From his father-in-law he gained huge advantages, particularly with the unions involved on the growing number of building sites he became interested in, but it wasn't only a one-sided covenant. Michael Clifford was one of the major providers of finance for both the Provisional Army in the island of Ireland and later the National Socialist German Workers' Party. Herbert was expected to contribute, which he did. His monetary contributions were made directly to a bank account in Switzerland managed by none other than the German minister for economics, the vice-chancellor of Germany; Hermann Göring, Shaun.

In 1942 both Earl and Haynes were overseeing the building of the so-called Secret City at Oak Ridge Tennessee. A site previously owned by Michael Clifford, thereby evading conscription into any military arm of service. Neither son knew of their father's financial arrangements with Nazi Germany, nor did the FBI. Nothing has changed as far as the FBI is concerned, but for Earl and Haynes things altered when Germany began to realise that they had lost the war."

"Does Penni know any of this, Leeba?" I asked lamely, hoping I would get a chance of asking about her pre-war days in Vienna.

"No, nor will she. I have lived too long with the shame of this family to allow it to spread and infect her."

"What about anyone else, other than Haynes of course?"

"I'm not sure that he knows it all, Shaun, but I know someone who does and another person who knows most of it. Want me to carry on with the story, or want me to take you again?"

"I want all that you can offer, Leeba. More on the Manhattan Project in Tennessee if you have it, but it can wait."

"I have nothing directly on that, Shaun. I have something far more interesting than atomic bombs to tell you of." Finally I had the opportunity I'd been waiting for.

"Is it anything to do with Vienna, before you arrived in New York?"

Late Afternoon In London

Chapter Twenty-Two

Scrambled Lives

One job that Dicky had expected to do on his return from the Home Office was to ring *Group*; however, some of his fading time was saved as that necessity had disappeared. On his desk was Archie's sealed buff dossier and marked *Directors Eyes Only*. He opened it and began to read:

1) The operational names of Horace and Butler have been used twice before, but separately. Neither had the appendage of Sir added. We do not believe that to be a simple accident or oversight. The first time that name cropped up was in 1940. *Butler* was the name given to the transportation of the Duke of Windsor from Portugal to the Bahamas. It saw life as a War Department program after Group, not I of course, uncovered a Nazi plot to kidnap the ex-King and take him to Spain.
2) We cannot conclusively say who initiated that directive, but Admiral Sir Maurice Curtis (Daniel Cardiff's uncle) was on the Privy Council, serving at the War Department in a supervisory position. He would at least have been consulted. I have confirmed that Barrington Trenchard was acting as his chargé d'affaires.

3) The Admiral served no time at sea being seconded straight from Dartmouth College, at the outbreak of hostilities, to the Special Operations Executive where he stayed until the cessation of the war. Six months on from then he was appointed Private Personal Secretary to the then Philip Mountbatten.
4) *Horace* was the 1944 code-name given to the extraction order mounted in Slovenia at a place called Divača. It was not sanctioned by any subordinate agency within the accepted intelligence services of the day, being solely a War Department independent sortie. A company from the Special Boat Squadron were landed by submarine four miles from the town and successfully lifted Yugoslav Marshal Josip Broz's (Tito) estranged wife Herta Haas and their three-year-old son "Mišo" from a German holding centre under the command of troops from Ante Pavelić. It was expertly done with no casualties on either side.
4A) You may well be wondering why we and not Tito's own forces were engaged in that operation as I was until I discovered that Herta Haas had genetic links to the Battenberg family. She was a cousin of His Royal Highness Prince Philip, Duke of Edinburgh. She died in 1970 and is buried at Frogmore.
5) We have found three operations, emanating from offices other than our own integral intelligence services, where the word *Sir* has prefixed the code name. The one we discussed into Vietnam led by Jack Price; Sir Geraint. One in 1954 under the umbrella of Kenneth De Courcy's private security company into Malaysia; Sir Garwin and the third; Sir Tristan, thirteen years ago into Kenya. All three of these had an extraction element as had been the case with Horace and Butler, but they differed in a significant way. They all had fatalities.
5A) In the Vietnam operation none of ours were harmed, however, it was reported by US forces on the ground that as JP's group broke cover with the evacuated subjects, three missiles were launched from an unmarked helicopter on a North Vietnamese position. We know that JP had three helicopters pre-

scribed from covert ordinance, we also know that he had several AGM-12 Bullpup missiles, but what's unusual here is that if an air to surface strike was made by British forces against the Vietcong it was the first time such a missile had been launched from a helicopter. If JP was responsible for this action he was acting in direct conflict with Parliamentary dictate.
5B) In Malaysia, several Chinese guerrillas were killed outside of Kuala Lumpur by De Courcy's mercenaries. They also suffered losses in the evacuation from a rubber plantation of an unnamed British dignitary thought to have been Richard Levine. Levine was at one time Her Majesty Queen Elizabeth's private secretary.
5C) In Kenya a detention camp holding hard-core Mau Mau rebels was raided one night by loyal natives who mutilated and then clubbed to death eleven inmates. The operation seems to have emanated from the War Department (unconfirmed) as the camp's commander (directly employed by WD) said he had orders from Whitehall not to intervene. Again, no orders were issued by accredited intelligence agencies that we could find. But we did find something. All of those that were killed were being held for the rape and murder of a coffee farming, land owning family named Holyport. That wasn't their real name. That was the place where their grandfather had lived. They were in fact descendants of Louis Mountbatten and the Queen Consort of Sweden.
6) It is our belief that all operations with the names *Horace, Butler* or *Sir* had Royal accreditation. If this is true then it follows that the present operation involving JP is a similar one. The only conclusion we draw is that whatever *Sir Horace Butler* is, the taking, or loss, of life has been approved by Royal consent.
7) We can find little of note about Patrick West. However, there are two entries of interest:
7A) He was allowed to take his finals at Oxford, even though he had dropped out of university three months prior to the examination date (unusual, but not unheard of). He gained a first in both chemical analysis and psychology, with meritorious distinc-

tion being awarded for his thesis on *The Good and Evil of Man.* It was a paper in which he argued that no utopian society could exist without incorporating the two opposing spectrums of human nature. We have had time for only a 'scan' read. A more detailed analysis can be supplied if requested (thirty-six hours).
7B) West's father, Harry West, served in the Royal Artillery, 8th Army Corps, through the North African Campaign, the invasion of Sicily and the occupation of Italy. At the battle of Monte Cassino he was promoted to the rank of Lieutenant when his battery commander was killed in action. When the Italians surrendered he was again promoted. He was given the rank of Captain and posted to Squadron 21. This was a field-intelligence unit that he commanded. When discharged from the army (full set of campaign medals, three mentions of gallantry, one mention of hospitalisation and a glowing report from the discharging officer) he was employed at the War Department until his death in 1971 (same year his son joined Met Police) There are no records remaining of the work that Harry West conducted in the army intelligence corps in Italy nor his duties at the War Department.
8) Daniel Cardiff is to meet with the present Private Secretary to HRH Prince Philip this coming week. Fraser Ughert's department is providing the legend that will gain him admittance into *the Firm.* Your operation. No details logged at Group as requested.
9) Job: Real name Scott Muller. Born 3/06/1931 in Durban, South Africa to an English father (serving in the Diplomatic Corps) and a Dutch resident mother. His father was recalled to England in 1950, leading to the son volunteering for active service that same year. Enlisted and enrolled as a second Lieutenant into 29th Infantry Brigade (Royal Gloucestershire Regiment) and sent to Korea in 1951.
9A) One of only 39 who escaped Chinese capture at the Battle of Injin River (suffered a severe facial wound) and one of two servicemen (a holding operation against 10,000 enemy insurgents) to receive the Victoria Cross for extreme bravery. He was in

Malaysia in '54 with De Courcy, and in 1959 he was attached to the Kenyon Police Force at the detention camp at Garissa, East Kenya. He had arrived the day before the massacre, leaving the continent of Africa the day following. His flight was scheduled to land in Berlin, but, guess what, it never did. Scott Miller resurfaced once. MI6 made the identification when Job departed for Vietnam. His military record has been sealed.

10) Until this week neither JP nor Job have been active on any continent that we are aware of. We are unable to trace either person's financial issues.

11) The C11 report from Scotland Yard is marked as awaiting.

As he reach the end of the report his telephone rang. He lifted the receiver.

"I have the product you ordered, sir." It was Fraser Ughert.

"One moment, Fraser, I'll have the call transferred to a private line," he replied curtly.

Two-seconds later, after pressing the button marked S on the terminal that connected all four of the telephones on his desk, the phone he held made a 'pinging' noise, the same sound as an underwater sonic device would make, only quieter.

"Will she be ready for tonight, Fraser?" Dicky asked nervously.

"Yes, sir! Only I don't know the target."

"Contact Sir Archibald at *Group* and liaise with him, particularly on backdated membership details. In his report, that's on my desk, he says you're in charge of the covers. How's that going?"

"Out of towners up for the weekend. I understand that it is an exclusive club where they are to go."

"It is! Her escort is named Daniel Cardiff, with Annabel's, Berkeley Square the first point of introduction. Make sure they both adhere to the strict dress code. It's an unusual place for that sort of thing. Is she up for anything?"

"The very best I've got, sir. I've heard it said that she could tease the last penny from a Scotsman's pocket by simply smiling at him."

"Both she and Cardiff will have to do more than smile tonight, I fear. Is there anything else?" Dicky enquired.

"Only a name for the operation, sir, to keep things tidy as it were."

"Echo, I think sounds appropriate. The echo of a Cardiff choir in the Welsh valleys. Powerfully evocative stuff, don't you think?"

"I do indeed, sir. Goodnight to you."

The hour hand on the wall-mounted ship's clock, a relic from HMS Victorious his father's last sea command before the ship sunk off the Netherlands coast, moved past the five bells it majestically struck. There was no time to get home and change for dinner.

"Ah, Louise, I need someone to go to the Travellers to retrieve some clothes of mine I keep there for emergencies. Black suit, white shirt, grey tie sort of thing. Oh yes, pair of shoes. These need a good polish." His trusted secretary's eyes followed his to the dusty brown brogues he was wearing.

"I can have them polished for you, sir," she announced on standing.

"No, not necessary! Need black ones to match the suit. Cufflinks I'll need, plus clean black socks and of course the unmentionables in the company of ladies." Normally he would have smiled, as was his custom, but today was as far from normal as it could have been.

"You mean underpants, sir. Will you be requiring a clean vest as well?"

"I think you're coming to know me too well. Yes, please!" He turned and was about to re-enter his office when she next spoke.

"I will need your room key, sir. And I will see to it myself immediately."

"In that case I'll phone the club butler and inform him. Women are not normally admitted in peacetime and if there was a war you'd need a signed declaration from the PM to get past the foyer. He'll have a key and have all my stuff readied for you. I'll do that first before calling home. My wife will not be best pleased with me."

"The floor would like to wish you a happy anniversary, sir," Louise said as the door closed behind him. It never registered. His mind was not on anniversaries nor on his wife, it was absorbed by the game ahead and how Daniel Cardiff's life was about to be scrambled beyond his wildest fears.

Tuesday Night In New York

Chapter Twenty-Three

Revelations

We lay beside one another with her head on my chest and her hands stilled when more revelations were disclosed; but not the one I was seeking.

"No, Shaun, I was not about to mention Vienna and nor am I likely to. For thirty-five years I've lived peacefully without once being reminded of my last day there. I'm not about to change that for you or anyone. Now, if you want me to call a cab and go home you'll press me on the issue, if you'd rather I stayed and we continuing doing what I like best, you'll let it go and allow me to tell of Michael Clifford."

I know this sounds crazy but the only thought I had that moment was of Fianna and how she would have found some comical reply to make emanating from a misquoted film star. When my head cleared I gave the only answer any over-sexed young man would make.

"Far be from me to put an end to a beautiful relationship. I won't mention it again, Leeba." Without any perceptible change to her voice or manner she simply carried on as if nothing had happened.

"Michael Clifford and his son-in-law started their resettlement of Nazis in April 1945 days before the end of the War. Martin Bormann was the last man who went through their hands. The early ones, eleven in total, went first to Ireland and then to Argentina, but that route was closed due to a mistake made by a submarine commander who thought he was surfacing near his supply ship in the Irish Channel, only to discover he had mistaken the silhouette and was in fact beside an American frigate. After a brief exchange of fire the American captain rammed his vessel into U-513, rescuing the crew from the icy water as the ship was scuttled. On interrogation, later that day, it was revealed that Oberbootsmann Richter, who had a Vatican passport in that name in his kit-bag, was in actual fact Obersturmbannführer Hans Kwellër, a prominent SS supervisory officer on transportation to concentration camps. The non-appearance of Kwellër prompted Clifford's organisation to pack their things up and flee to South America themselves, but not before signalling Clifford who in turn sent a diplomatic message to the German embassy in Lisbon, Portugal. Bormann, with two other escaping Nazis, was put ashore off the coast of Rhode Island on the night of 30th April 1945. He was driven straight to Newport where he boarded a ship bound for Buenos Aires along with one of the others; an Erich Priebke."

"I don't know a lot about the Nazis, Leeba, but I thought Martin Bormann was found shot dead in Berlin when the allies finally advanced on Hitler's bunker."

"No, Shaun! Bormann's death is still being speculated on. Even his family have been denied the burial of any body."

"Have these men remained in Argentina?"

"I've no idea, but before I fall asleep let me introduce the man who might well be able to supply that answer. The one I implied knew everything. You've met him by the way. Dieter Chase is Karl Weilham's ex-commanding officer; Generaloberst Alexander Löhr." That was a shock and I wondered if Jack knew.

"Why did he stay in the States, do you think?" I asked.

"Again I've no idea. I only found out all this when Earl died. I knew Earl, you see. He was the last man I made love to before you."

"How did you get to know Earl?"

"Richard introduced us. He's the man I'm thinking of who may not know all that I'm telling you, but does know more than he's letting on."

"Tell me about your feelings for Earl and how you felt after he died."

She reached for her almost empty glass, drained it then poured another before kissing my lips, holding that kiss for seconds.

"There are several things I find seductive about you, Shaun, some are blatantly obvious, but others not so. I've never heard you speak about yourself which most men love to do. You're an easy listener and just what I need right now."

"If you drink much more of that whisky you'll need more than me in the morning, Leeba."

"But you won't want more than me, Shaun. You'll be begging me to stop."

I laughed, as the begging bit about stopping was already true, only I never knew how to stop her and what's more, I didn't really want to know how.

"Richard hosted a dinner party, which was an odd thing for him to do. He is a very private man, normally one to keep a fair distance from people, even ones he knows well. It was round about this time of year two years ago. Hot as hell, just like now. I think the last thing I wanted to do was eat a big dinner at that old house of ours, but he insisted that I come and play hostess, so I obeyed and there was Earl.

Handsome man, tall, slim, dark-skinned from the sun and deep blue penetrating eyes that cut straight to my soul. We didn't sleep together that night but it didn't take us long as I offered little resistance on that score. I was less brazen with him than I was with you, Shaun. Perhaps his death taught me not to wait for something I want. We were lovers for about six months, breaking off a few weeks before that car crash. It was he who walked away from me otherwise I might well have been in that car with him. He learned of Dieter Chase when his father died. That's when he dumped me saying that being close to him was going to be dangerous from then on. He wasn't wrong, was he? He was an honest man and I believe it was that honesty that cost him his life!"

There was a tear in those brown eyes as she drank from her glass, offering me a sip which I refused. Empathy was not the thinking behind my refusal. I was more interested in her warm body than the drink. For the next few minutes we were silent, being carried onto sandy beaches by waves of scotch whisky mixed with carnality. A heady combination of explosive adrenalin that required extinguishing.

"I think Haynes killed Earl, Shaun, and it wouldn't surprise me if my brother was involved too. His car had gone off the road at a sharp bend, that overhung a deep crevice, in the hills near his home in Maine. The thing that I found so odd were the marks in the road just before that bend; four straight-line, double groves indicating four tyres deflating simultaneously. He drove a car with tyres that if punctured stayed inflated, tubeless things. I looked up the specification and consequences of a nail puncture. The only thing that could have happened in my opinion was if someone had laid one of those tyres shredders across the road then took it away before the local police arrived. The FBI found nothing to indicate homicide, or so they say. Haynes has very influential friends who are capable of covering any amount of evidence. They never gave me an answer to those marks in the tarmac. I doubt they looked very far to find one either.

How did I feel when he died? I felt frightened, that's how I felt and I still do. That's one of the reasons why I'm telling you all of this. Another is that I'm jealous of Penina. I've been that way since I gave birth to her and Mayanna paid more attention to my daughter than she did to me. Penni always had the first pick of things. When you came along I wanted to know if she'd take you."

"It was you who made that easy."

"True, but I needed to be sure which way you swung, Shaun. The last thing I needed for my confidence was to be turned down by a twenty-three-year-old desirable man. I was playing games with your mind."

"I'll have to take your word about a tyre shredder as I've never heard of them being used back home. But there again you're always ahead of us over here."

"You were pretty forward when it came to Penina, She gave you a flowing report incidentally. I lied when I said I hadn't asked for the details. I wanted to know just how direct you were and how good you were."

"Strange that, as she was the first woman I'd been with," I lied. "Never got close to any before."

"Then I'm only too pleased to say that she was a good teacher," she declared approvingly.

"She rates as the primary school instructor and you the university professor, Leeba. I'd get a first class degree under you." Smiling as provocatively as I could, I replied. "Are you still playing with my mind?" I asked, not ready for any missing truth.

"I'm not, nor am I exaggerating when I tell you to watch out for Richard. I believe he's caught up in something he can't get out of. Weilham is the key, I'm sure of that. And I'm sure of one other thing, Shaun. You may well be the very last man I have sex with if I don't go to sleep right now. You've killed me. More of the same in the morning if you're a lucky boy. I think I'll take the day off tomorrow, spending the whole of it in your bed."

"If I didn't know better I'd think you were on drugs, because I found it hard to keep up with you."

"I could be smutty, saying that as long as I find you hard when I need to then all's well, but I shouldn't go that low. Or should I?"

"When it's done so well, why stop is what I would say."

"I'm falling asleep, but don't let that hamper you. If you're good then I'll tell you a big secret in the morning." Within seconds she found the place of her dreams.

Wednesday Morning In New York

Chapter Twenty-Four

Ghosts

She awoke just before seven o'clock feeling very much the worst for wear.

"I have a hangover to end all hangovers. Did you hit me on the head with something hard last night, Shaun?" she asked, shielding her eyes from the outside sun.

"No need, Leeba, You did it all yourself. You drank the best part of a bottle of whisky," I replied, smiling. There was one part of me that was pleased by her incapacity but another, perhaps stronger, that wanted the salaciousness of her to be activated.

"If you want coffee then I'm about to disappoint you. I've only shopped for clothes since being here, food has not been a priority."

"Have you been living off air?"

"No! Eaten out every day. Both you and your brother threw money at me." I laughed, but she was incapable of that.

"No eggs then, I guess." By now her eyes were open, squinting at me in disapproval.

"Not even a pint of milk in the fridge."

"Bloody hell!" she shouted, then rubbed her head trying to erase the loud noise she'd made.

"If my memory serves me right, and with my head it will be a surprise if it does, there's a deli on the main street in the opposite direction to the office. They serve coffee to take out. Get some wholegrain bread and eggs and I'll try to scramble them. I need a shower. I stink!" She did a bit, but needed a toothbrush as urgently.

"Do they sell toothbrushes and toothpaste as well?"

She cupped her hands over her mouth and nose and breathed into them.

"I do need one, don't I! I'll just use yours. That's if you have one, of course."

"We have them in Ireland and some of us use them."

"Do you use a razor for shaving or only for cutting one another's throats?"

"Are you insinuating that I need a shave, Leeba?" She fashioned a smile of sorts which creased her brow in discomfort.

"I am," she replied. "I hope you have a towel in the bathroom, Shaun?" I grimaced, as if I hadn't.

"Do you wash in restaurants as well as eat in them?" She took the bait.

"I have two towels and soap. I nicked them from the hotel I stayed in overnight. I'll even allow you the use of my toothbrush. You see, I'm really quite a civilised gent when you get to know me."

"Oh you're a funny man, Shaun. Now go get my coffee. Two double shot espressos might do the trick."

"What the hell is that?" I asked, genuinely not knowing, as she got out of bed naked and clutching her head.

"You'll find out soon enough," she replied.

"And will I find out what that secret is about when I get back, Leeba?"

"Just go, Shaun! My head is going to explode any second now!"

Outside the building the air was yet to be clogged by the exhaust gases of normal day traffic, nor was there the everyday noise of screeching sirens and raised voices, but instead of wanting to dawdle in the comforting absence of these city traits the opposite was true. The warm sun on my back reminded me of Leeba's sleeping body against my own. I wanted more of her and I wanted more information. The fact that I was thinking of how to test Jack's assumption that she had no recollection of who had raped her, sometime during the coming day, was not the reason that I was not concentrating on my immediate surroundings. I would like to say that I had noticed the motley grey painted van, with blacked out windows, parked about a hundred yards in front me, but I didn't. However, I did notice three men standing opposite who separated as soon as I had left my building. Two of them crossed the street behind me, whilst the other started to take the same route as I with only the width of road separating us. Instinctively I glanced back towards the Holstein Building but there was no one I could see following on my side of the street. I was a mere boy playing a man's game in a strange playground. What's more, I was just about to be told how badly I was performing.

"Miss Stockford will not be needing coffee, Shaun, she is no longer in your apartment," Job nonchalantly stated as he alighted from the passenger side of the van and stood before me. "Jack is wanting to see you," he added as he took hold of my arm.

Monday Evening In London

If Sheila Blythe-Smith was asked if she was annoyed that her husband would not be home due to his workload, she would have answered that she was not. In fact, she was pleasantly pleased. Sheila never enjoyed travelling with him on the town leg of their journey from their home in Wood Street Village not far from Guildford. The return leg was never as bad, as on most occasions it was late at night when the traffic was lighter, thereby causing his constant reprimands of fellow travellers driving behaviour to diminish into silence. The same relief applied to their driver, only he would never voice that opinion, not even agreeing with Sheila when she said as much.

"It's very peaceful tonight without Sir Richard, George. We should be at Claridge's with plenty of time to spare and our heads in one piece."

"We should, Madam," the emotionless George replied.

"How's that new baby of yours doing, Peter? What is she now, three weeks old, is it?"

George's front seat companion, Peter Widmark, was the proud father of Betty, born to his wife Elizabeth twenty-three days ago with him only seeing his daughter twice in that time due to his own work commitments. He was part of a team of nine, twenty-four hour, seven days a week protection officers for both her husband and herself. His opinion on Dicky's perennial soliloquy on the lack of driving skill associated with other people was marred by the fact that had Dicky arrived home in time he would have been able to see some of Betty tonight and not have to wait until Tuesday, as he would now.

"Just over three weeks, Madam, and doing fine," He paused slightly before gravely adding, "At least that's what my wife says."

George gave a sly glance towards both his passengers, but neither registered anything other than a stoical look on their faces. It was as though Dicky's ghost was locked inside.

Some of us are required to accept that pain is part of our sworn duty to protect the Realm. These people driving their metal boxes on four rubber tyres must literally relish living within its confines. Have you seen their faces, Sheila? Not a single smile on any of the buggers, unless they are making everyone else as miserable as themselves!

After a few miles of agitation-free driving, Sheila bridged the silence.

"Will my husband be on time, Peter, or do we need to call ahead informing Marco of his delay?"

"Sir Richard is on schedule, Madam. There's no need to worry."

New York

I, on the other hand, had plenty to worry about. The rear of the van was partitioned off from any sunlight that may have filtered in from the driving compartment, so I could make out very little of it before Job apologetically placed a hood over my head, but what I had managed to see was significant. There was a set of headphones in front of two radio receivers and a tape recorder mounted on a fixed side panel running from the front partition to the rear doors. Above them, a blacked-out windows from which it was possible to see out, but not inside the van. A soft padded bench was bolted to the floor in front of that ad hoc position and on this Job sat me.

We drove away quickly but smoothly, until after a short time the van began to quicken and make several violent turns, throwing me from side to side. It was just before one such change of direction that I heard Job speaking, but I could hear nobody else. A few moments later I heard the distinctive sound of a police car's siren closing on us and then fade away. "All's clear," Job shouted and the van slowed. With the siren now faint and seemingly stationary we drove sedately with no more deviations until we made a sharp right turn and stopped. I heard one of the front compartments windows being nosily wound down but no sound of speech. The window closed and we began a steep decline, zigzagging carefully over three large bumps before turning left, making a coarse tyre-screeching noise, and pulling to a stop. As I was helped out of the van I could smell the cool dampness of an underground carpark.

I had a million questions, but had asked none throughout that journey which had been filled with thoughts of Fianna. I wondered if a hood had been her fate on leaving, or did she have the privilege of knowing her destination. Where I had foolishly imagined myself to be in control of my destiny, it was she that was the professional and I a bungling fool who simply had been used for Jack's end. What rankled the most was my ineptitude in believing his cautionary tales about the matchsticks whereas he must have placed microphones in the apartment and covered that by his own tricks of the trade.

"I've been a fool, Job, haven't I?" I asked as, trying to find an ally somewhere, I got out.

"To be frank, Shaun, I've no idea. Jack doesn't say a lot to me. He doesn't keep fools around him either. He looks after those he keeps, when he knows their value."

We walked up three short flights of concrete steps before Job opened a heavy groaning door towards us. The cold and damp were still there. We walked a few steps forward before my hood was removed. Jack stood before me with that characteristic smile on his face. We were in a completely closed and empty concrete lined room with a bare fluorescent light above.

"You're good, Shaun. You're very good! I wasn't completely sure about you in the beginning. How could I have been as there are so many imponderables including sexuality? You're all I hoped you would be and more."

"You've used me, Jack, haven't you? Was I your plaything finding out about smuggled Nazis from another time? What have you done with Leeba?" I asked angrily.

"Used—maybe—but I'd prefer to call it tested. Just keep it in mind that you were recruited into the police by Trenchard before I invited you to join me. Leeba is being looked after, Shaun, that's all you need to know." He was strolling to and fro looking more at the ground than me. "I knew about Dieter Chase and the others, but what I didn't know was who outside of the Baxter-Clifford household knew. You've shown me that, so now we move on to Richard, finding out precisely what he knows."

"Where's his value when Michael Clifford knows everyone who was resettled from Germany? Is that who's Fianna after? Have you sent her there, Jack?"

"An interesting proposition, Shaun. Why would you think that?"

"Because they're both Irish and the IRA must be at the top of your list."

"Not exactly at the top. There are other departments dealing with those matters who are far better equipped than I. My interest lies predominately elsewhere." Before he had finished I added my own take on things.

"But I'm betting it overlaps in a big way and none of what you've told me up till now is the full truth. Why the need of a hood if I'm on your side, Jack? Try that for starters."

He stopped walking around and now stood looking into my eyes.

"Because where we are must remain a secret from you for the time being, Shaun. It's for your own good, believe me."

"That's the trouble isn't it? What can I believe?"

"I haven't told you the whole truth for reasons that you will understand eventually. Everything in this sorry tale is complicated beyond belief. I needed to know how you would react to certain circumstances as they unfolded. Now I'm satisfied, but I still must withhold some of the truth. That is solely for your own safety and nothing else. You have had another visitor inside your apartment apart from us and Leeba."

"How do you know that, Jack?"

"Because he never noticed our matchsticks, Shaun."

"Wasn't that a good trick you taught me." If he noticed how sarcastic I was trying to be he never showed it.

"I want you to carry a firearm from now on. It's only a small one and there is a permit to carry a gun in your name. I'm hoping it won't be necessary, but we can't plan for everything."

"Do you want me to shoot whoever it was who broke in, or is he, or she, likely to be firing blanks at me?" He laughed, but I found nothing amusing in my question.

"I take it that this mysterious person has a recording of me whispering sweet nothings in Leeba's ear?"

"We must assume that he has, Shaun, yes."

"Did you think to remove his equipment when you installed your own or did you leave it there to embarrass me, Jack?"

"Not to embarrass you, Shaun. I thought the lady was suitably impressed. It was left in place because I considered that prudent. No one is more important than,"

"Yes, both Job and I know what comes next, there's no need to say the word. Where is Fianna and who was it that broke into my apartment?"

"Fianna is with Michael Clifford as his nurse. She qualified in that vocation in Liverpool before we found Father Finnegan for her. She's perfectly safe."

"Is he though?" I asked, to which Jack never supplied an answer, but began strolling again.

"You should be concentrating on that intruder at the moment," he added.

"Do you actually know who it was and how all this ends or, are you making it up as you go along, Jack?"

"Nobody knows for certain how anything ends, Shaun, not even life. Some people believe that religion was invented to ease the minds of humans as to their physical end, giving them a reason to live a pious life in order to achieve a spiritual afterlife. I cannot vouch for that either way, nor can I change the rules of the church, but I can change the rules of my own doctrine. Job has the pistol. He'll give it to you before he drops you near your apartment block, along with the permit. For reasons best known to me he cannot drop you outside your building. He will provide you with a jacket to wear in order to conceal the gun whilst you're on the street. I am sorry about all this subterfuge and I would have avoided it if it was at all possible, but we have to move as and when circumstances dictate.

We didn't know how soon you would get Leeba into your bed, Shaun, and as I'm obliged to stay here in this building for a time I couldn't get to Salvatore's this morning, otherwise I would have met you there. I have a letter I need you to deliver in person to Weilham. Make sure he knows it's from Richard Stockford and that you're his assistant. His hands only, Shaun. Be meticulous in that. Job will drop you off outside his offices and from there you must make your own way. It's a short walk to your apartment. I want you to clear your things from Baxter-Clifford's rented apartment and move into the space above Sally's restaurant. Not as plush, but it will do for the time being."

"What if Weilham's not there?" I asked.

"He will be, Shaun," he answered emphatically.

"I was followed before Job lifted me from the street, Jack."

"Yes, they are on our side. When you leave here, and Job returns you, they will wait and see you safely to Sally's."

"I could find my own way," I said suspiciously.

"We don't want you wandering off, Shaun."

"The car that was following us on our way here wasn't one of yours was it?"

"No, it wasn't," he answered.

"Did it get stopped by a police car for a traffic infringement, or was your old mucker Aberman and his FBI colleagues anything to do with it?" I asked, but once again he avoided a direct answer. I tried my best at rocking his composure.

"I know Aberman never died, Jack. Your story didn't work!"

"Things are moving at a fast pace, they're about to get faster." He looked serious after delivering that statement.

"I have to go, but we will be meeting very soon when I'll clear up some of your concerns."

"Am I being set up?" I asked helplessly.

"If you haven't already figured that out, you're not the man I hope you are, Shaun."

At that Jack left the room by the door opposite the one through which I had entered. He walked up one short flights of stairs before stopping to take the medication prescribed by his oncology consultant. He was handling his liver cancer the best he could, not yet suffering any jaundice or unusual weight loss, although his appetite was fading quickly, which in one sense he welcomed; it had helped to stop his vomiting.

Often, when alone, he worried about the future and the speed with which the cancer had creeped up on him. The question of *how long can I go on*, was never voiced aloud, but that silence would not cover its existence nor provide a reassuring answer. Exiting the stairway he inserted his security card in the elevator button then pressed for the twenty-third floor. On arriving the abdominal pain was easing, as was his sluggishness.

He took a deep intake of breath before entering an office marked: Karl Weilham. Under Secretary to the United Nations. As he passed the reception desk Cilla Redgrave waved hello.

"Hi there again, Cecil, you weren't gone long."

"Luckily no, Cilla. I had to phone my mother in England. She's eighty today and would have worried herself sick if I hadn't called. The old dear doesn't sleep well until she's heard from me. I didn't want to abuse my position by using the office phone." She smiled and thought him a little eccentric along with silly, as no one cared about telephone bills.

"Oh, by the way! I won't be in tomorrow until after lunch, I have a hospital appointment at eleven. My cleaning supervisor knows of course, but I wanted to let you know personally in case you worry about our dinner date. You really are a lovely lady, Cilla. I bet you've broken millions of hearts in your time." Cilla blushed slightly before replying, "I'm so looking forward to tomorrow evening, Cecil. You will be up for it, won't you?"

"I swear by King John's beard that nothing will keep me away."

"It'll be my first time out with an Englishman. I'm so looking forward to it," she declared again as if the point needed emphasising, as he walked towards the locker room blowing a kiss in her direction.

Late Monday Evening In London

Chapter Twenty-Five

Fetishes

Daniel Cardiff's first meeting with Maria was not the most auspicious of all time. On entering the taxi, where both she and Fraser Ughert sat on the rear seat, he fell on top of her as the cab pulled smartly away from the kerb.

"Oops, sorry about that," he said. "I should have sat down quicker. I'm Daniel Cardiff by the way" he said directly to an indignant Maria.

"Well, I wasn't expecting James Bond for the night, but if I was then you're definitely not him," she replied, straightening what she called a dress and others would have said was a handkerchief.

Maria Frankel, who originated out of Chiswick, West London, descended from a former German prisoner of war and a Polish refugee who had both died in 1963 when Maria was fifteen. She was fluent in both languages, having learned German from her father and Polish from her mother. But before her father died she learned more than just a foreign tongue; she learned how to make money from sex.

"I hope whoever it is I'm going with later tonight is less clumsy than you otherwise it's going to be a real messy night and ain't that the truth!" Daniel was left with no illusions as to what sort of girl he was dating that evening, but not all was entirely amiss as far as he was concerned.

She was an absolute beauty. The light in the back of the cab had gone out by the time he had found his seat, but it never dulled the vision inside his mind. A strawberry blonde with green eyes, facial features that could grace any magazine cover and from where he sat, a figure that he could have only dreamt of touching. Fraser Ughert allowed no time for Daniel's imagination to get the better of him.

"Maria has done this sort of work a hundred times over so she knows the drill. You follow her lead, Cardiff. No going off at a tangent. Stay focused on the job and everything will turn out fine. We believe that the man and woman you will be meeting in Annabel's are the link between a US funding circle and the upper echelons of an IRA brigade command here in London. So this is damned important. You may know the two concerned, Daniel."

Cardiff's mind suddenly deviated from Maria's body to the here and now.

"What's their names, sir?" he asked.

"Lord Reginald Beaufort and his wife Lady Margret. I believe she's a lot younger than him. Know the names, do you?"

"I say I do, went to the wedding last year. She is an out and out stunner! You can't be serious about an Irish connection surely? He's PPP to HRH," Daniel exclaimed indignantly.

"Someone want to tell me what a PPP is and, come to that, an HRH?" Maria stopped checking her appearance in the hand-held mirror and asked.

"Personal private secretary to His Royal Highness, the Duke of Edinburgh," Daniel supplied the answers.

"Oh, kinky couple then if I know what's what. Had a gent earlier this year who said he was related to a Belgian King. Loved being chained and beaten, but his real turn on was—" She wasn't permitted to finish.

"That's enough, Maria!" It was Fraser who interrupted her. "You'll have Cardiff fainting in excitement if you elaborate." She laughed whilst Daniel smiled half-heartedly; somewhat disappointed.

"Better not give my trade secrets away, eh! How much older is he than her?" she asked, touching Daniel's knee.

"I think he's in his sixties and she can't be much older than thirty, but I'm not very experienced in women's ages," Daniel nervously replied.

"He is sixty-three and his wife is twenty-seven, Maria." Fraser gave the exact ages.

"Then I guess I'll have my work cut out to get him going, but if they like a foursome you should be alright, Danny boy," Maria placed her other hand on Fraser's inner thigh, moving it closer to his groin. He stopped her and abruptly pushed it away before deflating Daniel's dream.

"The rumour is that they swing both ways, with Lord Beaufort preferring to watch his wife performing with another woman more than participating in straight sex. I'm sorry, Daniel, but he prefers men."

"Oh dear, double-o seven here is in for a seeing to then." Maria laughed as Daniel grimaced.

"If he approaches you then play along with whatever he says, Cardiff, but if he doesn't approach you then you must approach him. Your storyline is simple. You are out for the night with a girl whose sexual favours you have paid for, already having a good time with more to come. When you get introduced to Margret that's when Maria takes over. There is a room under your name booked at Claridge's for the night. Get them back there and your job is done."

"As soon as we walk into that room, sir? Is that it?" Daniel asked, with a look of hope on his face.

"Don't be as daft as you look, Danny boy. Not until we've put on a show for the cameras can we go home." It was Maria who supplied the truth. "I hope the Queen is paying you enough to lose your cherry, as she certainly is paying me enough."

"Are you sure, sir, that there's no other way than this?" Daniel asked, pleading for his virtue.

"There isn't, Cardiff. We've looked at everything." A doleful look descended on Fraser's countenance as he continued. "This is the only

way we can be sure. You are doing a great service for not only this country but also yourself. This will put you in the spotlight for future counter-intelligence work. You'll go far if you pull this off!" Fraser said, neither believing nor disbelieving his reply.

"'Ere, I just thought of something." It was Maria. "The girl this lord married weren't an escort like me, was she? I might know her if she was."

Ughert laughed before adding, "If she was then maybe we wouldn't be in need of your skills, would we?"

"Suppose not," she replied, before opening her handbag and replacing her mirror, satisfied that all was okay with her face. Daniel made sure all was in place with her body, as once more his mind went into overdrive.

* * *

At nine-twenty pm precisely Dicky ordered his second apple crumble of the day.

"Had one of these at the Travellers for lunch. Bloody horrible thing, full of crumble and no apple. This one had better be different or I'll start to believe that someone in Europe has put an embargo on the apples from Kent."

"You must watch your waistline, Dicky. I'm fed up telling you not to eat so many sweet things. They're not good for you. I suppose you'll be having a brandy and cigar to finish?"

"I hadn't planned to, Sheila. It's been an extensive day with everything that's going on. Thought I might have a brandy with the cheese at the table and a smoke in the car going home."

"No, you don't! You know how much I hate being closed in around cigar smoke. In a room it's fine, but in the car, then no. And cheese after a crumble will only keep you awake." She turned from her husband to address the maître d'. "Sir Richard will take his brandy in the cigar room, Marco, and I'll have a large glass of port. One from your Dow's collection, please. I will, however, allow my husband a small part of the stilton at the table as it is our anniversary." She smiled in the way that only a woman who cared could, knowing all along that she was in control. Dicky returned that smile but not as brightly; he had other things on his mind, and his wife's predicable nature was not one of them.

Wednesday Afternoon New York

Thirty minutes after leaving Jack I was walking into Karl Weilham's office with both Richard's letter in my hand and the gun that Job had pushed upon me nestled in the rear waistband of my trousers, feeling cold and awkward against my skin. He was a tall, imposing man, short on hair but not charisma.

"It will be a wonderful day for the world when the two pharmaceutical companies merge, Mr Redden. A huge step forward in eradicating life threatening disease for the less fortunate in the poorer countries. Please, take a seat whilst I read what Richard has to say. Would you like a coffee while you wait?"

I declined his offer but not the invitation to sit, my curiosity allowed nothing else. A paperknife was used to slit open the envelope, then, with a pair of reading glasses balanced on the end of his broad nose, his thick fingers withdrew the sheets of paper and he began to read.

I could clearly see that the first sheet was a photocopied list of some kind with a blurred insignia at the top. Clipped to the back of this one was a black and white photograph. What followed was in type and unreadable from where I sat. As he finished with each of the three pages he placed them in a neat pile on the right side of his desk. He gazed at the paper pile when the task was completed, breathed deeply then spoke:

"It would appear that your employer has an appetite for power beyond the advancement in drug manufacture for the betterment of others." His elongated nostrils flared wildly as he removed his spectacles and glared at me.

"You can go now, Mr Redden, and if I were you I'd go far away from New York. By your association with Stockford's company you are compromised and therefore a target for retribution. My reach is long and my forgiveness is short."

Any sense of an increased security that the Smith and Wesson had given me disappeared on hearing his solemn dismissal and seeing the vehement anger in his grey eyes.

Monday Night In London

Chapter Twenty-Six

Annabel's

"My word, it's Cardiff isn't it? Old Mildred Cardiff's son Daniel if I'm not mistaken. Saw you and your mother at my wedding bash last month. Knew your uncle Maurice more than your mother, of course. Attended his funeral, poor chap. Sudden affair, wasn't it! What brings you to such a fleshpot as Annabel's, dear boy? Not your usual stomping ground, London, I wouldn't have thought. Marked you down as a member of some young farmers club more than a member of one of London's trendiest nightclubs." Lord Beaufort saw Daniel standing at the bar about to order his and Maria's drinks.

"Ah, you've caught m, Lord Reg. Membership here was one of my twenty-first birthday presents. I hope you don't mind the familiarity but it would seem pointless to stand on ceremony. I'll tell you what brings me here only if you promise not to ring Mother and spill the beans." Daniel took up the challenge with all guns primed and ready to fire.

"Mum's the absolute word in my business, Cardiff. I'm doing your late uncle's job now you know, looking after you know whose private concerns. Secrets are imbedded in every single syllable of my name."

Daniel smiled liked the expert he was becoming. *Keep the conversation moving*, Fraser had said.

"I came into a bit of luck at the racetrack on Saturday, backed the first four winners then cashed in before Lady Luck left me. Decided on a night of passion with the girl I came in with." Turning, he nodded in Maria's direction who waved dutifully back.

"That's her sitting at the table behind us on the edge of the dance floor. She came from a very expensive escort agency I was recommended to use by a university friend. Does all sorts of tricks! I've got a room at Claridge's where I've sampled some but as I've paid for her services for the whole night I thought I'd get as much out of it as I could. Must admit that she's got me horny as hell. I'm in two minds whether to stay here or toddle off to the hotel."

"Bully for you, young chap. I can quite understand where you're coming from on that score. Does no harm to shop around for a bit of fun from an expert before one settles down into the respectable charade of married life. My Margret keeps me busy on that score. She's in the middle of that crowd on the floor dancing away. A popular lady, my wife, if you know what I mean. Leads me into all sorts of trouble. Stay and I'll tell you what, why don't you and your lady friend join me at our table. It's in an alcove on the first terrace, bit out of sight. I'll get your drinks fetched over by our waitress. Put the night on my bill, Daniel. I might even go half with you on your friend if you're up for a spot of sharing. She's caught my interest by just looking at her."

"Wouldn't Margret get a mite peeved if she caught you looking, Lord Reg, let alone propose such a thing?"

"Oh no, dear boy! If she likes the merchandise, which I'm sure she will, she would want to do more than merely look. Likes to get her money's worth, does Margret. What's her name this escort of yours?"

"Maria, and she's half German. I requested someone into a spot of leather bondage, but perhaps I shouldn't have told you that."

"Au contraire! I'm licking my lips. Both Margret and I enjoy that fetish very much indeed. Margret actually employs it on occasions, but I have to have been a good boy for that to happen. If you're a good boy, Daniel, you might have two delectable beauties toying with you tonight."

As long as it's only the women that are toying with me, Daniel silently prayed, but if God could hear anything above the music being played in Annabel's that night he never answered Daniel's prayers. He returned to Maria and whispered in her ear, "We're on, he's taken the bait."

Moments later Margret joined the three of them in their booth. Both Daniel and Maria rose from their seats to greet her. Reginald sat gaping at his two guests in anticipation. It was Maria who opened the conversation.

"*Ein Vergnügen, zu erfüllen. Ich hoffe, was Sie sehen, gefällt Ihnen beides.*"

"Oh I'm sure you can please us with something, darling," Margret replied to Maria, kissing her passionately on the lips whilst sliding her hand down Maria's bare back.

When all were seated Lord Reginald leaned over to Daniel, placing his hand on his thigh before moving it to his flies and started to toy with the zip.

"Prefer me to do this or Margret, whilst I have first go at Maria in that room of yours? Either way, you can watch or join in if you want, only the wife and I do like a prolonged experience, dear boy, nothing finishing hastily."

"Would you like to dance, Margret?" a blushing Daniel asked.

"Only if you're imagining me naked and right now having sex with Maria," she replied.

"Getting hard, Daniel, are we?" Lord Reginald asked, moving his hand up and down Daniel's groin.

It was Maria who saved Daniel from his tormenter, at least for the time being.

"I'm sure you two are well versed in this sort of thing, but my client is patently not. I would suggest another round of drinks and a discussion as to my fee before we go any further. I was hired by Danny boy here. I was not told of a foursome which seems to have come as a surprise to him as much as it has to me. Offers on the table, please, or I'm taking my Danny off limits."

"She has a point, Lord Reg," Daniel managed to say.

"Yes, I can see that," he replied removing his hand and calling for the waitress.

"I'll match what he's paying you, Maria." Reginald opened the bidding.

"Not enough. I want double the fee he has paid. Three hundred and then you get my avid attention along with my practised skills." She reached down to the floor and retrieved her bag. Inside was a pair of handcuffs, leather gloves, mask and wrapped in a fishnet thing was a black whip of leather throngs.

"Does this lot seal the deal?" she asked, opening it just enough to tantalise Lord Beaumont's imagination.

Reginald looked at his wife, who nodded her approval before turning once more to Maria's lips and tormenting body.

At 10.43 pm precisely Daniel Cardiff led the way to the lifts in Claridge's foyer and then room 691 on the sixth floor. He had Margret on his arm with Maria and Lord Beaufort following. A minute later Marco delivered a message on a silver salver to Dicky, who had just lit his cigar and about to savour his second brandy.

"Anything important, dear?" Sheila asked.

"Nothing at all, darling. Thank you for a wonderful night and here's to another thirty-two-years." He raised his balloon glass in salutation.

"My absolute pleasure, Richard. For all your faults I wouldn't change a thing about you," she replied sincerely.

"Why don't you have another port, my dear. Unfortunately I must call General John over a matter both he and I are dealing with. I won't be more than five minutes, but perhaps I could book an overnight room for us so the evening doesn't have to end so soon, Sheila?"

"Are you stark raving mad, Richard? Think what another port would do for my diabetes let alone the cost of an overnight room here to our bank balance!" she declared emphatically, adding without an intake of breath. "Do stop calling that man General. I dislike it intensely."

* * *

"John, Dicky Blythe-Smith here, sorry to trouble you at such an hour. I have a delicate situation that I'm dealing with, but have to clear with you first."

"If you're already dealing with it then my approval would seem somewhat redundant. You have my attention, Dicky, fire away," General John unemotionally replied.

* * *

Some forty minutes later, Peter Widmark passed a folded piece of paper from the in-car fax machine to Dicky, who was sitting comfortably on the rear seat next to his wife on the journey home. It read: *Operation Echo is successful.*

The negatives show our people, but in the printed exposures we will obscure their faces. We have subject A sexually engaged with our man and woman, and A's wife engaged likewise. For good measure we have subject A in acts of pleasuring himself several times whilst engaged in an act of fellatio. All copies (including negatives) will be locked in my safe overnight. The cameras have a further hour of filming capacity.

To give praise where it is due, Sir Richard's first thoughts were not centred on how smoothly the sting operation had unfolded, nor on how he would proceed tomorrow with the accumulated photographic evidence. His initial concern was for Daniel Cardiff and how the experience of being sodomised would now affect him. He made an unintentional exclamation of *hmm*, which Sheila could not avoid hearing.

"Everything still alright, Richard?" she enquired.

"I'm afraid it's not, my dear. I have some business to attend to that won't keep until morning. We'll drop you off at home then I need

George and Peter to drive me on somewhere. I'm sorry about this. If you had allowed me to book that room at Claridge's then perhaps this wouldn't have happened."

"There's no point in lying to me, Dicky. You would have gone even if we were on the moon," his knowing wife replied.

Dicky sat there staring blankly out of the window, trying to forget the revulsion he felt for himself.

Chapter Twenty-Seven

The Past

Barrington Trenchard's doorbell rang a few minutes past midnight. He was just about to finish up in his study and head off to bed.

"Well, what have you got?" Dicky asked without preamble, or any of the normal niceties as the door was opened. He was not in a polite mood, nevertheless, this tiny detail escaped Barrington.

"One would have thought that us sexagenarians would need more sleep than we actually get, Dicky. I'm relieved to know I'm not the only one over sixty still awake. Good of you to enquire about my wellbeing, by the way."

"I don't give a rat's arse about how you are feeling. Did you send a report over to me or not?" Without an invitation both he and Peter entered.

"Do come in," Barrington said caustically as he stepped aside. "I gave it to that babysitter of yours about three hours ago, before leaving my office. For the past hour I've been dragging people from their beds to fill in most of the missing pieces. That one will be on your desk first thing in the morning," Trenchard replied emphatically, attempting to re-establish his competence and credentials. "To what pleasure do I owe this visit, Dicky? All rather unusual, is it not?"

"Tell me now what's in it. This cannot wait until the morning. Start with your man Miller."

"Dicky, I've been working on this since we met for lunch. I'm tired. It wasn't easy, you know."

"You're a fat fool, Barrington, but that can soon be put to rights by a prolonged spell in one of my secure units in some far flung corner of the universe. It will probably do your weight good. Did Jack know Miller? Yes, or no?"

There was no immediate reply from his adversary. He silently counted to three then said,

"Just concentrate your mind. If I have to waste my time reading that report of yours then you can wait several days without sustenance tucked away somewhere nobody will know about, or, you can tell me now and save the starvation. I'm not a patient man and in no mood to listen to your complaints, Barrington."

Dicky's method of interrogation was based around his skill at cards. He drew information from his subject either through subtlety, or dominating his prey. With Barrington, Dicky already held all the tricks.

"If you had told me that was your preference then I would have phoned it through to you, saved you a journey."

"Pointless. I was out. Get on with it. And by the way, you will include if you and Alhambra are currently sleeping partners, won't you."

Had Sir Richard been a romantic, or in the slightest way idealistic, then now would be the time that he would have expected Barrington to rush off, find a gun and blow his own head off, but there was nothing quixotic about Sir Richard Blythe-Smith nor honourable about Barrington Trenchard. The animosity between the two men went back to the time when Hitler's National Socialist Workers' party was becoming entrenched in Germany and the threat of war loomed over Europe.

Trenchard was an established name within the British elite, with Barrington's father being the Liberal Member Of Parliament for Beaconsfield and one of his uncles being Master of the Royal Hunt, living on the Royal Estate at Balmoral, in Scotland. Both he and Sir Richard served in military intelligence during the years preceding the war when that service was in its infancy, split into many separate smaller sections. It was during this time that the then plain Richard Blythe-Smith was employed on Twenty Committee; a collection of twenty military-minded individuals attempting to turn German spies against their own country and work for the British Empire.

The first one Dicky found was a Hermann Görtz, who had arrived in England in 1935 and was actively collecting information on the Royal Air Force base at Manson in Kent. He was unwittingly helped by a Royal Airforce pilot whom he told Germany and England would be on the same side if war was ever to break out. Görtz's landlady became suspicious of him when she found some detailed drawings of the air-field whilst Görtz had returned to Germany for a holiday. It was Dicky who was given the job of recruiting him and, so he always maintained, he would have done it had it not been for Barrington Trenchard, who then worked in the internal security section of Britain's wartime intelligence services. Trenchard was in charge of a contingent of police officers who arrested Görtz when he returned to England. He was sentenced to a short term of imprisonment, unbeknown to Dicky, before being deported back to Germany. That was the first time their paths crossed, leaving just the smell of annoyance in Dicky's nostrils. If it had never happened again then in all probability it would have been forgotten, but it did happen again; twice. It could of course have been a matter of simple coincidence, as there was little coordination between the various widespread ad hoc units of intelligence gatherers, but the name Trenchard had been planted in Dicky's mind.

In those days of war Dicky was a bit of a loner, working on instinct as well as analysis as all good intelligence officers must do; however, on many occasions he went far out on a limb for what he believed. One such instance was more than serendipitous in Sir Richard's mind. Without orders, and acting alone, he had attempted to recruit the daughter of the Spanish Ambassador to the Court of St. James's using all his young masculine charms and revelling in the challenge, when suddenly she was sent back to Madrid. He made extensive enquiries as to why that had been necessary, but found neither a reason, nor anyone responsible. Some months after her disappearance her father attended the funeral of Leopold von Hoesch, Germany's ambassador in London, and in the photographs of the cortège that appeared in the national press her father was speaking to Trenchard's Scottish based uncle.

"It's always been a regret of mine that we never got on better, Dicky. I could never understand that." All three men were in Trenchard's study.

"Would either of you like something to drink?" Both his visitors refused the offer so Barrington sat, anxiously eking out moments to think.

"I hope it was not my fault. It's a no to your question about Miller. As far as I can ascertain, Price only knew him as a casual acquaintance. Jack had a rented garret in Soho and according to West the two were on speaking terms. As of yet I've found nothing else," Trenchard replied, hoping that Dicky's unanswered question about his sleeping partners would miraculously disappear up the chimney through the unused fireplace in front of which he sat.

"It would seem that Price has set you up, old boy. Bit of revenge for some ancient wrongdoing do you think?"

"Not sure what you're implying there, Dicky. I'm not following you."

"If that's the case then I'd catch up as soon as I could, old thing. I would wait, but I'm miles in front and you're just about to fall at the first hurdle. You see, my lot had a little rummage through your office drawers tonight, looking particularly for mentions of Alhambra, who we both know does not run a jazz club, nor is the porno king of London. Surprise, surprise! Your written conclusions, based on your detective constable's report, have nothing about our Indian born friend, but the one he left at the Home Office does." He paused briefly, relishing the irony of it being a Spanish pseudonym that delivered the coup de grâce on Trenchard's fate.

"I'll ask again, in case you've forgotten that question of mine; are you and Gregory Stiles still sleeping chums, Barrington? Only it would seem that young West was more suspicious than you gave him credit for, and I'm betting that Price had money on him being entirely that. Perhaps we're missing something, like a different report you sent to the Home Secretary that's gone astray in the internal post?"

The panic was audible in Barrington's voice and that was not just because Perter was now within inches of him and Dicky was leaning on his desk in a threatening pose.

"I want my family kept out of this, Dicky. I don't care about myself. Do what you want with me, but they deserve more than being ridiculed because of what I've done."

"We will assess the situation as it develops, old fruit, but for now I have a few more pressing questions for you. Has Stiles re-emerged and is he in this country?"

"I'm not sure that re-emerged is the right word to use as he's never been far from the scene. He mixes amongst a different class of people to us and certainly he is not so involved in society as he was, but he still has many friends that are."

"Where's he been then for all these years?"

"He's been wherever the Windsors have been. For the last few years they and Gregory have lived in France, at a place you may have heard of; Gif-sur-Yvette. As far as I know the house closed after the Duke's funeral. Wallis moved out and into the centre of Paris, whilst Gregory went to stay with the Moselys in Orsay. In his last letter he said he had been working with Wallis's solicitor and needed to travel, but never told me where he was going. If you're after Gregory then I must warn you that he has a younger lover these days who I know to my cost will do anything to protect him."

Dicky ignored Trenchard's introduction of Stiles's lover, preferring to stick to the theme.

"Would the French atomic research laboratory at Gif-sur-Yvette be of interest to Stiles?"

"Not that I know of, but that's not to say that someone who he knows wouldn't have."

"Intriguing! We must discuss that very soon. For now I have a final question. Why was it necessary to give an anti-Communist, but not an outstanding neo-Nazi, the code name of a Spanish Palace, or any code name at all come to that?"

After attentively listening to Barrington's lengthy reply, Dicky fell silent for a moment, rubbed his eyes in tiredness and reached for the telephone. With his back to Trenchard he spoke quietly, asking for a car and escort to be sent from his transport pool.

"What's done can't be undone. It's not your headache now, it's mine. Think of the coming few days as a holiday, albeit it won't be anywhere warm and tropical. The days will pass more comfortably that way. Leave a note for that wife of yours saying you've been called away on important business. I'm sure you'll think of a convincing story. You might want to add that her brother and his wife Margret were in town tonight. Perhaps they could find her some young amusing things to keep her occupied in your absence. There are a couple of my people coming shortly, my man Peter will wait until they arrive."

Why have you done this, Jack, and why now? was the question pounding at Dicky's tired brain as George drove him home.

* * *

The disadvantage that Jack saw of his upbringing being spent in Bermondsey, South London, instead of Guildford in leafy Surrey, should not have limited every aspect of his life, particularly when it came to spotting a *wrong 'un*, as his mother would call those men who preferred the company of other men to that of a woman. In fact, it should have given him a distinct edge, as the ships that used the Port Of London, close to where Jack grew up, carried more than just womanising sailors amongst their crews, but it didn't. Up until his time at the Savoy he had never noticed anyone who looked *wrong*, or spoke *wrong*, or acted strangely as he suspected a *wrong 'un* would do. Leading him to often question his mother's wisdom as to their very existence.

"What should I look out for, Mum?" he asked her more than once.

"You'll know one if you ever meet one," she replied anxiously.

Tooley Street, Shad Thames and Jacob's Island hid no monsters that Jack stumbled upon in his newspaper delivering job early mornings, nor during the daylight hours to and from home and his school at Dockhead, neither did they appear in the shadows of dusk when running errands for his mother.

When he started work, in the more fashionable Strand area of London, that awareness changed one morning when Mr Snow handed him his daily three pairs of gloves and then, after dismissing the other pages, took him to one side.

"I noticed, Master Price, that you have been in conversation with a regular visitor of ours on several occasions recently; a Mr Campbell."

"I have, Mister Snow. Have I done something wrong?" the young Jack asked.

"Not wrong in any sense that you would know, but I must caution you in regards to that gentleman. He is not what he may appear to be. If he reserves a room in the hotel and asks specifically for you to deliver something then do not enter his room under any circumstance. If he enquires why that is, then tell him those are my instructions. Got it?"

"I have, Mister Snow, but why?" Jack asked, without hesitation or embarrassment. Although the post room had emptied, Mr Snow still felt the need for discretion.

"He's as bent as a nine bob note, as are most of his friends and if you're unsure what that means, I suggest you ask your dad." Mr Snow whispered, leaving a lasting jaundiced impression in the young boy's mind.

"My dad's dead, Mister Snow, there's only me and my mum," Jack replied painfully.

"Even more reason to be careful, Master Price."

Tuesday Morning In London - Wednesday In New York

Chapter Twenty-Eight

Plain Soldiers

When Sheila awoke in the morning Dicky was not in his bedroom nor anywhere else in the house. His car had arrived a few hours previously taking him back to London and number thirty-nine Lavington Street, the address where Barrington had been escorted. On finding some books and papers left untidily lying beside his crumpled, discarded blanket on the floor of his office, she silently mouthed her disapproval of the hours that his department demanded from her husband, then loudly proclaimed, "I wish you would change jobs, you'll live longer if you do." The housekeeper turned in surprise. "Do you mean me, Madam?" she asked.

* * *

When I left Weilham's office I considered trying to trace my 'kidnapping' van's route on foot, but quickly abandoned the idea as it would have been an impossible task. Instead, with Salvatore's two escorts trailing behind, I walked to Penni's riverside building hoping she was there. It was not my lucky day. Disheartened and feeling rejected, I decide to return to my apartment to collect my things as Jack had instructed.

On exiting the lift I made my way along the short, wide carpeted corridor towards my door which although closed had been opened, as told by the fallen matchsticks. If Jack was right to be cautious I could now be the target of a madman wielding a firearm. I turned the key in the lock with my heart in my mouth, but my gun in my hand. Sitting directly opposite the door was a stout man with a flat tartan cap on his head and a gun pointed directly at me.

"How thoughtful of you to return! There I was thinking that I might not get the pleasure of your company. Please drop the weapon, as I'd get my shot well before you could."

He was roughly forty years of age, deeply tanned with an elongated face and square chiselled chin. The gun, with a silencer attached, held my concentration and as the sun was at his back, shining through the haze of cigarette smoke that swirled around him, it was impossible to notice anything else other than his harsh voice. Job came instantly to mind, as I thought he had a similar Southern African accent.

"Where is Leeba Stockford?" he demanded as I obeyed his command, dropping my useless gun.

"I only wish I knew. When I left she was heading for the bathroom complaining of a headache," nervously I replied.

"That was when you were whisked away by the van, was it?"

"It was, yes!"

"And where did your friends take you, Mr Redden?"

"They were no friends of mine. They put a hood over my head then tried to frighten me off from seeing her again. If you were there you would have seen that." I've never believed in defence being the first line to any successful strategy.

"Is Shaun Redden your real name?" he asked as he rose from the chair, stubbing out yet another cigarette on the carpet beneath his feet before making his way towards me. "We need to talk," he said as he closed the narrow gap between us, beginning to raise the pistol in his hand to my head.

With the palm of my right hand I grabbed the hammer of the gun, at the same time forcing my thumb against it, then I brought my knee up hard into his groin. Now was the time to see if the instructions I'd undergone on how to deal with a revolver would work. Although he looked out of shape, he wasn't. He hardly flinched and still held the gun tight. With my other hand I aimed a punch at his throat, but being shorter than me he ducked under it, and I ended up hitting him high on the head to no effect other than on my arm which shuddered from the wrist to the shoulder joint. At that moment I saw a shimmering band of light on his fist which slammed into my cheek, forcing me backwards towards the open door. It was as I staggered I felt my hand lose its grip on his gun. All I could do was pull his hand away from me, pointing the weapon towards the floor. Through the open door I fell, onto the carpeted hallway just as the gun went off. I remember feeling a searing hot pain in my foot before passing out in the corridor.

* * *

As I regained consciousness I could feel soft fingers touching my wrist and a warm hand across my brow. I had no idea how long I had been unconscious, but I did know I was no longer in the corridor of my apartment block. When I turned my head towards that touch, I had an intense burning sensation all over my face similar to having been scalded by a rush of boiling steam. A short comely woman, aged about fifty, wearing a white habit with a red scapular across her shoulders, was standing beside the bed taking my pulse.

"Try not to move your head too much, young man. You have had surgery for a fractured cheekbone and eye socket. Don't bite hard on your teeth or blow your nose for a few days. The pain will soon go with no more discomfort once the jawbone is bonded together, until then the splint must remain in place.When the aesthetic wears off I'll give you some painkillers and some antibiotics. It might take a couple of weeks until you'll be kissing the girls again, but rest assured you will." She smiled as she gently placed my hand down on the crisp white sheet.

"Why is that tent thing over my foot, nurse?" I asked painfully, the splint hampering my speech.

"I had to amputate three of your toes on that right foot, the outside ones. An inch higher and you may have lost your entire foot." I stared at her, trying to concentrate on her words.

"Did you say you amputated my toes or did I mishear that?"

"You heard correctly, yes. I'm your surgeon come nurse. I changed from being a hell-raising heretic into a Sister of the Annunciation of the Blessed Holy Mary after qualifying as a surgeon, too many years ago to remember. I keep my hand in when I'm needed," she replied mysteriously.

"Was it the Devil who hit me?" I was still feeling the pain in my face but nothing from my foot.

There was another voice in the room.

"In a roundabout way, Shaun, it was. Name of Wilson Pérez. Originally from Chile, but now a worldwide mercenary for hire." It was Jack that I heard although I couldn't see him.

"I thought he was South African," I said as I ignored the pain, pushing myself bolt upright from the bank of pillows in the bed. "Ah, there you are," I said as I saw him. "Where am I, Jack?" I asked.

"Somewhere safe! We cleaned up at your apartment then brought you here. Job had left a man inside, but Pérez shot him. He's dead. Sally's two other men nabbed Pérez in the lobby on his way out. He'd been shot in the leg," he told me as he put my pillows in a more comfortable position.

"I never had a chance to fire my gun, Jack."

"No, we know. We found it inside your rooms on the floor. It must have been a ricochet from his own. He's been taken care of."

"By taken care of, do you mean that he's dead?" I asked.

"I mean taken care of, Shaun. Somethings are best not disclosed in too much detail."

The room was sterile white, lined by open shelved, glass cabinets stocked with various medical equipment most of which I'd never seen before, nor wanted to know their purpose. It was glaringly lit with two huge ceiling-mounted, movable spotlights beside an operating table to my left. There was a collection of scalpels and the like on top of it. I wondered which ones had been used to remove my toes, but as that thought was leaving me I wondered if she had lied, because I was sure I could still feel them as first I clinched, then wriggled what was there.

"We didn't want New York's finest finding you first. That would have meant a lot of questions being asked and time needlessly wasted. We clean up our own mess, if we can."

"You were expecting someone to pay me a visit, weren't you?"

"It was a possibility, Shaun, that's why I gave you the gun and took the precaution of leaving one of Salvatore's crew in your rooms. Unfortunately, we didn't give you enough protection," he stated laconically as he stood from the chair he occupied and made his way over to the only window in the room. He never looked at me, just stood there gazing out onto whatever there was beyond. The window was barred.

"I've not been safe since arriving here, have I? There's not much of your story that I believe you know, especially about Penni." The throbbing in my face would not stop me from speaking my mind.

"I think it would be more expedient to wait until we are alone, Shaun. Don't you," he cautioned me in a severely disapproving voice.

"That would appear to be a timely reminder for me to leave you two to discuss whatever it is you need to discuss. I will return shortly, but I have other duties to perform for now. Goodbye, gentlemen."

With that she was gone. Leaving only Jack's rhetoric to deflect my discomfort and the smell of antiseptic mixed with something else that I could not put a name to.

"The Hitler thing was a bit farfetched, but it served its purpose, Shaun," Jack resumed as soon as the door closed behind her.

"This whole affair has been the slow collection of tiny jigsaw pieces really, and it's only now that the final ones are starting to fall into place. How long did that have you fooled?" he enquired.

"I never really believed it. I couldn't see Hitler with a Jewish girl. But it did hold my fascination, that's for sure."

"What intrigued me the most was how long it would take before you quizzed me on that one."

"I may have done before now, Jack, but we haven't had much time to chat. Have we?"

"No, we haven't, but now time has been forced upon us. Let me ask you a question first, then you can have a turn. You have never pushed me on the question of why you were chosen for this adventure. That has puzzled me a lot."

"If I'm truthful I was trying to avoid the inevitable answer of just being thick enough to fall for your lies. I hoped you would eventually tell me a truth that I could cling on to, but now that I'll miss Richard's Saturday meeting I guess I'm finished in your brand of espionage before I started to enjoy it."

"Things have recently happened that throw that meeting into doubt, but we have it covered without you or Richard being required to attend. The letter you delivered to Weilham will cause him to re-evaluate his position."

"He thinks Richard wrote that and that implicates me, Jack."

"Yes, I know! That was the idea behind it. He is a dangerous man, Shaun, with even more dangerous friends. The Stockfords are our main priority. I'm sorry to admit this but your life comes a distant second."

My head hurt, every part of my face screamed in agony on speaking and the thought of not being able to walk properly would have added further to my troubles if I'd thought long enough about it, but that last confession from Jack Price hit me harder than any shiny knuckleduster could ever do. Before I could say a word, he turned around and faced me.

"I think it's time for the whole truth and nothing but the truth. No threats about onward disclosure, just trust from me. There are only two people in the whole world who know parts of what I'm going to tell you, there were more, but they have passed on, so, I'm putting you deeper in the shit than you've been. That's what I think you want and why you're not fighting to get back to dear old London. Your heart is stronger than your brain, Shaun. That's got to change, son, and soon."

He paused for a second, examining my face as if a dramatic change might suddenly appear. None did.

"The last piece of this jigsaw happened last week in a place called Trelew, in Argentina. The real truth behind that event will never be reported, but it's the future's headline, my boy. Right, let's start at the beginning shall we?"

He fetched the chair and sat next to my bed taking a cigarette from his packet and offering me one. One part of me wanted to smash him to pieces for all his lies, the other, the wiser part, tuned in its ears and listened.

"The Vienna meeting was real. Hitler was present but you're right. When told that Leeba was Jewish he indulged his passion elsewhere. Our abdicating king, although prejudiced against Jews, blacks and almost everything and everyone who was not of his own race and stock, held no such prejudice on matters of sex. All he saw was flesh and pleasure. It was he who fathered Penina, Shaun. Penni is related to our present Royal Family and what's more they know of her and have been concealing the truth with my help."

I said nothing to this. Not because I wasn't shocked or moved, but simply because I never believed him. Whether this confession, the ever-changing stories, or the mixing of lies and truth together was how Jack worked on dragging people into his web of deceit I did not know, but whatever was his technique it had drawn me into it. I should have wanted out, but the opposite was true. I wanted more. I was enjoying the cigarette but not his story.

"What does Stockford really know, Jack?" I asked.

"He knows very little. He was suspicious of Aberman from the very beginning, but mainly in regards to his mother. He believed they were having an affair. As to the truth of that, I have no idea. After the war ended he returned to Austria making enquiries as to meetings and attendees at the Chancery in the year they left to come here. He surmised that the origins of his family's departure started in that building. It took quite a time, the best part of twenty-five years to be precise, before he realised that it was impossible to fully uncover what I'd been told in that café, but he was able to put the twos and twos that he found out together, and he came up with four. When he and his family arrived in America he could speak very little English and had no qualifications to get a job. He was, after all, only sixteen. Within a year both of those disadvantages had been rectified. His first employment was at an apothecary's where he quickly became indispensable to its owner, a Thomas Lexington.

Richard was a dab hand at throwing together bunches of herbs that eased away the problems suffered by some ladies in the heat of New York or when disturbed by other things in their regular life. It wasn't long before he used that talent to mix various over-the-counter opioids into cures for routine illnesses such as headaches, but marketed under the Lexington label. Lexington was a brand of medication carried by the vast majority of New York pharmacy outlets and then it became nationwide. Three years after the end of the war, Thomas Lexington sold his proprietary name to Grenletech, then a subsidiary of Monsanto. Richard was kept on in the new company as assistant head of research. Now here comes the crunch. One of the early directors of Monsanto was none other than Michael Clifford.

When Richard decided to branch out on his own it was Clifford who put up the finance. But it wasn't just in the expansion of chemical science that his vision was set on, he saw an opening in applying patents for biotechnology development and Michael Clifford saw the opportunity. What has since been described as bio piracy became the core of Stockford Pharmaceutical Company and that's where his wealth comes from. Clifford now wants a huge return on his initial investment. If he gets what he's after it will shatter the balance of world power in his favour. Incidentally, before I get too far ahead of myself, Perez worked for Haynes. Just like Leeba, we also believed he killed his brother, Earl Baxter-Clifford. He probably would have killed you after you had been abducted and questioned. That, I believe, would have been his ultimate aim."

"Does Richard know what Clifford wants from him, Jack?"

"No, but I couldn't be entirely sure of that until you placed my letter in Weilham's hands."

"You're using both of us as bait, aren't you?"

"I was, but that's no longer necessary, Shaun. Haynes paid a visit to Richard's home last night, left him beaten and in no doubt what would happen if he went to the police. For the moment at least; you are thought to be dead."

I drew hard on the nicotine. From the inside pocket of his jacket he withdrew a hip flask from which I swallowed gleefully, but the pain of realising that I was not as clear-thinking as I thought only dulled the physical pain that started to grow on me.

"I'm going to need something for this pain in a minute, Jack. Is there a nurse you can call?"

"Sorry, old chap, but no, only me on hand. I've been left in charge of your treatment. There is some morphine, that I think I can inject," he exclaimed with no confidence. "If you can wait, then that nun is coming back in a couple of hours."

"Can't wait that long. Give it to me. I'll do it!"

"Which would bring me to the middle part of my story in a nice sort of way. Your father would be proud of you, Shaun; if he was still here and could see you now."

"My father," I repeated in utter surprise. Was I hallucinating or would he appear at the window with my mother at his side?

"Yes, your father. It was he who found one of the earliest pieces to this conundrum whilst working for military intelligence in Italy at the end of the war. He worked alongside my investigations in the War Department up until his death." No spirits coming through the glass or plaster then.

"You had better find a bigger bottle of Scotch and give me all the phials of morphine you have, Jack. I think I'm suffering from the bends."

For the first time since he had begun speaking he smiled that trademark expression of self-satisfaction as his eyes narrowed into his questioning mode.

"He never spoke to you of any of this, did he?"

"Not a single word, Jack. A very closed man, was my father."

"Ever mention a list of names he'd come across?"

"No! Nor did he mention the war."

"Thought not," he replied as his smile widened into almost a laugh. "I knew it," he added and his face lit up as if Christmas, Easter and his birthday had all arrived at the same time.

"There will always be a need for the common soldier, Shaun, and we are three of them, you, your dad and me. No war can be fought without us Tommies and no war is won without them either."

"If you say so, Jack, but my dad's dead and I'm laid up for a little while which means you're leading the charge without any reserves." I stabbed the injection into my leg and seconds later sighed in relief.

Later Tuesday Morning, London

Chapter Twenty-Nine

Hess

"I hope they have settled you in okay, Barrington, you should thank your lucky stars that it is summer and not the winter. Needs a drastic overhaul on the heating, but the intelligence budget is a mite stretched in these austere times. General John had a chap here last January doing what you're about to do when it gave up the ghost completely. After three days he was signing documents admitting that he murdered Elvis Presley and was behind the Guy Fawkes plot. Would have had him confessing to initiating everything that's gone wrong in the Western world if his handlers hadn't frozen their whatnots off and asked to go home. We don't expect that from you, old boy. We only want the truth and nothing but. We will start at the beginning with dear old Gregory Stiles. Where you two met, what he was doing and what drew you to him. But first we'll order some tea. After all, some traditions still take priority in this land of ours. Not savages in all that we do, are we?"

Although Dicky knew that Barrington was almost certainly aware of the methodical methods that would be used against him, he enjoyed picking at his adversary's bones.

The top floor room, which overlooked the elevated railway tracks emanating from London Bridge station, was shuttered and lit by a single suspended light bulb under which the two sat at opposite ends of a scrubbed wooden table de void of anything other than a recording machine which was running. There were four wooden upright chairs spread unevenly around the grubby, bare, white painted walls with one door, which was closed. In a corner of the small room was a single metal bed frame with bed linen and a mattress neatly rolled at one end. There was one other person seated in the room. When the tea was delivered that person left and closed the door.

"Stiles and I are roughly the same age, Dicky, we were both born in 1908. Where I had been brought up surrounded by people of my own class, education and pedigree as it were, he had been raised doused in money. Dripping in it, he was! It had bought him a reputation of lavish generosity along with trappings of grandeur as well as a directorship of the D'Oyly Carte theatrical company. It was when he was producing Gilbert and Sullivan's operettas that he stayed at The Savoy hotel and that's where I met him in 1936. I forget which operetta it was, but that's how we first met and the reason why."

"Were you there to see the show, Barrington, or were you part of the cast?"

"Neither actually, Dicky." He was annoyed, but in no position to forcefully show it. "I was there on company business gathering what I could on Mosley and Hitler devotees. You know of course that's where Campbell, and then I, ran Jack Price."

Dicky merely sipped from his teacup staring directly at Trenchard, neither nodding nor shaking his head to Barrington's rhetorical question.

"Is that where Jack's dislike of you first took root? Did you proposition him? Invite him to a soiree with the three of you, one in which he knew what would take place?"

"Is that relevant? I doubt Jack Price is fond of anyone in this life whatever their sexuality may be."

"Possibly, but it would be nice to know why he served you up so neatly bundled and wrapped. Never mind," Dicky said as Barrington was slow to respond. "put that one on the back burner simmering away until later. Was Stiles a Nazi sympathiser when you first met, and if so did he hide it?"

"That's an awkward one to answer. He was never that open in those early days. Definitely anti-socialist, and a staunch critic of anything commie Russian, but not an out-and-out fascist in that sense. The thing that stood out through all his flamboyance was his loyalty to the Crown."

"How long did it take you to discover that he was homosexual?"

Barrington laughed. Not loudly in triumph, but more as a way of saving face, as the stealthy degradation that Dicky had wanted to achieve was beginning to bite.

"I knew from the first moment we spoke. Just as I knew from the first time we met that you were not. It's a gender thing that some try unsuccessfully to hide while others find no shame in admitting what they are."

"Your own reasons for not declaring your sexual leanings are not at issue here, nor are the leanings of any others that will be mentioned during this debrief unless specifically asked about. We will stick to the path we are on. Please bear that in mind. Did Stiles introduce you to the Duke of Windsor?"

"Formally, yes, but I had met him once before. I was assigned to a special detail that reported on a visit the Duke and Mrs Simpson made to Paris, just before he abdicated and married her."

"When did you formally meet the ex-king?" Dicky persisted.

"Not until 1940, when he was living in Lisbon, Portugal."

"The Santo residence?"

"Yes! Stiles and Ricardo Santo were close friends."

"Was that when you became aware of Gregory Stiles's relationship with Nazi Germany along with his financial dealings with that country?"

"Yes, it was!"

"How?"

"One afternoon Gregory introduced the Duke of Windsor to a German agent named Walter Schallenberg. I was aware of that name through my work with Campbell and with Internal Security. He had been in London in 1933 at the German Embassy. Schallenberg pleaded with the Duke to return to Spain where the Germans, with the co-operation of Franco's secret police, would mount a covert operation taking him and his wife to Germany. He refused, going to Nassau in the Bahamas instead. Stiles was going to finance that evacuation to Spain; instead I saw him sign a cheque for seven figures in favour of the Duke."

"You had ties to the Spanish Ambassador during that time, Barrington?"

"How very astute of you, Dicky! Again not directly, but through a family member, yes!"

"Did you meet again?"

"The Duke of Windsor? No!"

"Stiles?"

"Not until I think it was in the late sixties, maybe 1969."

"Where did Stiles go when the Duke was ferried away from Portugal?"

"He went with the Royal party. That's when we lost touch, but I did hear through the grapevine that Gregory had paired the Duke up with an old friend of his; a Swedish millionaire who was visiting Nassau. I would think that it was then that that the idea to set up the quasi Royal Court in Sweden was hatched."

"But you don't know that for sure, Barrington?"

"No, I do not. Look, I suspect that I'm being more cooperative than you imagined. I hope you're taking note of that," Barrington proclaimed defiantly.

Dicky was fighting the fatigue that he felt which had been aggravated by the consumption of the best part of a bottle of brandy. If Sheila had known how much he had drunk the previous day and night then she would have enrolled him in the local Alcoholics Anonymous programme. He removed his brown leather gloves and rubbed his eyes. Although he was struggling it was a battle he knew he could overcome; however, the update he'd received from Catherine at section four, whilst still at home, was a completely different matter. That took him to places he would rather not go.

"Duly noted and filed away, Barrington. Tell me about Rudolf Hess; how heavily involved were you in the cover-up that followed his arrival in Scotland?" he asked.

"What the hell! How do you put me into that boiling pot? Way beyond my expertise, the unravelling of why he came to Britain. No one invited me to Scotland that weekend."

"Not even dear old Uncle Tobias, old chap?"

"My, you have been busy."

"Yes, I have, haven't I?"

"My answer remains the same."

"It's a hunch on my part based on the fact that you were so eager to show me how much you knew of the Duke of Kent's plane crash. You can be rather pompous and puffed-up at times when mentioning those you've rubbed shoulders with, Barrington. Often it's best to say nothing, but now it would more expedient to make a clean breast of what you do know. Share the knowledge, lighten the load. You will not only feel better for the experience, but also be better rewarded. Want something stronger than tea?" Dicky asked for his own sake, more than for Barrington's wellbeing.

Back in New York

"Amongst many that your father interviewed in Naples, Italy, at the end of the war, Shaun, was a German colonel who, when a captain, was one of the aides-de-camp of the Nazi Party's illustrious deputy Führer; one Rudolf Hess, of Spandau prison, Berlin fame. The colonel wanted a favour from the allies and more importantly, your father was willing to trade. What he had to offer was gold dust by the tonnage. Luckily for him, and us, your father was a bright, forward-thinking man. In exchange for an exact copy of the names of British sympathisers to the Nazi cause that Hess had carried on that plane trip to

Scotland in May 1941, he wanted to stay on the farm in Italy where he had been captured, marry the woman there and live out his remaining days drinking wine under the olive trees. Your father did not think that to be too high a price to pay, but did wonder who to divulge those names to. He copied the names from the document the colonel supplied, then took that copy to the chief of military intelligence in Rome; Wing Commander Douglas Finley. Before he left his field unit he carefully hid away the original document. A cautious man, your father. Unfortunately, he wasn't vigilant enough.

He did not know that Finley and the man that Hess had flown to see in Scotland had served in the RAF together and were close friends. Finley dismissed your father's report, saying that none of the names could possibly be connected with Nazism. He told your father to send the German colonel to the appropriate POW camp to await further investigations on whether or not he should stand trial at Nuremberg. On return to Naples Captain West resumed his duties, but, and this is where I come in, he was recalled to Rome three weeks later by my head of station. If you recall I told you that one of the reasons for my marriage breakup was due to my many visits abroad and this was one of them." He passed me another cigarette then continued.

Colonel Von Striegt, a prisoner of war detained under military orders signed by Captain H. West at Camp12, Pozzuoli, near Naples, had been found shot dead. He had suspected he might be, and had left word with another prisoner to that effect. I met your father one month after meeting Aberman in Vienna, Shaun, and it all started to fall into place.

"What was he like in those days, Jack?"

"He was a man of honour and integrity. Just like yourself."

London

In Lavington Street that's what Dicky was after; honour and integrity along with lashings of honesty.

"We are going to do another ten or fifteen minutes, Barrington, then I will leave you in the capable hands of Ughert's lot. They will address some of the finer points in more detail than I. A lover of exactitude, is Mr Ughert. His men can be a tiny bit messy at times but they get there in the end. I'm to see the Secretary of Defence in company with the Home Secretary. We will obviously be discussing you and what treatment you deserve. Personally, I'd prefer it all to be kept as quiet as possible, save a few blushes that way. However, the next few minutes of your disclosure will determine whether or not that's my recommendation. Are we clear on that?"

"Perfectly, Dicky," Barrington declared.

"Let's get that little courtesy out the way to start with. From now on you will refer to me as Sir Richard. I am no longer your one time colleague, I am the person in charge of your interrogation and arbitrator on all matters to do with the Trenchard fraternity. Further statements, both verbal and written, will be made with due deference to my position." Dicky sat back in his chair waiting for Trenchard's response. He didn't have to wait long.

"Yes, Sir Richard."

"Hess, how involved were you?"

A heavy, laden sigh was followed by the withdrawal of a cigarette and a request for an ashtray.

"Stub it out on the floor. Everything gets swept and burnt after you leave, Barrington. You have never been here." Trenchard muttered a quiet *okay* before carrying on with his story.

"Hamilton, that's the man Hess wanted to see in Scotland, phoned me the afternoon he was called to the hospital where Hess had been admitted. He'd suffered some minor injuries when he parachuted from his plane over Hamilton's estate. Hamilton said he would fly down to London and meet with Churchill, taking the list with him. I asked whose names were on it. Some were obviously well known in Whitehall, but there were others that would not have been suspected, let alone known."

"What did you do?"

"I told Hamilton to tell the Prime Minister of Hess's arrival, but to cover up those unsuspected names. *'Give him the Duke of Windsor, the Duke of Kent and Lord Louis Mountbatten, but those others don't warrant being slandered just on the word of a Nazi, Douglas. They will never survive the scandal,'* is roughly what I said.

"Was Douglas Hamilton a fellow supporter of the Nazi ideal?"

"If he was then I knew nothing of it. I believe he was mistaken to be one by Hess because they shared an interest in aviation. Douglas had attended the Summer Olympic Games in Berlin in 1936 and had dinner whilst there with the German Foreign Minister, Joachim von Ribbentrop, but he was part of a travelling parliamentary group and not there under his own steam."

"Wasn't he later invited to inspect the Luftwaffe by Hermann Göring at about the same time that the Duke of Windsor was in Berlin?"

"You seem well versed on things. I know nothing of that, Sir Richard. We weren't that close."

"Really! Then that phone call of his the day the deputy Führer arrives on his estate must have come as whopping great surprise to you?"

"We went to the same school and had some of the same friends, but that's all there was. He probably knew I was with the intelligence services and figured I could help."

"We might have to come back to that at some point, but for now I'll accept your word. What were the names that you persuaded him not to divulge?"

"Arthur Stangate; who sat on the Privy Council and had been First Lord at the Admiralty. Leonard Turner, 1st Baron of Eastfield. His family were major ship owners, Earl Bingham of Tangier, one time supreme Allied forces commander, and finally one time Admiral of the Fleet, Sir Ernest Hatfield.

"Just the four?"

"Along with the two dukes that you're aware of and Lord Louis, then yes, just four."

"Did the list that Hess carried contain the names of serving Nazis that would actively support a union between Britain and Germany if certain conditions could be met?"

"I see where you're going, Sir Richard, but no. The Jewish question was not a prerequisite to peace. As the once king of the British Isles had voiced no problem with Hitler's proposed Jewish solution and indeed Hess was one of the primary orchestrators of that policy I can't imagine anyone objecting. Hess, however, must have known of fellow-thinking Nazis."

"Into whose hands did that unabridged list end up, Trenchard?"

"Douglas was asked to hand it over to Kenneth de Courcy, which he did."

"And who did the asking?"

"The then Chief of Combined Operations; Lord Louis Mountbatten!"

"But of course you and Douglas Hamilton were not that close. Were you?"

"We kept in touch over the affair."

"Hmm, interesting!" Dicky leant across and stopped the recording.

"What, in your opinion, was the benefit for those esteemed men giving up the sovereignty of this country to Germany, Barrington?"

"Two, mainly! One would rest with the Windsors being of German descent, as are our present Royal Family, and the second was what Hitler offered. The guarantee of holding on to the British Empire by reinforcing its military presence with Axis troops when he had won the war. As you know, Sir Richard, we couldn't hold on to any of it with American hands picking our pockets and drafting our foreign policy for us."

As Barrington Trenchard finished his reply, the recording was turned on again.

"Why did you send West to see Price? What was the reason behind that decision of yours?"

"In truth, one reason was vanity. I saw his name on a statement and wanted West to find out what he was up to and before you ask, no, I never linked Jack to anything. When I read West's report on Saturday that's when I worried. It had a smell about it with Jack muddying the waters that until then had never been stirred. What I didn't know was that there was a second report, the one that dropped me right in it. I don't know that much about Jack's war years, but I do know his quartermaster comes out of Italy. Want to know his name; Sir Richard?" Barrington stressed the '*sir*.' The intended insult did register, but brought only a tiny rebuke.

"Stop playing games, Trenchard. Now's not the time for pass the parcel."

"Salvatore Guigamo. He was a colonel in the Italian 8th Alpini Regiment, but somehow or other wangled a softer posting when the main part of that Alpine Division joined Hitler's invasion of Russia. Jack uses him for his muscle."

"Happen to know in which country this man is now, do we?"

"I don't know for sure, no, but I helped Jack with the immigration papers in 1945. The idea put forward was that Guigamo would become active for us in America. When he and some family members left Italy he was heading for New York."

"Did he provide any intelligence that you're aware of?"

"I wasn't privy to any of that. It was shortly after that I was kicked upstairs to Special Branch."

"Funny that. Never saw Special Branch as a promotion, old fruit!" *Game, set and match to me*, thought Dicky.

"Who was debriefing Price when you knew him?"

"Ah! There's the thing that has mystified me forever. Never could find out who Jack worked for. Questioned his loyalty once."

"That must have made him fond of you, Barrington, particularly if, as seems highly likely, he already had your number filed away for future use."

"I can't answer for Jack, in truth I never really knew him well."

"Did Jack ever met Stiles?" Sir Richard continued with his crisp questioning.

"I very much doubt it. From a completely different class, was our Jack. He was the type who wore his lower-working class as a badge across the heart. How goes that saying; you can take the boy out of the gutters but you can't take the gutters out of the boy." Dicky merely frowned in a disapproving way before continuing.

"During your stint in Ireland did you ever work closely with Sir Archibald Finn?"

"Why, is he suspected too?"

"Just answer the question, please."

"Not closely no, but I was aware of him."

"Was Jack Price over there at the same time?"

"Can't answer that one. If he was then I wasn't privy to that knowledge."

"One final question for you, Barrington. Have you ever heard the name of Aberman before?"

Up until now Trenchard's replies had been sharp, concise and quickly delivered. To this question he both paused and prevaricated.

"Aberman, er, I don't think so, Sir Richard. If it's a place somewhere, then I'm unaware of it. Sounds like some Swiss mountain pass. On the other hand, if it's someone's name then it rings no bells with me. Sorry!" he replied with effort.

Dicky rose from his chair, angrily looking down upon his prey.

"That's disappointing, old chap, as I don't believe you. You would be wise to reconsider that answer before I meet the gentlemen I spoke of earlier with whom I will be discussing your future. Ughert has his box of tricks, but it would serve you well if you volunteered the information than wait for him." He turned towards the door and was just about to call for its opening when Barrington spoke.

By the time he finished both men were drained physically and emotionally, Barrington by the weight of confession, and added to Sir

Richard's weary body was the nervous tension of a hunter stalking an animal, knowing that one mistake would send it running.

"You will be given a telephone to enable you to call that wife of yours. Make it simple and to the point. It will be monitored, Barrington. I don't want to hear any elaborate explanation, nor any phrases that could be thought of as a code. Plain language and short. Do you understand?"

With the first recording tape safely tucked inside his jacket pocket, Dicky walked for a while with an armed escort a few paces behind and his car slowly following the two of them. Light rain was falling as the sun broke through the clouds, but he hardly noticed.

Late Wednesday In New York

Chapter Thirty

Negotiations

"It was when I read that list that I realised how important the now named Stockford family would become if the birth of an illegitimate daughter of the Duke of Windsor was ever known to fanatics following the idealism of the Nazi movement."

"Do you think it is known, Jack? I asked, still dazed by morphine and news of my father, as well as heady from the cigarette smoke.

"I honestly can't be sure."

"How come my father gave you a sight of the copy and not his commanding officer?"

"You would have to ask him that as I have no answer other than it was through a sense of patriotism and a belief in the good of our country."

Hello there! Captain Harry West I presume. I'm Jack Price. Come to see about a German Colonel you interned to Camp 12 and who was murdered the other night. Yes, he was murdered alright. I'm attached to Special Operations Executive based in London but working over here trying to clear up any loose ends. I understand you paid a visit to your HQ in Rome a few weeks back. My boss was wondering if that visit had anything to do with this murder.

We researched his name you see, seems that he was on Rudolf Hess's staff at the beginning of the war. I'm not sure you would be aware of this, but Hess defected to us about four years ago spouting a cock-and-bull story about some of his lot and some of ours wanting a peace treaty before it all got as ugly as it did. This Colonel didn't mention that to you, did he, and that's why you went to Rome? Before you answer let me assure you of something that may have crossed your mind. I'm not military, nor is what I do connected to any military unit. My department's role is purely of a national interest nature. The suppression of dubious assumptions would come under our remit, as would the prosecution of treasonable acts. Sorry if that sounds a little heavy, but other research we were able to do showed that Squadron Leader Finley and the man whose estate Hess parachuted onto are old acquaintances. We wouldn't want to think that either of you might have unwittingly stumbled into something that you cannot adequately deal with yourself. Or, perish the thought, you are both part of a plot to withhold the truth!

There is, of course, another scenario. If this colonel had something embarrassing to Finley's friend, like a list of names, and that's what led to his murder then who knows where that might stop. Probably it's all just coincidental, but you know what intelligence gathering can do to a person, you end up seeing a conspiracy around every corner, don't you. My boss and I would hate to see such an intuitive and honest man as yourself get caught up in any internal conflicts when it comes to demob day, nor do we want you to rat on your commanding officer.

The war in Europe is over, with the one going on in the Pacific finishing soon, so, your job in Italy will very quickly be null and void. It would be terribly unjust to label you as uncooperative over a matter of national security and thereby slur a previously unblemished military record. I would urge you to be honest over any list. It would be for the greater good if you did, Harry. My boss is a far from unreasonable man. He has instructed me to offer you a life-long position in the War Department or the Ministry of Defence if you're ever in the need of one. Always room for a true patriot as yourself. Did that late colonel leave anything with you?

"I've got to ask you this, Jack, because it's intriguing me. There you are, one of only three people still alive in 1945 who could possibly know that our one time king had fathered a child, and then later in the same year being one of only a handful having a list of names that had wanted to undermine Britain. Is that about right?"

"I'm not that good at sums, but yes, I guess you're not that far off, Shaun."

"Did you ever think of extorting money from any of those who stood to lose so much?"

"Why, is that what you would have done, resorted to blackmail?"

"I honestly don't know. What you had must have been highly volatile dynamite to some."

"Yes, if any of it could have been proven, but I'm not in that sort of game. I work with rumours and hearsay. Seldom do I deal with truth, as the people I mix with wouldn't know what that is. I'm a collector, as I said. I deal in what might result from actions taken by others."

"So you gave the list that my father gave you to your boss, Jack."

"I did!"

"That brings me to another intriguing question that's on my mind. Who exactly is your boss, Jack, because it's not the head of any intelligence service in the UK is it."

"I told you that I resigned from British intelligence. Barrington Trenchard was responsible for that. He showed me the depth of incompetence in the service that I'd tried hard to gloss over."

"What happened to the names on that list, Jack, and was Trenchard one of them?" He had that *I know all the answers and you know none and I won't tell you until I'm ready* look on his face. He supplied no answer.

"To use your phrase of not getting too far ahead of ourselves, can I recap on last Friday's tour of Soho, Jack?"

"I'm yours to enthral, Shaun."

"As Edward Heath was a figment of your imagination, Jack, or so you say, is Miller really on the take?"

"Yes, he is and so are many more in the Metropolitan Police, I'm sorry to say," Jack replied.

"How about this Alhambra bloke? Does he exist?"

"He does, but not under that name. That was the name given to his file by *5*. He comes in at the end of my story, so I'd prefer to speak of him later."

"The end, you say. When does that come about, and am I included at the end or do I make up part of that end?"

London Mid Tuesday Morning

"Well, this had better be good, Dicky. The Prime Minister has enough on his plate without any controversy surrounding Scotland Yard's head of criminal intelligence being kept in The Tower for subversion. I'm not sure what would take precedence in the newspapers; Trenchard's arrest or that of Arthur Scargill and his coalminers. The Trade Unions will topple this government if we're not careful and then what will you get, a bunch of quasi-Communists under Harold Wilson and his socialite alter ego Roy Jenkins. Yours will be one of the first departments to be shafted. No need for international security when the Labour Commies are in Number Ten!

Are you in with all this Peter? Writing the script alongside Sir Richard, or have you been stuttering through this garbage like me?" Martin Redman held aloft the hastily stapled report that Dicky had garnered on his flying visit to Century House. He had slept, but uncomfortably, for three hours on his office sofa bed before his secretary's arrival and the awakening chimes of his ever present desk alarm. Peter Rawlings, Secretary of Defence, muttered, "all new to me Home Secretary," then proceeded to look interestedly at page seven of the report.

"Anything you wish to elaborate on from that page, Dicky?" Martin asked.

"Which page, Minister?" Sir Richard replied, lost in thought.

"Page seven of course. The number's at the top."

The meeting of the three men was held in the lead-lined security capsule suspended from floor and ceiling by insulated carbon steel wires in a sub-basement approximately eighty foot below Parliament Street. The retractable staircase had been withdrawn and now lay flush with the floor.

"No! That's all part of Ughert's appraisal of the situation, Minister."

"I trust you have more than mere thoughts, Richard. Could this affect the Government?" Martin asked.

"The Government?" Dicky screwed up his lips as if he had tasted something unpleasant. "Hmm, I think not, but the House of Windsor and all that entails then yes, possibly. If that then impacted on HMG, who can say." His eyes fell to the metal table as Peter looked at Martin and all three fell silent.

"Does any of this reflect on the Queen directly, Richard?" The Home Secretary broke the impasse.

"Yes, Minister, it could. If, as we suspect, Mountbatten is one of the leading conspirators then that drags in Philip and as a consequence Her Majesty."

"Tricky situation all round. You say that you believe this man Stiles to be in America, although you don't give any reasons for the belief. Could we not enlist the FBI to either confirm or rebuff that belief? If you're right then they would be able to tell us of to his movements and who he's in contact with."

"We could, Minister, but it would take them some time to accumulate useful information. However, I would warn against requesting their intervention. We would be better placed to handle this predicament away from the press without their participation. The American agencies do tend to be a bit press-orientated and theatrical on occasions."

The Home Secretary nodded his head in agreement to Dicky's truism as another question was asked of Sir Richard.

"Do you know who Stiles intends to contact in New York?" It was Peter who asked this question.

"I'm pretty confident on that score, yes. I expect some results by this afternoon. It is *Group's* analysis that there is an outside chance that a British operative is in place and handling this affair."

"Outside chance! Are you saying that there's an agent that you know nothing of, Richard?" Martin drew first blood.

"Do you know this operative personally, and if so is he a friendly?" Peter opened the wound further.

"I know of him," Richard wearily replied. "As far as I'm aware he is certainly not anti-British, nor would I add are any others in this whole mare's nest that we face. However, *Group* and I firmly believe that his first allegiance lies with the Palace and not us."

"Is 5 involved?" the Home Secretary asked whilst looking to find any reference to General John in Dicky's report. He found none.

"No, sir. Neither do I think it wise to include them. I discussed this with both Sir Archibald and the head of the Civil Service. You were out, Minister when I called on him. The fewer people who know about this the easier it will be to clear it away."

Martin Redman raised no objection. In fact he was pleased that the decision had been taken in his absence.

"Has the time arrived for a ministerial briefing of the PM with a visit to the Court of St James in mind, Richard?" Martin asked, thinking ahead towards repercussions.

"I think I can avoid that at the moment, Minister. There are a few cards to play before that would be my recommendation."

"What's to become of Trenchard?" Peter Rawlings enquired.

"I want to hold him until at least the beginning of next week. A week could prove to be a long time in this matter. After that I wash my hands of him. I cannot see how a public scandal of this dimension would benefit anyone. My suggestion would be early retirement through ill health, a signed declaration of silence from him in return for a full pension with the stringent denial of any frills such as knighthoods or the like." He paused whilst the enormity of the situation was fully digested by the two others before continuing.

"There is one other thing. I would be very grateful if you, Peter, could delve into a little matter that the Ministry of Defence are probably in a better position to do than my own department."

"Is that another confession, Sir Richard? Do you mean to say that your tentacles stop at someone's door that you should have the key to?" Peter always reverted to sarcasm when the chance arose and Dicky was well aware of it.

"No, that's not what I'm saying at all. I'm being courteous and nothing more, Minister. Up until recently there was a Harry West working at a desk in the War Department. As that falls within your area of responsibility I was hoping you would supply details of his work interest to my department without the need of us circumnavigating your in-house regulations and come crashing through your front door! I wanted to divert responsibility away from you." Dicky sat back with a stony stare on his face.

"Of course, Richard. We can do that for you," Peter replied, sensing that now was not an occasion for hilarity.

The Home Secretary was becoming impatient. For the last eleven consecutive Tuesday mornings he had allowed himself the indulgence of a creamed waffle followed by a strong cup of heavily sugared coffee to wash it down. He suffered from high blood pressure that normally forbade such treats. Those last eleven Tuesdays were different. No longer was there a Mrs Redman to prevent his childhood favourites returning to his diet. She had left him on a Tuesday, finding, as she announced in the note she'd left him, a more thoughtful man to care for.

Why do I have to take notice of her anymore? he would volunteer to anyone who mentioned his dalliance from not only her more circumspect dietary regime, but also away from her stereotypical unimaginative bedroom control. He wound the meeting up in expectation of sweeter things.

"If the condition remains unsettled we shall reconvene here next Monday morning at ten am. By then I hope you will have discovered more details allowing me to decide on Trenchard's fate. Keep him well hidden until then, Sir Richard." At that he pressed the floor-mounted, black, round button for the staircase to ascend and when secure, they left the capsule.

At the foot of the stairs Martin Redman waved Peter away, taking Dicky's arm and whispering conspiratorially into his ear.

"Are there no records of this Harry West, Dicky?"

"None that we can find, Minister."

"Are you preparing to shove your umbrella of blame up poor old Peter's backside?" the Minister asked.

"I would say that if there were blame to lay for missing documents the ultimate responsibility would rest at the Home Office, Minister. I'm trying to avoid opening umbrellas up anywhere. Trenchard is in my view beyond saving, sir. He has been in the wrong places too many times for my or anyone's satisfaction not to escape blame, but it's in no one's interests to hang him high in the public view. I believe what is going on in America at this moment is beyond his knowledge. However, that makes it much harder to deal with. All I can do is mitigate and manage the effects. That will require some drastic and unorthodox measures, Home Secretary. One further consideration you should take into account is that if we are too heavy-handed in this, the Palace will cover their backs with anything they can find. Trenchard will be dumped on your doorstep which by implication will muddy General John's."

"Take whatever action you think best, no matter what. No rules. But I want all this tucked away behind the highest screens possible, Richard. You do understand that, don't you?"

"Only too well I do, Minister."

New York

"I can't understand why you're so fatalistic, Shaun. I'm a serious judge of talent. I know a good one when I find one. I've given you one of the best cover stories that has ever been devised yet you still have doubts."

"I was found though, Jack, wasn't I?"

"Not because of the cover, Shaun, because of the operation! That happens at times."

"But which cover is going to save my life? Patrick West doesn't exist over here and Shaun Redden is linked into the mess. Where should I go for the next one?"

"You'll never need another one. Shaun Redden cannot be traced conclusively. No living parents, no relatives, no friends, no ties, nobody looking under paving slabs to discover his past. Can you see the similarity with your real identity? The two of you are the same." Pleased with himself, he sat back into his chair, then continued with his eulogy. "You're so good that I've recommended your name be pencilled in as my successor. You're a natural. When this operation is all over I'm retiring. Sorry, meant no pun with the operation reference. Toes and all that! Anyway, spent enough years away on behalf of someone else's business. Time to read a book and watch the world pass by before I'm too senile to enjoy it. I'm too old now, Shaun, and well past my best. Do you know how to tell that you're getting old, Shaun?"

"No!" I replied with as much enthusiasm as a young child would have when being regaled a story from an aged relative in which there is no interest.

"When a young lady, who is ahead of you in the queue at the bus stop, waves you to pass her when the bus arrives."

"Never thought of you travelling by bus, Jack. Thought you'd be a limousine passenger when on the move."

"And I never realised that you were such a snob, Shaun. I do a lot of my best thinking aboard buses. By the by, I'm becoming more fond of the name we gave you rather than your real name. Prefer Shaun to that of Pat. Ah, perhaps I'll write in for the Poet Laureate's job when I retire after that rhyme of mine," he laughed, but I didn't share in his humour.

"Are you sure that you want me and not Adam Berman? Is his name not on the shortlist, Jack?"

"There you are, you see. My faith in your ability was not misplaced. What do you know of Adam?" Jack asked.

"Only what you're willing to tell me, Jack."

"I can go one better than that, my boy, but first get some much needed sleep. You're perfectly safe here. Salvatore's men are outside the building and down the corridor. Believes in safety first, does Sally. Tomorrow you'll meet Adam, and the two of us will fill in all the missing details which will answer most of the questions you're dying to ask. Exciting times ahead, eh! By the way, there is something you could be doing whilst you're lazing around here." He passed me a piece of lined writing paper with the names of some chemical components written upon it.

"Have a look at these, while I'm gone. See if you can come up with the same answer that we have. It will give you something else to concentrate on instead of just your injuries."

Chapter Thirty-One

Reputations

Sister Monica Kelly, my surgeon-cum-nurse, arrived seconds after Jack departed. If I believed in conspiracies then she could have been eavesdropping in the next room waiting for her appearance cue. As it was, I neither suspected any conspiring nor questioned her motives. For perhaps the first time since arriving in New York I was in the company of someone who I did not feel threatened, intimated by or thought was a liar. She was charming, efficient and apparently cared.

"I've had the initial blood test back and there is no infection, but I will take another blood sample tonight to monitor that, Mr Redden. I expect you're feeling a bit weak and disorientated, but that's nothing to worry about. The stitches in your foot will have to remain for at least ten days during which time you'll probably find a walking frame useful and less cumbersome than crutches. After all's mended it will be more comfortable to wear a reinforced shoe or boot. I'm afraid one of the expensive shoes you were wearing when you were shot had to be cut away. When I get the time I will ask one of the burly men outside to supply you with that frame. They look as though they could get you absolutely anything, one way or another. I'm hoping to remove the splint by the weekend. For now I'm going to give you a sedative to ensure you sleep and don't get out of bed and overdo things. I don't want you smoking or speaking too much. Walking will feel awkward until you get used to the block, or something similar, fitted into a shoe. But no footwear until those stitches are out. I'll get one of my brother's men to get that frame."

"By that, do I take it that Salvatore is your brother?"

"I thought you knew," she declared in surprise.

"I didn't. No! You don't even have much of an Italian accent to your voice. There's a trace now that you've told me, but not really noticeable."

"I took on another surname when I joined the order. It was better to distance myself from what he does. I didn't have such a tough time as he did when I arrived here. He had it hard. He still dislikes strangers. I understand the gentleman that's just left helped him out with one or two things. It's complicated, Mr Redden."

"Were you in Italy during the war with your brother, Monica?"

"Yes, I was in Italy, but not with Salvatore. He was in the army."

"On the wrong side, I presume?"

"There were only two choices open to any man in those times: the side of Mussolini and Hitler, or death by the firing squads. When the Allies landed in Scilly he was drafted back to Italy from the Balkans. Things started to change after the standoff at Cassino. The subsequent amphibious attack on Anzio opened the road to Rome. Salvatore was stationed south of that attack. When the Italian soldiers were caught between the two-pronged attack of the Allies, true Italians turned on the Germans. My brother was one of the leaders of that revolt."

"Did Jack, the man who just left, help your brother to leave Italy as well as settle in here?"

"That's for either Salvatore or your man to tell, Mr Redden, not me." She had her back to me, preparing the syringe.

"I met a niece of yours a few days ago when I changed my hair colouring. Bit of a tyrant that one, not as polite, nor as gentle, as yourself, I have to say."

"I heard about it. Salvatore was full of himself when he told me. You gave as good as she did, I understand. She can be very much like her father that one, bombastic and overwhelming, but there's a good heart somewhere. Maybe I'll find it one day. Let's find a vein for this sedative, shall we?" She tapped lightly on my arm until one met her approval for the insertion of the needle.

"Where am I exactly?" I asked.

She sighed heavily before replying. "If your colleague has not told you then there must be a reason that I can only wonder at. You shouldn't be asking me to take on the responsibility of telling you something that he obviously won't."

"You won't tell me?" I asked, astonished.

"I was not asked to, Mr Redden. I do what I'm asked and no more. It is said that all of life is a test, perhaps, this is another one in your life that you've come across."

"If you won't answer that one, would you answer this? Why did you treat me in the first place? You must have been suspicious."

"During my life I've seen many men shot for what they believed in that someone else didn't. I've never judged a wounded man by his beliefs, I can only see the injuries. I understand that life is not always as straightforward as we would want it to be, nor what the law states it should be. Some of the things the 'law' allows to happen are morally wrong. Evil should never be assessed by legality. My brother doesn't ask me to do anything illegal. He asks that I'm here for his friends when the morality of their actions is better off not being addressed by legal agencies. God accepts sinners into Heaven as well as saints, so why can't both be treated without prejudice? Now don't you go fussing over things you don't need to worry about. Just relax and take the next few days easy. Besides, it's raining outside so you're in the best place. Nice and warm and dry. Very humid out there. Shall I put that paper you're clinging onto somewhere safe, Mr Redden, as it's time for you to fall asleep?"

"No, I need to put it under my pillows," I pleaded then explained.

"When I was at university, cramming all manner of things into my head, I used to put books or the papers I was reading under my pillow at night believing that the words would jump off the pages and into my brain when I was sleeping."

"Did it work?" she asked.

"I did pass most exams, but you'd have to open up my brain and see what's there to completely answer that one. Don't go planning any visits to neurosurgeons without asking me first though, will you. I'd like to keep my head on if that's okay with you." As she took my arm in readiness, I asked my final question.

"What is that smell I keep breathing, Monica?"

"It's burning frankincense, mixed with holy oil. Can you fathom out where you might be now, Mr Redden?" She was smiling as she slid the hypodermic needle into me.

London

Just before midday that Tuesday, the second request Dicky made after ordering black coffee was for his doctor. Top civil servants, along with senior government officials, although having their own medical practitioners provided for them also have the advantage of being able to call upon a staff of standing medical doctors supplied from the public purse on call twenty-fours a day, seven days a week. All those doctors were covered by the same Hippocratic Oath sworn by their civilian counterparts. The only trouble was that their oath did not apply to internal government-driven investigations. No ethical secrets were safe if the doors were being knocked down by sledgehammers wielded by employees of the security services. While he was waiting for the duty doctor to return his secretary's call he telephoned Fraser.

"I need two things at the moment, Fraser. As quickly as you can, old fruit. One would be the chasing up on Peter Rawlings at the MOD over anything he may have on a Captain Harry West. *Group* have all the details on that one. Make sure that when he comes back having found nothing you stress just how disappointed I will be. Lay it on strongly, please. Second; I need Daniel Cardiff here in my office a.s.a.p. How is he by the way? Heard anything this morning regarding Echo?"

"Mr A and wife left straight after breakfast. He kept his word over paying for the room and bites, so accounts won't be raising hell over any expenses spent on this one, sir. My first lady left about ten-thirty with her handbag full of the usual souvenirs from the bathroom and Cardiff called in half an hour or so later. I'm told he was near to tears, sir. He's in an anteroom of our Lambeth building. We've fed him and drowned him in tea. Seems to have recovered his composure somewhat. Shall I courier the photographs over, sir?"

"I want the negatives as well, but I also want you to do something for me first. Find out from the Palace what's in our subject's diary for today. Use the Home Secretary's name for that. Give me a call as soon as you find out about that."

"I will try, sir, but those at the Palace make me feel so uncomfortable if ever I have to speak to them. Can't we get the Home Secretary to enquire?"

"I wish I could, Fraser, but that's out of the question at the moment," Dicky replied.

Twenty minutes later he phoned *Group*. Sir Archibald took his call.

"I've instructed Ughert to put Cardiff on this evening's flight to New York. An hour or so ago I gave GCHQ the name of a Haynes Baxter-Clifford who we believe may have some connection with the IRA. Joseph reliably informed me that he'll be able to work something up at his end in order to monitor the situation. I want Cardiff on the ground as our contact if we need first-hand information of collaboration. There's one other thing that you can help with me. I need the file drawn on an operation I was caught up in way back in 1946; name of *Agatha*." Sir Archibald interrupted.

"Palestine issue was it not? Montgomery thought it up after some Zionist underground organisations had blown up several bridges. Were you there, Dicky?"

"In a very minor capacity, Archie, I was, yes. How do you know of it?"

"I was on Monty's staff at the time. A humble captain in the Royal Ulster Rifles. We were being amalgamated with two other regiments and I seemed surplus to requirements, so they shunted me off to him." Archie gave a self-deprecating laugh at his modesty.

"Sadly my memory is not as good as your own, Archie, otherwise I wouldn't be asking," Dicky replied curtly, far from being in a jocular mood. "There was a chap I ran into during that escapade who worked in our High Commissioner's Office. I'm afraid I need reminding of his name. Could you get someone to delve into it and send me a list of those attached to Cunningham at the time?"

"Of course! I'll get someone on it at once. I must, however, question that decision of yours to use Cardiff so soon and on such an assignment, Dicky. Have you no one in situ that could do the job? Can't you use the New York station? And another thing, Cardiff has no cover whatsoever. He will get made as soon as he steps off the plane. If not then, as soon as he opens his mouth. He's never been in the field before." *Exactly*, Dicky thought, but never voiced that opinion.

"He'll be fine after the doctor I've sent for sees him, Archie. I'll wrap him in a blanket of goodwill for good measure. You won't forget Joseph at the doughnut, now will you? Just give him another nudge."

"I will, Dicky. Leave it with me."

He just had time to take a tablet for his drowsiness and a quick shower before his secretary called.

"The duty doctor will be about fifteen minutes, sir, and a Daniel Cardiff is pulling into the underground carpark as we speak. Is there anything I can do whilst you are waiting for the medical officer?"

"Ply me with coffee until he's here and interrupt my meeting with him after about three minutes with an urgent message that needs my immediate attention, Louise. Knock and enter with that news, please."

"Cardiff is in the lift, sir, and I have GCHQ on hold. Will you take their call, or shall I tell them you will return their call after your meeting?"

"Put them through and hold Cardiff until the security light goes green, then show him straight in."

Daniel Cardiff was twenty-five-years-of-age, over six foot tall with brown hair, hazel coloured eyes and of presentable appearance. There was nothing handsome nor ugly about him, neither was there anything physical that distinguished him from most of the other young men that were recruited into the subversive world of espionage, but there was something that separated him from a lot of that pack. He had found a home at *Group* through patronage, not from the divine summons of an enlisting agent.

"I knew your uncle, Admiral Sir Maurice Curtis, Daniel. Fine man indeed!" Dicky lied as he rose from behind his desk to greet Cardiff. After exchanging a handshake he continued.

"I hope you realise just what a huge contribution you've made to this department. If it were possible for me to publicly acknowledge your dedication then believe me, I would, but that's an impossibility as I'm sure you know."

Dicky guided his guest to one of the soft armchairs that stood beside his well-stocked mahogany drinks cabinet in front of a window overlooking St Thomas' Hospital and Big Ben, the other side of Westminster Bridge.

"Would you like a drink Daniel? Tea or alcohol? Your choice?"

"I'm okay, sir, but thank you for your kind words and the offer."

He was far from okay, thought Dicky, taking the other chair, trying to hide his disgust at what had happened to the decency behind the ashen face that stared starry eyed in his direction.

"Was this your first assignment, Daniel?" Dicky asked, knowing full well that it was.

"It was, sir. Now I'm worried that having done what I did it will be on my file as a trademark if you understand what I mean. It was my first time with a man, sir, and something I don't want to repeat. I do want to get on in this job that I know my family orchestrated for me but, well, I guess I'm stuck with the reputation now, aren't I?"

"Your good name is not tarnished in my office! Your reputation as a devoted member of *Group* is firmly cemented in my mind, young man. However, I'm afraid that there is one more painful ordeal that I have to ask you to undertake, but this one is for your own welfare. In a few minutes the in-house doctor is to arrive. I want him to thoroughly examine you. I'm told that there are various diseases attributed to anal sex that can be treated successfully if diagnosed early. He'll take some blood samples and ask a few questions. That's all, nothing to worry about, but I would advise that you make a clean breast of what exactly occurred."

"Am I finished in field work, sir?" Cardiff asked, leaning forward in his chair, directing his gaze towards Dicky's shoes.

"Very far from it, young man. You're just starting. In fact you are to go to New York this afternoon as my eye's on the ground in an operation we might be running over there. On leaving here you're to report directly back to Fraser's department. He is processing all the necessary paperwork now. You will have plenty of time during the flight to assess the information he'll give you. There are two simple rules to follow once you are over there. One: if someone contacts you, never invite that person into to your room. Always, and I stress this, Daniel, always meet in a public place for the first time. Second: never open your hotel room door to anyone who is not staff of that hotel. Tell them you're taking a shower and you'll be ten minutes or so. Then get a name and meet in the lobby. There you are. Easy enough to follow, now have a brandy with me. I'm having one. Won't you join me?"

"I'm not a queer, sir, if that's what's everyone is thinking," Cardiff blurted out as he began to cry.

"It never crossed my mind that you were," Dicky replied honestly, adding, "Make sure you tell the duty doctor that, Daniel, it will help in the long run."

Chapter Thirty-Two

Trelew

The doctor had left Dicky's office by the time Fraser Ughert telephoned at 12:43.

"Apparently our subject is a man of fastidious routine, sir. Every other Tuesday afternoon he has his haircut at three-fifteen at Truefitt & Hill, the barbers at the Palace end of St James's Street then takes a cab to Waterloo Station catching the four-eighteen to Weybridge. He's due his fortnightly trim today. We are not in possession of any facts regarding the Weybridge end. I think it's either got to happen in St James's Street or at Waterloo. If it's an immediate reaction you're after then it has to be the barbers. That way we can almost guarantee his return to St James's Palace for a secure line. We could lose him at Waterloo, and Weybridge would be too loose for my liking."

"Give me a moment," Dicky replied, then placed the telephone receiver on his desk beside the framed photograph of the Queen. At that moment Daniel Cardiff rose from his chair and made to leave the office.

"No, not you, young man. I was addressing the man on the phone. You stay where you are for the time being."

Sir Richard walked to his window, looked out, then muttered, "Okay, here we go." Cardiff, although now seated, again moved. "Stop being so jumpy, dear boy. You have a role to play and nerves to keep in check."

Dicky did not sit. He spoke to Fraser standing and peering into the space before his view.

"This is what I want done, Fraser, to the letter, mind you, and no deviation. You find the most unnoticeable employee in the building and give him an unfolded photo in a sealed addressed envelope and enough money for some cab rides. First he takes a taxi to St Paul's where he alights, then walks for a few minutes down Ludgate Hill into Fleet Street. Once there he hails another taxi. He gives the envelope to this cab driver and demands that it's delivered into our lord's hands. Tell him to make absolute sure that it's for the addressee only; no one else. Not the receptionist nor a barber, but Lord Beaufort himself! I want this done when our man is in the chair. I also want someone outside the premises to make sure it's all gone smoothly. Oh yes, one other thing. On the front of the envelope write, *From a close friend. For your immediate and earnest attention.* Is all that quite clear, old fruit?" He raised his eyebrows in the direction of where Cardiff was sitting as if asking him the question he posed to Fraser. Cardiff fashioned a subservient smile in response.

"Perfectly, sir," Fraser replied confidently.

"And the tickets, etc, all dealt with?"

"Yes, they are. We've booked him on the six-thirty flight this evening. British Overseas Airways of course. Then I've placed him in the St. Regis Hotel. There's a dossier he can study on the flight of known IRA fundraisers, makes boring reading material but it gets him started. I followed your instructions regarding his passport. You were right to check, as he never had one. We pushed the buttons and had it issued an hour ago in his name. All we're waiting for now is Cardiff himself, sir. I've laid on a police escort for him to the airport. That should put a smile on his face."

"Champion stuff, Fraser. While you're on the line get that messenger of yours to fetch me the first three hours' tape recordings of our man in those dwellings of yours. Has our man mentioned any more about Jack, do you know?"

"Not to my knowledge, sir. We've been concentrating his mind on his middle years in the service as you requested. Would you like us to take his mind back a few?"

"No, that's not necessary at this moment. I'm sending our young hero back to you any minute now. Fax Louise that hotel address, would you. We might need to reach out to him whilst he's there. He'll need to go home to gather somethings together before being taken to Heathrow. Can I leave that in your capable hands?"

On getting confirmation that all could be done, Dicky turned to Cardiff.

"Right you're all fixed up. Police outriders all the way. You will remember those names I've written down for you, won't you?"

"Yes, sir. Salvatore Guigamo and Jack Price," Cardiff replied without looking at the sheet of paper Dicky had handed him.

"Good boy! Guigamo you'll probably find listed in a telephone book. Could be many, of course, so it might take you a while. Price, on the other hand, could be easier. Never known to use an alias. The photograph I'm giving you is out of date, but I doubt he'll have changed much. There is another man, much more recognisable. His picture I've included in that pack." Dicky pointed to the buff envelope that rested in Cardiff's hands.

"Has an unmissable scar on his face and goes by the biblical name of Job. By the look of him I wouldn't have thought that patience was his strongest point. Right then, we'll take one last brandy to wish you well on this adventure of yours, young man, then it's off you go. All system green as they say on the TV." He poured two small glasses.

"Down in one, dear boy. Here's to you in America! Sorry, but I think I forgot something," Dicky announced, replacing his glass on the tray on the cabinet.

"Of course, how silly of me to forget. Find a minute to call whoever it is you're supposed to work for at the Ag and Fish. Spin them a line about a member of the family popping off unexpectedly. You're taking a spell of leave to grieve, give solace and all that paraphernalia."

"I will, sir, but I'm not sure I'm due any leave yet. I've only been there a month or two."

"Minor details, dear boy. There must be some regulation in the Civil Service handbook that allows for compassionate absence from duty. Leave that to the mandarins to worry about."

"There is another thing that crossed my mind, sir." Dicky gave him his avuncular look, but was becoming anxious in regards to time.

"Fire away, Cardiff."

"Is the department that is looking after me providing a cover name and legend, or is *Group* doing that?" Cardiff asked Dicky apologetically.

"I really don't know who's in charge of that, but I'm sure someone's on to it. Might take a few days to be absolutely positive it's the right one for you though. Don't worry, there's no need. You have my assurance that even if you travel under your own name all will be fine. We can always paint a picture for you when you're in place. Time's of the essence, young man. You had better get your skates on if you're to catch your flight."

Ten seconds after Cardiff left, Dicky was on the telephone again. He dialled the direct number of The Foreign and Commonwealth Office linking him to his boss, the Foreign Minister, Charles Matkins; deputy head of the Joint Intelligence Committee.

"An hour ago, Charles, we had a 'heads up' from the NSA listening station at Bad Aibling, in Germany. There's been unusual activity at Trelew, in Argentina. We have exclusivity on that for the next two hours before other agencies are informed. I have just received confirmation from Sir Joseph Walters at GCHQ and forwarded the communique to Group."

"Sounds intriguing, but isn't there always something odd happening in Argentina. Come to that, in the whole of South America. Always a revolution or forced change of government going on somewhere. To be perfectly honest, Dicky, the whole region is one big melting pot of insurrection and unrest. There is some highly jingoistic rhetoric being monitored at the moment about the Falkland Islands. Nothing will come of it, of course, but there's mention of possible retrievable oil reserves and one never knows when there's revenue involved. The intricacies of world politics are perplexing to say the least, Dicky. Can't say I've heard of Trelew though."

"The Foreign and Commonwealth Office were briefed in 1945 and then again in '53. I have the relevant papers on my desk, Minister."

Always best to be respectful when administering a reprimand to a senior, Dicky would often advise his close family adding the over-rider – *especially if you are peddling a lie.*

"What the file's name, Dicky, I'll get a runner to search for it."

"Sorry, Minister, I've no idea how the Civil Service at the FO store their data. Ours is number O78JZ9/Reich."

"Don't like that word, Reich, Dicky. Would you kindly elaborate, please?" Matkins asked uncomfortably.

"Certainly, Charles." Confident in the knowledge that the Foreign Secretary would not go looking for a non-existent dossier, Dicky began to elaborate as requested.

"In the first directive, dated the twelfth of June 1945, the Foreign and Commonwealth Office were notified that an ex-Nazi chemical engineer had informed our counterparts in the CIA of a varied assemblage of Nazis who had been smuggled out of German at the war's end. The CIA along with numbers from my department verified this in the July of that year. They were, in the words of one American agent, openly parading around federal offices in Buenos Aires obviously among friends!

"The 1953 report was commissioned by the then Foreign Minister, Lord Rennie. It detailed additions to the community and most importantly, it advocated the site's surveillance to be handed over to the Israelis. In essence, we wiped our hands of it." Dicky held the telephone away from his mouth and counted to five. "I firmly believe, Charles, that had you been in office in 1953 you would have reacted differently. By reading between the lines it's my appraisal that the Americans were applying pressure on Rennie in order to appease the State of Israel. You would have stood stronger on the issue than Rennie did, Minister, and refused Mossad meddling in affairs best dealt with by us."

Never harms to flatter someone whose bank account you're just about to raid.

"That's all well and good, Dicky, but what's the point of this conversation?"

"The point, Minister, is that all known Nazis previously pinpointed by the two directives I've quoted from, were rounded up and shot in a prison camp at a place named Trelew earlier today. Both GCHQ, at my department's behest, and the NSA have been working in tandem having permanent ears on the situation since '53. Eleven days ago a known Mossad agent arrived in the capital of Argentina and hooked up with a team already on the ground. I was told that he went up country and we left it there. Not on our priority roster, or likely to be. Because," Dicky repeated his previous procedure of counting to five, "we had no direct instructions from your office. What we had, was wiped from the operations board in 1953."

"You've put me on a spot, haven't you, Dicky. No doubt that's what you intended. Look, if I comment on the existence of right-wing fanatics in Argentina I'm tantamount to confirming our duplicity in this. Argentina are on the *friends* list and not yet on the uninvited guests one, although that may change at any moment. There is a military regime in that country who support whatever suits them. Their allegiance changes with the wind, Dicky. Can you cover the fact that we knew about this group of Nazis?"

"I can ask the CIA to block forwarding it on to other partners most certainly, Charles, and the Israelis are highly unlikely to admit their knowledge of the whereabouts of escaped Nazis for so many years without acting on that knowledge, so yes, I believe I can silence it all, but that brings me to another discussion I must have with you. A rather delicate one, Charles, involving a man of noble rank. I want it kept strictly between you and me, Charles, you understand."

"I fear the worst. Are you about to coerce me into something, Dicky?"

"Only for your own good, Minister, and that of the Government in general. You have my word on that."

"I hope I'm not going to regret this, Sir Richard. Where do you propose having this conversation?"

Within ten minutes of replacing the telephone receiver Dicky was driving into King Charles Street in the back of the blacked out London taxi cab he had taken from the car pool at Century House. Charles Matkin joined him seconds later. It took three circumferences of St James's Park for the Foreign Secretary to be fully cognisant of the severity facing Dicky and as a consequence; his government. He raised no objections to the plan he was presented with.

On Dicky's return he dialled *Group's* extension.

"Archie, I need a huge favour, but first I have a few questions for you." Not waiting for a response, he ploughed on. "First: was it Trenchard who told you that Price was active in London or someone from his section in Scotland Yard?"

"It came directly from him, Dicky."

"And did he speak with you or someone on your staff?"

"Not me, I'm afraid. Called at 19:17 and left a message for the duty officer's log. I was notified at home that night."

"What were his words to your duty officer?"

"Only that he needed me to call him."

"Okay, fine. My next question then. Who did your man follow after Price and West parted last Friday?"

"I detailed two watchers from *burners*. They followed them both, but I had no others on the ground for a full scale alert. Had I have done so then we wouldn't have lost contact with Price overnight. Both men decided to stay *eyes on* each entrance. There was no other option open to them."

"Yes, I appreciate that. I wasn't aiming blame anywhere. And where did West live? I don't know why I've never asked that question before, didn't seem important and I'm not sure if it is now, but nevertheless?" He never finished that sentence.

"Are you okay, Dicky?" Sir Archibald asked his old friend, concerned.

"Yes, I am. Sounding a bit tired and stressed, am I? It's just that I believe time is running short for what I must do."

"Does clairvoyance run in your family, Dicky?" Archie asked.

"Why?"

"West walked to a residential building in Covent Garden. Number six, Rose Street, which he entered and stayed the night. At approximately eight-ten Saturday morning he left that building and went to the Home Office, via the twenty-four-hour post office in Trafalgar Square. After that he reported to Trenchard's place in Suffolk Street. I'm reading that report from my screen. I'll tell you why that's so. Three minutes ago GCHQ flashed the name *Eva* to the Foreign and Commonwealth Office and every SIS department's communications system. General John has been on the blower asking for my breakdown. That's why my screen is lit up. *Eva* apparently is the code name SIS gave to a Viennese Jew named Alain Aberman back in 1945. I'm working on the reasons for that, but for now I can tell you that number six Rose Street was owned by a Brian Alaname; an anagram of Alain Aberman. It hit me as you rang."

Sir Richard fell silent, causing Archie to enquire again if he was okay.

"That was his weakness, Archie; cryptic crosswords. He was doing the one in the Times when I bumped into him in the King David Hotel in Tel Aviv. Have you that list I asked for handy? The Agatha one?"

"I have! I was just about to fax it over when *Eva* flashed up. Hold a second and I'll find it."

"You're the expert on anagrams, Archie. Take your time," Dicky replied patiently.

"lan Balearman, is that the Johnny?" Archie shouted down the phone line excitedly.

"That's him! Said he had something big on our Royal Family. Something money couldn't buy!"

"Look Dicky, I'm not sure what's going on here but Matkin's put an embargo on 5 over this *Eva* thing. *Stay off the roundabout in the Playground. It's all 6 until further notice*, was the wording. What shall I tell John?"

"Tell him what Matkin said, Archie. Keep the pseudonyms to ourselves for the time being."

"Fine, you have it. Now what was the favour you wanted?"

"Arh, I'm sorry about this, but I have to, Archie. I asked my head of Section Four to trace an old acquaintance of yours. She came up with her whereabouts, but no means of contact. I'm hoping you will help me with that. It's a favour, old boy, not an order, you understand."

"This sounds ominous, Dicky! Ask away."

"Bridget Slattery. I think we may have need of her."

"As soon as I saw Price's name I wondered how long it would be before she was mentioned. Old wounds, Dicky, very old wounds!"

"Are they healed and mended, old chap? Enough to get your hands burnt again?"

"I'll wear asbestos gloves this time and carry a fire extinguisher." Dicky burst out laughing and inwardly sighed in relief.

"Have you a way of getting in touch?" Dicky asked, hoping against hope that he did.

"There was a way that we had, but I'm not sure that it will still work. I don't know if she gave up looking."

There was someone else Dicky asked to do some searching on his behalf; Catherine Dullas, head of historical research at Section Four had another coded message for her-eyes-only from him.

When I saw Alain Aberman posing as Ian Balearman he must have been in his mid-forties. Search before and after the war and find every name he has ever used.

Tuesday Afternoon London

Chapter Thirty-Three

Shepherd Market

At 3.37 that afternoon Fraser rang Dicky who took the call whilst smoking one of his favourite Cohiba cigars seated in one of his two soft armchairs with the windows wide open onto the street seventeen-storeys below. He had seldom been this nervous.

"Lord Reginald is blowing a gasket, Dicky. He's after blood and Cardiff is his target. He's phoned three ministers and about six permanent under-secretaries looking for him. The Home secretary's number two has rung me twice."

"What's he been telling all that he's phoned for the reason behind his request, Fraser?" he replied calmly from under a cloud of cigar smoke.

"Says the boy has done him a great injustice and he wants recompense. He didn't elaborate on how that would play out. Lionel Phillips, at the Min. of Ag and Fish, was really concerned. Asked me outright if Cardiff had screwed Reginald's wife. I almost burst out laughing at that one."

"Has Lord Reginald left a number where he can be reached, Archie?" Dicky asked.

"Quoted as saying that he won't leave his offices at the Palace until Cardiff is traced and his head is served on a platter."

"Is it an open line that he's on?"

"It's not secure in the sense that you and I know, Dicky."

"Leave him to stew for a while then phone and tell him you're sending a car to pick him up. Take him to that place *Group* has in Shepherd Market. Put him in a room on his own, nice and comfortable with a drink in each hand. Tell me when he's there and I'll take a slow walk over the bridge in the afternoon sunshine and have a chat with the old fellow. When you call inform him of these arrangements, only don't say to whom it is that's he's to speak. If you have to tell him anything say that Cardiff is being delivered. Make sure that any cameras are empty of film, Fraser. I don't want to give him any more problems than he already has. One tape and one tape alone. Another thing whilst you're here. Have you passed on that directive of mine to GCHQ requesting the rerouting of any communiques appertaining to young Cardiff to Special Branch yet?"

After Fraser confirmed his compliance with all of his instructions Dicky telephoned an old friend at the American Embassy in London.

"Good afternoon, Irving! Sorry to be a pest but I wondered if you had found that chap I was looking for yet. I realise your offices must be busy with internal matters, so, if not I'll quite understand."

"As a matter of fact, Sir Richard, we have found him. They came back to me early this morning. Just hadn't gotten around to calling you. He owns a restaurant opposite Columbus Park on Worth Street. Applied for and was granted citizenship in 1945. There is a minor conviction recorded against his name in 1951, but nothing that would warrant our attention. If it's not an indelicate question, why did you need to know?"

"No reason other than nostalgia. We ran into each other at the end of the war in Europe and I have a young friend flying in to New York tonight for a short period of recuperation. He's been under a lot of work-related pressure of late. Wish I could say more, but you know how hairy things can get at times. Added to his burden is the recent loss of a close member of family. It never rains but it pours, as they say. Anyway, my wartime friend's name jumped into my mind from out of the blue. Thought I'd give him my old pal's address to young Cardiff in order to pass on a long belated greeting, and of course one never knows if one might get some decent coffee sent back as a token of friendship. Hands across the water and all that. Thanks for your help in this, much appreciated. If I can ever reciprocate, et cetera, et cetera. Could I be a real pain and ask if you would fax that address to Daniel Cardiff, care of Lionel Phillips MP, Ministry of Agriculture and Fisheries, old sport? Lionel will see that it reaches my friend."

"Did you want a 'meet and greet' reception laid on for him, Sir Richard? I'm sure I could lay that on with a tour of the city thrown in. Mind you if it was yourself we would go the extra yards for sure! Full red carpet, the lot. Wonder why it's a red carpet and not a blue one?" Irving asked, seemingly lost in his own thoughts.

"No, no, no, old chap. Far from necessary. It's only a short break he's taking to regain his confidence. All that fuss and palaver might not be wise. Had a doctor see him earlier today, said he was badly suffering from a stress-related illness and recommended a peaceful break. You know how seriously that can debilitate a chap. I thought of New York and its renowned hospitality, but the lavish entertainment you greet people with is way too much for my young colleague, plus I can't afford to be without him for too long. He's thought very highly of at my end. I can perfectly do without you lot greasing his hands with temptation. That would never do." Dicky left the carpet question for another day.

Sir Richard drew heavily on his cigar in jubilation, the tiredness now replaced by the onset of adventure. He smiled, satisfied in himself. *First parts almost in place. I hope you caught the name, Irving,* silently he reflected.

For the next hour Dicky busied himself in procuring all that he thought he would need for the following day.

Louise was summoned and instructed to find an unused office in the basement and fill it with the list of files he gave her. She was to remove her name from Wednesday's roster adding: *special assignment duties* in the space provided, then report to that office the next morning armed with her notebooks and pens.

Whatever I say tomorrow morning, gibberish or not, I want you to note it down cross referenced with the file I'm reading from. I might need you to run a couple of errands for me as well, so, carry your top-floor security clearance pass as usual and some petty cash. It could be a long day. A flask would come in handy. Make it big enough for three. We'll have company! I will need an in-house pass. In catering I think. At least that way we can get more tea and sandwiches when your flask runs out. He laughed in a boyish fashion; a laugh of pleasure. Next came Fraser Ughert.

"Ah, Fraser, glad I caught you. I was after the best man your department could offer me, but then I realised that it was you, old chap." He laughed again. "Care to join me in a little escapade I have planned? It will mean a trip abroad with a bit of trade craft and canniness thrown in. Count you in on board can I?" Dicky needed a running mate and there was none better than Fraser.

Ughert was a deceptive man, although another portrayal would include the word; deceitful. The deception arose through his physicality, or rather his lack of it. He had always been slight of build, but since his capture at Singapore, and the forced labour he endured under the Japanese on the Burma railway, it had worsened, never to recover. It wasn't a sense of patriotism that had saved his life in that state of brutal slavery, nor any devout belief in the sanctity of life itself, it was pure Scottish doggedness alongside the self-denying upbringing of an ascetic childhood. He would give nothing away freely, especially his survival.

His lack of build was accentuated by the loose clothing he now chose to wear. Jackets that hung awkwardly, collars two sizes too big, and trousers pulled tight at the waist by belts that bunched up the excess material. But he was far from weak in any physical sense. The outward librarian appearance of a pale almost pasty complexion coupled with the black, thick-rimmed spectacles worn below his grey balding hairline hid a determination that a heavyweight boxer would envy. Fraser was not a man to take lightly, particularly when it came to a fight.

The deceit that he proudly proclaimed as one of his characteristics had also come from his early childhood raised in the tiny Scottish village of Cambuskenneth, on the outskirts of the City of Stirling. Through those tranquil, initial years he smelt the perfume of trade, above the newsagent-cum-grocery shop his mother and father owned pervading through every nook and cranny of the three-storeyed weather-boarded building that his father never did find time to paint and renovate as he often told his son that he would like to do. Just one of many things that remained unaccomplished in his dad's uneventful, but duplicitous life. The essence of vanilla and pear drops, mingling with soap powders and cheese, spilt milk and disinfectants found space in Fraser's memory, alongside another that carved out his youth and built his character. The marginally dilapidated but essential village store, catering for the needs of the nine hundred or so fellow villagers, had a small-time thief as its owner.

Always douse the fruit and veg thoroughly with water, son, before you put them out. That way they weigh more than they ought to. And another thing when it comes to weighing. Never leave those brass weights within the reach of customers. I've fiddled with some to them. It's only pennies I know, but it's the small things in life that make the larger ones all the more enjoyable.

The adherence to the details needed in the art of successful skulduggery aided Fraser throughout his association with the security services and the long-running partnership with Dicky leading to the shared respect of each other's capabilities. Having Fraser's acquiescence to his proposal, Dicky prayed for the early morning rain that had beset London for the last few days to continue to fall tomorrow and left Louise, walking towards the uncertainty that awaited him.

At five minutes past five o'clock the narrow front door of number sixteen Shepherd Market was opened from the inside and Dicky came face to face with an incandescent, raging Lord Reginald Beaufort.

"Ah, it's you! I hope you have an answer to this outrage, Mister director," he shouted, "and I hope I get my hands around Cardiff's throat within the hour." His face was drawn tight with his upper lip white with rage.

"If he thought he'd get money from me then he has an enormous lesson to learn," he exclaimed, waving his clenched fists at Dicky.

"My sexual preferences are well known within my collection of friends. I take it you know what I'm talking about, Smith. I'm just about holding off accusing you of putting him up to it. Your career is finished along with his if you are involved!"

Dicky could smell Beaufort's breath and perspiration as he threw the envelope, containing the damning photograph, in his direction. It fluttered rather than slammed to the floor, much to Lord Reginald's dissatisfaction.

"If that had been Cardiff then he would have gone through to the rat infested basement!" he raged.

Although the room was well furnished, Lord Reginald was not seated. He preferred to pace up and down with heavy stamping steps. The shapely bottle of Hennessy XO brandy had not been touched nor had the plate of assorted sandwiches, brought from the café across the road.

"I don't think you are in any position to threaten me, Reginald. It wasn't me captured in a photo buggering Cardiff. Before you start lambasting my department let me offer you a solution to this problem you and your wife have. I know where Cardiff is now and where he'll be later tonight and for the next few days. He will not be in this country, which, if you're sensible about all this, is to your advantage. Shall we sit and parley, or do you want a ridiculous squabble?"

"So, you are behind it," Lord Beaufort stated calmly, taking a seat after opening and pouring a glass of brandy. Dicky took a glass and followed suit.

"I want something, Reginald. Something only you can give me. In exchange I will give you every copy of that photograph that now lies on the floor along with the negatives that we hold. If you don't give me what I ask for then those copies will be sent to every tabloid newspaper in this country and we will keep the negatives. The fact that your appetite for eroticism is known to your fellow participants is of no consequence to me. It will be the astronomical embarrassment it will cause the Royal Family that will end in your downfall.

You will be dumped quicker than a hot knife slicing through butter and in all probability your peerage will be rescinded. Emigration could be the only solution open to you after you've been blackballed in every respectable club in town. Somewhere in deepest Africa might be best place to consider. Don't look so shocked. Philip might condone what you do in private, but I doubt very much that he, or any other member of the Royal Family, will have a good word for you after the publication. Do you?" He took a large sip from his own glass whilst Lord Reginald tried to gather his thoughts.

"You're taking a huge risk, Smith. The Palace would slam a D notice on every editor of every paper. Then where will you be?"

"Even you can't control the European press, old boy, and then of course there are the former Colonies. You know how much America loves our Royal Family. A bit of British rump on the front page of the New York Times will fill their coffers admirably. I might get you on the cover of Vanity Fair with a bit of luck. Your wife might like that. Incidentally, she has a superb body. Everyone said so."

"What is that you're after?" Reginald poured himself a second glass.

"We want to know precisely how you lot are mixed up with one Jack Price, once affiliated to both my department and the department now chaired by General John Mark Hampton. We want to know where he is, why he's there and how what he's doing impacts on the establishment that you so skilfully preside over."

"Never heard of him," Reginald replied defiantly.

"Oh dear! I'm obviously not making myself clear enough. That is not the response of a sane man, old sport. Give me what I want then nothing of this sordid affair will ever reach the ears of those you're protecting. You have my word on that. Sit there and commit hara-kiri then I will supply the dagger you can fall on, starting off with tonight's two evening papers, and to avoid your D notice I'll keep you locked in here whilst I do. I know Jack personally. I know him to be patriotic to such an extent that he would die rather than betray this country. And if he did die through betrayal of England he'd rise again to defend the Crown. Whatever he is doing on your behalf he believes passionately in it. His loyalty would, I believe, lead him to kill to cover up anything that besmirches the good name of our Royals. He is too good a man to throw to the wolves, which I suspect maybe an option for you lot.

Now to the point where your brain comes in, Reginald. He has recruited someone for a particular purpose that I'm not aware of, but I can, and have, guessed what that may be. If you think this whole thing through then there is a way out of this dilemma for both Jack and yourself. If Jack is in New York then that's the place I've sent Cardiff. Cardiff is not of the same material as the man Jack recruited. I want Jack and Patrick West both home safely untarnished by whatever is going on. Cardiff is another matter. If you supply me every detail that I've asked for, old boy, then I concede complete freedom to you to deal with Cardiff however you wish. I'm going to put the question about Jack on hold for a second and start with Gregory Stiles as I believe they're joined at the hip."

One and a half hours later nothing remained of two people being cosseted at the address in Shepherd Market. Lord Beaufort caught a cab to Waterloo Station and Dicky took possession of the only tape recording of their conversation. Louise was waiting on his return. She handed him a small brown parcel containing all that he required for the following morning.

"I've checked the weather report, sir. Light rain starting around five and clearing by eight tomorrow morning," she reported. He nodded in her direction, but never spoke.

Signing out in the day book at Century House, he added: *Away fishing. Back Sunday if all's well.* He smiled at the two porters, sitting behind their desk in the front entrance hall and departed in his departmental car, with Peter in the front beside George his driver.

"Home, George, and don't spare the horses. You two have a pleasant five days to look forward to without me around to bagger and harass you both. I'm off on a few days' holiday. Have fun, won't you!"

"No night-watch nor personal security going with you, sir?"

"No, not necessary, Peter!"

Not once on that homeward drive did Dicky mention erratic drivers, in fact, he was silent for almost all the journey. He had Tuesday's decoding card on one knee and Fraser's coded message on the other. It was Barrington Trenchard's list of serving police officers who had the Commander of C11 in their back pockets, but there was no contradiction to his answer about how he had known of Jack witnessing the robbery. As George indicated to turn off the motorway, Dicky suddenly asked a question.

"Why tell a blatant lie if one knows it will be discovered?" The two men in the front looked at one another as though a bolt of lightning had struck the car.

"Are we expected to answer that, or, were you asking yourself, sir?" It was George who reacted first.

"Yes, please do answer. All help appreciated."

"Maybe if the person telling that lie wants you to know they're lying, sir?" It was Peter who supplied that answer.

"But why, Peter, why?"

"Because there's a truth hidden in that lie. Perhaps they want you to find it without making it obvious that it's them telling the truth," Peter explained not really understanding what he was saying.

"Or, perhaps the person telling the lie believed it to be the truth." Dicky thoughtfully replied.

"You are a grade one bastard, Jack, aren't you. Screwed him twice without him even noticing," he said aloud, staring out towards the setting sun, to which neither man added a single comment.

Wednesday In London

Chapter Thirty-Four

Blessed Rain

The weather forecasters had been correct. There was light rain falling when Dicky, in a brown trench coat and wearing his favourite collapsible matching fishing hat pulled down around his ears, showed his security pass to the disconsolate sentinel at the 'Employees Only' gate set in the rear of Century House. It was five minutes to seven, five more minutes of tedium before the shift changed and War Department Constable number 643 could make his weary way home to Dartford in Kent. The pass was scrutinised, but not Dicky's face. He punched in the security code and passed through the glass doors making his way down three flight of stairs to room number D twenty-five; Catering Accounts/Storage. He unlocked the blue gloss painted door, entered and locked it when inside. He breathed in the musty smell of paper, composed himself then looked around.

"It's been a long time since I've done anything like that," he announced with a boyish grin on his face to the two bare wooden tables, one stacked high with an assortment of colour files. "I didn't know I could still do it! In my childhood I would creep into Dad's office holding my breath to steal a boiled sweet from the glass dish on his desk whilst he had his back turned. He never did catch me."

"Are we here for your confessional, Sir Richard?" Louise asked as she hung her sodden outer coat over Dicky's on the door coat hanger.

"Highly unlikely, Louise, far too sordid for your ears! I was simply reminiscing about bygone days. Strange though how things go around in life. I started in the intelligence trade in an office just like this. A couple of tables and files everywhere. Let's hope it does not end it here."

"You got away with stealing those sweets, so why think you won't get away with this, sir? I left the flask at home, but brought a small kettle, cups, milk, sugar and teabags instead. Oh, and three cheese and tomato sandwiches for good measure! Would you like a brew now, or shall we wait for Mr Ughert?" The door opened as she spoke.

"Mr Ughert at your service, Madam. Pour away and by the look of all this we'll be needing plenty more. Where do I sit, sir, and where are the nearest loos!"

"Have you a car, Fraser?" Dicky asked.

"Yes, sir, as you instructed. Parked in a council estate within walking distance." Fraser expression mimicked his two conspirators; the look of excitement and worry children carried when playing truant from school.

* * *

Sir Richard's own upbringing was not so far removed from that of Jack's. His family had been in trade, that of book publishing, but not in the upper bracket of that profession. However, his father had met and nurtured associates mainly through his mother's ability to write profitable novels on travel and housekeeping. Those connections had helped Dicky to get a start in his career but not enhanced it to a level that he did not deserve.

Like Jack, his education had finished at grammar school level, and like Jack, his first days in the SIS were spent in the shadows of his university educated, Surrey residing peers and overlords. There the similarities ended. He worked inside the security services from the start, not as Jack in repeating gossip, but analysing and investigating information from both English speaking nationals and from foreign sources that he came across or were introduced into his circle of interest.

He was fluent in German, French, Italian and Spanish by the age of twenty-five, joining the staff of the Admiralty in 1935 as a translator at the British Embassy in Madrid, just in time for the civil war that broke out a year later. When Germany invaded Belgium, Dicky was again a naval attaché, this time in that county's British Embassy and was one of the last to leave before landing at Blighty and a slow but steady progress within the secret world. When the war was over, and duties with Twenty Committee ended, he found himself on active field duty in Berlin, spying on contingents of the Red Army occupying most of the city. He came home in 1949 and it was in the summer two years after that recall, when he headed up an obscure department in the newly united intelligence services, that his path crossed one that Jack Price was travelling along. Jack was in London working as a freelance journalist, ostensibly investigating why abandoned military camps were being ignored as sites for the Labour Governments proposed rehousing and rebuilding policy. He had, what Dicky was told, an *overactive* interest in unused military bases and in particular; HMS Centurion, the empty naval shore establishment at Haslemere, Surrey, forty miles outside of London.

Jack was propping up the bar in the Wig and Pen Club, opposite the Law Courts in The Strand, engaged in a heated conversation with his companion, a tall brown-haired woman in her forties dressed in a black barrister's gown when Dicky made his entrance.

"This bloody government needs its arse kicked and I for one won't shed any tears when it's gone. Do you know that even though they're a bunch of lily-livered pacifists we have the second largest standing army in the world and the biggest proportion of national income per head spent on defence outside of America. Our Navy is the largest in the world and the Air Force is not too far short of being the biggest. But when it came down to action, what did they do, I'll tell you, sent a handful of troops to Korea as a token. We had a chance to cut Stalin's head off in '45. Churchill knew

that, but Attlee; spineless! They've been banging on about rehousing all those still living in the slums and bomb damaged houses since they were elected. Nothing's been done about it though, has it? Do you know we have still got over two thousand military bases in the UK, most of which aren't being used and never will. Why don't they turn them over to public housing?"

"I've no idea, Jack. Perhaps you should ask them," she replied, picking up her well-worn, yellowing wig from the bar top, replacing it with her empty glass containing a partially chewed lemon slice.

"Excuse me, but I couldn't help but overhear some parts of your argument there, old boy. I might be able to help you in some small part. I'm David Lewis by the way," Dicky announced himself.

"And I'm Audrey Goldsmith," the brown-haired barrister replied. "Pleased to meet you, David, but I'm sorry, only popped in for one G and T. Due back in court in ten. Must away. Bye, bye, Jack, I hope you sort the government out soon. See you another time, then." She departed, waving over her shoulder as she left.

"I hope I didn't lead to that lady's departure by barging in like that, Jack. We still have you down as married on the company books."

"Have we met... old boy?" emphasising the old boy, Jack sarcastically replied.

"Briefly, but obviously I left no impression. You were working at Harwich sorting out the imports from the exports. Barrington someone introduced us. He spoke highly of you as I remember."

"Either he was drunk or you were. Can't stand the fellow. He represents all that's wrong in this country of ours, Dave."

"What's all this about Haslemere, Jack? You're making alarm bells ring in every fire brigade station in London."

"Have the brown nose brigade got each other's wives knickers in a twist? Worried about the poor of London being housed next door to their Guildford mansions are they? Sent you to tell me off and smack my hands no doubt."

"If I hadn't heard you lambasting Clem Attlee I would now be thinking you'd joined the Fabian Society donning a red beret every Sunday

morning at Speaker's Corner, Jack. Should we notify the Soviets that you might be joining their side? What's your real beef, old boy?"

"I just hate the snobbery. They act as though they own the world, but they don't, do they? All they own is the shit that comes out of their mouths and the only ones they care about is their own. As you're on the same pay-roll as them you can buy me my next pint!"

"Gladly, if you tell me who's paid for all the others? Only we haven't seen any published articles under your name for some time, old boy."

"I sell my stories to the highest bidder. Sometimes that means my name is removed from the article in favour of the editor. Would you like me to send you an eloquent piece on the Porton Down research lab, or some samples of the banned chemicals they're working on, Dave? Perhaps you'd rather I send my jottings to The Times? No? Didn't think so. Don't you worry about where my loyalties lie. I wear a Union Jack handkerchief on my head whilst paddling at Bognor Regis on my hols. My money has the Queen's head on it just like yours, only mine might be fresher than yours. I quite like people who were born into power, it's those that have power by self-ordained decree that I object to. Pilchard, or whatever his surname, was a crap agent who should have been shafted along with loads of the other ponces. It's his breed that perpetuate the class system that this country is riddled with."

"You don't mince words do you, Jack, but I'm only the messenger boy. All that is way beyond me. It might be in your best interests to keep away from the subject of abandoned military bases and it will definitely be in your favour not to mention Porton Down again to me, or anyone else. I'll tell the powers at be that you took your rap across the knuckles without a murmur of protest and leave it there. Allowances and expenses untouched. What say you?"

"What did you say your name was again?" Jack asked, as the barman placed his pint of Courage Best in front of him.

"David Lewis, old boy."

"I'll look out for you, Dave. That's if you last! You're brighter than the rest and that will worry them. They don't like bright lights burning in the dark corners they inhabit."

"You really should watch out for that inverted snobbery of yours, doesn't do you any favours to wear that chip so prominently. I doubt we'll meet again, unless you misbehave of course, and if happens I might be the person who stops that allowance of yours. I'd hate to do that," Dicky countered, frowning as he turned to leave.

"Do what you like, Dave, old boy. I'd still get paid by people far more powerful than you, or any of those in Whitehall come to that. Don't waste time worrying about Jack. Jack can look after himself, David, old boy."

* * *

For three long hours Dicky alternated between sitting at his table and prancing to and fro reading from those files then placing them, relevant page face up, at a space on the floor in an order that left Louise and Fraser mystified. He listened to the tapes of Trenchard and Beaumont, both standing over Louise whilst she wrote notes and sitting whilst she read them back.

"Whatever it is that they're covering up happened in Vienna, of that I'm certain, but what was it? Let's go through it all again and look at the facts, shall we?"

"Are you inviting my analysis, as I'm not really qualified in that area," Louise replied, somewhat embarrassed.

"I'm supposed to be amongst the best in the country, but this has me baffled, so why not throw in your comments. More minds on the job the better."

"You said that Lord Beaumont did not know the whole truth. You added that it's because it's too important. It could also be that it happened before his time."

"Yes, obviously, Louise. Go on."

"Well, this Gregory Stiles worked for the Duke of Windsor who died last month, so, if the secret involved the Duke in his younger days then Beaumont might not know about them."

"I'm listening."

"Price, you say, loves the Royal Family." She looked at Fraser who nodded back at her. "He would keep a secret about the Duke, but now the Duke's dead is the secret still needed to be kept?"

"Yes, I believe it would be." It was Dicky who answered her question.

"Not if everyone who knew of the secret were dead."

"We're on parallel lines, Louise. Keep going."

"Are you following Louise's hypothesis, Fraser?"

"I am, sir, but not too sure I'm liking where it's leading."

Louise gave him a puzzled look which neither man could understand.

"I'm going to give away my age here, sir. Please don't repeat what I tell you to any in my section upstairs, I'd die if you did."

Dicky sighed with his eyebrows raised in a look of understanding that he would normally reserve for Sheila when hearing about mischievous behaviour either by, or exacted upon one of his children.

"When I was younger I had a crush on Edward VIII. I read every story about him in all the women's magazines I could lay my hands on. I never thought that he would marry that ugly Wallis Simpson, especially if he'd met me. I know how that sounds and I know it's rubbish, but that was me. He was a dish, sir, and to put it bluntly had an obvious attraction to women. What if he fathered a child who's alive as we speak? That would be some secret to keep."

"I came to the same conclusion, Louise, with the man I met in Tel Aviv telling Jack of the secret when Jack was in Vienna working for this department. But there's something else working its way through those two that connects to Argentina. Aberman is closely connected to the disappearance and probable murder of several ex-Nazis. Where for example do Jack and Patrick West fit into that? Aberman, that's the man I met in Israel, is in New York along with Stiles and Price. I'll stick my neck out and say that he was blackmailing the Windsors, but I'd sell my soul to the devil before I'd believe that Price was in it with him. Price knew West's father who was in Italy at the end of the war interrogating captured German troops. We must assume that

Harry West found out something important and told Price. The only thing that I can think of would be the list of sympathetic names carried by Hess when he landed in Scotland. If the names on that list were discovered, and then subsequently interrogated, they would no doubt comprehensibly incriminate the Duke as being the leading light in appeasing Hitler. That could explain why Price found Captain West a position in the War Department and all records of what he worked on were erased by the Palace.

There's nothing that leads me to conclude that Price told Aberman of that list. If there was, then those who went under the hammer would have screamed like pigs by now and Beaumont would have heard. No, Jack's not into any blackmail scam and I'm pretty sure not involved with ex-Nazis. As much as the Court of St James disapproved of the Duke, with the Queen's mother blaming him for her husband's early death, they would certainly agree to pay to keep the birth of an illegitimate child from the general public as well as those in ministerial offices. Stiles would make the perfect go-between, not Jack. But what if Stiles told Jack something and Jack is trying to tell me?"

"How can you find out, sir? Louise asked, looking up from her notepad.

"We have to go and ask him."

"We, sir?" Louise's eyes almost flew out of their sockets.

"I was thinking of Fraser going with me, Louise. I think he has more expertise for this one." With a beaming smile on his face Dicky directly addressed Louise, who blushed slightly in embarrassment.

"Will he tell us, sir, if we ask him nicely?" It was Fraser's turn to ask a question.

"I think he will as I think he needs us."

Fifteen minutes later the two men left Century House by a service exit which was surrounded by garbage bins, and drove to Lavington Street in Fraser's white Ford Cortina. Barrington was already awake. Dicky thrust the report containing the names of corrupt police officers on the table as Trenchard rose to meet them, but he never got to his feet. The report was left unopened.

"Tell me again how you knew of Price's Soho address. As nobody can find that statement of his that you mentioned."

"Well, I saw one. Saw his signature with the capitals P and R of his surname. That's how I knew where he was living and where to send West."

"You sure it wasn't Gregory Stiles who told you?"

"No, it was not!"

"You are in a bad mood this morning, Barrington, aren't you. Had a restless night, have we? We're sorry to add to your woes but on the table is a list of all those other custodians of the law who were bent and you knew of. When you sent West looking for Price were you so dumb as to think that your complicity would remain undiscovered? Someone, presumably Price, has made off with that statement leaving you looking somewhat naked when it comes to knowing of Price's whereabouts. Where is the rationale in sending West to expose an endemic corrupt practice that you're bang in the centre of? As dumb as you are I cannot believe you signed your own suicide note without a compelling motive. Care to expound on that, old chap?"

"Gregory was to look after me. We both decided that my time was up and I needed to get out. Neither he nor I saw you in the picture, Sir Richard. I'm to blame for that. Had I of known that it would be you on the case then I would not have underestimated your tenacity. Could I have something to drink please, I feel a thirst coming on."

Fraser pulled the hip flask he carried from his jacket pocket, placing it on top of the all accusing papers that lay undisturbed on the table. Trenchard reached across for it, then went to unscrew the lid. He was stopped short by Fraser's hand on his arm.

"Truth is always the best way of alleviating the lump of a lie in one's throat, Barrington. First your capitulation then you get the whisky as a treat." Fraser stepped back holding the flask.

"I met Gregory at David's funeral at the beginning of June this year. The Duke of Widsor was buried at the Royal burial site at Frogmore, Windsor. We hadn't seen each other for about three years, so his letter of invitation came as a complete surprise. I'll be extra truthful here, and admit I was elated, over the moon in expectation, but he had changed considerably. His cheerfulness had disappeared along with all other aspects of his conviviality and intoxication. At first I put that down to the occasion, the solemnity of it all and his personal loss. He loved that man before anything else in this world.

If you're thinking that they must have been lovers then I can neither confirm nor deny that, but my opinion would be that they were. I asked him outright about that once. The only reply I got was that he wished they were. It was said in a way that carried no element of regret, nor hope, more as a way of defence and defiance. Anyway, the reason for his change was not what I first thought. As the ceremony was ending he took hold of me, leading me away further into the gardens. That's where this plan of ours was hatched.

Aberman, the Jewish man you mentioned, Sir Richard, was blackmailing the Duke. Asking for astonishing amounts of money that Gregory raised on his behalf from our present Royals. Aberman is not the most careful of men. He talks a lot. Early into their monetary relationship he mentioned that he had an accomplice. Said that if anything untoward happened to him then Jack, yes, he actually used that name, would take up the reins to the money cart and drive it harder. Now, he said, that the ex-king is dead, is the time to even the books on them both. He wants to kill them, Sir Richard, and needed my help to flush them out.

Over the years of that extortion, Gregory had found Jack's full name, mainly through Patrick West's father's involvement in operations run through the War Department. Mountbatten had inside knowledge on some and others, who knew Gregory from his former gregarious days, helped in the rest. The Palace were not directly involved in a hands-on fashion, but they covered all traces of West's work in the WD in case of any recriminations at a future date. Very thorough, are the ways of the Royal Court. You would fit in well there I'm sure of it!"

"Take time out to have a swallow, Barrington, but don't let it interrupt where you're going in this highly interesting story. You have the undivided attention of us both, old chap." Dicky nodded to Fraser, who handed Trenchard the whisky.

"I knew I'd be caught in any inquiry into police corruption, but he faithfully promised to get me out before any shit hit the fan. I believed him, as I wanted to get out, but as I said, I hadn't reckoned on you." Barrington took a hard swallow and lit a cigarette.

"It was Stiles that led you to recruit the young West, Barrington."

"Yes, it was his idea."

"Why?" Dicky asked.

"In his role as the Duke's and Mrs Simpson's confidant, Gregory had plenty of time on his hands. One thing you can depend upon with the Army is that they keep immaculate records. He found a German officer whose name he recognised being interrogated and interned by Captain Harry West. He simply had to follow that lead, adding up the numbers, finding Jack's highly probable connection in the profit column. You had me turning somersaults when you mentioned Hess's name to me, sir Richard."

"Did he think that the elder West told the younger one then?"

"He said it was a possibility that he couldn't ignore, Sir Richard."

"Has he gone to New York with the resolve of murdering Jack, Patrick West and Aberman?"

"Yes! But it won't be he who fires the bullets. It will be his newfound lover who does that."

"Does Stiles know the name and whereabouts of the child that the Duke of Windsor fathered?"

"No, he doesn't. But he wants to find that out before he does away with Price and the Jew."

"Does Price have any idea that Stiles knew of West's father?"

"Not that I'm aware of, no. But Price won't be able to protect West. Gregory is somewhat unhinged when it comes to David and Mrs Simpson. He will cover all the angles to preserve the Duke's reputation; even murder. Up until this point he has been exceptionally thorough in that."

"Now would seem an opportune time to explain why Gregory was given that code name of Alhambra, Barrington. It has intrigued me for many years." Barrington took another swallow before he contritely continued.

"Gregory was in Spain during the Civil War on the royalist side. He had a nephew of the King of Spain as his lover. One night, and I do not know the details why, he cut off the boy's penis and then stuffed it down his throat before he garrotted him. It all happened in the gardens of what the Moors described as a pearl set among emeralds. Gregory had a nickname for the boy. He called him the emerald of Alhambra."

Dicky looked hard and long into Trenchard's eyes searching for a flaw in his conviction, but there was none to be found. There was only the obdurate strength of certitude.

"Give Fraser the name of Stiles's lover then finish the Scotch if you want, Barrington. I'm going to take some air. A walk in the rain might just clear my mind over what to recommend about you. It could be a long walk indeed."

* * *

"Did you notice that there was one enormous answer missing from Trenchard's lips, Fraser?"

"I didn't, sir, no." Fraser replied.

"It's the one that's still puzzling me and I believe only Jack can supply the answer."

The drizzle had turned into a downpour that neither men noticed as they walked in careful thought.

* * *

At three-thirty that Wednesday afternoon a Mr David Lewis and a Mr Fergus Andrews boarded the Pan American flight leaving London to New York. They touched down a little after six pm, New York time.

Chapter Thirty-Five

Arrivals

When Daniel Cardiff's plane touched down in New York late Tuesday night he followed Dicky's instructions to the letter, after all they were not difficult, relying on impression rather than results. On exiting the subway in Manhattan, he walked to the St Regis Hotel where Fraser had made the reservation. He checked into his lavish room on the seventh floor then showered and, whilst watching a pre-recorded game of baseball on the TV, dived into the telephone directories searching for the name; Salvatore Guigamo. It took him under an hour to find the address and fifteen minutes in a cab to arrive outside Salvatore's restaurant on Worth Street.

"It looks all kosher to us, sir. He rode the subway into town then a leisurely stroll to the Regis. He never looked over his shoulder once. Came straight here from his room, a swanky great penthouse suite. No cheap chicken run this affair. It's as you said, sir, he's a top ranker. He's shaking hands with Salvatore Guigamo as we speak. Yes, they're in full sight of me as I'm in a kiosk across the road. Joe is taking a few snaps. He's not intending to stay as the cab has still got its flag down. They ain't trying to conceal anything, sir." The Bureau agent announced to Henry Cavendish who was seated at his desk in the FBI headquarters building.

"I don't trust the Brits. This is too easy. I reckon they're playing us. I'm sending two agents to the Regis to work alongside you two. When you're back there point him out, then you two relieve them in the morning. He certainly has enough of my interest to keep tabs on."

That Wednesday morning, after taking a light breakfast of fruit and cereals at the hotel, Daniel again adhered to Dicky's instructions as though he was made of super-glue. He took a cab from the front entrance to the British Consulate. It was a little after ten when he passed through the foyer. On signing for the diplomatic pouch and then placing it in the brown leather briefcase he'd brought with him, courtesy of Fraser Ughert, Daniel retraced his journey, but this time only as far as number 351, West 38th Street where he rang the entrance bell for apartment number eight on the second floor. After giving the occupant of that apartment the unopened diplomatic pouch, Daniel walked back to his hotel on 5th Avenue carrying the now empty briefcase. He had never heard the word 'tradecraft' nor was aware of any procedures he could have taken to assess his position. None were necessary. *"Impression is everything,"* Dicky had told Daniel. The fact that Joe and Harold found it easy in the extreme to follow him would have widened even the most prodigious of smiles in Dicky's impressive portfolio.

Unseen by anyone, including agent Harold Lawson who had stayed watching the front door of 351, a heavily built figure of a man emerged from a rear window on the second floor of the block that Cardiff had entered and silently slid down the drainpipe, then made his way to Pennsylvania railway station where he stoically waited for the 12:03 arrival from Hartford, Connecticut. He never had long to wait.

* * *

"Ah, there you are and here am I. 'Tis a long time since I've cast my eyes on your ugly mush, Raymond. Wish I could say that I've missed you. But hey, we're all on the same side nowadays, isn't that the truth.

A man we both know told me that you would have a little something for me?"

Raymond lifted his gaze from the stone floor and vacantly stared at the haunting heart-shaped face with deep-set eyes that glared back at him, whilst both recalled the times when they would have been on opposing sides during the bloody days of aggression still being fought between warring Irish factions from which they'd escaped. He didn't want to hang around exchanging memories.

"I'm thinking it was James Joyce who said it, but I could be mistaken as I'm not a man who reads much, and it could have been some drunk on the Falls Road; no man's an island, Miss Slattery. Time marches on and thankfully some of us survive."

"That it does and no mistake. Me, I'm thinking that it was James Cagney who said that line along with; 'I'm On Top Of The World, Ma'."

"Well, someone has to be, don't they and by the look of things it's neither of us, that's for sure." Raymond replied as he handed over the parcel then turned his back and left.

* * *

The journey and arrival of David Lewis and that of Fergus Andrews differed greatly from Daniel's. Whereas he had been awake through his seven-and-a-half hour flight reading useless information, theirs had been one of both sleep and study. As the first complimentary drinks had been finished and cleared away, David handed his travelling companion four folded, closely typed, sheets of paper.

"I came across this earlier today, Fergus. It's a breakdown of Sir Archibald's brief association with a former Irish insurgent who he successfully altered course towards us. Name is Bridget Slattery. She's also worked alongside Job and Jack. We gave her a present a few years back which she devoured with great gusto. Very messy table manners! Have a close study reading between the lines as you go, Fergus. Archie became very attached to her. Very attached indeed!"

"I will, David." Fraser then hesitated slightly before asking a question that bothered him from the outset. "Is it okay if I shorten that to Dave, as we might get the Duke of Windsor and yourself mixed up a bit, sir?"

"Fine," Dicky replied and promptly fell fast asleep.

* * *

Bridget Slattery breezed past the outside tables, now dressed with white tablecloths and festooned with lighted candles, their flames dancing beside the late diners carrying their conversation into the almost starless sky, and entered Salvatore's restaurant.

"Looks like rain," she said to Luciano, the night-time maître d', who acknowledged that fact with a sigh of resignation.

"Is he in?" she asked.

"In *la cucina*!" Luciano replied.

The preparation of food in the kitchen had ceased, leaving all but a few staff clearing plates from the deep sinks and stacking them away on stainless steel shelving whilst others wiped surfaces and replenished stock cupboards and refrigerators. There was a faint sloshing noise of a mop in the distance.

Sally sat alone in a corner checking table receipts. He had a large balloon glass of red wine in one hand and a fat cigar in the other.

"*Buona sera, signorina. Come stai?*"

Dispensing with pleasantries, Bridget went straight to the point.

"Where's Jack, Sally?"

"He is at the Chiesa di Santo Stefano with my sister, signorina."

"Is he hurt?" she asked incredulously.

"Not him, no! The red-haired man who came with him is though. He was shot."

"Badly?" Bridget was distressed.

"Lost some toes, I think, but he'll live," he replied as he shuffled the receipts.

"Was it an accident, Sally?" She enquired, slightly calmer, but still agitated.

"It was an accident that the man who tried to kill him was shot and it was an accident that your friend still lives."

"Is that man now dead?"

"He is, signorina!"

"Where's Job?"

Sally stopped his work, put down the glass of wine and looked at his garish wristwatch.

"By this time he should be at a smelting factory in Newark stoking the furnaces, signorina. Can I get you something to eat?" he enquired.

Early Thursday Morning In New York

Chapter Thirty-Six

The Return

The sedative must have been a heavy dose, as I didn't wake until almost eight o'clock to a bright sunlit, morning sky with no evidence of the overnight rain that Monica had mentioned. I could still taste the anaesthetic in my mouth and that sensation was heightened by the absolute quietude I awoke to. Passively I lay there for an unquantifiable passage of time. It could have been seconds or minutes but for whatever length it was, all I did was stare at the ceiling not recognising what I was looking at. Suddenly I remembered an image I'd had during the night of someone examining my foot. It was an indefinite figure, blurred at its edges and ghostlike. I wriggled my toes. It was then that I remembered where I was and why I was there.

With an uneasy feeling I sat upright, throwing aside the bed linen covering my right foot, but I couldn't see anything other than a wide, crêpe bandage where the toes would have been. *I thought she said only three toes were amputated,* I silently thought having nobody to ask. The thought of undoing the bandage crossed my mind just as I could smell brewing coffee which served only to remind me of the pain in my face. I swore out loud as my stitches stretched inside my jaw, adding the word *hell* after the usual profanity.

"My, you are a noisy person first thing in the morning as well as during the night, Shaun. Feeling out of sorts, are we?"

It was Fianna, who was curled up under a blanket on a chair in the corner, out of my eye-line.

"I know what you're thinking. You want a look at your toes, don't you? Well, you can't. I changed the dressing whilst you were asleep last night, so leave it alone," she said as she flung back her makeshift covering and made towards me.

"How long have you been there?" I asked without emotion, thinking only of the discomfort of my face.

"I came when you were in dreamland, Shaun. You looked a mess then and you look even worse now you're awake."

"That's all I need. A bossy red-headed sister scolding me when I haven't done anything. Where are we, Fianna?" I asked as if I was a schoolboy seeking favour with his teacher.

"We're in an annex of the convent behind Saint Stephen's church in Brooklyn. If you're quick you can catch an early confessional. But I bet it's not that you're wanting. You'd rather find a greasy cafe and have me spoon-feed you a fry-up for your breakfast, crispy fried bread with all the trimmings?" she laughed in derision.

"What on earth made you get shot in the foot? Were you running away?" This time she added the insult of imitating someone running away in fear.... *Don't shoot, don't shoot me, please, please,* she added, still giggling her head off as she ran backwards and forwards across the small room with her arms flailing in all directions. I couldn't help myself but laugh at the sight. It didn't last long because of the pain.

"Oh, hell! I need the bathroom. I think I'll wet myself if you don't get me there quick," I shouted.

"There's nothing quick that you'll be doing for a long time, peg-leg. Hold on to it, because I'm damned if I will." This time we were mimicking each other's laugh, as I eased myself from the bed and took the first tentative steps since being shot.

"Here, take my shoulder," Fianna offered. "I hope the seat is down as you won't be able to stand on your own and I'm only your nurse not your concubine."

"I'm so pleased about that. Had enough of sex for a while, thanks very much," I replied.

"Not with my Penina, I hope?"

"You were way off in your guess with that one. Straight as an arrow with some lovely kinky bits thrown in." My turn to laugh first. "Then there was her mother, Leeba, and the girl at—" I wasn't allowed to add the name of my female acquaintance at the Tat & Tail club.

"Sounds as though I've arrived in the nick of time, not only for your sexual wellbeing but to save the maidens of New York. Although I wouldn't include Leeba in any definition of maidenhood. She's old enough to be our mother, Shaun. Was it a lover of one of those ladies that mistook your feet for your head?" Another burst of laughter accompanied her admonishment.

"Stop bragging and get in there," she added as we stood outside what appeared to be a utility room stuffed full of boxes, with a toilet pan added as an afterthought.

"Love the sanitation in this hospital. Was it better at the Clifford residence? Solid gold taps with parchment as loo paper I expect?"

"Not quite, but something along those lines," she declared as I stumbled towards the pan.

"I did only have three toes cut off didn't I, as everything is wrapped up down there, Fianna?"

"Only three, Shaun. All will be as right as rain when the stitches mend. By the way, there's a pair of open-toe sandals back in that room of yours with some fancy clothes that were brought over from an apartment I'm told you have here in New York. I would say that since you arrived you seem to have landed on your feet, but that's not really the case now, is it? A one footed playboy just doesn't cut it somehow," another laugh.

"How do I hide this face of mine?" I asked. "If it was ugly before, it's more so now!" I had caught sight of myself in the mirror above a sink that was also in the room.

"Stop fishing for compliments and concentrate on what you're doing. I don't think the nuns here want to wipe-up your spillage," she replied.

"It's good to see you, Fianna. At least I think it is," I said, more of an apology than a heartfelt greeting.

"Well now that's a relief as here I was wondering if you welcomed me being back or I embarrassed you. You're not wearing that ring of mine nor am I hearing friendship in your voice, Shaun. You did get that letter I left you, didn't you?"

"Yes, and I read it. The ring was a bit tiny for my fat fingers so I left it in a bank deposit box along with a few other things. I knew that you were in deep with Jack, but it wasn't until now that I realised just how deep. You've been in this building many times, haven't you?" There was no hesitation to her reply.

"I have that, and what's more it's no secret. 'Tis the truth you're after I'm thinking, well, in that case here goes. This was the first place I came to when I escaped from England. I wasn't waiting on any sacred floor for the police to find me covered in Father Finnegan's blood after I killed him, I came to America. That was the first time I used the name of Fianna Redden. I was here for a short time working for Jack before going back to the England. From then on everything I've told you is the truth minus a few details that are none of your business. The one thing about Jack Price that you can always rely on is him being thorough. Whatever story he tells, he tells it with conviction and enough passion that even his mother would believe it. I've worked for the IRA and against them. I'm working this op now and next week, or next year, maybe something completely different, but in the back of my mind is the knowledge that Jack has thought it all through to the tenth degree and beyond. As far as I know there are only the two of us that he uses regularly; me and Job. From Salvatore he gets all what he needs to cover the edges. But, and this is a big, enormous but, I don't think he is in charge. There's at least one other Johnny in all of this, if not more."

"Let's see if I've got this story right. Jack gives you Finnegan as a reward for all your great work for the security services of GB but flatly denies working for them? Then he flies you here to settle a debt on their behalf. All a bit odd, Fianna, don't you think?"

"I've never asked who signs my wage slips, Shaun. I don't care who pays me just as long as I'm paid!"

"What's happened to Michael Clifford, is he dead?" I asked.

"If by that you're asking if I killed him on my way out, then the answer is no. But if you're asking if he's dying, then the answer is yes, and that will occur very soon if it's not already happened."

"Have you poisoned him?" I asked quite calmly.

"You're too damn pleasant talking about death for my liking, Shaun. I won't answer that question of yours. That's something I don't see you having the need to know."

"I might be in that position of needing to know if Jack is right and my name is in the line of ascendency for his command, Fianna. He told me he has put my name down as his successor."

"Now there's a thing, to be sure! Personally I wouldn't want you to take his job, but you're your own man, so if it's what you want go for it. But again you're wrong. You're missing a huge point here. If I did poison Clifford, and I'm only saying if, then Jack would not want to know. Do you know why?"

I had finished in the makeshift washroom and was tentatively making my way back to the bed, holding onto her arm.

"No, but I'm sure you'll tell me."

"Because he would have issued the orders and would already know that I wouldn't be here without carrying them through, that's why." Angrily she glared at me.

"Job doesn't inform Jack every time he picks his nose. We follow orders, Shaun, and never mess up. I can see the sense of keeping this group small. When he quotes that thing of his about equality what he's saying is that the responsibility of what we've each done separately is held by us all. Not one of us escapes the blame of another's actions. Let's say you're right and I did poison Clifford, am I to blame, or, is it Jack's fault for telling me to?" she asked.

"Both of you are equally guilty," I replied.

"Right! But what about Job? He's involved in the whole thing so does he carry some responsibility?" she asked, delving into my theory-based morality with her questions.

"Yes, he does and by applying that rule of guilt by association then so do I," I replied with self-examining honesty.

My physical weakness was being pounded upon by a reality of a different kind. True, I'd wanted adventure when Jack proposed my inclusion in his maze of truth and lies, being stretched in what I could achieve beyond the strict rules contained in that Instruction Book of the Metropolitan Police, but now I was included in a plot where perhaps a person had been killed on the pronouncement of an individual I knew so little of. There wasn't enough time to minutely examine my inner soul to find any logic as to why I had remained before I was hit by another blow. This one could have taken my head off my shoulders had it been a punch.

"There's the rub, eh. What was the title of that thesis you wrote when you lazed away under the spires of Oxford, the one on morality? Was it called; *The Good and Evil of Man?*"

I had once read a brief outline on how acupuncture can cure certain pain. Put in simple terms it outlined how one medieval battleground injury would take away the pain of a previous one. Apparently it was developed by the Chinese who up until that point I had respect for. Her knowledge of my written thoughts did not wound me in the way that a spear or sword would have done, but not only did it take away all the thoughts about my face and foot, but also my sinking pride. I had not locked my suitcase, and what's more, someone had taken a good old look through the contents.

"Did you read any of what was in that paper, Fianna?" I asked, still shocked.

"Only the opening lines, Shaun. How did it start? Oh yes, how could I forget." With a patronising smile on her face she began to recite the first two short paragraphs of my work from a piece of paper she withdrew from a pocket.

There is no Right in this world. No seraphic conscience that guides our decisions in a righteous direction towards what is implied to be; the right way. There is only Wrong. Wrong never deviates, nor can it be complicated by conscience.

The reaction to the effects of any action upon collective humanity are not governed by an inbred spirituality. The response is based solely on an individual's, or government's, ability to assimilate the cost to himself, or country. Be that life or death, war or peace, or truth or lie.

The failure to respond to Wrong is not wrong. It is the natural progression towards the acceptance that there is no Right.

"I gave up after that, far too intellectual for me. I used to find Enid Blyton too difficult."

"Did Jack read that?" I enquired painfully.

"He did and then he made me write it down."

"I'm so pleased you both found it so absorbing. I'm impressed," I managed to reply, confused and agitated at the same time.

"Did Jack tell you of my being wounded and ask you to return?"

"Not exactly, but he does know I'm here. I think I may have given him more to think of, Shaun."

"That sounds ominous."

"Have you a gun?" she asked with the pain of life that I first saw in Twickenham lining her face with its intensity in her eyes.

"I did have. It should be with the clothing I was wearing."

"It's not now! Nor do those look like worn trousers and shirt." She indicated the newly pressed garments hanging from a cupboard door.

"That's all new stuff. Perhaps you were covered in the gunman's blood."

"Jack said he was wounded so, that could be right. Do you know what's happened to him, as Jack was his usual vague self?"

"He's dead, Shaun!"

"And I need a gun, do I."

"I'm of a mind to think that you do, yes. Luckily for you I have two."

"Am I to guess that Jack doesn't know that?"

"You'd be far from wrong by thinking that."

"Okay, then whose side is Jack on and come to that whose side are you on, Fianna?"

"We have a saying in Ireland that goes—your feet will carry you to where your heart lies. I'm here, so pick the bones out of that, brother dear."

"You haven't answered about Jack."

"He's on the side of right, but according to you there is no right, or, have I got that wrong?" she smiled deliciously.

"You're in no danger from Jack, Shaun. Have you taken a look at that list of chemicals that he left with you?" she asked as the subject was changed from the future to the here and now.

"Only a quick look, before I nodded off. I'd like to get a shoe on this foot of mine and have something soft to eat before giving it my full attention. I'm starving and thirsty as hell," I replied.

"We're back where I came in. Hell again," she smiled and I returned that smile. Only mine was forced whereas hers looked pure and honest. Where did I go from here, I wondered as I desperately tried to gather what thoughts I had left making sense of a situation I was still trying to understand.

"It's a fifty-yard walk from here to the street outside. I'll turn my back while you dress and then, if you're up for it, we'll wander out and catch a cab to Sally's. I'll stand you breakfast. Are you up to having that splint removed? If not I'll leave it on, but you'll find it difficult to eat and drink with it there, Shaun." She gently touched the side of my face, sending shivers down my back and making the hairs on the nape of my neck stand on end.

Mid Morning In New York

Chapter Thirty-Seven

The Wait

I had recovered the list from under my pillow then dressed and with careful steps, aided by a walking frame, followed Fianna to the street. The splint was off, but the pain was still there. When we arrived at Salvatore's I waved her on before me as I paid the cab fare. She obeyed under protest, carrying on with her complaint as I caught up with her inside the restaurant. She was at the counter ordering.

"That stubborn side of yours could have led to a fall, Shaun. How does your foot feel?"

"A little sore, but on the whole, fine, thanks. Can I get some water to go with that coffee, I'm gasping!"

"How about your face?" she asked.

"I'll manage with a straw. I'll tell you more after I've eaten."

"I've ordered you some porridge."

"I hate porridge! Lumpy wallpaper paste! Anyway, I thought you said we'd miss breakfast?"

"It's about all you can eat for a few days, besides, it's good for you," she stated to my obvious annoyance.

"These Americans eat it all the time. I'll get that water of yours brought over. I'm going to use the Ladies and leave you to have a ponder on that list of Jack's. See if you can fathom it out. Be back in two shakes of a bee's bum."

"And how long is that?"

"Depends on the size of its bum, Shaun." Her golden smile turned towards the washrooms leaving the shrill of an Irish laugh lingering, as the only other person in the restaurant rose from the end table he occupied and left. I watched as he crossed the road to use the same phone kiosk that Jack had used. Even allowing for my anaesthetised mind the coincidence did not escape me.

Around the corner from Sally's was the same Ford van that had taken me on that hooded trip yesterday, only this time Job had company inside with him listening in to the wiretap he had on that telephone; it was Alain Aberman.

"The man who had Leeba in that apartment is not dead. He's in Guigamo's with a tall broad with red hair. No, they're the only ones in there!"

When Haynes Baxter-Clifford next used his telephone it was to call Karl Weilham, who took the call and then hurriedly made arrangements to leave.

* * *

There were more people interested in the comings and goings at Salvatore's this day other than Alain and the man who worked for Haynes. Henry Cavendish had an agent taking photographs from a car parked down the street. However, his camera was never pointed at the two figures that approached on foot. There was no need. One was Daniel Cardiff and the other, agent Harold Lawson.

Fraser Ughert had parked the car he had rented under the name of Fergus Andrews much earlier that morning then walked the block, noting both the Ford van and the FBI agent with a camera. He was now sitting inside his vehicle also watching the front entrance to Sally's. He had misgivings on seeing Cardiff, ones of a professional nature, but Fraser was not fully aware of Dicky's plans. He might have been more worried if he did know.

* * *

As the tables on the pavement outside began to fill with lunchtime customers and the noisy conversations penetrated inside the building, I started my examination of the list. It was extensive and complex. There were chemical compounds such as corticosteroids, which could cause depression or induce euphoric mania. Mescalines which were common hallucinogens. Methamphetamine which can act as an aphrodisiac, or as another euphoriant, but it can also send a user delusional and psychotic. Another inducer of sleep; benzodiazepines, but overuse of that drug can cause strong dependency, along with memory loss and aggression. There was one chemical compound that I had no knowledge of, and not having access to a periodic table, I had no way of finding out what it was. It could either have been a hybrid, or something recently discovered. To determine what all this added up to needed experiments conducted under laboratory conditions where the combination of the available structural formulas could be supervised, preferably on recipients of some kind. Either the bee had a small bum or Fianna's phone call to Jack, with an update of my condition, was short and compact.

"Come to any conclusions, Doctor Mengele?"

"That's a very strange name to use, Fianna. Why him?" I asked.

"Just the first name that came into my foolish head, brother dear. How's it going? Have you cracked it yet?"

"Nowhere and no, are the short answers to that, sister dear. All I could possibly do is to guess. This is just a list with nobody telling me how it's been put together. I'd need to see the whole package. But even then, without trials, I would not be able to reach a definitive conclusion on what purpose it serves. If Jack's on his way here for an answer then he'll be disappointed. Where did he get this from, Fianna?"

"Sorry, Shaun, but I've no idea. He just asked that when awake you took a look. He is on his way, only he has things to do before he can get here. He wanted me to apologise on his behalf for keeping you waiting."

"Has it anything to do with an Argentine town called Trelew?" I asked.

"Nope, sorry! Not told about that. Care to fill me in?"

* * *

"Wow, what a sight you make, Shaun! Straight out of a horror movie without the need of makeup, but at least you're walking unaided," Jack declared as he saw me standing at the counter of Salvatore's ordering two more coffees. He looked flushed in the face as though he had hurried from somewhere else. He also looked odd. Dressed in blue overalls bearing the white logo of a cleaning company; Wiped Out Cleaning.

"It's all good with me, Jack. How's it going in your world? Found a new occupation, with more clearing up to do?" I replied.

"I wear them now and again just to keep my clothes clean, Shaun. Job has a plentiful supply if ever you need a set."

* * *

Cilla had been a complication that needed fixing after their planned evening together had fallen through because of my injuries. Jack had wanted one last visit into Weilham's office on Wednesday night to set his recording machines to tape Richard Stockford, the chairman of the German pharmaceutical company, Karl and his South African wife in conversation. Now that the coming together was no longer a proposition he had visited the UN building on his way to Salvatore's this morning.

"They kept me in the hospital, Cilla. I'm so sorry, but I had no way of letting you know. If only I had been a little less English and asked for your phone number. Anyway, too late for that now! It turned out that I

have a slight heart murmur that requires some investigating. They let me loose on the world an hour ago when it turned out to be not as serious as they thought. I've got to go back in a week's time for an ambulatory electrocardiogram. No, don't look so worried, it really is nothing. Just a tiny machine strapped to me that measures my heartbeat as I go about a normal day's activities.

The only trouble is I'll have to tell my supervisor for insurance purposes, you understand. Look, I know it's a bit much to ask, but as it's Thursday today I need to work to get a full paid week in, otherwise they dock my money and quite honestly with all this going on I can do with every penny, oops, cent! I wouldn't have this problem back in the UK with their National Health and all that, but when in Rome as they say. Anyway could I borrow your keys? That way no one should know that I'm late on parade, as I can get straight on without signing in. I'll spin some line about forgetting to, when I sign out. I'm sure I won't be the first who's forgotten.

What's that, you will! You're an angel, Cilla, and no mistake. How about we have a drink after work, then perhaps a walk in Central Park in the setting sun? If tonight is as good as it has been, then it should be lovely."

"I would so love that, Cecil, but only if you really want to. No pressure at my end."

"That's a date then, and thanks again for the keys. I'll catch you later and arrange the time, Cilla."

It was then that he made the wax impression of her master key, rather than last night.

"Everything's hunky-dory with me, Shaun," he said, as he passed a small tin box to Salvatore.

"Make anything of that list of chemical elements I gave you?" he asked.

"Nothing, Jack. Told Fianna the same."

"Know anything about a country called Namibia?" he quizzed me, with that characteristic, supercilious smile on his face.

"Other than it's next door to South Africa, then no again."

"Part of South Africa nowadays in reality what with apartheid in that country. Let me grab a coffee and I'll join the two of you. I have some points of interest to explain that might tie a couple of knots up for you," he volunteered mysteriously.

"Is what's happened to Leeba on your agenda, Jack, or did her disappearance come as a surprise? And while we're on the subject of loose ends how about that man of Haynes Baxter-Clifford? Fianna tells me he's dead. Are there any more waiting to shoot me before I get to go home?"

"In one way you should be grateful to Haynes. It was after all his concrete floor that saved your life, Shaun. If it had been made of wood then he wouldn't have wounded himself and in all probability he would have shot you dead. Why the mention of home? Fed up with excitement already, are you?" he laughed and I caught myself joining in. He turned and ordered his coffee.

Whilst he stood at the counter, Salvatore approached him and whispered in his ear. Jack appeared to be halfway between elated and puzzled, but whatever it was it did not remove his smile.

"Good to see the two of you having fun." Fianna took up the conversation whilst he still waited.

"Next thing we'll all be on Broadway in a threesome production of *Hair*. I could be the Irish equivalent of Sally Eaton. That's if no one notices I've got red hair. Why did you get the colour of that beautiful hair of yours changed, Shaun? Blond doesn't suit you at all," Fianna complained.

"Blame him," I pointed at Jack, adding, "and he sent me to a mad woman to have it done." I spoke quietly, not because my face ached but trying not to offend Salvatore.

"You're not about to tell me of another of your conquests are you, cos if you are then I'm covering me ears, unless you agree to performing in *Hair* with me," smiling she tried to entice me.

"If it involves any dancing then I'll sit that bit out," I replied, caught up in her euphoric mood. But not for long.

"Has Richard been frightened off from meeting Karl, Jack? Or, will he go in the end?" I asked as he returned, coffee in hand.

"There was I thinking that your broken face might have stopped your questions long enough for me to get a few words in. Seems not even that can stop you. Good job you're not a dog. You would have chewed my leg off by now if you were." *Anything to avoid the subject*, I thought. I persevered.

"What was the topic they were going to discuss, Jack? Care to fill us both in?" He sipped his coffee and lit a cigarette, and both Fianna and I followed his lead. It was then that he slowly started to reveal the truth behind the façade he'd built around that 1937 meeting in Vienna.

"There was a settlement at a place called Karas, about five hundred kilometres east of Bloemfontein, in Namibia, that up until Tuesday of this week was the home of some three hundred or so souls of the Nama tribe. Today not one of those are alive. Want to know why, Shaun?" Fianna was puffing vigorously on her cigarette, not looking at either of us as I answered.

"I would think it's something to do with that list you gave me. From what I can gather I would say they become delusional with either depression or severe euphoria then either killed each other or killed themselves. Whichever way their lives ended it was neither pleasant nor painless. I'm guessing of course as there was one element I'd not seen before; CID 3355. I have no idea what molecular formula that refers to."

"It's a high-powered painkiller, Shaun. The strongest that's yet been discovered. You're wrong about them dying painfully. They never felt a thing! The experiment took three days. That's what Karl, his wife and their chums were to discuss. Mrs Olivia Weilham brought the results to New York this morning. Benzine of some description was added so I'm told, not sure why though."

"Was it sprayed over that settlement?" I asked.

"Yes, it was. One thousand gallons of the stuff delivered on consecutive days with differing amounts of methamphetamines added along with the chemical you couldn't pin down. Notes were taken of the results from a fair old distance. Behaviour, tolerance, resistance, that sort of thing. Some of those affected would have walked through machine-gun fire to kill anything. They who looked on were very clinical. It was Olivia Weilham's company who supplied the planes, observers and then it was her men who counted the bodies before burning them." His face was of a tortured mess, squinty-eyed, channelled brow, clenched teeth, all moving and changing as the tale became more terrifying.

"I asked about the spraying because the benzine could have made it atmospherically heavier, Jack. Plus, if it was an ethanol-based substance it could have made it sweeter to breathe. Like sniffing a good cognac or whisky. I'm surprised your lab technician never told you that. If you knew what the whole thing added up to why give it to me?"

"Simple, Shaun, I wanted you to know who and what we're dealing with. If this stuff had been manufactured indiscriminately then whoever held the formula had life or death hanging over us all."

"There's a lot of past tense in that remark of yours. Have you stopped the manufacture?"

"We think we have, Shaun, and we believe we have the only copy of the compound. We now have to deal with those who wanted it in the first place. Do you want a role in that part of this operation?" he asked.

"Can't see as I'd be much use to you, Jack."

"You're not usually unsure of what you want. Sidestepping was a word I never thought I'd aim at you. What's put the doubts in your mind?"

"Fianna did. I'm not sure that I want to be involved in Clifford's death by whatever method the two of you devised. Incidentally, the gun you gave me is no longer in my possession, Jack, so, if you're thinking of asking me to shoot someone I'm afraid I'll have to refuse. Will that put me on the next plane home?" I was fishing to see if he knew that Fianna had given me a replacement.

"Not keen on you flying in your condition, painful around the jaw I would think. No, I want you here."

"Would you care to elaborate on where that concoction was put together? My mind is telling me South America. How close is that?"

"That's better! You might have got hurt a bit, but you're up for seconds, Shaun, aren't you? Generaloberst Alexander Löhr is ours. We turned him in our direction two years after he arrived in America. It was the easiest job we've ever done," I interrupted.

"I think that's the second time you've used the word 'we,' Jack. And now you've added a time period to it. I know your *we* can't be Fianna. She's not old enough, nor do I think Job is. Let's get some facts on the table, shall we?" I emphasised my use of the word *we*.

"There has only been one other person who could have been on point with you in all of this. Do you want to do the honours in declaring his name, at least for my benefit? I expect Fianna already knows?" She looked in my direction with sad, cold eyes that I couldn't read, as Jack replied.

"And confirm what you have already worked out, Shaun, then yes, I'd be delighted to do that; it's Alain Aberman."

"Okay, I'm all ears." I caught sight of a grin from Fianna as she lit another cigarette.

"When Alain first came to America he worked for the FBI. He didn't do much because they never asked much. Theirs was a long term strategy aimed at placing him inside Mossad but working for the CIA. By now you probably know that I helped Salvatore and his family to exit Italy. I suggested London, but he wanted New York. Apparently he knew half the mafia here and the other half knew of him." Jack laughed, I smiled, determined not to be diverted by his ability to seamlessly change track.

"Okay, Shaun, you've obviously gone off my jokes. Never mind, I'll just carry on then. Sally saw Löhr opening a limousine's door one day and clocked the number. He told me, I told Alain and he traced it to old man Baxter-Clifford. It was, as I said, a simple squeeze, but it had a sting in its tail. We told him that he faced either a night-time snatch, then smuggled off to Israel to stand trial or, if he chose to cooperate in pinpointing all escaped Nazis along with continuing information on what they were getting up to we would cover his back. Alain told the FBI. That was done to protect Löhr from any subsequent discovery. Didn't want him spotted by some returning GI and turned in to the local plod, so we in effect grassed him up first. The agency developed an interest in the wheeling and dealing of the Baxters and the Cliffords because of what we fed them. Yes, Shaun, we made up lies. I bet you never thought I'd admit to that. Löhr didn't lie though. He was the coordinator of those escapees and proud of it. Knew them all and what's more, tied his benefactors into the swindle. This, of course, we kept to ourselves." He paused to order more coffees and I jumped in.

"How did he do that, Jack?"

"In the simplest way possible, Shaun. He told them that the Bureau had made him and were attempting to turn him into a grass. If he vanished the FBI would know why that was and where to look for clues, but if he stayed then he could work the system in favour of their interests and not those of the Bureau. They had very little choice. He supplied low-grade information to the FBI, but managed to give Baxter and Clifford some useful stuff on what the FBI were doing or watching. They did quite well on the exchange. In the end it came down to who Otto feared the most; Mossad, with Sally's lot hovering in the foreground, or American justice. Guess what he chose?"

"Aberman is Mossad's man then, Jack? Was Löhr connected to Trelew? Is that how you knew?"

"You're racing, Shaun. Yes, it was. Alain has had a cadre in Argentina since we turned Otto. We had a chance to change the world, Shaun, Alain and me. We could have rounded them all up, thrown them to the wolves, sat back and congratulated ourselves on a pretty superb piece of intelligence gathering, or, done what we did. Leave them in place, watch them relentlessly and gather more. Now's the time we sell our investments and close the company books."

"How does our Royal Family's heritage fit into this thing you have with Alain, Jack?" I asked. "And where the Hell does it all lead for Fianna and me?"

"I'm not sure how you arrived at that first question, Shaun, as the two operations are separate, merely being handled by the same two men, but I guess you will explain how you came to that conclusion at some point. You and Fianna can go as far as you wish within my organisation, that decision is entirely up to you two. Look, I'm sorry, but I'm only on a lunch break. I have to get back. I have a date with a lady after work, but I won't be detained long with her. I need to finalise certain things and then, when everything is tidied away, I'll come clean with you, Shaun. Just trust me for a few more hours and wait until you've heard it all before you jump ship or decide to carry on. Okay?"

"I think I've heard too much already to have that choice, Jack. There's no way you allow me to walk from this knowing all what I know, nor, come to that, can Fianna walk away." As I looked at them both I couldn't decide who I trusted the least.

I felt trapped inside Jack's warren of lies and inside Salvatore's restaurant. I wanted to walk freely and feel the sun on my face. I wanted not to feel the stitches in my mouth pulling the skin tight and making it so uncomfortable, but most of all I wanted the truth but I had no idea where to look for it, let alone find it. I decided to start with Fianna, but that intent didn't last long.

"Let's stop messing around, Fianna. I'm getting lost in all these stories from Jack, I would hate to think that you're telling me stories as well. How was that you knew I'd been shot? I'm thinking that the news of that never came from Jack. If I'm right then how did you hear of it?"

"Okay, Shaun, it's a bit before I wanted to tell you, but as you've asked; here goes. In that letter of mine that I left you I told of how the British got hold of me. Well, I became attached to that chap who was old enough to be me father in a big way. Yes, I was having sex with women then, but with him I was different. Please don't ask me how that was, the difference I mean, it just was. He told me he was a widower, but he wasn't, he was married and in love with his job not her nor me. There was no space for anyone else in his life. I broke off our relationship by crossing over and dropping him right in it. I told the high command of the Provos where they could find him. I wanted him dead, Shaun, but couldn't go through with it. I tipped him off. Sent him on his way back to England with a bullet from me gun in his arm. Told the brigade commander a pack of lies, smiled at him, said three Hail Mary's and got away with it.

Later on down the road of Irish troubles I met a man who knew my man very well he said. Said he'd broker a deal; my liberty for agreeing to keep in touch and working for the Brits if my profile fitted any of their particular nasty schemes. I did a few things for them. Yes, okay, I killed for them, laying the blame on the Republicans. They got their money's worth and I thought I was free. Then I get a message from that man I mentioned; said *Sir Horace Butler in trouble. Your help needed.* I tidied up at Michael Clifford's, a little sooner than intended, and caught a train back to New York. It was Salvatore who told me that you'd been shot. Jack confirmed it when I saw him in the early hours of today."

"My head is spinning, Fianna, and not because of the pain in my face! What sort of trouble is Jack in?"

"All I know is what I read on a sheet a paper I took out of a diplomatic pouch last night along with the two guns I told you I had. It said that someone, no name was mentioned, was over here intent on retribution for some unstated reason. He had targeted Jack, you and Alain Aberman. Jack was instructed not to tell Aberman of this. Contact was to be made sometime today or tomorrow by a senior British intelligence officer. It was signed Porton Down. When I gave it to Jack he just smiled and said nothing for a minute or more, then he said I could tell you, but not to scare you because if he knew anything about David Lewis then we are all in safe hands. *The very best the English have got, Bridget, the very best!*"

"I wonder who's David Lewis when he's at home, Fianna?"

"Beats me, Shaun. Would you tell me what Jack meant when he said that you'd explain about the Royal heritage bit you spoke of, only that left me standing?"

"It wasn't Hitler who fathered Penina, it was the Duke of Windsor."

* * *

Throughout this forty minutes or so Daniel Cardiff had sat quietly at the same window table where I had first spotted Jack sitting. He looked disconsolate with an elbow on the table in which he rested his head. Having eaten a more than adequate breakfast at the Regis where they served a rather good pot of Darjeeling tea he wondered what he would order at this Italian restaurant other than the obvious coffee for which he had little liking. Eventually he'd settled on a glass of fresh orange. When Jack arrived he almost lost the glass from his grip as all his concentration was focused on the man who until then had only existed in the photograph that he carried in his jacket pocket.

At last I'm in the game, he thought as he tried not to look in Jack's direction too often.

Chapter Thirty-Eight

An Introduction

The walk from the cab had more effect on me than I first realised. As I went to stand from the table, my leg gave way and I almost fell. It was Fianna who stopped me.

"You're doing too much too quick," she said. "Sit awhile longer, Shaun, there's no rush," she added.

"I need air. I feel suffocated in here, besides it's getting busy and we can't sit here all day." With the aid of the frame and despite her protests, I ventured back out onto the street.

As we exited the swinging doors the first thing I noticed was the intense heat that almost took my breath away and then the raucous comments from Sally's men gathered around the outside tables which did nothing to restore my pride. Perhaps there were some that I had seen there the first time I'd visited his restaurant, but my mind was otherwise engaged to bother to look. Then I heard an unmistakeable, "Ouch! I bet that hurt," spoken in clear, unbroken English. I instinctively turned and for no logical reason replied, "It still does, but you should see the other man. He's laid out in the morgue."

"I don't think that's true, but if it is then it wasn't you who put him there, was it, Shaun? My name is Alain Aberman, but Jack tells me, that you have discovered one of my other names; Adam Berman. I have many, but we'll save that topic for another time. One will be of immediate interest to you though. The Secret Intelligence Services in London christened me as Eva. If you allow, I'll have a stab at explaining that as it has a direct bearing on why you and I are here."

I had played mind games with his name ever since Jack had first told of it. When I was younger I had a fictitious elder brother who I named Alan. He was my shining knight in armour who was a champion at the jousts in lance and sword. A defender of the faith and all good egg to younger relatives in trouble. When I was growing up, often I would confide in him when alone in my room. He was my hero. Perhaps he represented all that aspired to be, or, perhaps I was simply lonely and in need of company. Whatever the reason *Alain* came close to my make-believe brother's name so it brought comfort and reassurance to my playful mind. Aberman had strength too. Able-man, capable of things that others were not. A man's man. A crusher of walls and all round dependable figure. The actuality of my imagination now stood before me; the manifestation was disappointing.

He was a short, slim man with a tanned complexion, brown well-cut hair, deeply set blue eyes with thick eyebrows above a prominent sloping nose. The laughter lines that were etched into a drooping face with heavy jowls gave the impression of a happy disposition. It was a well-worn face that had lived through many lives but now looked exhausted. By any description he was immaculately groomed. Two things was obviously clear; he was not as old as the birth date I had read ascribed to him; being no more than middle sixty, not the seventy-nine he would have been if born in April 1893, and secondly he was no warring knight in armour.

He took up his introduction as soon as our hands parted from his initial enfeebled greeting.

"After the war finished in Europe I had a keen interest in a man named Ante Pavelić. He ended up in Argentina advising Eva Perón's President husband for a time, hence my coded name. The two of them shared some right-wing fascist views that were abhorrent to me. Unfortunately, those views are in play as we speak. The situation requires brave men to end it. Jack sings your praises in that regard, Shaun. That's why I'm here; to meet the man Jack has selected to eventually take his place."

Fianna suddenly turned squarely towards me with her back to the opposite pavement. As she did so I caught sight of a man with a camera trying to find a better position to take our photograph. Alain's gaze followed mine, but he was not perturbed by this sight. Fianna obviously was.

"My car is on the corner, Shaun. There's a place I want to take you that's not far from here, but an awful lot more secure for what you need to know and I'm able to tell you. No, don't look so cynical. It's not that I have things that I won't tell you because of some subterfuge of mine, it's just that I don't know it all. I only know what has involved me directly. That I'll disclose without holding back on anything, I promise. I'm not Jack. He has to work in circles surrounded by mirrors and whispers. I'm different, I'm a native here. Don't blame him for being what he is, as it has been those unusual methods of his that have kept him alive and out of everyone's sight for so long." Momentary taking his eyes from mine and looking at Fianna, he added,

"I expect you both have heard that nonsensical saying of his about all being equal and of the same importance without me having to rack my brains and repeat it." His attention returned to me without one word said in recognition of her.

"He really does believe it, you know. No doubt it will be the sermon he preaches when he dies and goes off to wherever he goes, or, it will be the epilogue engraved on his headstone. Certain to be one of the two at any rate. But listen to me! I'm rambling on whilst I guess all you want to do is give me the third degree and draw blood from my veins in the form of information."

He took a step backwards and to one side, allowing for a wider passage along the footpath.

"Owing to logistical reasons I cannot invite you, Fianna, I can only take Shaun. If that's okay with you, then; shall we?" He extended his right arm by way of an invitation to walk to the awaiting car.

"In that case, Mister whatever your name is, you'd better hold his arm. First day up walking without all his little piggies, is my lovely brother. Oh, and don't go offering him a slap-up lunch either, nor any of that whisky stuff he's so fond of. I need to look after him for a couple of days and get him relatively well." Fianna let go of me and turned and walked away with an unmistakable scowl on her face.

"I fell in love with your letter writing, Fianna. It almost made me cry." With sincerity I called out to her, but she either never heard it or never felt it, as she never turned around.

After a twenty-minute drive, where I sat in the back of the car and Alain sat next to the driver simply looking straight ahead, without speaking to either of us, we drove through two high, thick steel gates manned by two uniformed armed guards on the outside, then once inside, four more waited in the courtyard. Flying above the stone white-painted, palatial building was a white banner, with two horizontal blue lines with the blue Star of David in the centre. I was in the grounds of the Israeli Embassy. Before alighting from the car he spoke.

"If the need arises that I must deny you ever entered this building then I will. Nobody of importance knows that you're here. The Americans film us, but we are able to disfigure their images when necessary. What I tell you inside this building will also be denied if that occasion too arises. You are, so Jack tells me, a signatory to the UK Official Secrets Act; that act obviously does not cover Israel, so I'm trusting you, not something I easily do, Shaun. I'll use that name in all our dealings, present and future, but I know all about you and probably more than Jack knows. For example, I had you followed last Saturday morning when you left your lodgings in Covent Garden. Why did you not tell Jack that you went to your Home Office before reporting to C11?"

"I didn't trust Jack nor Trenchard, Alain. Would you have?"

"So you gave a copy of the police report you'd compiled on corruption to the Home Office and your commanding officer?"

"I did. Whoever you had following me probably told you that I used the copying machine in the Post Office at St Martins Place on the way."

"You were seen going in, but we could only guess at what you were doing. That report you put to the Home Office has caused a few ripples inside Scotland Yard. Your Commander Trenchard has gone missing and the head of MI6 has been scurrying to and fro across London for no apparent reason. I was wondering what might have caused those two events? Jack tells me that he gave you the name Alhambra. Did you report that name to both places?"

"Yes, I did. Shouldn't I have done?"

"No, of course you should have. I'm just pleased that's been cleared up. We can now start at the beginning, but first let me say this. What started in Vienna ends in New York here and now. We are already writing that ending, there will be no second chance to come nor forgiveness if we fail."

We took the escalator to the top floor and then entered a spartan, white coloured office at the rear of the building. Once inside I heard the distinct sound of a lock automatically operated on the door through which we'd come. There had been a noticeable absence of other people inside the embassy which I mentioned to him.

"Is it normally this empty, Alain, only I find it weird not to see people scurrying around?"

"We have what we call a 'lock-down' system in operation. Within seconds of a stranger being admitted through the outside gates all corridors are cleared and the offices automatically locked down. It's an anti-terrorist strategy, Shaun, and nothing for you to worry about. This door has now locked and will remain so until I unlock it. All the other offices have reopened and normal service has returned to the embassy. When we leave here, there's a time delay allowing the procedure to cut in again." I was impressed, but didn't tell him that.

All four walls were lined by acoustic tiles only broken by two small windows which were barred and translucent. Our light came from winding fluorescent tubes masked by the panels of a suspended ceiling. It was subtle lighting, but perfectly adequate. We sat either side of a low, solid, grey block of polished aluminium, that served as a table, on two of the four matching red leather swivel armchairs that were new and unused. In my opinion it was a room designed for a discussion, not an interrogation. On top of the table was a writing pad and a pencil for each of us, as well as two empty glasses and a covered water jug. Alain had no notes to refer to, relying solely on his memory. We were alone, with no sign of anyone watching or listening. The air conditioning whirled efficiently away as he spoke.

"I'm going to start by explaining what Jack has fabricated slightly. Most of what he's told you is true, only he mixed some fiction into the reality adding romantic substance to a far from boring story. Firstly, that meeting in 1937 did take place with the people that he spoke of being there. As was I. I was ordered to supply Hitler and your ex-king's entertainment. That meant I met, and then coerced, the Jewish girls who were shot when the meeting ended. It was I who had to take them to the German Waffen-SS Oberführer in charge of the firing squad. He saluted me, Shaun. Can you imagine how nauseating that made me feel? To this day that scene has haunted me. I can recall the pain on each of those the girls' faces in every detail, their names and what that officer looked and smelled like. He wore a cologne that reminded me of walking on wet cedar bark and being surrounded by the perfumed air of the pine trees. I'll never forget that smell." He paused for a split second and looked down at the table.

"No matter how all this plays out none of those memories will disappear, nor can I take enough lives in retribution to wash away my sin. All I can do is try to give justice to those innocents that I allowed to be damaged and then destroyed. It's been my only purpose since that day."

"Yes, I can understand that feeling of blame and guilt, Alain. But if it wasn't you who carried out that edict from Hitler then in all probability you'd have been shot and someone else would have been ordered to do what you did."

"Most definitely! I have no doubt of that. However, then I'd have died with pride instead of living with the disgrace that has forced me to keep alive. Yes, if you're wondering, I considered turning myself in and hoping for the best when the Nazis annexed Austria, after all, everyone knew it was coming. When I heard of the fate of others who had adopted that policy I contemplated using a hanging noose to finish my life, as a lot of fellow Jews had done, but I couldn't. I don't think I had the strength then, and I never found it. After a while I decided that the only course I could follow was the path of revenge. With your understanding of the human psyche you might well say that it's my guilt that I'm redressing and not doing it on behalf of the victims. To be honest I've lost hold of the reasons that persuaded me to carry on, it's been a long time and now I'm no longer sure. All I know is that I've arrived at my destiny and met a new friend in you. But that's enough of my soul searching, that's not what I promised."

"It wasn't, no, but it's lifted the lid on what drove you to keep alive. I'm grateful for that insight. I never doubted Jack when he told of the meeting, but I did doubt that Hitler was Penina's father. I had many other doubts about his story including how you were hidden for the duration of the war by a priest who Jack subsequently had murdered. The motive I was given sounded too contrived and manufactured to be the truth. Care to address that one next?" I asked.

"I know of the story he told you and you're right, it was contrived, but that was to conceal a tale too unbelievable and dangerous to be told to anyone who was in authority back in those days. Many ex-Nazis were used in high positions of governments in Germany and in Austria. They were volatile days." He leant forward and poured from the jug then sipped from the glass.

"I was not hidden by anyone from the Catholic faith, but I did hide in many of their churches. Father Finnegan is not a figment of Jack's imagination; there was a priest, however, Finnegan was not his name! I'll come to him after I explain how I stayed out of the Nazis' hands. My principal place of hiding was in St Augustine's Cathedral, on a street named after it; Augustsplatz. It was an ancient church with extensive catacombs and a museum underneath it. The interconnecting tunnels ran for miles in every direction. Some followed the sewers, others not, but one of them came up under St Peter's about two hundred yards away. I used both of those churches and a few others, along with various places I found, or made, along those passages of sewage. That was the main reason I was never found by the dogs the Nazis used to track down Jews who had not been captured. My aromatic smell flummoxed them." For the first time since the street he smiled.

"Your fictional sister did kill a priest who was helped to leave Vienna by the Vatican; he wasn't the only person the Vatican helped escape justice, but as I say his name was not Finnegan, nor was he Irish and nor was it in Liverpool that the murder took place. You were told the story for a purpose, Shaun, and that purpose remained until this day. We wanted to see if you would research into it further for some motive unconnected to us, but endangering us. You didn't and we were pleased. Calmed our minds as to where your heart was. You haven't failed us in any way, so far. If you have any questions ask as we go along. The paper was put there to make notes and then refer back to then, but it seems more sensible to be spontaneous rather than structure a separate session to expand on any puzzling items. Anything unclear up till now?" he asked, rising unexpectedly from his chair and walking towards the door.

"None at all," I replied. "But I do have a request. I smoke and would like to, if that's acceptable. It takes my mind off this busted cheekbone for a while."

"You must blame that on my old age. I'm sorry but I'd forgotten that you did, otherwise I would have had one here already. I've never smoked, so it's not normally something I think of. But I thought I detected some agitation in you, that's when I remembered and got up to fetch an ashtray. While I'm at it I'll get a bottle of Bells. Jack tells me you like that variety of Fianna's forbidden fruit, but as she isn't watching, what harm can it do."

He returned after a few minutes with both the things he had promised, waited patiently for me to light a cigarette and taste the whisky then began again. It was his story that cancelled the pain I felt.

"Let's start at the Catholic church, shall we?" he suggested, as he too poured a small measures of Scotch.

"The priest that I came to hear of in Vienna was called Der Hammer. I never knew his real name, but I saw him enough times to draw his face on a piece of white cotton with a child's crayon that I found in a bin outside a school where I used to scavenge for food. I scavenged at night at first, but after a few months of living underground, amongst rats and effluent, nobody came near me on the outside if I was careful to avoid the places which the Germans frequented more than others. I wasn't always lucky though. On one particular occasion, when I was stopped by two soldiers, I was left for dead in the street. They hit me with their rifles, their helmets and fists then kicked me for good measure. It was my smell that made them stop. I heard them say that regulations dictated that someone had to stay with my body until collected if I was dead. Neither of them fancied doing that. I didn't eat while I healed, but I did move about in the tunnels, I had no other choice. It was on one of those nights that I heard the screams that led to me seeing Der Hammer and what he was known for.

I was many miles from the Cathedral, but never knew exactly where I was. I couldn't just leave those cries of agony and ignore them; perhaps I should have, but I didn't. It was late as any sign of the sun creeping into the tunnel had stopped hours ago, so I chanced it and lifted a storm drain cover. I saw the street sign; Hoher Markt, predominantly a former Jewish area now deserted other than a few billets for senior German officers who had moved in before war was declared. There was only one building that was lit. It was in a side street to the main road, something you English would call a mews. It must have taken me an hour to reach that house, a three-storeyed affair that was in good order and well maintained. There were flowering window-boxes and hanging baskets. For all appearances a home where a caring couple lived in comfortable surroundings."

He stopped speaking to replenish our glasses then regained his seat.

"The screams ceased then began again throughout that hour with no one coming to investigate. I hadn't seen the basement area until I was almost on top of the place. It was lit by three candlesticks that were placed on the window shelf." He swallowed the contents of his glass in one gulp then breathed in deeply through an open mouth.

"On the floor I could see two young bodies; one a girl, the other a boy. Difficult to tell their ages from where I was but at a guess I say neither was older than twelve. Both were nailed down, Shaun! And the man that had done this was walking in between their naked bodies holding a builder's hammer. Their arms were spread out horizontally, but it was their feet I couldn't look away from. They were grotesquely broken at the ankles as if they had been first nailed standing up before being forced backwards to the floor. There were thick, protruding nails sticking out of the flesh of their hands and from those small, tiny, broken feet. I was violently sick." Once more he stopped to compose himself.

"The animal who did this was naked himself apart from his clerical collar. When I met up with Jack in the Cafe Landtmann we made a pact. I would tell him where the mother of the child of his one-time king was, when he told me 'the hammer' had been killed. It took a long time, Shaun. The Vatican had many secrets they wished to conceal forever, but when both ends of that bargain had been met, it opened up an entirely different affair that led us directly to where we are now." He stopped speaking and leant back in his chair, inviting a question. I jumped in.

"I have an immediate question for you, Alain, that maybe you are about to address, but if not, here goes. When and how did you verify that this man was a priest as you haven't explained that so far?"

"I found out when the Russians came to Vienna in, I think, late March 1945. Austria as you know was not invaded by Germany, as were the Balkans, France and all of Northern Europe along with countries that are now part of the Eastern Bloc. Austria was Hitler's birthplace and as such the Government officially invited him to take over. However, as early as 1943 the Allies had decided that we would be handled in the same manner as any other country that the Nazis had overrun; as a liberated and independent state whenever the war finished. Vienna was to be divided between Russia, America, France and Britain, the same as Berlin, but before that happened the Red Army committed heinous crimes on both Austrians and any German troops they found in Vienna and throughout the countryside. It wasn't until the end of July 1945 that the Allies had set up their regions of control in the Capital. When they stopped raping and murdering in Vienna, the Russians returned to another favourite activity of theirs; getting drunk. Whilst the rest of Austria was bleeding, the surviving Viennese people came out of hiding and we talked. Names were put forward to form the government, gossip was exchanged, those who collaborated more than was thought acceptable were pointed at and a Catholic priest who regularly nailed Jewish children to the floorboards of house behind Hoher Markt was exposed. That's when the Archbishop of Austria stepped in and called his friend the Bishop of Rome for help."

"But you never heard his real name, Alain? That I find surprising."

"He was called by many names, Shaun. Everyone, apparently, had either seen these atrocities or been told of them and each of those had a different name for him. I, however, had my sketch. That was all I needed. I had, and I'm pleased to say, still have, an exceptionally accurate memory. When I eventually re-entered normal life I was able to draw a precise depiction of that man."

"Are you responsible for whatever it was that rattled Jack? He mentioned a town in Argentina called Trelew, but never told me what happened there?"

"Wow! I thought it was only the Americans who rushed their meals. You English must also suffer from indigestion, wanting the whole dinner before the hors d'oeuvre course is dispensed with." We both laughed, which I found refreshingly honest. Often I had shared in laughter because it seemed to be the right thing to do but it had been manufactured to suit the time and the audience, now was different. I felt different.

"If it's all the same to you I'd prefer to sip the whisky, taking time to savour it. We will arrive in Trelew, but at my pace, okay, Shaun?"

I raised no objection to his proposal, only raising my glass as an acceptance of the inevitable.

Chapter Thirty-Nine

An Explanation

"Although the Russians were in the whole of Austria they could not control all that happened there. It was full of troops who had either deserted from the German Army, or had been left behind when the main body had withdrawn. There were also anti-Communists and many others who hated the Russians. They all fought for their freedom, paying a great cost. There were also personalities who wanted to lose themselves in that kind of chaos. Allow me to make plain what I excel at and what I'm absolutely not cut out for. I'm what you might call a collector, or a collator like you have in Scotland Yard and I believe; every divisional police command. I'm like them, collecting information, piecing it together then passing it on. I'm also a facilitator, making it as easy as I can for others to act on the information I gather. I don't run people as spies do. I listen and ask questions. I draw conclusions from what I hear and advise on an appropriate course of action. Rarely do I participate in the execution of my recommendations.

Ante Pavelić left Yugoslavia in a hurry. Twice he had been sentenced to death in his absence. He didn't want to hang around in any country that had been liberated by the Allies and be executed when Tito took over the Balkans. In mid-April 1945 he, with Löhr, along with a large contingent of Ustaša troops arrived in Vienna. Karl Weilham was with them, but kept himself apart from them. Before the war began there were over one hundred thousand Jews living in Vienna, Shaun. When the Nazis withdrew, and those that had evaded the concentration camps re-emerged, there was about one percent of that number still alive. Some I knew from the old days. A few I remembered from my employment as the Chancellor's private secretary. Those I did not know soon became as close to me as all those others that I did. We were a family who had shared Hell and survived. I soon found clothes, they were more plentiful than food, and I started to appear respectable again. I was able to engage with previous government officials, some of whom were setting up a provisional ruling party that would deal with both the Allies and the Soviets. The trouble with that plan was that because the Russians had arrived before the others, Allied Command would not accept a government that the Russians already approved of."

"Is that when Schuschnigg returned from the camp he was held in, Alain?" I asked as I leant across towards the bottle of Bells in mind to refill our glasses. He held his hand across his own and shook his head to my invitation. That wasn't his only reaction.

"I must clear away any misconception that you're under about our previous Chancellor. Jack's overworked imagination went into full throttle regarding Kurt Schuschnigg. He does not figure in this story other than it was he who presided over the 1937 atrocity and passed the orders. We will not speak of him again. Is that understood!" His voice rose several decibels when delivering that final command.

From nowhere he had changed from an engaging, expansive communicator into a bad-tempered authoritarian. I nodded my agreement and stressed it by adding a harshly spoked, "*yes*." There was no explanation, nor apology for his drastic change of character. After a second of calming himself he continued in his narrative as though nothing untoward had disturbed him.

"To solve this problem the proposed leader of our representatives turned to me. He and I had met on many pre-war occasions over government agendas and proposals; usually I was able to end the discussions in favourable terms that all parties concerned found agreeable.

He asked that I find a way to pacify the Allies' fears whilst maintaining the Soviets' approval and thereby guarantee his appointment as the post-war head of state of an independent Austria. I was successful, and Karl Renner became President of Austria in October 1945. Later that year Leopold Figl was appointed as Chancellor. He and I remained close friends until he died in May 1965. He was a truly great diplomat, Shaun. I learned a lot from him in many different ways." He decided to overtake me in the whisky consumption, pouring twice as much as I had poured into mine into his own glass.

"You never struck me as a drinker, Alain, and your previous refusal only reinforced that opinion. Jack and I have shared a few this past week. The two of you are leading me into bad ways." I smiled hoping his bad temper had disappeared completely with his more congenial side permanently returned.

"I don't drink as much as I did, Shaun, and I never drank as heavily as Jack, even when I was younger. We won't be leading you anywhere you don't want to go, my friend, but we will, and have been, opening your young eyes on things that only the old should have experienced." He was back where I preferred him to be.

"The war was bad, but what is proposed to happen now is far worse than anything that took place during that six-year period. Karl Weilham, with Haynes Baxter-Clifford in the forefront, mean to administer death and terror upon millions in a much shorter timescale than that. I try to bury my memories by whatever ways are open to me. Yes, by that I do mean bury in the literal sense of under the ground. I haven't any fond memories to balance things, so I use artificial ways to cover that remorse, drink is one way. I shan't elaborate further, I might shock you." His laughter had returned, but his attention never altered, nor had mine. He hadn't mention Michael Clifford, from which I deduced that he knew of his death. Equally obvious was his pain in recalling the war years spent in Vienna.

"It was during my dealings at the Allied high command centre that I became aware of a system being choreographed by the Catholic Church in Austria to support the evacuation of Nazi war criminals in their escape to both North and South America, notably, New York, as in the case of Generaloberst Alexander Löhr, or Dieter Chase as he's known, and Pavelić, with others, to Buenos Aires. The State of Israel did not exist then. There was no central organisation to collate that intelligence, nor follow those criminals. Resources were non-existent. I knew that New York could never be the final place for a permanent home for those escapees so after gaining citizenship here I travelled to Argentina and I attempted to chase a cold trial. You know about how Löhr was discovered, Shaun, don't you?"

"Yes, Jack told me that Salvatore confirmed who he was after he was luckily spotted acting as the chauffeur to the Baxter-Cliffords."

"Yes, that's correct! Sometimes all one needs is a bit of luck, something you can't rely on though. Whereas, if one nurtures friendship and has a friend who knows what you would like to know, then the willingness to share that knowledge can be relied on, yes?" I agreed, sipping from my glass as I continued trying to weigh him up, but I couldn't decide whether all of what he told was true or a diversion away from Leeba and Penina.

"By the time I got to Argentina, Buenos Aires was effectively the new Berlin. Ante Pavelić, along with the highest echelon of ex-Nazi leaders had their apartments and houses in the city or immediate surrounds. By late 1947 I had established a permanent network of ever-changing trusted agents watching and noting everything they ever did, including whether they stood or sat when taking a pee. Pavelić traded knowledge, contacts, manpower and building materials with Michael Clifford and Henry Baxter's construction companies. All three of them used their property developments to funnel escaping Nazis into and out of Argentina posing as structural engineers. By 1951 they owned their own shipping company; Kelp Shipping Lines, or KSL for short.

"Then why did it take you so long to kill them, Alain?" I asked, genuinely puzzled.

"That wasn't the reaction I was expecting, although perhaps I should have. Jack told me that he thought you emotionally empty when it came to death. I'm starting to believe he was right." There was no smile this time, but at least I was gathering reactions.

"The first answer to your question lies with the international premise that murder is a crime. Do you agree with that moral position, Shaun?"

"At one time I would have answered that question that I absolutely did, but now I'm not so sure. I can now accept that there are some reasons why murder can be a justifiable response to certain circumstances." He made no comment.

"The second reason to why they were not dealt with sooner lay in what they were developing. It puzzled us for years. Then, two years ago, a complex was built in Trelew, into which most of them moved. Unfortunately, we had neither luck nor a friend who knew that purpose until last week. It was designed with the sole purpose of developing a chemical gas that would ultimately decimate those parts of humanity who they did not consider suitable to enjoy life in the fascist-ruled utopia of an Elysian Fields." He downed his scotch in one flowing gulp, then, as he meticulously placed his empty glass on the metal table added,

"It arrived on board a KSL registered boat in South Africa last Friday. Sunday was the first day of experimentation; by Tuesday that experiment was over. Later that day my crew closed Trelew, scattering the ashes of those Nazis who had lived and worked there on the tail end of a burst of cold pampero wind. My team killed twelve, including three you probably know; Josef Mengele, the Angel of Death, Martin Bormann, Hitler's private secretary and Ludwig Stamfrid, a biochemist." I interrupted.

"I have heard of the first two. In fact, Fianna mention Mengele just before you arrived, but I've never heard of Ludwig Stamfrid."

"No matter, you'll never meet him now, Shaun! I struck a deal with some people in Argentina before that destruction. For the removal of any evidence of Nazis ever being in their country they would sanction the action and not be showered with both photographic and documentation evidence of their support for escaped Nazi criminals. It would have been a diplomatic mess had I released all the information we'd collected. They really had no alternative but to agree. All twelve skulls are on their way to be buried on German soil. It's not important that they are discovered, convenient yes, but not essential. However, I will deliberately allow one or two to be found in the not so far off future.

For internal news coverage, Trelew has been converted from a secure hideaway into a penal institution where the guards had no option than to kill armed convicts who were attempting to escape. If the story is covered internationally, and as all Nazi-connected evidence has been removed, not only will we have achieved a successfully outcome but also sent a message to any unknown co-conspirators of our power and influence. It's been two days since that incident at Trelew and nobody here in New York has a clue about it, but Dieter Chase will not be able to keep it a secret for much longer. I think today will be our final chance to clean up all that began in 1937. One could think that the job's almost over, Shaun." He poured two more glasses before adding, "but it's a long way from that, I fear." I wondered why the reference to 1937 was necessary, as what happened in Argentina did not start in that year, but eight years on from then.

"Are you saying that Karl Weilham, Richard Stockford and friends are planning to spray this toxic gas over populations that don't met a certain genetic strain that's acceptable to Nazi idealism, Alain?"

"No, on three counts. It wouldn't just be a physicality that would be targeted, but a religious and political following as well. Secondly it wouldn't be restricted to a gas, if that were the case then it was already available. We believe the idea is to produce a tablet, or add this formula to existing medication, then target who they no longer want to live. A pharmaceutical company would be needed to manufacture that drug. Someone high up in the United Nations would be a great ally in targeting the distribution. Who would question medication sanctioned by them? And lastly, we don't believe Richard Stockford was aware of that intention."

"Jack told me you have the only copy of the formula, Alain. Is that so?"

"I believe that is the truth, Shaun, but we can't be sure that we have all the chemical. I had a small team in South Africa who were not able to sit on every canister that came off the Tangerine Rose when she docked in Durban. If one canister is still active it would only take an analysis to break it down into its chemical constituents and then—" He never finished that sentence, leaving me to guess how devastating that result could be. I was not seeking the answers to speculative guesswork. I was after facts.

"What's happened to Leeba and her daughter, Alain?"

"Yes, of course, that must have been a very complicated relationship for you. One in which you must have wanted to share some of what you knew perhaps?" he asked.

"No, that never entered my mind. I tend to put separate issues into separate boxes. A secret is a secret from those who shouldn't know, but shared with those who told it. I haven't had a real chance to ask Jack about them as he's always in a rush. I am worried though."

"Why worried, Shaun? Have you found a sense of commitment to one or other of those women?" His eyes narrowed and he became more fixed in his stare. A chameleon in the ways that he changed character to suit the occasion. Now he was the interrogator and I his victim.

"Not the sort of commitment that you mean, Alain, just a commonplace sense of care and wellbeing for fellow humans. After all, theirs is the kind of manipulated innocence that you are trying to protect, is it not?"

"So it's still 'you' and not 'us' is it? You're not aligning yourself with Jack and me, Shaun?"

"Not if Leeba and Penni are dead. If they are, then to stop me going straight to the local police station at a rapid hobble you will have to kill me too."

"They are both alive and together." He checked his watch before continuing. "In approximately thirty minutes' time they will be boarding a plane to their new home where they will assume new identities.

You will never hear from or see either again. You have my word that their future is secure."

The only trouble with his stated assurance was that I had heard similar before.

"When I was about ten years of age I had a friend named Coln, I forget his last name, but he was Irish like me, living in the street next to ours, going to the same school as I. We also shared a love of wrestling. We would fight each other, or any that challenged us, at every opportunity that we could. One day he unexpectedly never appeared at morning assembly. I asked a teacher about him and was told that he was ill and being kept at home. I called at his house a couple of days later and was told by his father that not only wasn't I to be allowed in, but to stay away and never call again. For two, maybe three weeks, I asked my mother where he was. All I got from her was the repeated story about him having an illness that confined him to bed. One afternoon, when I arrived home from school, Coln's mother and father were in our sitting room talking to my mum. When they left, my mother told me that Coln and his family were to take a holiday.

Coln is going on an aeroplane to a country a long way from England with cleaner air than London, Patrick. They are all going to live there and start a new life together.

A year later I found out that my friend had died as a result of the polio epidemic that had ravaged London in the late fifties. You will not be the first person to use a story of travel to cover up a death and I doubt you'll be the last. Any of the others connected to all this likely to be flying off somewhere and permanently retiring from view, Alain?"

"Another thing I'm not is a fortune-teller Shaun." His evasiveness was annoying, so I decided to take a chance with my next question.

"Are you doubling up with the FBI, or is that something Mossad are unaware of and you'd like kept a secret?" As I asked my question I scanned the room again looking for microphones. The fact that none were on view did not mean that there weren't any.

"If the service I've given my life to since leaving Austria were unaware of my credentials and this place did have capability to overhear and record this conversation, then now would be the time for me to run, would it not? Thankfully neither of those two scenarios apply. Did you hear a police siren following in the distance when Job carted you off in his van yesterday, Shaun? Of course you did. Someone as fundamentally inquisitive as yourself would not have missed that. It was I who had the car that was tailing you stopped by the New York police. That was because of my ongoing connection with the FBI and it's how your destination and meeting with Jack was not compromised."

"Why is it then that you have not gone to the FBI with all you have on Weilham and the Cliffords, Alain? I would have thought that would have been your first port of call!"

"Strange expressions you English have—'port of call.' It was hard enough to follow some of Jack's idioms, but not as strange as to still think of you an idealist, Shaun. I would have thought you'd have got over that by now. The FBI can deal with their own and I will deal with what's mine."

"I'm going to hazard a guess here and say that the Stockfords will not be included on either list? If any of them were then your actions would be heavily criticised and possibly investigated. Ultimately you and Jack could face imprisonment, particularly if anyone dies."

"Richard is safe, Shaun. He was offered the same chance as were Leeba and her daughter. He declined. He wants to keep his pharmaceutical company and indeed press on with the amalgamation. There is no reason why that cannot happen. But not at this moment and certainly not brokered by Weilham. When the dust settles, that business transaction will take place overseen by more ethical authorities than are handling it right now."

"And would it be fair to say that the Israelis might have some future interest in that amalgamation, Alain?"

"As well as being no clairvoyant I'm also not a politician, Shaun."

"That listing of you as Adam Berman arriving from Belgrade was a serious oversight of yours, Alain. Care to elaborate on that one?"

"It was early days into this secretive world, Shaun. As you say; it was a stupid mistake."

Lunchtime In New York

Chapter Forty

Different Courses For Different Horses

When Jack left Salvatore's Daniel followed him, but being no artisan in that craft he was too simplistic for a seasoned veteran such as his prey. Within two blocks Jack had slipped from his leash. It took two changes of buses and an in-and-out at Macy's, on Herald Square, where he removed the blue overalls in a men's room, to shake off the one remaining FBI agent of the two who had followed Daniel. Fraser Ughert accomplished more than the others who had left Salvatore's. He caught up with Jack as he was passing the Chrysler Building.

"You're slipping, Jack. I doubt I could have crept up on you that simply in the old days. David Lewis sends his regards and requests a chin-wag in the not too distant future."

"To whom am I speaking?" Jack calmly asked.

"Just a foot soldier of small importance delivering his master's message."

"Well, Private whatever your name is, we obviously never trained on the same pitch. I spotted you leaving your car near Salvatore's and again when I came out of Macy's. At first I thought you were one of four, but after I lost that first plonker and one of you lot tailed off to follow him, I started to think you were on your own. The other Fed was easy enough to lose, which left only you. I had received a message from David Lewis so it was logical to assume you were with him, but

I was beginning to think that I might have to hire a boat and cruise the East River for you to catch up. You're good but I've known better. Has Dicky hyphen whatever, had words with Barbecue Pilchard on matters of state?"

"If you mean Barrington Trenchard then we both have," Fraser replied.

"Ah, so, you're not a foot soldier after all. You're of officer rank. Over here with the full battalion, or, are you just a raiding party sent to collect prisoners?"

"Sir Richard will explain, Jack. When's your earliest free appointment?"

"Sir now, is he! In that case if I'd have stayed on in your line of work I guess I would have replaced you as his batman. Did he tell you that I met him once? That was enough to mark him down as different and I told him the same. It took me three weeks solid to find out who David Lewis really was, but that was way back when he was no one special. I thought he'd go places. Didn't realise we'd all come together on foreign soil. Happy days, eh! Seven o'clock tonight at this address." Jack thrust part of a business card into Fraser's hands, and he studied it carefully.

"Where's the other bit, Jack?" Fraser enquired. Which seemed to pass over Jack's head, as he never supplied an answer.

"No more games of hide and seek, okay, officer, sir. I have affairs that I must attend to. Can't play the fool with you all day. Tell the boss to fetch some brandy with him, that's all he'll need. Tatty bye for now, sport. See you both later!"

"Before you go, Jack, Sir Richard said that it could be beneficial if both you and your man Job came armed. Purely precautionary, you understand. He extends his invitation to Patrick West, but suggests that he remains untouched by our business. He added, in the strongest tone, that it would be to no one's benefit to either bring anyone else or to tell anyone else. My name's Fergus by the way, not 'sport' and Sir Richard is David whilst we're here!"

"Who was the first guy following me when I left Salvatore's, sport? One of yours, or a stray that's got himself lost?"

Jack's question went unanswered as so many of mine had done. He stood and watched as Fraser hailed a passing cab on his way to his and Dicky's remote hotel. When it had disappeared from view Jack took up his own journey, apprehensive about the future.

* * *

Alain Aberman gave me a choice over where to be taken on leaving the Israeli Embassy: Salvatore's or St. Stephen's. I chose the church. Drinking as much alcohol as I had done was hardly conducive to keeping a clear head in company, but I needed more than just rest to make sense of all I'd been told. At least the pain in my face had disappeared, however, my foot did not appreciate the form of medication I'd self-administered as much, it throbbed like mad. Fianna was seated on a bench facing the gateway in the gardens at the front of St. Stephen's.

"Where's that walking frame I found for you, Shaun? Lost it, have we?"

"Oh shit! I've left it in that cab!" As I turned, hoping to stop the cab from pulling away, I fell awkwardly to the grass. I heard a shrieking whistle that any traffic cop would be pleased with, then Fianna ran past me in a blur of white. A screech of brakes followed, as I saw her open the rear door and retrieve the metal frame.

"You'll be needing this after we sober you up. We're off to a meeting in five hours' time so we'd better get started on that, Shaun. By the way, I forgot to ask, did you ever look for that Patty Ann of yours?"

"No, I didn't, but by the way you're looking I don't think I have a need to," I declared as she helped me to my feet and her sweet perfume filled my lungs with honey and lavender. She was wearing makeup. Blue eye shadowing with soft red lipstick. Tight fitting white shorts with a loose matching man's shirt replacing her usual denim jeans and scruffy T-shirt.

"Get away with you," she blushed as she said it.

"Is that one of my shirts you're wearing?" I asked as I regained my balance.

"It is, as I had none of my own to wear and it wouldn't do to walk around this place naked. Now would it?" she replied in a teasing fashion.

"You wrote in that letter of yours how you could fancy me yourself if it wasn't for your lesbian tendencies. I'm thinking that they aren't as strong as you make out. You're stunning, Fianna!"

"I seem to remember telling you that last Saturday. I also said no to your advances. What makes you think I've changed my mind?" she asked."And if I had, why would I want that conversion supervised by a cripple?" she added as an afterthought.

The Hotel Near The Airport

To Dicky's logical mind Gregory Stiles would not choose anywhere other than a prestigious hotel to take up lodgings during his sojourn in New York. He started with the very best. It took just one phone call to trace his, and his travelling companion's, whereabouts. He was staying in the Royal Suite at the Waldorf Astoria with Oscar Stannic, the twenty-eight-year-old great-grandson of Count Leopold Stannic of Prussian blue-blood ancestry. There was another person that interested Dicky also booked into that hotel, having arrived late the previous evening.

To the many great attributes that made up Sir Richard's character a least one weaknesses had to be added; his impatience. Fraser had left their hotel on Rockaway Boulevard before Dicky had risen, leaving him the tasks of trying to enjoy an insipid breakfast kept warm in soulless, warming cabinets devoid of human beings and that search for Stiles. He had listened to Barrington's confession over and over again, Beaufort's revelations held no more surprises and the files he had brought with him made poor companionship with the meticulously scrutinised lines. He composed his letter of inducement and set about the part of his plan he had devised in London and kept hidden from Fraser Ughert.

Dear Mr. Stiles,

Sir Horace Butler would be honoured if you would meet with him to discuss a matter of mutual interest at your earliest convenience. He can be contacted through: Mr Daniel Cardiff, Room no 765, St. Regis Hotel, East 55th Street.

He signed it, *Daniel Cardiff, a dutiful friend.*

Having placed it in an envelope, he took a cab from the rank outside the Best Western Hotel.

"I want the Waldorf Astoria, please. Once there I need you to wait for me then take me on to the St. Regis. I may be quite a while in that hotel. It will depend on whether the chap I need to see is in his room or not. This is my name." Dicky passed the driver a slip of paper. "You can confirm that I'm staying at this place if you're worried at all."

"I'll do that, Mac, and because you look an honest guy I'll only take a reasonable deposit from you when you get out. If you're worried about your money my name and badge number is written in plain view next to me. We okay on that, chief?"

Having already experienced some local dialect, Dicky was not concerned by the driver's reference to either *Mac* or *Chief,* making no comment other than a polite; "perfectly" in acceptance of the driver's terms.

On arrival at the St Regis Hotel, Dicky positioned himself in front of the mirrored wall and relaxed in a soft chair reading one of the daily newspapers that were scattered around on table tops. He had taken Sheila's advice and brought his favourite fishing hat with him and with that loosely on his head he settled down to wait.

"I've heard the heat in New York can melt the tarmac during the summer months. Take that horrible fishing hat of yours to save what hair you've got from being singed, Richard."

Within a few minutes he'd spotted four definite federal agents and two possibilities; one a woman, with blonde hair in a pink linen dress wearing a lightweight, blue short-sleeved jacket, the other, a man in a grey suit with a brief case on the table before him. It was the distinctive figure of Oscar Stannic who first tried to make contact with Daniel Cardiff.

Stannic, once a first soloist with the Kirov Ballet before he defected to the West when preforming at Covent Garden, was easily recognisable. The story of his defection was covered by all the international press causing great embarrassment to the Soviet Government and thereby increasing the Joint Intelligence Committee's interest with MI6 in the vanguard. It was one of Sir Richard's departments who vetted him and the name of Gregory Stiles first crossed Dicky's path.

When Stannic asked at the reception desk Dicky spotted the concierge signal to one of those agents, who in turn signalled to his three colleagues. The pretty, colourful girl was one of them, but the grey-suited man was not. The next unrehearsed moves were all beyond Dicky's influence, he had achieved what he had set out to do and to stay would have been foolhardy, but he couldn't resist. On being informed of Cardiff's room number, Stannic used one of the lifts to the first floor and Dicky figuratively held his breath. Fortunately his concerns were unfounded. His pupil held fast.

From the lift nearest to where Dicky was sitting, Stannic emerged a few moments later. He inwardly breathed a sigh of relief, then, riding his luck, decided to stay and see if Cardiff followed. He did.

The tension amongst the FBI agents was almost tangible as the two shook hands as if old friends reunited. The pretty girl in the pink dress was using one of the telephones on the wall to Dicky's right. He wanted to listen to the conversation, but this time resisted the overwhelming temptation. She put the receiver down and meandered over to where Stannic and Cardiff were sitting, at a middle of the floor table.

You're doing brilliantly, son. Carry on as you're going, he said under his returning breath, feeling his heartbeat slowing to normal.

The girl bent slightly towards Stannic holding a cigarette in her right hand, which, after mouthing a few words to him, she put to her mouth lifting his hand toward herself as she accepted his offer of a light. Stannic never saw her left hand in the jacket pocket, but Dicky did. He saw the tendons in her forearm tension as her thumb pressed the camera button which was then clearly outlined. Dicky allowed himself a smile, a small one but nevertheless a self-congratulating one. The fish had taken the bait.

Play the role, Daniel, if Horace Butler's name crops up, which it will, mention your uncle Sir Maurice Curtis and your job is done. It was not only Dicky who was to have a busy time ahead, but Henry Cavendish as well.

Late Thursday Afternoon In New York

Chapter Forty-One

Saint Stephen's

"Do you remember Richard Stockford giving me a letter when we left his office the day you went to Hartford, Fianna?" She was beside me on the bed as naked as God had intended her to be.

"I do," she murmured in reply.

"In it were details regarding those inquiries of his into meetings held in the Vienna Chancellery on the day of his family's departure to America. Although he found all the names that Jack told us, he never found any mention of Alain Aberman being Kurt Schuschnigg's secretary."

"Did he look?" She turned around to face me.

"I don't know, but I did!"

"You've got something to tell me haven't you, Shaun?" she asked, now sitting upright.

"Not before I ask you a question."

"If it's going to be about sex and your performance then don't. I'd hate to disappoint you," she laughed, and playfully prodded me in the chest.

"It's about pregnancy, Fianna."

"God, you are a forward thinker! Is it a baby I'm meant to produce for you, cos if it is I'm in no mood to be starting a family, Shaun."

"No, Fianna! Be serious for a while. When I was with Aberman in the Israeli Embassy I mentioned Schuschnigg and he went off on one, turning nasty without any apparent reason. It made me wonder."

"Wonder what?"

"About that meeting."

"You saying that it never took place?"

"No, but I did question who did what."

"Did, as in already done?" With a grave look on her face she knelt on both knees then pushed me flat to the bed.

"Listen to me carefully, Shaun. You committed a cardinal sin when you shot that IRA commander in London. You are a walking dead man if your profile ever rises outside of our little community. If you start to dig away into people like Aberman you'll be hung out on a wire with IRA Killer written all over your lacerated body. You won't find a friend with a sticking plaster anywhere. Before you kill a man you must prepare a very large hole to hide the body. That's what people like Jack and Aberman do. You couldn't. Your killing happened in public view. It won't go away, Shaun. If you have spooked Aberman he will use it to ruin your life."

"Do you know something that could have spooked him, Fianna, and you're not telling me?"

"No, I don't. But if the name of Schuschnigg got him riled then he's on your case already. Be careful, is what I'm saying."

"I want you to do something for me, Fianna. It does not involve Aberman nor Jack, but it has a fundamental importance with far-reaching consequences if I'm right."

"Ah, I'm just a simple girl at heart and easy to please. Go on then. At this moment I'd do anything for you other than have your child." At that she fell on top of me.

A few minutes later there was the faintest of knocks on the door a millisecond before it opened and Jack stood framed in the doorway. Fianna and I were not playing tiddlywinks.

"I see you two have become better acquainted. The trouble with convents, monasteries and most churches come to that is that they have few doors with locks on. Time to get dressed. Places to go, hands to shake and truths to tell."

As he went to leave and Fianna pulled all the bed linen over herself leaving me completely exposed, he added, "Did either of you see the news headlines an hour ago?" We both shook our heads. "CNN have the best coverage. Karl Weilham's plane, with his wife on board, is missing somewhere over the South Atlantic, believed crashed into the ocean!"

"Wow! That wasn't planned was it, Jack?" I asked, hastily pulling on my trousers.

"Not by me, no! I planned to hand him over to the American authorities, Shaun. Had it all in motion. Did Aberman take you to his home address from Sally's or did you go to the embassy?"

"The embassy," I answered

"So, you don't know where he lives in New York?"

"No, Jack, I don't," I answered, wondering where this would end.

"Thankfully I do. I've written the address down for you. I want you two there and I want you, Fianna, to take a car. Job has left one outside."

"I have something to do for Shaun first, Jack," she replied, sitting up in bed still covered by the sheets.

"Do you indeed. Shaun pays you now, does he?"

"I can assure you that it's vital to this whole affair, Jack." I intervened before any innuendo was misinterpreted.

"Vital, eh! Well, you'd better do it, but I need you at that address by six-thirty at the latest. That gives you three and a half hours. Okay?"

The Hotel Near The Airport

As a sympathetic human being Dicky regretted the demise of Karl Weilham with his wife Olivia, and as head of British overseas intelligence he took note, but the scant notice he'd given that bulletin changed dramatically on hearing Fraser's report

"Price carried on to the UN building, but I don't know where he went when inside. He's got a job in a cleaning company that has a contract with several of the floors there. He was inside for just over an hour then went to St. Stephen's Church in Brooklyn. That's where Bridget and Patrick West are. West looks as though he's been twelve rounds with Joe Frazier and he had his right foot heavily bandaged. Only able to walk with the aid of a frame."

"Jack never saw you, Fraser?"

"No, sir! I left him under the impression that I was an imbecile. It wasn't hard to do as I believe he thinks that everyone other than himself is one!"

"Yes, he did suffer from that tendency. Mind you, he was mostly right! I guess things haven't altered much in his world." Dicky pushed the hotel window wider. "I hate this air-conditioning contraption, not good for you, you know."

Fraser wasn't listening, he was reading the file headed 'Daniel Cardiff'. It was one he had not seen before.

"Does it really go that far deep, sir?" he asked when he had finished.

"A vastly complicated matter, Fraser, isn't it. I wish I could have dealt with it differently, but I never knew how complex it was when Cardiff first appeared. Catherine Dullas compiled the data only after Claridge's, by which time it was too late to pull out. There's someone else who's not on our radar behind all this and it's them pulling our strings!"

"I had a thought, sir."

"Go on, man. I'm bereft of them."

"If Stiles was to kill Jack, Aberman and West how on earth will he get away with it and if caught, which seems highly likely, how will the whole story be kept out of the press?"

That was precisely what Dicky had been thinking of since Catherine had made her report.

"I've given things a little nudge. A little unorthodox but necessary in my view. Cardiff is with Stiles now in the same hotel as Lord Beaufort.

His Lordship arrived late last night. As cover I made it easy for the FBI to swarm all over Daniel. The only trouble that I can think of is, will Stiles see them? I'm totally reliant on his once active service." Fraser interrupted.

"He's been inactive for donkey years, sir. That's a huge gamble."

"You may be right, however, I believe he has kept his hand in because of Aberman. Remember Trenchard's reference to Gif-sur-Yvette?"

"I do recall that, sir."

"What if Aberman had Stiles steal a few French secrets?"

"Where's the evidence of that?" Fraser asked.

"There is none, but if I'm right it will put him on his guard and if I'm wrong I can sow seeds of doubt with the French and more to the point; with the FBI."

"What about Cardiff?" Fraser asked.

"What about him?" Dicky replied, adding, "I'll do what I can for him, but his destiny is out of my hands."

* * *

Henry Cavendish was at the NSA headquarters in Maryland, begging Admiral Frank Meade to be shown information garnered from their *Echelon* project on the British Royal family.

"This man Gregory Stiles has no fixed role within the Royals, but as far as I can ascertain he's been at the Duke of Windsor's side both before he abdicated and until his death a month ago. Lord Beaufort, who arrived at the same hotel last night, is connected to the Royals in a big way. I want to know what they're up to. Stiles has also been looking after Wallis Simpson. Now even I know that she was mentioned when Charles Bedaux was arrested for treason. I should do, as my department were holding him in custody when he committed suicide."

Deputy Director Frank Meade was pulling faces that showed that he was far from impressed. Henry played his trump card.

"The Duke, alongside Wallis, lived in a French chateau at a place called Gif-sur-Yvette of which I'm sure you're aware of, Frank. Yes, that's right, the atomic research laboratory the French have. It's our opinion in the Agency that this Stiles has some information from there and is passing it on to the British intelligence operative my men were tracking before we discovered Stiles and Lord Beaufort."

"You said the head of British Intelligence gave you the name of his operative, Henry. Why do you think he would do that?" Frank asked, his interest having risen a few notches.

"The only thing we came up with is that they want to avoid the embarrassment of another scandal. There was huge controversy when Stiles's lover Stannic defected. They want us to do their dirty work for them in finding out if the French were compromised."

"Possibly, but I don't buy that," Frank retorted.

"Look, Frank, I know how protective the NSA are over *Echelon*, great work you've been doing on that, I understand, but what if the French had something that the Brits knew of, that we didn't? Your surveillance program is going to come a poor second to good old ground work which costs a lot less when the budget is drawn up!"

Frank's early countenance of bored indifference changed instantly into something a fierce bulldog would be perfectly at home with. He almost snarled his reply.

"I'll give you six communication specialists from 70th Operational Support Group and add more if you need them. Get me what the Brits know that the French have before the rest of the world know what we don't, Henry!"

"Eyes on *Echelon* as well?"

"You have it!" Meade emphatically replied.

Thursday Evening

Chapter Forty-Two

Turtle Bay

Fianna parked the silver BMW outside a house being renovated, about twelve houses south of number thirty-seven, 48th Street, switched off the engine and slid along the bench seat to be closer to Shaun. She put her arm across his shoulder and gently kissed him. It was the first intimacy between the two since Jack had disturbed them and left with Job. It had taken them under the three and half hours deadline to achieve all Shaun had asked, but he had shown no joy on her discovery, only a strong sense of regret. In the time they waited Shaun did not speak a word despite several prompts by Fianna who too was sombre, but her loyalties were being stretched by differing forces than Shaun's. His problem could only be rectified by himself.

At two minutes past the hour two men mounted the steps leading to number thirty-seven and knocked on the door. It was Fianna who stated the obvious.

"That must be the man Jack spoke so highly of, Shaun."

It was Job who opened up, waving them past as he stepped into the evening air to stand watch. Jack was waiting at the end of the wide, carpeted hallway seated beneath a painting by Piet Mondrian: The Gray Tree.

"A lovely place you have here, Jack. I compliment you on your taste in art. Is that an original?"

"No idea, Mr man from Guildford, all this belongs to our friend Alain Aberman. Spying for Israel obviously is well paid. You're playing on the wrong team, David."

"Has this place been swept at all?" Dicky asked.

"Yes! I had it vacuumed when we arrived over an hour ago. Found them all, so real names are allowed. Can I now address you as Sir Richard or stick to David?" he asked.

"Dicky is fine, Jack. When is Aberman expected home?"

"He's tied up on Agency business, won't be home for at least a couple of hours. Plenty of time for our conversation. Did Fergus tell you to fetch the brandy?"

"He told me what you said, Jack, but I declined the invitation. Preferring you sober throughout the evening. It has never been a quality of mine understanding drunken fools."

"Sorry to disappoint you but I've made a start on Alain's stock. Care for one?" Jack rose from the black leather armchair, leading the way into the spacious, well-appointed lounge. "Please choose your spot, Dicky. I'm sure Fergus could do the honours."

For almost an hour Jack told Dicky the story of the 1937 gathering at the Viennese Chancellery, his meeting with Aberman in '45 along with his knowledge of the Nazi sympathisers that Patrick West's father had supplied him. He covered Aberman's account of the priest called 'The Hammer' and how he collaborated with Sir Archibald Thomas Finn in securing Bridget Slattery for the murder of the priest known as Father Finnegan. His animosity towards authority had gone, which both amused Dicky and caused him to worry. His first question was to be the one he'd noticed Trenchard not answer: Why he selected Patrick West to assist in his operation, but he chose to address Jack's newfound cooperation instead.

"You've changed considerably, Jack. I expected the firebrand you were when we first met, but I have a burnt out squib seating before me. Fraser said he'd met with your characteristic aggression when he ran you down earlier today, so, please tell me, when did the conversion take place?"

"Fraser, is it now? Well, I wasn't aggressive with you, not my style at all. I leave aggression to Job. He does that sort of thing with aplomb." He spoke directly to Fraser who was sitting nearest the drinks cabinet.

"If I caused offence then that was not my aim at all. My objective was to slightly annoy you. Enough so you'd believe that I'd finished with you and would not be looking over my shoulder. But I was looking and you were being played, old sport. Thought I'd put you wise on that count just in case you get too big-headed. Hope you don't mind." He smiled that condescending smile I'd come to know so well, only I was not there to see it. Then it left him and was replaced by a reflective gaze and a humourless reply.

"I'm on the way out, Dicky. Got liver cancer past repair. I was given one year to live back in early June last year. The bell rang on my time weeks ago, drinking up time has gone as well." He held his empty glass towards Fraser who instantly looked at Dicky as if asking the question - should I? Dicky nodded in affirmation and Fraser poured.

"Did that have anything to do with you choosing West to become your partner in the protection of these secrets, Jack?" Jack gave a small laugh on accepting his replenished glass.

"You know me too well, Sir Richard, but that's what puts you head and shoulders above the other Guildford crowd. You have empathy where they were empty of everything bar the love of power. To answer your question then, yes, it was. As I've said, I knew his father. First in Italy then I got to know him better in London when he worked at the War Department. He had morals, Dicky, a high sense of duty with loyalty and honour. A truthful man who I respected. He had been wounded in Africa when a bombardier in the Royal Artillery. Do you know they stripped him of his rank when he was hospitalised because it saved the War Department money! He never complained about that, just accepting it as par for the course. His promotion to captain came about because they saved even more money. First when his battery sergeant was killed in Scilly and then his commanding officer copped one at Monte Cassino. Neither were replaced. He never had a bad word for anyone, did Harry West. If he couldn't say something good about a man he simply kept his opinion to himself. I wish there were others like him, but it don't seem to be a commodity easily found in our trade." He paused for a swallow before continuing.

"Job and I were perfectly capable of seeing this operation through to the end and I was up for doing just that, until I heard about Alain blackmailing Gregory Stiles. That's when I planned all this. I prayed that it would be you who picked up the scent and I prayed Patrick West had a lot of his father in him."

"I wouldn't have, had it not been for West's second report he delivered to the Home Office. That was quite fortuitous, Jack, don't you agree?"

"If he hadn't then there was always the old anonymous phone call routine, Dicky, but I needed to know the boy had originality and boldness."

"Okay, you got lucky. West had balls, but where did the reasoning come from for outing Trenchard through the Alhambra link?"

"Two reasons really. The main one being my disgust for him and the other knowing that you would recognise the code name. I wanted your attention, Dicky, and I wanted it in double quick time."

"An interesting reply. Disgust, not dislike, Jack?"

"You know my history at the Savoy, you also know about Trenchard's homosexuality. I'm not going to spell it out for you with every syllable highlighted. For all I know old Fraser here might like it and jump me. Only joking, sport. I can tell you're a ladies' man." He winked at Dicky who smiled back.

"Why did you need it done in 'double quick time', Jack? That I'm confused with."

"Are you stringing me, Dicky? Trenchard must have told you by now, otherwise the 'hands off Aberman' would not be the order of the day. Please, treat me with the same respect I give you and we'll get along just beautifully."

"Barrington did tell me about meeting Stiles at the Duke's funeral and how that led to Stiles revelation about the extortion, but what I don't know is how you knew of that, Jack. Care to enlighten us on that one?"

"Okay, you have me. I first heard over a year ago, from the man I approached back in 1945 and who signed me on at the Palace. I definitely need a refill for this, Dicky and I'll get it myself, Fraser. You're a typical Scotsman when it comes to generosity." He withdrew his cigarettes and after both Sir Richard and Fraser refused, lit one, drawing heavily on it as he poured a large measure of brandy into his glass.

"The Lord Chamberlain, the Earl of Cliveden. I didn't mess about with just anyone, Dicky, I went straight to the head man. I had to wait for Aberman to disclose the name Stockford for about eight years I think, but when eventually I had it, I was up and running with Cliveden as my boss. With him on board I had carte blanche to do anything. He opened the doors which I walked through to nick the family silver as it were."

"I imagine you had a field day, Jack?"

"No, I was extremely circumspect when it came to the Royals. They had my trust and admiration, but less of me. Time marches on, back onto your subject of how I knew. The Duke of Windsor was more or less hanging on to life over the last year. His body was riddled with cancer far worse than mine and he had more courage than me. Cliveden called me to St James's one day. It was before I had my diagnosis, I know that much, and I have the impression of blossom hanging on the trees, maybe the spring of 1970. Cliveden came straight out with it.

Your friend Alain Aberman is turning the screw on the Windsors and it's The Palace who are digging into their pockets to fund him.

"He babbled on a bit about whether I was in league with him or not, then asked me if I could do anything about it. I told him I could but I wouldn't as there was something happening in Argentina that Aberman was controlling and could not be removed from. I never disclosed what that was, Dicky and he never pressed me on it."

"Has that anything to do with Weilham's disappearance, Jack?"

"Everything I suspect. It's also what Aberman's doing now. There's an intermixed family of the Cliffords and the Baxter-Cliffords. They were funding the development in Argentina of a chemical that would wipe mankind from this earth if not stopped. Alain put an end to their plans and is now at the Baxter-Clifford mansion with his FBI chums either arresting Haynes Baxter hyphen, or going through the place with the proverbial. I gave Alain the tapes I had running in Weilham's UN office earlier today, thinking that he too would be arrested, but I believe Alain had rather more dramatic ideas for his demise. There's also Weilham's ex-Nazi commanding officer working for Haynes, who I suspect Aberman will turn in to the Agency if only to add weight to his condemnation of the UN under-secretary. He'll get away with the double murder, Dicky. Make no mistake on that!"

"Was that the occurrence at Trelew, Jack?"

"Yes!"

"And the Weilhams, where did they fit in?"

"Her planes, engineers, pilots, his influence and power."

"The ex-Nazis, have you names?"

"Of course I have."

"All dead in the water, is it?"

"Nice pun, Dicky, congratulations. There was I thinking you had no sense of humour. As far as I know, yes, but Olivia Weilham's South African ranch could do with a going-over if you've a mind to. Argentina is clean. Bormann was one of them Nazis out in the wilds. His skull is going to be buried in a disused Berlin railway site that's due to be redeveloped later this year. Apparently Aberman promised the Argentinian Government he'd do that for them, throw the hounds off the track kind of thing."

"It would seem to be a good place to stop and recap one particular part, Jack, and if it's not too much to ask of you, Fraser, coffee would go down well whilst we do."

"Certainly, sir, I can do that. Do you take milk and sugar with yours, Jack?" Fraser asked.

"No to the sugar, Fergus! Type one diabetic, me old son. Bet that was not down in my file, eh, Dicky?" Looking at the waiting Fraser he added, "In our day they never asked questions like that, but now, so I'm told, they ask if you have a temper and if you admit to having one they kick you out of play. I thought that would be a prerequisite to being selected." Fraser had no time to reply as Sir Richard fired another question.

"I'd like to re-examine your relationship with Earl Cliveden, Jack, if I may. Was it under his influence that the Police Commissioner instructed Trenchard to approach West with an offer to join?"

"Yes, Dicky. I was there when he made the phone call."

"One other small point whilst we're alone and before our brain-reviving coffee is served. What exactly did Harry West do for you when he was assigned to the War Department? Only there are no accurate recordings of his work. I'm guessing you know why, Jack."

Jack took another cigarette from his packet. On the first exhalation of smoke he sat firmly back in his chair with his eyes fixed to the ceiling.

"There are some things I cannot tell you. Note I did not say I won't tell you, but I can't tell. As far as I was concerned Harry facilitated certain things for me. Passports, visas if needed, and money. He provided secure phone connections to my man here; Salvatore, who in turn procured travelling documents and the means to travel. Harry, on occasions, got me the right papers, with the right signatures on them, for War Department equipment. Once he provided classified equipment for an overseas operation. His records and files were expunged of all that by a person I cannot name and quite honestly, Dicky, you'd do well to avoid."

"One last question for you, Jack, a personal one. What was it do you think that made young West jump from a steady, reliable job in the police to one with a questionable future?"

"I think the answer is in your question, Sir Richard. He is how we were. We never grasped the steady and reliable when there was the unpredictable waving at us."

Chapter Forty-Three

Who's Who

It was Fianna who broke the silence.

"What are you thinking of, Shaun?" she asked.

"Right now I'm wondering what's happening inside that house and whether or not I should go over there with the information you found, Fianna."

"You found it, not me."

"I thought of looking, but you found it." I replied sternly.

"Why so angry? It's not your fault, so why blame yourself?"

"I was slow in recognising its worth. That's why I blame myself. If I'd taken notice sooner instead of dreaming, then who knows where we'd be now. Perhaps sitting on a beach in Honolulu drinking cold beer and watching the world go by."

"Maybe we'd be spending all our time in bed, Shaun. Have you thought about that?" She tickled me around the waist then ran her fingers through my hair, but not even that could distract my thoughts.

"Look, Shaun, if you're so worried then go over there and tell Jack. You will have to one day."

"Yes, but not when he's with someone he has such obvious respect for. You were there when he said it - the best they've got, this David Lewis! How will it look, if I burst in saying you've been had, chum, and I'm here to show you up?"

"You know what they say about thinking of something you can't change, Shaun, don't you?" I did, but I allowed her to carry on.

"No, go on I'll buy it."

"Simple, change the way you're thinking about it. In other words accept what you got and move on. How about visualising me naked in a field of four leafed clover? Can you do that?" she asked.

"No! It's raining in my imagination," I laughed out loud but the joke was lost on her. I soon found out why.

"That car coming in our direction is the same kind that you and Aberman drove off in earlier today, Shaun. They like their cars big over here, I know, but that's bigger than big, it's enormous."

"It felt as though I was getting into a truck, but it handled like a car and looked like one inside."

Alain Aberman was at the wheel as he passed us, his attention diverted presumably looking for somewhere to park.

"What shall we do, Shaun?" Fianna asked.

* * *

Fraser had re-entered the room carrying the cups of coffee on a small, polished wooden tray.

"How did Barrington know of you witnessing the robbery last Thursday and subsequently your London address, Jack? I'd very much like to clear that question away."

"Haven't you found my statement yet, old boy?" Jack replied sarcastically.

"Funnily enough no, we haven't. Rather a cruel trick to play on old BT, don't you think?"

"Not at all. Deserved every moment of sweat and tears, did that one! Bet it made you think though, eh. Did I get Pilchard in trouble for telling porky pies? Shame if I did." Jack laughed whilst both Dicky and Fraser smiled.

"Now that the Duke is dead, Jack, what arrangements have been made regarding the girl he's said to have fathered? Are you in charge of that or is Aberman?" Dicky resumed his interview process whilst sniffing the coffee aroma.

"Alain's job, not mine. He's flown both the mother and daughter to Israel. Offered the brother the same, but he elected to stay on in America where he owns a pharmaceutical company. It was his chemical plant that Weilham planned to use in the manufacture of the toxin used in Namibia. There was a German chemical company called KGA being courted as a possible partner with Stockford's, but neither they nor Richard Stockford, knew about Weilham's plans."

"You're full of surprises today, Jack. We in London knew nothing of this and nor do I suspect did the South Africans. All this written down somewhere, is it?" Dicky asked, more hopeful than expectant.

"Job has the address of where I've left a detailed report à la recommended by good spy manuals. It's perfectly safe with him."

"Bit of a character, your Job."

"Eaten bullets for me, Dicky! It will take a bull elephant at full charge to kill that one." Jack poured a little brandy into the remnants of his coffee and offered the same to Dicky.

"Don't you think you should leave the brandy alone, Jack?"

"Why? Will it add years to my life if I did?" Sir Richard frowned and never supplied an opinion to that.

"What do you think Aberman will do when he walks in and finds us waiting for him?"

"Not sure really. I haven't given it any thought," Jack replied.

"I think you have, Jack. I think you'll try to kill him."

"It was you who suggested Job and I came armed, Dicky. I think it's you who want him dead and I'm wondering why that is."

"Did you know that he used many aliases throughout your partnership, always based around that name of Alain Aberman?"

"I was aware of that. Did you discover it when tracing West to his flat in Covent Garden?"

"That was one we found, but I came across him in the Middle East under the name of lan Balearman. Heard that before have you?"

"I think so, yes. Where's this going exactly, as I doubt he'll be long now?"

"Alain Aberman was never at any meetings between Hitler and our Duke of Windsor, Jack." Dicky stared at Jack, waiting for a reaction.

"That meeting in November 1937 took place, Dicky, I saw the notes!" Jack vehemently announced, looking directly at Sir Richard as if it was the devil taunting him.

"Oh yes, the meeting took place, of that I have no doubt, Jack. But it was under his real name that Aberman attended it. Ever heard the name; Képesszemély, András Képesszemély before?" Jack's violent, absorbed expression instantly altered to a look of incredulity and astonishment.

The intoxicating atmosphere was shattered by the reverberation of a crash of metal somewhere near, but outside the building.

"The Irish girl has rammed Aberman!" Job shouted as he filled the doorway. Squealing tyres proceeded another crash.

As all four dashed towards the street there was the unmistakable sound of two gunshots before the night was reclaimed by its previous silence.

Chapter Forty-Four

A Time To Die

Aberman could find no parking bay available on his first drive-by. I watched in the mirror as he turned his four-wheel-drive vehicle around at the end of the street to make a re-run. As he neared our car he slowed to a crawl near a gap behind us, but decided not to attempt to park there and drove on. He slowed again, twenty yards in front, but repeated the action he had previously taken. It was on his third attempt that he spotted Job, who this time was too slow to duck. He picked up speed.

I shouted at Fianna to ram him. With screeching tyres and the acrid smell of burning rubber she reversed, hitting the car behind, then accelerated from the kerb into his path. His larger vehicle slammed ferociously into ours, slewing our car across his path. He had nowhere to go. This time it was he who reversed, but only far enough for another run. Smash! Our windshield shattered on the impact created by his car and the already damaged vehicle behind. Now he had created enough room to pass. But that was not all he had in mind. I saw his gun and withdrew mine. Instinctively my brain measured speed, distance and angle of the shot. I cannot say with any certainty which one of us fired first. Perhaps the two shells passed equidistant in the closing space that separated us; no matter, they both had the same effect. Mine had gone through his open side window and into his head, killing him instantly and stopping his vehicle just past our shattered BMW. I turned to Fianna who was slumped over the steering wheel. The damage caused by his shell was extensive and deadly. Half the back of her skull was missing, most of which was splattered over the rear seat behind where she had sat.

The towering figure of Job was tugging my door open, then seemed to scream into my left ear.

"Has she a gun?" he asked and I answered, "yes, she does." He took my gun from my hand, wiped the grip, trigger, guard and barrel with a handkerchief then leant across me and pressed it firmly into Fianna's hand. It fell to the floor.

"Take her gun and give it me." I obeyed without thought.

He dragged me from the car, hoisted me upon his shoulder and began to run in the direction Aberman had intended for his escape. We reached his parked van.

"Get inside and hold tight when I drive off. Got to do something first."

I stood leaning against it without any feeling of remorse, sadness or regret, just idly watching him as he felt for a pulse inside Aberman's Jeep Wagoneer. The gun shots had caused a sudden deafness, but as I swallowed hard my ears started to clear and slowly I began to recognise the silence that follows death.

Back at number thirty-seven Jack and Fraser were busy cleaning surfaces, cups and glasses, Dicky was wiping anything they overlooked.

"Is there a back way out?" Fraser asked Jack.

"Not that I know of," he replied.

"Right, it's a run for it. Our car is up the street a bit. Meet you at the Best Western on Rockaway Boulevard near JFK in about—" Dicky checked his watch. "We have just over two hours until there's a flight, so you'll have to make it snappy, Jack."

"Got it!" he shouted as he exited the room.

It is said that very few witnesses to a crime or traffic accident fully appreciate the totality of the scene. Their vision is focused on one aspect and one alone, in this case the two cars were the primary concern. This was evident as doors of adjoining homes were opened and residents appeared, gazing steadily at the mangled mess of metal on the normally quiet street. It was the crash that fixed their attention, not the running figures making off in both directions from number thirty-seven

When Jack arrived at Job's van I calmly opened the side door and followed the instructions of holding on.

"Have you got your passport, Patrick?" Jack shouted at me as he jumped inside. It was the use of my real name that registered first in my clearing eardrums, then came the realisation that I was about to leave America.

"I have, Jack. I sent Fianna to the bank where I kept everything this afternoon and she emptied my box. She's dead, you know!" It was then that the pain of separation set in.

"You will have to get a shoe on that foot of yours. You won't be allowed on any plane with that injury on show along with the state of your face."

That's all he said. No mention of the woman I had belatedly come to know so well and who had died in a cause that was not her own. I wanted to scream at him. Vent all the anger that had built up on the back of his ludicrous storytelling when only truth was needed to be told. But something held me back.

Rockaway

Chapter Forty-Five

Flying High

When Job with his two passengers found the room that Dicky had told of, both he and Fraser were packing their bags in an orderly unhurried fashion. The television on the wall was broadcasting the local evening news and to anyone who may have opened the door onto this scene there was nothing to indicated what had happened a mere thirty-five minutes ago in an otherwise peaceful part of New York. Dicky was the first to notice me.

"I wish we could have met under different circumstances, young man, but alas that's not been possible. Allow me to introduce the two of us to you. I'm Sir Richard Blythe-Smith; head of what's commonly referred to as MI6. This gentleman is my colleague, Fraser Ughert. You might not believe it at the moment but we came to America to rescue you and Jack. I'm sorry it ended in such a messy way. Unfortunately there is preciously little time for us to discuss all that needs to be discussed. We must move as swiftly as humanly possible. There is a flight to London leaving at nine-fifteen. Fraser has booked reservations for the four of us. We have thirty minutes before we must collect our tickets and present our luggage at departures." He took a stride backwards to examine me, and satisfied with what he saw, he continued.

"You must have a million and half questions you wish to ask me. Believe me when I tell you I will answer them all to the very best of my ability. Have you all that you need to travel, Patrick?"

"Yes, sir, I have," I answered, catching Fraser staring intently at me.

"And how does your face feel without the splint?" It was he who asked that question.

"It's a bit sore, but I'll survive," I replied more in hope than certainty.

"I have four syringes of morphine on me, Dicky. Just in case Pat needs them." It was Jack who spoke. "Recently I've been in the habit of using them more regularly."

My head was about to blow up and concentration was an effort I could have done without. *Did he say he's been using morphine?* I asked myself silently.

"I have a spare pair of shoes that should fit you, Patrick. Here, try them on." The voice was Fraser's, but nothing was registering in my brain. I was miles behind the conversation as I stared dumbly at his offering.

"Was the morphine for your illness, Jack?" Same voice but what illness?

Suddenly I was acutely aware of what was happening.

"Are you dying, Jack?" I asked without any emotion.

"I am, Patrick. Liver cancer, beyond redemption!" he calmly replied.

There was that condescending smile of his and the moment I saw it I knew why I could not have screamed at him or lessened my pain by striking him and rendering him as dead as Fianna. He was lovable, was Jack Price, in a manly way, you understand. The affection that one man can have for another without the complication of sex. As that reality hit me, both Sir Richard and Fraser turned their attention to the television.

News is coming in of a possible argument over road space in the Turtle Bay area which has left a woman aged in her late twenties and a man about sixty dead from shots to the head. We hope to have more of this in our 9pm bulletin.

As the two turned from the TV set, and continued with their packing, another death was announced.

Earlier this evening a young United Kingdom national was found dead on the walkway outside the St. Regis Hotel on East 55th Street. It is believed he jumped from the seventh floor. A local police spokesman has said that he was known to suffer from depression. No one is being sought in connection to this incident. His relatives in the UK have yet to be informed.

I saw Fraser look at Sir Richard and he returned the same glance. That shared look convinced me that the body on the walkway had not committed suicide. I told myself that he, whoever he was, was the man sent to kill me and someone had got to him before he had succeeded. I needed something to believe in.

"What exactly is that bandage on your foot covering, Patrick?" Sir Richard asked with his back to me as he closed his suitcase.

"I've lost the three toes, sir. They were shot off when a man tried to kill me," I stated, trying to announce it as casually as I could.

"In that case try a pair of mine. I have them made as I have a wide foot." he replied, as if it was everyday conversation.

Fianna's dead you dead know, and my brother Alan killed her. I wanted to shout it. Open my mouth and come to terms with the fact that Alan was a murderer. Or was it Alain dead and Fianna had shot him? *What am I doing?*

I was sitting on a bed with Sir Richard on his knees adjusting the bandage around my foot so as to slip into a pair of brown brogues previously worn by the head of MI6. If ever I wrote a book, I told myself, I must include that. My mood was lightening in more ways than one. As I bent to tie the laces, Jack stabbed his morphine-filled syringe in my thigh.

Chapter Forty-Six

England

I never told Jack or anyone else what Fianna had told me on the night she died, it would have benefitted no one if I had. I saw him again only the once.

On arrival at Heathrow I was taken to a hospital just outside of Brighton, and ordered by Fraser Ughert to remain until fully recovered without moving from there. Jack passed away three weeks after landing back in England believing that he had saved the Duke of Windsor's honour, and I was not going to change that view. I had telephoned Century House, asking Sir Richard Blythe-Smith for permission to see Jack in his home at Woolwich, South London where he was being cared for by, of all people, Gloria from the flat below his in Romilly Street and Bethnal Green, along with Amelia, also known as Jimmy, from the wine bar in Soho.

In the corner by the window of his lounge stood his yellow triangular chair and on the mantelpiece was the chiming slate clock with the two framed photographs either side of it.

"I told you Soho had heart, didn't I, young whatever name you're going by nowadays." He smiled as he greeted me, but it was not the same smile, it was edged by death and marred by disappointment. We chatted for a while about this and that but never once touched on

Fianna or her death and how that left both of us. So, when I was leaving it came as a bolt from the blue that he asked about her jade ring. I showed him it, hanging around my neck on a gold chain.

"It's not lucky that thing, you know. *Se fossi in te, avrei sbarazzarsi di esso*," he said incomprehensibly, then immediately added the translation; "I'd get rid of it, if I was you."

There was no reason that I knew of for him to say that, but one thing I was certain of and still am, he was a generous man and I was privileged to have known him. I have never looked back on the events that happened in my life due to the association I formed with Jack Price with anything but a sense of pride. I believe that Fianna would have approved and shared in my view. I attended his funeral. The service was held at St Michael's Church, Plumstead and he was buried in the cemetery beside that church. There were eight other mourners, all from Soho. I asked each of them if they knew of his son or daughter, but none did.

The task I'd asked Fianna to do the afternoon before she was murdered was to use my key to gain entry to Leeba's office and check the photograph she had shown me of Penni standing beside the birthday aeroplane. It was dated third of July 1970 and said—Pennia aged thirty-two. Leeba was at least seven or eight weeks pregnant when she boarded the plane from Austria. To my eternal shame I had taken no notice of it when first shown.

Jack's inverted snobbery had led him to trust an abused figure of a man who had lied purely for his own ends. Penni's father was Alain Aberman who was not, as Richard Stockford believed, parting from a lover that night he saw his mother and Aberman say their goodbyes; in all probability he was confessing his sin and asking for a forgiveness that not even a flight to freedom could provide. As to the question of why Leeba had no recollection of who it was that raped her when she was thirteen, then only she can answer why that was never openly discussed. Some answers are best locked away from sight; forever. I never saw or heard from her, Penina or Job ever again.

* * *

I did see Sir Richard though. When fully recovered I was driven from my nursing hospital to the Travellers Club in London by Fraser Ughert. We exchanged no more than common pleasantries on the journey, avoiding all mention of New York as though it would cause an epidemic of disastrous proportions to break out in our wake if we had. The conversation at Sir Richard's club began no differently. It was stilted and awkward for the both of us but perhaps more so for him. Eventually, after the studying of menus and the summoning of waiters, the subject of why I had been invited was broached.

"Shall we get down to business, Patrick? I bet you're dying to get back to work. Your position in the police is assured. Enhanced in fact. Your leave of absence was marked down as a special assignment by the new head of C11 at the Yard. Trenchard took early retirement and has emigrated to far away lands. It was thought best that he went quietly with no fuss being made in the press. You'll be pleased to know that as a direct result of your action abroad you have been awarded the George Medal with instant promotion to detective sergeant." I noted that there was no specific mention of New York. He stopped speaking as our lunch was served, but he never looked at his plate, he just stared at me waiting for a response. I had none.

"I am embarrassed by what I have next to say, but it is my duty and I'd fail in my responsibilities if I did not. Everything you heard from either Jack, Fraser, myself or the unfortunate Miss Slattery is classified, Patrick. You are legally bound by that Official Secrets Act that you signed when you joined the police service. I hope I do not have to spell out the consequence if you breached that Act." Again the pause and the stare.

"I'm aware of that, sir, and have no desire to speak to anyone."

"Good to hear, young man. I thought as much. I have an offer of a job to put to you. The details are in this envelope." He withdrew an envelope from his jacket pocket and wedged it between the salt cellar and the pepper shaker in the middle of our table.

Now it was my turn to stare at him. The ease with which bad memories can be wiped away were in that envelope, my bribe for staying silent.

"The remuneration is at a grade three level in line with the Civil Service pay structure, but it has additional benefits that far outweigh any in the private sector, or what the police can offer you. It's not, you understand, in my department, but it is of a similar nature." I was unmoved by his offer and he could see it.

"There's absolutely no rush in this. Read the contents and give it some thought, Patrick. You're not expected back in any capacity until you feel that you are ready." Our wine was being served when he next spoke.

"I can recommend the apple crumble here. They have changed the pastry chef recently, but if anything this one is even better." he exclaimed cheerfully.

"If you wouldn't mind, sir, I have a question for you over something that occurred in New York and has caused me some restless nights since getting back."

"I'm sorry to hear that, young man. I only hope I can put your mind at rest. Ask away and I'll answer if I can, of course."

"On the plane coming home, Jack mentioned the name András Képesszemély to me several times. He seemed obsessed with it. He said that you had brought it up when speaking of Aberman inside that house on the night of the shooting. I wondered what it had to do with all that went on over there?"

"News to me, Patrick! I really have not heard that name before. Do you think that maybe Jack was slightly delusional because of having to share what morphine he had with you?" Was that an attempt to make me feel guilty?

"That could be the answer, sir, only I don't think so." It was my turn to study his expressionless face as our waiter left with our plates.

"You don't? Then what's your explanation?"

"In his will, Jack left his house in Woolwich to me. He also left some money to be shared with two other people. When I told those two that I would be leaving the flat that was rented out to me, one of them knew the owner of the whole block in Rose Street. His name was an anagram of Alain Aberman; a Brian Alaname."

"Yes, we knew of that, Patrick, but I don't see the connection with that other name you claim I said to Jack." Sir Richard was fidgeting with his dessert spoon and fork.

"At first I was simply intrigued by Aberman's use of a pseudonym, but then I remembered what Jack had said on the plane and did some investigation. Képesszemély is Hungarian, sir. Its literal English translation means; capable person. Substitute Ableman for Aberman then capable person is not dissimilar, is it?"

"I see your point, Patrick, but again I must reiterate that the name never came from me. Jack, as you know, was an extremely inventive person with an imagination as big as the universe, and remember he must have been in pain."

"Never a truer word spoken, Sir Richard, but there's more I'm afraid. I'm an impatient man, Sir Richard, and the time I had on my hands recently would have drove me insane had I not had something to do. I looked up the Képesszemély family and do you know what I found, sir? Of course not, how could you if you'd never heard the name before. The Képesszemélys and the Schuschniggs were related by marriage. I'm totally sure you would have heard of that last name. The Schuschnigg one?" He had stopped fidgeting, but declined to answer.

"It bothered me for ages why Aberman had almost imploded when I mentioned the name Schuschnigg to him in the Israeli embassy. But all became so much clearer after my research. Still no recollection of that Képesszemély name, Sir Richard?"

"No, Patrick, nothing is stirring upstairs for me."

"Kurt Schuschnigg was András Képesszemély's uncle, Sir Richard, and according to a genealogical tree I had drawn up for me, Kurt is related to someone living in a very big house close to where we are now sitting. Shall I go on, sir?" It was at that moment our dessert was served.

"Ah, the crumble, Patrick. It's always important to enjoy the cream, don't you think? He said as he reached for one of the bowls at the side of his dessert. "Although, by that look of contentment on your face you seem to be lapping it up already."

"Cream is indeed nice, sir. By the way, I almost forgot to congratulate you on the announcement of your upcoming peerage. Have you selected a title yet?"

For a moment the apple crumble became less important than my question.

"I haven't, Patrick, and thank you. I wonder what my dear wife would think of Lord Richard and Lady Sheila Blythe-Smith of Woolwich. It has a certain - ring about it, don't you think!"

"I remember little of my father, sir, but one thing I do remember is a saying of his - *if you have to tell a lie, son, make it a big one!* There seems to be many that have been told surrounding the secret of Vienna, sir."

* * *

Lies are the currency of life. They move effortlessly through every corridor where the spoken word is the favoured method of communication. The endemic proportion of the insidiousness of lying has become essential to civilised human existence. It sustains the very essence of life installed in us all from birth - You are important - That's the biggest lie ever spoken, written or assumed. The truth is - You are unimportant.

People such as I, Jack Price and Fianna, or Bridget if you prefer, were hostages to lies. We, like you, once believed that there was a virtue in truth. We were encouraged to seek it out and follow its lead to the salvation it offered to our soul. But it led to a hollow grave where those that are important occasionally visit to hear the echo of insanity crying; 'listen to me, I'm important. I have an opinion. My vote counts'. Their derision slowly drowns the noise to a whimper that no one hears as nobody has the time to deflect away from their envy of the perfection offered by lies. It's the lies that are not heard but kept as a secret that own us all.

The best Westerns, the cowboy variety, end when the good guy defeats the bad one in a gunfight. Fianna's and my own trip to America ended in a gun battle of sorts. I'll grant you the fact that it was more modern but nevertheless similar to the old fashion showdown type. However, I'm not sure if it was the good guys who survived the fight or the bad ones. What I am convinced of is that my thesis was correct in its assumptions: There is no Right, there is only Wrong.

The End

About the Author

Danny Kemp, ex-London police officer, mini-cab business owner, pub tenant and licensed London taxi driver, never planned to be a writer, but after his first novel —The Desolate Garden — was under a paid option to become a $30 million film for five years until distribution became an insurmountable problem for the production company what else could he do?

Nowadays he is a prolific storyteller, and although it's true to say that he mainly concentrates on what he knows most about; murders laced by the intrigue involving spies, his diverse experience of life shows in the short stories he compiles both for adults and children.

He is the recipient of rave reviews from a prestigious Manhattan publication, been described as —the new Graham Green — by a managerial employee of Waterstones Books, for whom he did a countrywide tour of signing events, and he has appeared on 'live' nationwide television.

http://www-thedesolategarden-com.co.uk/

Lightning Source UK Ltd.
Milton Keynes UK
UKHW042249010620
364212UK00020B/115